A PET DINOSAUR?

Who didn't fantasize about dinosaurs as a child? Whether your dream was to own one, be one, or conquer one, you'll find your fondest fantasies—and many more you never even dreamed of—fulfilled in this all-new collection of stories about those long-ago rulers of the Earth.

"Dino Trend"—When dinosaurs are all the rage, a real fashion statement, sometimes being human just isn't enough. . . .

"One Giant Step"—Why did the dinosaurs really disappear? Maybe it had something to do with time travel. . . .

"Rex"—When your daughter's pet starts eating you out of house and home, something—or someone—has got to give. . . .

DINOSAUR
FANTASTIC

DINOSAUR FANTASTIC

EDITED BY

Mike Resnick
and Martin H. Greenberg

DAW BOOKS, INC.
DONALD A. WOLLHEIM, FOUNDER
375 Hudson Street, New York, NY 10014

ELIZABETH R. WOLLHEIM
SHEILA E. GILBERT
PUBLISHERS

First Printing, July 1993

1 2 3 4 5 6 7 8 9

DAW TRADEMARK REGISTERED
U.S. PAT. OFF. AND FOREIGN COUNTRIES
—MARCA REGISTRADA
HECHO EN U.S.A.

PRINTED IN THE U.S.A.

To Carol, as always

And to Patrick Read Johnson

ACKNOWLEDGMENTS

Introduction © 1993 by Mike Resnick.
Just Like Old Times © 1993 by Robert J. Sawyer.
Disquisitions on the Dinosaur © 1993 by Robert Sheckley.
Dino Trend © 1993 by Pat Cadigan.
The Greatest Dying © 1993 by Frank M. Robinson.
Revenants © 1993 by Judith Tarr.
One Giant Step © 1993 by John E. Stith.
Last Rights © 1993 by Mercedes Lackey and Larry Dixon.
After the Comet © 1993 by Bill Fawcett.
Rex Tremandae Majestatis © 1993 by Kathe Koja
   and Barry N. Malzberg.
The Skull's Tale © 1993 by Katharine Kerr.
Cutting Down Fred © 1993 by Dean Wesley Smith.
Shadow of a Change © 1993 by Michelle M. Sagara.
Wise One's Tale © 1993 by Josepha Sherman.
Curren's Song © 1993 by Laura Resnick.
Whilst Slept the Sauropod © 1993 by Nicholas A. DiChario.
Rex © 1993 by David Gerrold.
The Pangaean Principle © 1993 by Jack Nimersheim.
On Tiptoe © 1993 by Beth Meacham.
Betrayal © 1993 by Susan Casper.
'Saur Spot © 1993 by Kevin O'Donnell, Jr.
Pteri © 1993 by Lea Hernandez.
Chameleon © 1993 by Kristine Kathryn Rusch.
Fellow Passengers © 1993 by Barbara Delaplace.
Thirteen Ways of Looking at a Dinosaur © 1993
   by Gregory Feeley.
Evolving Conspiracy © 1993 by Roger MacBride Allen.

CONTENTS

INTRODUCTION

It would be untrue to say that dinosaurs have *always* fascinated us. After all, they weren't discovered until a couple of centuries ago.

But from the day the first oversized bones were unearthed, human beings have been totally captivated by these prehistoric "thunder lizards." In fact, the notorious "bone wars" between the two great American paleontologists of the nineteenth century, Edward Drinker Cope and Othniel Charles Marsh, in which each mounted expensive digging expeditions, constantly raced to publish their theories first, sabotaged each other's finds, smeared each other in the press, and even got Congress to pass laws favoring one over the other, captured the public's attention as has no other battle between scientists.

Paradoxically, the farther we move along the river of Time from the dinosaurs, the more popular they seem to become. They attract more interest today, among all segments of the public, than they ever have before. Canada's magnificent Tyrell Museum is the first such edifice built strictly for the display of dinosaurs; movies abound with them; cartoons revel in them; everything from gas stations to breakfast cereals are named for them; amusement parks wouldn't dream of opening without them; not a month goes by without a new coffee-table book about them; and almost every child has at least one toy in the shape of a dinosaur.

Fantasy and science fiction writers, always in the vanguard of the popular culture, have been examining dinosaurs in all their many aspects for more than a century. Edgar Rice Burroughs put them in *The Land That Time Forgot,* spread them throughout his Pellucidar series, and even put them in modern Africa in *Tarzan the Terrible*. Not to be outdone, Sir Arthur Conan Doyle took time off from writing Sherlock Holmes stories to send his other hero, Professor Challenger, to *The Lost World*. Ray Bradbury and L. Sprague de Camp wrote classic dinosaur stories in the 1940s and 1950s, dozens more followed in their footsteps—perhaps most notably Harry Harrison with *West of Eden*—and more recently, Michael Crichton's *Jurassic Park* made the national bestseller lists.

And yet, despite the constantly growing interest in dinosaurs, there has never been an anthology composed exclusively of original stories about them. Until now. When this lack was mentioned to the good people at DAW Books, they made up their minds to change the situation, and here is the result: 25 all-new stories by some of the finest fantasy and science fiction writers in the field.

—Mike Resnick

JUST LIKE OLD TIMES

by Robert J. Sawyer

Robert J. Sawyer won Canada's 1992 Aurora Award for the best science fiction novel of the year.

The transference went smoothly, like a scalpel slicing into skin.

Cohen was simultaneously excited and disappointed. He was thrilled to be here—perhaps the judge was right, perhaps this was where he really belonged. But the gleaming edge was taken off that thrill because it wasn't accompanied by the usual physiological signs of excitement: no sweaty palms, no racing heart, no rapid breathing. Oh, there was a heartbeat, to be sure, thundering in the background, but it wasn't Cohen's.

It was the dinosaur's.

Everything was the dinosaur's: Cohen saw the world now through tyrannosaur eyes.

The colors seemed all wrong. Surely plant leaves must be the same chlorophyll green here in the Mesozoic, but the dinosaur saw them as navy blue. The sky was lavender; the dirt underfoot ash gray.

Old bones had different cones, thought Cohen. Well, he could get used to it. After all, he had no choice. He would finish his life as an observer inside this tyrannosaur's mind. He'd see what the beast saw, hear what it heard, feel what it felt. He wouldn't be able to control its movements, they had said, but he would be able to experience every sensation.

The rex was marching forward.

Cohen hoped blood would still look red.

It wouldn't be the same if it wasn't red.

* * *

"And what, Ms. Cohen, did your husband say before he left your house on the night in question?"

"He said he was going out to hunt humans. But I thought he was making a joke."

"No interpretations, please, Ms. Cohen. Just repeat for the court as precisely as you remember it, exactly what your husband said."

"He said, 'I'm going out to hunt humans.' "

"Thank you, Ms. Cohen. That concludes the Crown's case, my lady."

The needlepoint on the wall of the Honorable Madam Justice Amanda Hoskins' chambers had been made for her by her husband. It was one of her favorite verses from *The Mikado,* and as she was preparing sentencing she would often look up and reread the words:

> "My object all sublime
> I shall achieve in time—
> To let the punishment fit the crime—
> The punishment fit the crime."

This was a difficult case, a horrible case. Judge Hoskins continued to think.

It wasn't just colors that were wrong. The view from inside the tyrannosaur's skull was different in other ways, too.

The tyrannosaur had only partial stereoscopic vision. There was an area in the center of Cohen's field of view that showed true depth perception. But because the beast was somewhat wall-eyed, it had a much wider panorama than normal for a human, a kind of saurian Cinemascope covering 270 degrees.

The wide-angle view panned back and forth as the tyrannosaur scanned along the horizon.

Scanning for prey.

Scanning for something to kill.

*   *   *

The Calgary Herald, Thursday, October 16, 2042, hard copy edition: "Serial killer Rudolph Cohen, 43, was sentenced to death yesterday.

"Formerly a prominent member of the Alberta College of Physicians and Surgeons, Dr. Cohen was convicted in August of thirty-seven counts of first-degree murder.

"In chilling testimony, Cohen had admitted, without any signs of remorse, to having terrorized each of his victims for hours before slitting their throats with surgical implements.

"This is the first time in eighty years that the death penalty has been ordered in this country.

"In passing sentence, Madam Justice Amanda Hoskins observed that Cohen was 'the most cold-blooded and brutal killer to have stalked Canada's prairies since *Tyrannosaurus rex . . .*' "

From behind a stand of dawn redwoods about ten meters away, a second tyrannosaur appeared. Cohen suspected tyrannosaurs might be fiercely territorial, since each animal would require huge amounts of meat. He wondered if the beast he was in would attack the other individual.

His dinosaur tilted its head to look at the second rex, which was standing in profile. But as it did so, almost all of the dino's mental picture dissolved into a white void, as if when concentrating on details the beast's tiny brain simply lost track of the big picture.

At first Cohen thought his rex was looking at the other dinosaur's head, but soon the top of other's skull, the tip of its muzzle and the back of its powerful neck faded away into snowy nothingness. All that was left was a picture of the throat. Good, thought Cohen. One shearing bite there could kill the animal.

The skin of the other's throat appeared gray-green and the throat itself was smooth. Maddeningly, Cohen's rex did not attack, Rather, it simply swiveled its head and looked out at the horizon again.

In a flash of insight, Cohen realized what had happened. Other kids in his neighborhood had had pet dogs or cats. He'd had lizards and snakes—cold-blooded carnivores, a fact to which expert psychological witnesses had attached great weight. Some kinds of male lizards had dewlap sacs hanging from their necks. The rex he was in—a male, the Tyrrell paleontologists had believed—had looked at this other one and seen that she was smooth-throated and therefore a female. Something to be mated with, perhaps, rather than to attack.

Perhaps they would mate soon. Cohen had never orgasmed except during the act of killing. He wondered what it would feel like.

"We spent a billion dollars developing time travel, and now you tell me the system is useless?"

"Well—"

"That is what you're saying, isn't it, Professor? That chronotransference has no practical applications?"

"Not exactly, Minister. The system *does* work. We can project a human being's consciousness back in time, superimposing his or her mind over that of someone who lived in the past."

"With no way to sever the link. *Wonderful.*"

"That's not true. The link severs automatically."

"Right. When the historical person you've transferred consciousness into dies, the link is broken."

"Precisely."

"And then the person from our time whose consciousness you've transferred back dies as well."

"I admit that's an unfortunate consequence of linking two brains so closely."

"So I'm right! This whole damn chronotransference thing is useless."

"Oh, not at all, Minister. In fact, I think I've got the perfect application for it."

The rex marched along. Although Cohen's attention had first been arrested by the beast's vision, he slowly became aware of its other senses, too. He could hear the sounds of the rex's footfalls, of twigs and vegetation being crushed, of birds or pterosaurs singing, and, underneath it all, the relentless drone of insects. Still, all the sounds were dull and low; the rex's simple ears were incapable of picking up high-pitched noises, and what sounds they did detect were discerned without richness. Cohen knew the late Cretaceous must have been a symphony of varied tones, but it was as if he was listening to it through earmuffs.

The rex continued along, still searching. Cohen became aware of several more impressions of the world both inside and out, including hot afternoon sun beating down on him and a hungry gnawing in the beast's belly.

Food.

It was the closest thing to a coherent thought that he'd yet detected from the animal, a mental picture of bolts of meat going down its gullet.

Food.

The Social Services Preservation Act of 2022: Canada is built upon the principle of the Social Safety Net, a series of entitlements and programs designed to ensure a high standard of living for every citizen. However, ever-increasing life expectancies coupled with constant lowering of the mandatory retirement age have placed an untenable burden on our social-welfare system and, in particular, its cornerstone program of universal health care. With most taxpayers ceasing to work at the age of 45, and with average Canadians living to be 94 (males) or 97 (females), the system is in danger of complete collapse. Accordingly, all social programs will henceforth be available only to those below the age of 60, with one exception: all Canadians, regardless of age, may take advantage, at no charge to themselves, of government-sponsored euthanasia through chronotransference.

There! Up ahead! Something moving! Big, whatever it was: an indistinct outline only intermittently visible behind a small knot of fir trees.

A quadruped of some sort, its back to him/it/them. Ah, there. Turning now. Peripheral vision dissolving into albino nothingness as the rex concentrated on the head.

Three horns.

Triceratops.

Glorious! Cohen had spent hours as a boy poring over books about dinosaurs, looking for scenes of carnage. No battles were better than those in which Tyrannosaurus rex squared off against Triceratops, a four-footed Mesozoic tank with a trio of horns projecting from its face and a shield of bone rising from the back of its skull to protect the neck.

And yet, the rex marched on.

No, thought Cohen. Turn, damn you! Turn and attack!

Cohen remembered when it had all begun, that fateful day so many years ago, so many years from now. It should have been a routine operation. The patient had supposedly been prepped properly. Cohen brought his scalpel down toward the abdomen, then, with a steady hand, sliced into the skin. The patient gasped. It had been a *wonderful* sound, a beautiful sound.

Not enough gas. The anesthetist hurried to make an adjustment.

Cohen knew he had to hear that sound again. He had to.

The tyrannosaur continued forward. Cohen couldn't see its legs, but he could feel them moving. Left, right, up, down.

Attack, you bastard!

Left.

Attack!

Right.

Go after it!

Up.

Go after the triceratops.

Dow—

The beast hesitated, its left leg still in the air, balancing briefly on one foot.

Attack!
Attack!
And then, at last, the rex changed course. The triceratops appeared in the three-dimensional central part of the tyrannosaur's field of view, like a target at the end of a gun sight.

"Welcome to the Chronotransference Institute. If I can just see your government benefits card, please? Yup, there's always a last time for everything, heh heh. Now, I'm sure you want an exciting death. The problem is finding somebody interesting who hasn't been used yet. See, we can only ever superimpose one mind onto a given historical personage. All the really obvious ones have been done already, I'm afraid. We still get about a dozen calls a week asking for Jack Kennedy, but he was one of the first to go, so to speak. If I may make a suggestion, though, we've got thousands of Roman legion officers cataloged. Those tend to be very satisfying deaths. How about a nice something from the Gallic Wars?"

The triceratops looked up, its giant head lifting from the wide flat gunnera leaves it had been chewing on. Now that the rex had focused on the plant-eater, it seemed to commit itself.

The tyrannosaur charged.

The hornface was sideways to the rex. It began to turn, to bring its armored head to bear.

The horizon bounced wildly as the rex ran. Cohen could hear the thing's heart thundering loudly, rapidly, a barrage of muscular gunfire.

The triceratops, still completing its turn, opened its parrotlike beak, but no sound came out.

Giant strides closed the distance between the two animals. Cohen felt the rex's jaws opening wide, wider still, mandibles popping from their sockets.

The jaws slammed shut on the hornface's back, over the shoulders. Cohen saw two of the rex's own teeth fly into view, knocked out by the impact.

The taste of hot blood, surging out of the wound . . .

The rex pulled back for another bite.

The triceratops finally got its head swung around. It surged forward, the long spear over its left eye piercing the rex's leg . . .

Pain. Exquisite, beautiful pain.

The rex roared. Cohen heard it twice, once reverberating within the animal's own skull, a second time echoing back from distant hills. A flock of silver-furred pterosaurs took to the air. Cohen saw them fade from view as the dinosaur's simple mind shut them out of the display. Irrelevant distractions.

The triceratops pulled back, the horn withdrawing from the rex's flesh.

Blood, Cohen was delighted to see, still looked red.

"If Judge Hoskins had ordered the electric chair," said Axworthy, Cohen's lawyer, "we could have fought that on Charter grounds. Cruel and unusual punishment, and all that. But she's authorized full access to the chronotransference euthanasia program for you." Axworthy paused. "She said, bluntly, that she simply wants you dead."

"How thoughtful of her," said Cohen.

Axworthy ignored that. "I'm sure I can get you anything you want," he said. "Who would you like to be transferred into?"

"Not who," said Cohen. "What."

"I beg your pardon?"

"That damned judge said I was the most cold-blooded killer to stalk the Alberta landscape since *Tyrannosaurus rex*." Cohen shook his head. "The idiot. Doesn't she know dinosaurs were warm-blooded? Anyway, that's what I want. I want to be transferred into a *T. rex*."

"You're kidding."

"Kidding is not my forte, John. *Killing* is. I want to know which was better at it, me or the rex."

"I don't even know if they can do that kind of thing," said Axworthy.

"Find out, damn you. What the hell am I paying you for?"

* * *

The rex danced to the side, moving with surprising agility for a creature of its bulk, and once again it brought its terrible jaws down on the ceratopsian's shoulder. The plant-eater was hemorrhaging at an incredible rate, as though a thousand sacrifices had been performed on the altar of its back.

The triceratops tried to lunge forward, but it was weakening quickly. The tyrannosaur, crafty in its own way despite its trifling intellect, simply retreated a dozen giant paces. The hornface took one tentative step toward it, and then another, and, with great and ponderous effort, one more. But then the dinosaurian tank teetered and, eyelids slowly closing, collapsed on its side. Cohen was briefly startled, then thrilled, to hear it fall to the ground with a *splash*—he hadn't realized just how much blood had poured out of the great rent the rex had made in the beast's back.

The tyrannosaur moved in, lifting its left leg up and then smashing it down on the triceratops' belly, the three sharp toe claws tearing open the thing's abdomen, entrails spilling out into the harsh sunlight. Cohen thought the rex would let out a victorious roar, but it didn't. It simply dipped its muzzle into the body cavity, and methodically began yanking out chunks of flesh.

Cohen was disappointed. The battle of the dinosaurs had been fun, the killing had been well engineered, and there had certainly been enough blood, but there was no *terror*. No sense that the triceratops had been quivering with fear, no begging for mercy. No feeling of power, of control. Just dumb, mindless brutes moving in ways preprogrammed by their genes.

It wasn't enough. Not nearly enough.

Judge Hoskins looked across the desk in her chambers at the lawyer.

"A tyrannosaurus, Mr. Axworthy? I was speaking figuratively."

"I understand that, my lady, but it was an appropriate observation, don't you think? I've contacted the

Chronotransference people, who say they can do it, if they have a rex specimen to work from. They have to back-propagate from actual physical material in order to get a temporal fix."

Judge Hoskins was as unimpressed by scientific babble as she was by legal jargon. "Make your point, Mr. Axworthy."

"I called the Royal Tyrrell Museum of Paleontology in Drumheller and asked them about the tyrannosaurus fossils available worldwide. Turns out there's only a handful of complete skeletons, but they were able to provide me with an annotated list, giving as much information as they could about the individual probable causes of death." He slid a thin plastic printout sheet across the judge's wide desk.

"Leave this with me, counsel. I'll get back to you."

Axworthy left, and Hoskins scanned the brief list. She then leaned back in her leather chair and began to read the needlepoint on her wall for the thousandth time:

My object all sublime
I shall achieve in time—"

She read that line again, her lips moving slightly as she subvocalized the words: "I shall achieve *in time* . . ."

The judge turned back to the list of tyrannosaur finds. Ah, that one. Yes, that would be perfect. She pushed a button on her phone "David, see if you can find Mr. Axworthy for me."

There had been a very unusual aspect to the triceratops kill—an aspect that intrigued Cohen. Chronotransference had been performed countless times; it was one of the most popular forms of euthanasia. Sometimes the transferee's original body would give an ongoing commentary about what was going on, as if talking during sleep. It was clear from what they said that transferees couldn't exert any control over the bodies they were transferred into.

Indeed, the physicists had claimed any control was impossible. Chronotransference worked precisely because the transferee could exert no influence, and therefore was simply observing things that had already been observed. Since no new observations were being made, no quantum-mechanical distortions occurred. After all, said the physicists, if one could exert control, one could change the past. And that was impossible.

And yet, when Cohen had willed the rex to alter its course, it eventually had done so.

Could it be that the rex had so little brains that Cohen's thoughts *could* control the beast?

Madness. The ramifications were incredible.

Still . . .

He had to know if it was true. The rex was torpid, flopped on its belly, gorged on ceratopsian meat. It seemed prepared to lie here for a long time to come, enjoying the early evening breeze.

Get up, thought Cohen. *Get up, damn you!*

Nothing. No response.

Get up!

The rex's lower jaw was resting on the ground. Its upper jaw was lifted high, its mouth wide open. Tiny pterosaurs were flitting in and out of the open maw, their long needlelike beaks apparently yanking gobbets of hornface flesh from between the rex's curved teeth.

Get up, thought Cohen again. *Get up!*

The rex stirred.

Up!

The tyrannosaur used its tiny forelimbs to keep its torso from sliding forward as it pushed with its powerful legs until it was standing.

Forward, thought Cohen. *Forward!*

The beast's body felt different. Its belly was full to bursting.

Forward!

With ponderous steps, the rex began to march.

It was wonderful. To be in control again! Cohen felt the old thrill of the hunt.

And he knew exactly what he was looking for.

"Judge Hoskins says okay," said Axworthy. "She's authorized for you to be transferred into that new T rex they've got right here in Alberta at the Tyrrell. It's a young adult, they say. Judging by the way the skeleton was found, the rex died falling, probably into a fissure. Both legs and the back were broken, but the skeleton remained almost completely articulated, suggesting that scavengers couldn't get at it. Unfortunately, the chronotransference people say that back-propagating that far into the past they can only plug you in a few hours before the accident occurred. But you'll get your wish: you're going to die as a tyrannosaur. Oh, and here are the books you asked for: a complete library on Cretaceous flora and fauna. You should have time to get through it all; the chronotransference people will need a couple of weeks to set up."

As the prehistoric evening turned to night, Cohen found what he had been looking for, cowering in some underbrush: large brown eyes, long, drawn-out face, and a lithe body covered in fur that, to the tyrannosaur's eyes, looked blue-brown.

A mammal. But not just any mammal. *Purgatorius,* the very first primate, known from Montana and Alberta from right at the end of the Cretaceous. A little guy, only about ten centimeters long, excluding its ratlike tail. Rare creatures, these days. Only a precious few.

The little furball could run quickly for its size, but a single step by the tyrannosaur equaled more than a hundred of the mammal's. There was no way it could escape.

The rex leaned in close, and Cohen saw the furball's face, the nearest thing there would be to a human face for another sixty million years. The animal's eyes went wide in terror.

Naked, raw fear.

Mammalian fear.

Cohen saw the creature scream.

Heard it scream.

It was beautiful.

The rex moved its gaping jaws in toward the little mammal, drawing in breath with such force that it sucked the creature into its maw. Normally the rex would swallow its meals whole, but Cohen prevented the beast from doing that. Instead, he simply had it stand still, with the little primate running around, terrified, inside the great cavern of the dinosaur's mouth, banging into the giant teeth and great fleshy walls, and skittering over the massive, dry tongue.

Cohen savored the terrified squealing. He wallowed in the sensation of the animal, mad with fear, moving inside that living prison.

And at last, with a great, glorious release, Cohen put the animal out of its misery, allowing the rex to swallow it, the furball tickling as it slid down the giant's throat.

It was just like old times.

Just like hunting humans.

And then a wonderful thought occurred to Cohen. Why, if he killed enough of these little screaming balls of fur, they wouldn't have any descendants. There wouldn't ever be any *Homo sapiens*. In a very real sense, Cohen realized he *was* hunting humans—every single human being who would ever exist.

Of course, a few hours wouldn't be enough time to kill many of them. Judge Hoskins no doubt thought it was wonderfully poetic justice, or she wouldn't have allowed the transfer: sending him back to fall into the pit, damned.

Stupid judge. Why, now that he could control the beast, there was no way he was going to let it die young. He'd just—

There it was. The fissure, a long gash in the earth, with a crumbling edge. Damn, it *was* hard to see. The shadows cast by neighboring trees made a confusing gridwork on the ground that obscured the ragged opening. No wonder the dull-witted rex had missed seeing it until it was too late.

But not this time.

Turn left, thought Cohen.

Left.

His rex obeyed.

He'd avoid this particular area in future, just to be

on the safe side. Besides, there was plenty of territory to cover. Fortunately, this was a young rex—a juvenile. There would be decades in which to continue his very special hunt. Cohen was sure that Axworthy knew his stuff: once it became apparent that the link had lasted longer than a few hours, he'd keep any attempt to pull the plug tied up in the courts for years.

Cohen felt the old pressure building in himself, and in the rex. The tyrannosaur marched on.

This was *better* than old times, he thought. Much better.

Hunting all of humanity.

The release would be *wonderful*.

He watched intently for any sign of movement in the underbrush.

DISQUISITIONS ON THE DINOSAUR

by Robert Sheckley

Robert Sheckley has been science fiction's leading humorist for four decades.

1. THE DINOSAURS OF ANCIENT ROME

Nero was very surprised when one day his freedman Pallas announced that there was a person who wanted to talk to him and wouldn't take no for an answer.

"Who is this person?" Nero said. "I don't talk to just anybody."

"You'd better talk to this guy," Pallas said.

"Why? What is it about him? He something special?"

Pallas rolled his eyes.

Nero knew that when Pallas rolled his eyes, it meant something very special indeed.

"Where is this guy?" Nero asked.

"He's outside, in the waiting room. But he said he wasn't going to wait long."

A sudden flash of fear coursed through Nero's body. He had a good-looking body. In fact, it was one of the best-looking bodies in Rome that year. A little fleshy, perhaps, but topped with glorious hair of a tawny color. Nero was one of the best-looking emperors there had been so far. Gaius, whom they called Caligula, had been a good-looking emperor, too. But he'd been crazy. In fact, poor old Uncle Claudius had been crazy, too.

"He's waiting," Pallas said.

Nero looked around. He was in a room made entirely out of marble. There were beautiful vases on the table. Etruscan work. You couldn't get any better.

27

"I don't really feel up for this," Nero said. "Why couldn't this guy have sent in a papyrus requesting an interview, like other people?"

"How the hell should I know?" Pallas snapped. His tone of voice was really ugly. Nero recoiled.

"What's the matter with you?" Nero asked.

"Nerves," Pallas said. "It's been getting rough ever since . . ."

"I know," Nero said. "Don't even mention it."

"I'm not going to mention it," Pallas said. "But really . . . Burning down Rome!"

"I told you not to mention it!"

"And why did you have to burn down the Freedman's Club? People like me haven't got a lot of places to go to."

"I didn't set that fire," Nero said.

They were referring to the fire that had recently burned down three quarters of Rome. It had been a very bad fire. There was a lot of evidence pointing to the fact that the emperor had started it himself. Nero swore that he hadn't. But, of course what else was he going to say? They had managed to put the blame on the Christians. The Christians were a very tough sect. Everyone knew they were capable of anything. But no one believed that they had started the fire that had burned Rome. What the hell, they'd lost a lot of their own stuff in that fire. A dozen proto-churches had burned down. That was not nothing. So it always came down to Nero. He was the one who was always talking about "burning with a hard gemlike flame." And Nero kept on saying, "I didn't do it." And since he was emperor, it was hard arguing with him. But since everyone knew he did it, it was hard to believe him when he said he didn't.

"Okay," Nero said, "show him in."

"Thank God," Pallas muttered under his breath. But not so softly that the emperor didn't hear it. He made a mental note: *this freedman is getting mighty uppity. He's got to go. As soon as I find another freed-*

man to take his place. But not now, because he needed Pallas to announce new people coming in.

Pallas went out of the marble room into the waiting room and returned with a tall man wearing outlandish clothing. Nero had never seen anything like this clothing, and if Nero hadn't seen it you could be pretty sure nobody else in Rome had. The guy was wearing what would later be recognized as a three-piece business suit. Slate gray. Enameled cuffs. Notched lapels. Regimental tie.

The guy said, "Ah, Nero, about time."

Nero could see at once that there was going to be a lot of trouble with this guy. As a rule, the emperor had a pretty quick way of handling people who had any potential for causing trouble. He had them killed. But this person oozed power from his every pore. The stranger had hair of a glittery blond color. His eyes were like lasers, which Nero hadn't seen yet, but which he had imagined in some of his worst nightmares.

"Welcome to Imperial Rome," Nero said, in what he hoped was an affable tone. "What can I do for you?"

"Look," the stranger said, "I got no time to fool around here. We're going to change things a bit."

"We?"

"Me and the boys. You'd call us gods. Actually we're just scientists, but to you we're gods."

"Oh my God," Nero said.

"That's the idea," the guy said. "Now the fact is, things have gone along pretty well up in what you'd call heaven but we just call Control Central. It's been getting pretty dull and we've been thinking of introducing a few changes. To liven things up. So what we're going to do is we're going to introduce dinosaurs into Rome."

Nero gaped. Then he collected himself sufficiently to close his mouth. "Dinosaurs?" he said. "I don't think I've met anyone of that name before."

"Think lizards," the stranger said.

"Ah, lizards! I've seen them."

"But these are big," the man said.

"Yes, of course," Nero said.

"No, no," the man said. "I don't mean just big. I mean humongous big. I mean really *huge*. You know the size of the Apollo that stands near the Parthenon?"

"Oh, certainly," Nero said. "I saw that on my last trip to Greece. Divine, wasn't it?"

"I don't know anything about that," the stranger said. "Art is not my field. But it's big, isn't it?"

"Oh, yes," Nero said. "It's at least twelve feet tall, not even counting the base." Nero was figuring in Roman feet, which were somewhat larger than English feet, so that was very big indeed.

"Well, that great statue," the stranger said, "would make no more than a baby dinosaur from one of the smaller species."

"Okay," Nero said, "I think I got what you mean. You mean really big."

"I mean big," the stranger said. "These things will really fill a city street. Think of a dinosaur as equivalent to a herd of elephants."

"Elephants," Nero said. "Yes, I've seen those."

"Try five or six times bigger, and armored all over, and they got huge jaws and teeth."

"And you want to bring these things into downtown Rome?"

"You got it."

"But why?"

"Ah, don't ask why," the stranger said. "When you can do these things, there's no asking why. Let's just say because it would be amusing."

"I don't think it would be very amusing," Nero said.

"You'll love it," the stranger said. "Any guy who can burn Rome ought to love dinosaurs."

"I did not burn Rome!" Nero said.

In his next proclamation, Nero said, "Let all Romans knows by this message that I have had a visit from a representative of the gods who tells me that Rome is going to be singularly blessed by a visitation, one might almost say an infestation, of dinosaurs. These will be free range roaming dinosaurs, and they will be our honored guests. It is your emperor's pleasure to grant these dinosaurs the rights of Roman citizens. They are not human beings, but I have been assured that they are intelligent and in their own way quite tractable. Please be on your best behavior with these dinosaurs. This is only a temporary measure. Everyone will have to watch the traffic patterns because there is going to be a little trouble until things have been sorted out. Faithfully yours, Nero, Emperor of all the Romans."

There was a lot of discussion about this throughout Rome, as you might expect. People said, "The emperor will do anything to get people's attention off the burning issue. But we all know he burned Rome."

A lot of people didn't believe anything was going to happen. "Dinosaurs," they said. "Who ever heard of such things?" Still, a very good crowd showed up the first day when the first assembly of dinosaurs was declared. The dinosaurs were going to march into town along the Viale Victor Emanuel II, or where that great street would be some centuries later.

At first there was a cloud of dust from off toward the Appian Way, then a stamping of feet, and then they came, the dinosaurs. They came marching through town in their ones and fives and their threes and their sixes. Handbills had been printed to identify some of the main species, because the gods, or the guys who were passing themselves off as gods, had decided that people really ought to have a program for an event like this. There were line drawings so the main outlines of the main dinosaur species could be identified. This was before the invention of the printing press, of course, but what the hell, once you start the anachronism thing you might as well throw caution to the winds and try at least to be clear.

The dinosaurs came in their astounding variety. There were allosaurs and trogodonts and flying nimichisaurs and big lumbering protosquabosaurs, and small nimble nimblokides, and there were chiron-

prontes walking in threes as they always did, while
overhead the pterodactyls soared with their long thin
beaks and their short leathery claws. And the crowds
lining either side of the great boulevards, chewing gar-
lic and onion sandwiches which had been passed out as
free party favors by the dinosaur advisory commission
hoping to make a good impression at the very start,
applauded wildly as some of the bigger beasts came
by. And watching all this from the imperial bandstand,
Nero thought it seemed a pretty good idea after all,
because, as the god guy had told him in a private
conversation, this was certainly getting people's minds
off the burning of Rome and was even better than
gladiatorial games. It's true it didn't leave much room
for Nero's artistic initiatives, and that was always a
matter dear to his heart. But still, it was something,
and Nero thought it might work out very well indeed.

2. DINOSAUR LETTER

Dear Atherwell,

In answer to your recent psychic communication:
Your ancestor, George, whom you were asking about,
was a medium-sized tyrannosaurus, weighing about
nine tons in his prime, who lived in southern Italy.
He was born in the late Cretaceous, probably toward
the end of the Campanian Age (records were a little
sparse in those days). His family, the Atherwells,
(same name as you, my darling!) were socially prominent reptiles, members of the ruling council for the
Campanian region. Of his immediate biological family, little is known, except for one sister, Aethra, who
became a fairly well-known artist in her day. We know
a little about his associative horizontal family, the list
of associations by which dinosaurs have always
grouped themselves. They include several stegosaurs,
one brontosaurus, a small tribe of triceratops who
lived by themselves near Lodi, and several archeopt-
eryx. So you can see that your uncle was by no means
"a nameless dinosaur of no social position," as has
been alleged by some of his detractors.

Your other uncle, Anchides, was one of the first of

the tyrannosaurs to arrive in Rome. He took up residence in a very large stone barn which had been built just where the Spanish Steps would be some centuries later.

The biggest problem in Rome at that time was keeping the streets clean of dinosaur dung. Dinosaurs, even civilized ones, are quite unconcerned about where they deposit their dung. And although dinosaurs have many fine and even endearing qualities, one that they do not have is that of cleaning up after themselves. "As sloppy as a dinosaur," was a popular expression in the ancient world.

A special class of men, known as dinosaur sweepers-upper, had to be enlisted. These quickly formed a labor union of their own with their own rights and privileges, and soon, their own ancient rituals, special feast days, secret handshakes, and holiday songs.

Traffic regulation was a formidable problem. Luckily, the dinosaurs picked regular hours to go back and forth in and out of the city. Most dinosaurs liked to live outside of Rome, in the green fields and the pleasant meadows out on the Appian Way. This was a good deal, especially for the herbivores among them. They had big appetites. Especially the brontosaurs, who weighed fifty or sixty tons and could in a day's browsing put away half or more of their own body bulk. Fast-growing grass species had to be imported from Asia, where they had such things. No one knows what we would have done if it hadn't been for the carnivores among them who kept trimming down the brontosaur population. This worked to the advantage of the Romans, too, who in the normal course of things were supplied with a great deal of brontosaurus meat. Brontosaurs tasted a great deal like buffalo but with a certain tang that reminded you of wild duck. It was pretty tasty grub, and that was good because there was really a lot of it.

Huge clouds of dust arose as the dinosaurs migrated in and out of the city, following the major routes like the via Flaminia. But the situation wasn't entirely satisfactory. A lot of people got trampled to death before the Romans got the hang of the new traffic patterns.

The arrival of the dinosaurs changed Roman and European history. In the east, the Parthians broke through the Armenian line but decided against invading Rome when they heard about the dinosaurs. They decided they had enough problems of their own without adding dinosaurs. The Germans and Gauls who were invading Italy across the Alps at this time decided to adopt a wait-and-see policy. Even if they did conquer Italy, what would they do with the dinosaurs?

With the dinosaurs wandering freely around Rome, the Romans found themselves with a really difficult upkeep problem. The dinosaurs were so big and clumsy, they were always chipping the cornices off buildings. And even with all the handbills available, most people didn't know one dinosaur from another, so they couldn't tell which dinosaur was responsible when they brought their complaints to the local dinosaur control boards.

It was inevitable that dinosaurs would be introduced to the gladiatorial games. It seemed a natural. But there were difficulties.

3. A CONVERSATION WITH THE DINOSAUR MASTER AT THE GLADIATOR SCHOOL

"Hail, Rufus."

"Hail, Lepidus."

"What success have you had with this afternoon's training?"

"Not too much, sir. We expended twelve gladiators against two allosaurs. The results were not impressive."

"Were you able to score any points against the dinosaurs?"

"Since, as you told us, sir, the dinosaurs are too expensive to be killed in practice sessions, but must be kept alive for the main event in the Colosseum, we observed great care not to harm them, attacking only with blunted swords and spears without metal heads. Our precautions were unnecessary, however. These dinosaurs are well able to take care of themselves. Even bowmen are unable to provide any hits that might have proved fatal. These creatures are extensively armored, as you have noted, sir, and not even a direct shot to the eye or down the throat could be counted on to prove fatal. In fact, my lord, I have my doubts as to whether any number of my gladiators could be counted on to kill the big dinosaur they call The Tyrant."

"Nonsense, Rufus. Of course they can do it. It will simply call for teamwork. One, or better still, several of the gladiators, must distract the beast while others run in and hamstring him. They must run in behind him and cut the muscles in his thighs. The dinosaur must be immobilized, then he will be easier to deal with."

"Yes, sir," Rufus said. But he wasn't convinced.

4. NERO TALKS WITH THE DINOSAUR MASTER

Not everyone agrees that the gods brought the dinosaurs to Rome. Some say that the dinosaurs were brought to Rome through purely Roman efforts, as a result of finding a hidden valley in the Alps where a strange foreign man was found keeping watch over a small clutch of dinosaurs. This man, who claimed to be a dinosaur-keeper from the future, was taken to Nero and the following interview took place.

"You are the master of the dinosaurs?"

"I am the one associated with them. Not the master, no, I don't think any man could be considered their master."

"You perhaps are ignorant of the accepted form. When you address me, you call me Your Majesty, or Excellency, or at least Caesar. I do not normally stand on ceremony, but it would be churlish to not insist upon a common and respectful form of address."

"I am sorry, Caesar. I am still overawed by being

in your presence. I never thought I'd get to see ancient Rome and a Roman emperor.''

"That's better. I think they said your name is Silas? Now, tell me something, Silas, about the place where my soldiers found you when they went hunting for dinosaurs. How did you happen to get to the past, as you call it?"

"It is very difficult to explain, Caesar. We do not have a common vocabulary about these matters. I still do not know how your soldiers came to the Time-Locked Valley where I was observing the dinosaurs.''

"I thought you had been informed as to that. When we rescued the last of the sibylline books, before the hag in whose keeping they were had a chance to burn them as she had done with the others, we looked in it and found spells for the passing to a place of great mystery. This mystery was described in detail, and there were descriptions within it of the monsters to be found there. The details as to how we got there have been mentioned by some of our writers. Our wise men, with a half legion of soldiers to protect them, invoked the spell and went to the place. There, in a great valley of ferns and strangely-shaped trees, they found the dinosaurs and you. Now then, where was this place, Master Silas?''

"You must understand, Caesar, that I am not a man of your own time. I come from a different age. It is several thousand years in the future from this time. This is not easy to understand. . . .''

"I understand it perfectly well. You claim to come from the future. Please go on.''

"In that future, Caesar, we have learned how to travel in time. It is an ability we use only rarely. There are dangers involved. When you go to the past, there is the possibility that you will change some important fact that our own time, your future, depended on. It is known as the Butterfly Theory. The trembling of a butterfly's wings, this theory goes, can discommode the entire progress of a civilization.''

"That is very fanciful, no doubt.''

"Not at all, Excellency. It is the simple truth. It is what I have been trying to warn you about."

5. THE DINOSAUR MASTER WROTE A LETTER TO THE FUTURE, THE CONTENTS OF WHICH ARE HERE REVEALED FOR THE FIRST TIME.

Dear Linda,

I doubt there will be any way of reaching you with this letter. Yet I must try it anyhow, and, even if it is impossible to think of it being delivered, I need to unburden my heart. You can imagine my surprise when, one afternoon, I was examining my parasite specimens in the little laboratory which the society constructed for me, and looked up to hear loud noises. They weren't the familiar bellowings of the dinosaurs, or any other natural sounds. Instead I heard the clash of metal objects, and the hoarse voices of men.

At first I was utterly dumbstruck. There was anger in those voices, and dismay. My immediate thought was that a change of administration had taken place in our own time, and that a crew had been sent to dismantle the laboratory and remove me from the Pleistocene. This project has always been controversial, and there have always been those who say we should not be maintaining a presence in Earth's past, not even under present circumstances, when we have walled off this past from the main line of Earth's present and future.

So, expecting to find a scientific group put forth by the new administration, I went outside, and there beheld a group of about fifty Roman soldiers of the classical period. They were small men, wearing leather uniforms upon which were plates of bronze. They wore helmets and tunics, and heavy marching sandals. Each man was armed with the pilum and had the short sword on his hip. I am by no means an expert on the classical period, or any other period of history, since my work is as a general biologist. But I had studied the period enough in university that I could make some guesses.

6. EXCERPTS FROM THE CHARLES A. BAXTER LECTURES IN COMPARATIVE FOLKLORIC DINOSAURICITY.

There are two important matters in dinosaurology which we will go into today. The first has to do with why the stegosaurus had a hindbrain, situated in the area of its hips, in addition to its forebrain, which was in the usual spot, its cranium.

The second question has to do with the use made of the very small front arms of the tyrannosaurus. Following our usual practice, we will answer the second first.

The tyrannosaurus, though a hulking twenty-foot-tall monster weighing some ten or fifteen tons, had very tiny forearms not much larger than a man's. The question has been raised, what did it do with these forearms, and why were they there at all?

The answer should come as no surprise. The tyrannosaurus, with its small forearms and its long dainty fingers—inacurrately called claws—was the preeminent cardplayer of the archaic world. The fingers of his hand, even without the presence of a true opposable thumb—something over which people make entirely too much of a fuss—were inadequate for tearing and rending, but were perfectly suited for holding cards.

Cards themselves were not a dinosaur invention. Playing cards were introduced to Earth, along with toilet fixtures and neckties, by the very first alien race to come to this planet; a race that traveled here long before the development of mankind. This race—the proto-Atlanteans—came from Arcturus, a large star with very pretty coloring.

The Arcturans could be distinguished from true humans by their possession of double opposable thumbs, which made them twice as clever as the single-opposed-thumbed humans who were to evolve later. The Arcturans had brought along with them certain subhuman servants with a shambling gait and strange coloration. These eventually became our ancestors.

The Arcturans landed here in early Paleolithic times, back when the climate was warm and mild and there was plenty of real estate around for everybody. That was before the Age of Flowers. The Arcturans didn't mind; they brought their own. Their flowers gave birth to our own Age of Flowers. Which stands to reason, of course. Where else would flowers come from? Certainly not from ferns, which are dreary things. Just as their subhumans eventually developed into our humans, as you would expect.

When the Acturans got here, they found there was nobody around to talk to except the dinosaurs. The dinosaurs were a lot smarter in those days. They looked like they had a great future. Size counted for a whole lot back then. And there were some really big ones. The bones found lying around are mainly of some of the smaller species. The big, smart dinosaurs didn't leave any bones to give themselves away with.

There were a lot of big old dinosaurs in those days, stamping and galumphing around. Galumphing is a technical term that refers to a dinosaur's natural way of progressing.

The Arcturans came down and built their tent cities and looked around for something to do. They were a card-playing race—one of the most advanced—and soon after building latrines and dance halls, they got their familiar card games going. Their game was duplicate bridge, though hearts ranked second, and there were always earnest contingents of rummy players.

The tyrannosaurs used to kibitz these games. In fact, "kibitz" is an Arcturan word meaning to watch and make snide comments. After a while, the Arcturans noted that the tyrannosaurs were making small squealing sounds through their noses during certain plays. At first the Arcturans thought this was merely a nervous mannerism. But then, checking more closely, they saw that the giant reptiles were trying to encourage certain lines of play and discourage others. Independent scientific studies by independent scientific groups verified these findings. The tyrannosaurs had a rudimentary but natural card sense, one of those prodigal endowments that nature sometimes casts upon a species.

After that realization, it was a small step to letting the big dinosaurs sometimes sit in on a game. Although their card sense needed training, the tyrannosaurs were naturals, and first-class competitors. They learned rapidly, though they had to be trained not to open four-card majors, a trait which seemed almost like an inherited predisposition. (And also to not trump their partner's ace. Something wrong in the genetic material, embedded in the DNA, no doubt, accounted for these small faults. But this was soon corrected by training.)

The tyrannosaurs proved not only adept at bridge, but to have a strong natural propensity for it. They took to it by the thousands, and then by the millions. As Russians play chess, so tyrannosaurs played bridge. It became their national sport almost at once.

Soon the tyrannosaurs couldn't be bothered to go out and kill creatures for their living. "Just send something in," they told the Arcturans. They hired some of the smaller card-positive reptiles to forage for them, rewarding them with scraps of information as to the best strategies in playing hearts, although they wouldn't pass on their bridge secrets for anything.

It was at this time that the first of earth's industries was begun. This was creating tables and chairs for tyrannosaurs to play bridge at. Typically, these were made of stone, since woodworking equipment hadn't been invented yet. You could get tables in limestone, basalt, granite, or a variety of other nice stones. Special chairs for tyrannosaurs to sit in were also an early industry. These came in two models—tail up and tail down. They were made by the subhuman Arcturan servant class, whose knowledge of this craft has persisted to the present day. It culminated in our present line of office furniture.

During those first years of card-playing, tyrannosaurus gaming skills advanced rapidly. In the beginning there were only a scattering of Junior Masters. But after less than a decade there were a thousand Life Masters in what would become North America alone. The tyrannosaurs engaged in bridge tournaments with the Arcturans and proved themselves more than a match for their far-traveling friends.

Encouraged by their first big wins, which took place at the town of Neanderthal in what would someday be Germany, they entered the next galaxywide competition and placed a very respectable third against all contestants. At the first opportunity, the tyrannosaurs decided to pursue their luck to the limit, and went to the first great all-cosmos tournament held near Deneb. There they came away with a first prize.

The tyrannosaurs were on their way to becoming the bridge champions of the universe. Unfortunately, upon returning to Earth, they inadvertently brought with them some gas-producing bacteria from Deneb that festered and grew and multiplied in the low, dark, dim places of Earth. Great clouds of the stuff came forth, and so came to an end the Age of the Reptiles.

Nothing was ever found of the playing cards of the Tyrannosaurs, because these were made of water-soluble material and did not survive the various floods that swept the Earth. Scientists are still looking for the primitive scorecards which were made of sheets of limestone with the numbers of the games scratched on them. We still have hopes of finding these things. And this is the story of what the tyrannosaurs did with their tiny forearms.

As for the stegosaurs, these big lumbering creatures with their armored and plated backs came into existence with two brains, one in the cranium, in the normal position, and the other in the back of the body, between the hips, some twenty or thirty feet away from the head. At first it was impossible to tell what this hindbrain, as it was called, was for. Nature never makes a mistake, but sometimes her purposes are a little obscure. And so it was initially with the stegosaurs' two brains. Early on the stegosaurus simply used its second brain as a kind of storage device for memories that it didn't want to lose but didn't need immediately on tap in the limited capacity of its forebrain. Here it stored old songs, rarely-used phone numbers, and recipes for special holiday foods.

It seemed pretty natural after a while for the stegosaurs to use their hindbrains as places to register information about what was going on around them, i.e., in the area of the hips and tail. It was, after all, quite a distance between the rear of a stegosaur and its front. Sometimes there could be quite a difference in what was going on in the two areas.

The hindbrain let the stegosaur know when its rear quarters were in water, for example, or on fire, without bothering the forebrain about it, since the forebrain had more than enough to keep it occupied, the Pleistocene being the sort of place it was.

The hindbrain became an important survival instrument. It was useful for finding dry, clean quarters to sleep in at night, because the forebrain had so much on its mind that it never got around to thinking about things like that. There were always new things appearing before a stegosaur's eyes, and these needed thinking about. But who was there to think about the hindquarters and what they were up to? The hindbrain served this purpose admirably.

The hindbrain early became aware of its own value and started to resent being called "hindbrain." It found the term deprecating and patronizing.

Since the hindbrain was involved in where the creature had just been, it became a specialist in memory and contemplation of the past. When combined with writing skills, the hindbrains of stegosaurs became Earth's first essayists.

These writings of the stegosaurs were the earliest flowering of nostalgic writing on the face of the Earth. The stegosaurs were the first writers with a sense of the past, of where they had come from.

The stogosaurs didn't do their own inscribing, of course. Their forepaws were not well adapted for this. Instead they enlisted certain small, agile lizards to do their writing for them. These were the amanuensoids, also known as the secretary reptiles. No one knows what the secretary reptiles got out of it, but they served an important function in the diffusion of dinosaur culture.

All might have been well with this development and this division of labor between the stegosaurus' two brains. But unfortunately the hindbrain began to develop a sense of ego, and to take umbrage at the idea of being always considered hindmost. It insisted that there was a purely abritrary definition of meaning between front and back. The hindbrain insisted that the back could lead just as well as the front. In fact, the hindbrain preached a doctrine known as Positive Retrogressionism. It was aided in this by the development of rudimentary visual apparatus in the monsters' buttocks. These were of soft tissue and have not survived in fossil form.

Soon an impasse was reached in stegosaur psychology. Every stegosaur was a split being with two egos, one in the head and one in the ass.

The situation became acute. No progress could be made. Locomotion in any direction became impossible. These vast reptiles could be seen lying on rocks arguing with themselves.

"Let's go forward."

"No, backward."

"Where do you think you're taking us?"

"Just shut up, it'll be fine."

"No, I need to have my say."

"We can't go on this way."

"Exactly what I'm saying."

And so on.

Tedious, heartbreaking conversations, during which time the poor creatures often starved to death. Before a solution could be found, the dissemination of bacterial gases from Deneb wiped out the entire dinosaur race. Ironically, this occurred just before Nature had time to make its next logical development—a third brain for the stegosaur.

This third brain was already developing in the mid-spine. There is no telling how far the stegosaurus might have come if this had had a chance to come to fruition.

DINO TREND

by Pat Cadigan

Pat Cadigan is a Hugo and Nebula nominee, and won Britain's Clarke Award for the best science fiction novel of 1992.

"The tyrannosaurus body is so popular, the cultural elite's scurrying to look up other, less vulgarized varieties," Marcia Durant said to her partner, Randall Quinn.

"What, already," said Randall.

"Sure. It's the Age of the Nanosecond as well as the Age of Nanotechnology. Every time we get something that works fast, our attention spans get shorter."

"Huh?" said Randall, looking up from the jar of Bronto-Cream she had brought home. They were sitting in their living room which was currently in flux as it became the bedroom; Randall was feeling affectionate. These days, they could have afforded to annex another room, but they had both agreed: why bother? Why bother changing location when the location could simply change for them? Then they didn't have to interrupt whatever they were doing or saying. One room was very time-efficient, and the nano-transformers changed it often enough to keep it from getting too boring. And they could use the money to buy better nano-transformers. It was a policy that fell in line with their general agreed-upon philosophy, *Do only things that make sense*.

"Do you really want us to be brontosauruses?" Randall asked her. His magenta face acquired hazard-yellow stripes along his cheekbones; doubt indicators. Color semaphore also made sense to them. They had, in fact, met through a color semaphore group. "Won't the tails kind of get in the way dragging along behind

us, maybe knocking stuff over whenever we turn
around?"

"It's just a free sample. They were handing the
jars out downtown and I took one," Marcia said,
shifting to her left as the carpet rose like yeast and
absorbed the chair she was sitting in to become the
bed. Randall had placed himself a little better and
was already leaning against the headboard while his
clothes dematerialized. Marcia's silver face took on
a row of concentric orange circles across her forehead, for frowning.

"I thought you got rid of the nanostim elements.
You know that made me uncomfortable. There are
some things I'd rather tend to myself."

Randall's yellow stripes disappeared as the deep
purple spots of embarrassment appeared all over his
face. "I did get rid of them. I'm afraid it's a reflex
now. As soon as my clothes go, *ba-da-bing!*"

A red lightning bolt of displeasure cut from Marcia's
left temple to the right corner of her mouth. "Where
do you pick up those antiquated expressions? Have
you been on the tiresome computer net again?"

"No," he lied, handing the jar of Bronto-Cream to
the nightstand as he reached for her.

She looked down and flinched. "Jesus, I'm just
never going to get used to that."

"It works fairly well for a lot of the animal kingdom," he said, rather smugly.

"For *dogs*," she insisted. "*Dogs* have ones that—
telescope." Wavy blue lines of distaste appeared
around her mouth, disappearing almost immediately,
but not too quickly that Randall didn't see.

"When are you going to give me a break?" he demanded, falling back against the pillows, white curli-
cues swimming down his face. "You know it wouldn't
have happened if you hadn't insisted on us trying the
nano-ticklers. I know, I know—" he put up a hand as
she started to protest "—there was no way *you* could
have known they were defective any more than *I* could
have. But I *still* say I'm lucky to be alive. They could
have eaten the rest of me away, too. As it was, I had

a bad time with the trauma, and I expected *a lot* more understanding from *you*—"

"Hey, I was traumatized, too, you know," Marcia said. "I'll never forget the sight of you laying there while your—"

"All right, all *right*!" Randall pulled the sheet over himself.

"What," Marcia said, looking pointedly at the covered lower half of his body.

"It's customary to cover the dead, excuse me very much." He stared away from her. "You had to *insist* that I get rid of the 'stims. And worse, *I* had to listen to you."

"Fine," Marcia said tonelessly, and took the Bronto-Cream from the nightstand.

The cream had been loaded with pixie dust, which glittered a lot for the sake of special effects but was otherwise inert. Marcia's body was transformed within ten minutes. She made a rather small brontosaurus, of course, but she was an exquisite jewel-tone green.

"Nice tail," Randall said, impressed in spite of everything. He picked the open jar up off the bed where Marcia had left it. She couldn't pick anything up herself now. "Boy, not much left here. I guess I'll have to just watch tonight."

She gazed at him with her flat, reptilian eyes and wiggled her toes.

"Well, what?" he said. "Do you want to go out now or something?" He laughed. "Remember, it's just a body. If you have a craving to wade in muddy water and eat seaweed off the bottom, it's strictly psychosomatic."

"I *know* that," she growled, her voice sounding slightly muffled and slurred. "I guess I'll go out to one of the new dino clubs. Unless you have some objection." He didn't; she plodded toward the front door. It dematerialized, parting for her like a curtain, and then resolidified as soon as the tip of her tail disappeared.

"I don't know," Randall sighed. "I just don't know anything any more." He looked over at her side of the bed.

"You were supposed to beg her not to go," said Marcia's side of the mattress, a little chidingly. "Either that or say you wanted to go with her, and stop on the way and get a dino body."

"Oh, shut up." Randall drew the blanket up on her side. "Everything's so easy for a mattress. You ought to try it walking around out here where you actually have to put it all on the line every day. I bet it wouldn't seem so simple then."

"Any time you want to switch, say so," came the mattress' voice faintly from beneath the sheet. "I bet you wouldn't think my job was any picnic either."

"Don't be ridiculous, you're not even intelligent. You're a goddamn answering machine that fell into the bed one day and got lost. In case you've forgotten. *I* haven't. It cost enough to get a new one."

"A *much* better model, however," said the new answering machine from the nightstand.

"Shut up, shut *up*!" Randall said, irritated. He jumped out of bed and threw a handful of clothing matter at himself. Two minutes later, he was covered in a suit that seemed to be made of dinosaur hide. "Now look at that. A trend already. Don't answer that!" he added quickly, addressing both the mattress and the new answering machine. "There was a time when people didn't have to engage in stupid conversations with their possessions. The dinosaurs, too, were thusly blessed."

He headed for the door, expecting it to dematerialize and hit the woodlike surface nose first. "Oh, come *on*." He glared at the bed. "You didn't slip into the door, too, did you?"

The mattress sat up. "No, it just has strong feelings for Marcia."

Randall turned back to the door. "I'll get an *axe*."

The door promptly dematerialized for him and he stomped out.

The streets were filled with a mixture of fancied-up

people and dino-people. The sight of the dinos mixed in with everything else wasn't unexpected, but he found it depressing just the same. Maybe it was because those reptilian heads all had a built-in snobby air, with those strange flat eyes and strangely-placed nostrils, or maybe it was because he couldn't tell whether any of the brontosauruses were Marcia, if indeed *any* of them were.

She couldn't have gotten very far very fast, he reasoned, since she didn't seem able to move too quickly as a brontosaurus. None of the brontosauruses he could see were in a hurry, but maybe that was because she knew he wouldn't be able to pick her out. Maybe this was her way of breaking up with him. Declaring their relationship extinct, so to speak.

Well, that *was fast*, he thought unhappily. One moment they had been getting ready to make love, the next she was starting a new life as a plant-eating reptile.

Age of the Nanosecond. Every time we get something that works fast, our attention spans get shorter.

As if to underscore Marcia's remembered words, the pavement under his feet changed from a toasty-golden color to a shiny black, the change sweeping along like a chromatic tidal wave.

"Well, that's *terrible*," complained a nearby allosaurus in a strained and slightly muffled female voice. She lifted one mighty-looking hind leg and then another. "It makes the whole street look like a *tar pit*. Why on Earth would anyone think we all wanted to walk in a *tar pit*?" Her foreclaws opened and closed in distaste. Randall blinked at her, then rubbed his eyes. Horrible as it was to contemplate, the allosaurus looked good to him. So Marcia had been more correct than she knew, he thought; he was going along with the trend in a slightly different way. Or rather, the trend was hijacking him. No, *hacking* him—it had found an access to him and entered there, working a few subtle alterations in his *Weltanschaaung*. He sighed, but that didn't make the allosaurus look any less good to him.

Maybe it's because she's a flesh-eater and that association appeals to me more than a plant-eater, he thought, sidling closer to the allosaurus. It was strange, since he and Marcia had both been vegetarians. But then, the allosaurus also had limbs that would serve as hands, whereas Marcia was now limited to going around on all fours. Why hadn't Marcia thought of that?

Or had she?

Now he was getting on his own nerves with his paranoia. He looked at the allosaurus, who was regarding him with what appeared to him to be speculation. Or . . . hunger?

"Um?" he said. The allosaurus wasn't actually any bigger than he was but it *felt* bigger. *Stronger.* Well, it *looked* stronger.

"Excuse me, miz." A hadrosaur with navy blue accents and a badly-fitting Sam Browne belt materialized at Randall's side pointedly looking only at her. "Is this biped bothering you?"

"I was just going," Randall said and hurried down the sidewalk, weaving between the dinos and the still-recognizably-humans. When he dared to turn around and look back, he couldn't really see anything except the top of the allosaurus' head, and even then, he couldn't have sworn it was the same one.

"Tyrannosaurus cream?" someone said close to his ear. He turned and found himself looking at a man who might have been the result of a crocodile-human liaison.

"Were you giving out brontosaurus cream a while ago?" Randall asked suspiciously.

"All gone," said the man apologetically and licked his chops. "After this runs out, I think they'll give me some stegosaurus ointment. Bronto-Cream will probably be going on sale at the nearest nano-boutique any minute now—"

Randall resisted the urge to lunge for his neck with both hands. It was a thick neck and there were entirely too many teeth in the man's smile. Instead, he walked on, feeling so morose and frustrated that even his semaphore had subsided.

Maybe he should just follow Marcia into whatever dino club she was frequenting these days. Except he was pretty sure that if he wanted to be any kind of dinosaur, he'd choose one with hands—or whatever—so perhaps their relationship had been doomed after all.

"Everything comes to an end," he said, sighing.

"Pardon?" said a passing iguanodon, looking at him suspiciously. Or just looking at him—the reptilian face looked suspicious as a matter of course.

"Nothing," Randall said, "I was just talking to myself."

"For god's sake, *why*?" asked the iguanodon, gesturing with its claws.

"Boy, you know, people as dinosaurs are a lot nosier than they were as people," he said.

The iguanodon motioned at itself. "It's like a full-body mask. Both liberating and concealing." The voice was so strained, Randall couldn't say for sure whether it was a man or a woman, and he couldn't bring himself to look closely at the physiognomy to find out. Dinosaur throats weren't made for talking, he thought. *What if people stop talking, what will they do?* he wondered. *Perhaps they'll take up sign language—those that have the right kinds of forelimbs.* . . . He thought of Marcia; what about her species and those like it?

The dinosaur population on the street seemed to be increasing as he stood there and, as Marcia had mentioned, an awful lot of them were tyrannosauruses. Nanotechnology and the nanosecond. Marcia had always had a lot of insight to offer about modern life; he was going to miss her.

And what was he doing out on the street anyway? If he wasn't going to get to a nano-boutique for the latest in makeover trends, he might as well go home and wait it out. Even if there wasn't anyone to wait it out with anymore.

*   *   *

When the door dematerialized and let him back in, he found himself hip-deep in swamp water. Whether it was a swamp from the Jurassic or the Cretaceous, he didn't know, but he knew the brontosaurus standing in the middle of the room where the bed had been.

"I thought you were going to a dino club," he said, taking a step toward her.

"Was," Marcia said with some difficulty. "Then I decided it was no fun without you." She swung her head from side to side. "I redecorated. I know, I know, it's psychosomatic, but it makes me feel better. If you really hate it, we can change it, or even switch it back later."

"Actually, I could get used to it," he said, looking down at the water. "It's nice and quiet without the answering machines jabbering and interrupting the way they used to. But I feel a little out of place."

Marcia swung her long neck toward something that looked like an antediluvian rubber plant. There was a jar on top of it. Randall picked it up.

" '*Camptosaurus,*' " he read. " '*One of the first of the bird-hipped dinos, herbivorous, bipedal.*' " He looked up at her, touched. "It's got *hands.*"

Marcia's head bobbed up and down slowly. "Even when I'm a dinosaur, I understand you. And—well—certain features have more appeal for me now. You know, some things just seem more appropriate on a reptile."

"Yeah. I know." He sighed, thinking of the allosaurus. "Well, okay. But later, do you think we could switch to meat-eaters?"

The brontosaurus looked hesitant. Or maybe it had no expression at all. The color semaphore had not survived the transformation and he wasn't used to it yet. "We can talk about it, but frankly, I don't think the apartment is big enough."

"We could add another room now," he said. "Doesn't that make sense?"

"Let me give it some thought," she said.

He considered asking if they could reinstate their color semaphore as well and decided against pushing things for the time being. He would wait until they became carnivorous. But the trend was extinct before they got that far, and when they became mammals again, they broke up after all.

THE GREATEST DYING

by Frank M. Robinson

Frank Robinson has been writing science fiction and main-stream for four decades; two of his novels have been made into highly successful movies.

Under the lab light, the piece of amber glimmered with a soft rosy glow. Reid Locke turned it over with a pair of tongs, then held it up so it was illuminated from behind. He'd put it under the 'scope in a minute but for right now he wanted to get a rough idea of what had been entombed within. He adjusted the magnifying glasses on the end of his nose and moved the chunk of resin closer.

The usual shreds of dirt and grasses and thin strips of what he assumed were bark. He started making notes on a pad, meticulously listing every detail of what had been frozen in time. There was something else in the center, partly obscured by surrounding detritus. Locke squinted, trying to make out what it was.

A moment later, he put down the piece of amber and leaned back in his chair. It was cool in the lab, but he was a big man and sweated easily and he could feel a thin film of perspiration on his forehead. He'd have to put the amber under the 'scope to make sure, but there wasn't much doubt about it. Cradled in the middle of the piece of resin was a tiny claw from a finger bone and . . . maybe . . . something else.

He sighed and riffled through the papers that had come along with the amber. Like much research amber, it had originated in Peru high in the mountains which, millions of years ago, probably hadn't been mountains at all but a pleasant valley fringed by an ancient forest. It was a huge chunk of resin—the largest he'd seen, almost eight inches long—but murkier than most.

How old . . . ?

He riffled through another few sheets of paper and stopped. The dating lab had been appropriately vague, not wanting to go out on a limb. But it was a preliminary report and no doubt they'd make a more detailed analysis later.

According to the lab, the amber dated from the late Cretaceous, some sixty-five to seventy million years ago. He'd heard of more ancient pieces of amber but had never seen one; it was certainly the oldest the museum had ever analyzed.

He mopped at his face, then placed the amber on a tray by the 'scope. He should probably notify Austin and Paschelke—he had a bitter feeling when he thought of them—but they were upstairs looking over the diorama that dominated the main hall of the museum. It would open tomorrow for public viewing and there would be the press as well as thousands of kids—the papers had already published drawings of the huge ultrasaurus rearing up on its hind legs for a total height of six stories, ready to trample on an allosaurus slashing at its feet. It had been a tremendous project, featuring replicas of the beasts themselves, complete with mottled "skins," angry eyes, and terrifying claws and teeth.

He hesitated. Notifying Austin and Paschelke right then would not only interrupt them, it would probably be premature and Paschelke, especially, would belittle him for it.

He reached for the piece of amber again, carefully measured its dimensions, then held it up once more to the halogen lamp. A small claw, all right, maybe two inches long and an inch wide at best. And . . .

He frowned, then maneuvered the piece of amber into the specimen holder on the stage of the 'scope. He leaned forward to the eyepieces, working the adjustments to bring the claw into focus. After a long moment, he leaned back, once again mopping at his forehead. No doubt at all. One claw, and at the tip of it, neatly skewered by the claw itself, a small piece of what looked like flesh.

The oldest piece of flesh in history, carefully dessicated and preserved by the amber which acted as a natural antibiotic.

He frowned, then flipped back through the pages of the dating report. Approximately sixty-five million years old, the end of the Cretaceous when the dinosaurs had suddenly disappeared from the pages of history.

He stared at the piece of amber, seeing in his mind's eye the broad savanna, with the small carnivorous theropod darting after its prey, spearing it with its claw and wolfing it down. Once having fed, it had wandered into the forest, pausing to scrape its claws down the trunk of a tree to rid itself of a tiny, tenacious piece of meat that still clung to the tip of one of them. The claw had stuck in the bark and, perhaps loosened in the fight, stayed there when the victor had jerked away. And shortly thereafter a glob of sap had oozed from the tree trunk, encasing the claw and the tidbit of meat and preserving them for aeons.

Austin and Paschelke should know, it would make their day, he thought sourly.

But a minute later, he was still hesitating. Austin and Paschelke didn't need to know right away and besides, he was . . . curious.

"How old is it?" the reporter asked. He paused with his photographer at the railing surrounding the small, sandy mound on which the ultrasaurus and the smaller allosaurus fought in silent fury. He stared up in awe at the beast that towered above him.

Julius Paschelke hooked a thumb in his lapel, knowing that it made him look more professional and authoritarian and hating himself—though only slightly—because it did.

"Late Jurassic, maybe early Cretaceous. About a hundred and fifty million years ago." He smiled. "Give or take a few hundred thousand."

The photographer shot away, crouching low on the

floor so the head of the towering ultrasaurus would appear even higher. Harry Austin was working with the photographer, occasionally glancing over at Julius and the reporter, and Paschelke felt uncomfortable, as he usually did around Harry. He was titular head of the museum and its chief fund-raiser and spokesman while Harry ran the "bone room" and the research staff. Harry was a brilliant man, he thought reluctantly. His own main asset was that he looked the part of an administrator—tall, professorial, with a neatly trimmed mustache and hair that was just starting to silver.

Harry, on the other hand, was black-bearded and shaggy, comfortable in baggy jeans and sweatshirts and happiest working in the bone room, cheerfully leaving to Paschelke the job of meeting the public. Paschelke knew he was at his best acting as spokesman and explaining the various dioramas of dinosaurs and stuffed mastodons and saber-toothed cats mired in a tar pit while Harry was more at home working on the fossils in the bone room and talking to the squads of schoolkids as they came through on guided tours.

The photographer was now taking closeups of the gaping mouth of the allosaurus, trying to get the light to glint off its huge, serrated teeth.

"They ruled the earth, right?" the reporter asked, scribbling notes.

"For a hundred and fifty million years," Paschelke nodded. "Quite a bit longer than we humans."

The reporter wandered over to a glassed-in diorama that showed several startled dinosaurs that had been feeding in a lakebed glancing up at a sky blazing with light.

The case was labeled: *The Great Dying*.

"And then they vanished, just like that?"

Paschelke shrugged. "That's the theory—they died in a mass extinction. A large meteorite struck the earth and changed the climate so much all the dinosaurs died—probably in a matter of a few months."

The photographer and Austin had moved over to

the imitation tar pit and were snapping photos of the mastodon and the snarling saber-toothed cat.

"How do they know?" the reporter asked, frowning. "About the meteorite and all."

Paschelke glanced at his watch. This was going to take another half an hour, more than he had allotted. On the other hand, the museum and its new exhibit would probably be the featured story in the "habitat" section of the Sunday paper.

"To be simplistic about it, you dig through the various strata of earth in dinosaur country and you come across a thin layer of what used to be mud called the K-T layer. It marks the boundary between the Cretaceous and the Tertiary. They're . . . periods of time."

The reporter hadn't jotted down a note.

"I know. I learned that in high school."

You could never predict how much they knew and how much they didn't know, Paschelke sighed to himself.

"To make a long story short, below that layer are all the dinosaur fossils. Above it, there are none. The layer itself contains some thirty times as much iridium as you would expect to find. And iridium is an element that's present in relatively high quantities in asteroids."

The photographer had circled the pit and was taking more photos of the huge cat, trying to find different and more terrifying angles. Paschelke smiled. He wasn't watching his framing, his editor would scrap at least half a dozen—too much of the rear end of the mastodon.

"They ever find it?" the reporter asked.

"Find what?" Paschelke asked, puzzled, then picked up the reference. "There're maybe a hundred and twenty large craters that we can make out on the surface of the Earth. We've been hit by meteorites as much as the moon, but our sites are eroded or covered with sediment with a very few exceptions. We've located two sites of enormous meteorites that might have struck at the K-T boundary, sixty-five million years ago. One's in the Caribbean, just off of South America, and the other is the Chicxulub crater on the coast of the Yucatan."

A moment of quiet while the reporter scribbled in his notebook. A dozen feet away, Austin looked over, tuning in to the conversation. With God's help, Harry would keep his opinions to himself, Paschelke thought hopefully.

"You said 'enormous,' Professor Paschelke. How enormous?"

"Probably a meteorite whose diameter was as big as San Francisco is across—maybe seven miles, maybe a little more—traveling at a hundred and fifty thousand miles an hour." He looked properly somber. "Enough to cause quite a bit of damage."

The reporter glanced up from his pad, waited a moment, then said: "I guess that's the heart of it, Professor. How much damage?"

Austin looked as if he were about to interrupt at any moment. Paschelke cleared his throat.

"It was the greatest catastrophe in the history of the world. Another name for it is 'the great dying.' Almost half the life in the world disappeared—vegetable as well as animal, a quarter of the marine life, most of the species of plankton, most of the marsupials." He smiled thinly. "On land, almost all animals that weighed more than sixty pounds were wiped out."

The reporter's pencil had wavered to a stop. Paschelke thought he looked a little gray.

"How'd they die?"

The reporter wouldn't get it right, Paschelke thought, and he'd have to spend the next week explaining it all over again to confused callers.

"At the point of impact, the shock and the fireball erased all life for miles around—the meteorite gouged out a crater maybe twenty-five miles deep and over a hundred wide. The amount of debris in the atmosphere obscured the sun for months and it wouldn't have taken long for vegetation to die and then the herbivores and after that the carnivores. If you were small, you might have been able to burrow and hibernate until it was all over. If you couldn't . . ." He shrugged again.

The reporter wrote furiously.

"Any other effects?"

Paschelke frowned. There was a danger the newspaper article would focus more on mass extinctions rather than on the museum and its new exhibit.

"The fireball would have consumed a lot of the nitrogen in the atmosphere and then acid rains would have killed off a lot of the vegetation, maybe affected the ph balance of the oceans. And if the meteorite actually hit off the Yucatan, that would have been a worst case scenario. The rocks in the area are mostly limestone which stores carbon dioxide. The impact might have released huge quantities of the carbon dioxide and then for the next few thousand years you would've had a mini-greenhouse effect. What hadn't died because of the cold and the darkness would have died from overheating."

He made a show of glancing at his watch.

"We still have time for the other exhibits—"

Austin had walked over and the reporter glanced up, realizing he'd heard the whole conversation.

"Any other theories, Professor Austin? Or do you agree with all this?"

Here it comes, Paschelke thought glumly. He might as well kiss an early dinner good-bye.

"Well, no," Austin said. "No, I don't."

In the bone room, Reid Locke leaned over his worktable, operating a high-powered dental drill, slowly carving the claw and the clinging bit of meat out of the amber. It was going to cost him his job, he thought, but on the other hand, it could also make his reputation. The fossil in the piece of amber was worth a fortune, not only to any museum in the country but to research institutions and medical houses as well.

The claw could yield up dinosaur DNA—possibly for the first time; he hadn't seen anything else in the literature. There had been the work by Poinar and the rather sensational movie, but now it could be a reality. DNA had been obtained from the scales of fish 200 million years old and researchers were well on their way to establishing a historical DNA map from the oldest to the most recent. Now they would have a solid link between the later dinosaurs and modern birds and who knew what else? And for once the credit would be his. . . .

He slowly cut through ancient leaves and shreds of bark and tiny insects that had been trapped in the amber with the claw. He had to be very careful that he didn't cut the claw itself, just rough it out—

My God, what am I doing?

He liked the bone room and his work there and he'd always thought he would be content to spend the rest of his life working there. But all it had taken was one small temptation.

Well, not a small temptation. A very large one.

For a moment he was blinded by the sweat from his forehead and fumbled for his handkerchief to wipe it away. The piece of amber was probably the most valuable artifact in the world and he was carving it up like a stick of butter. But it had been too late the moment he had made the first cut; there was no going back.

He made the last incision with the drill, then lifted out the rough form of the claw and the remains of its victim, still surrounded by a thin coating of amber. The next step would be the most risky of all.

He filled a deep, enamel pan with solvent and then located a bottle of preservative. The less exposure to oxygen, the better—no telling what it would do to either the claw or its final bit of dinner.

He made sure the level was high enough that the amber-covered claw would be covered, then lowered it in. He swirled the solvent slowly with a pipette, leaning close so he could watch the amber as it dissolved. The small shred of meat would be fragile; as soon as it was free of the amber, he'd have to put it into the preservative.

He leaned closer and squinted at the amber.

Now.

He fished out the claw with the tongs to drop it into the preservative, shoving slightly against the lab stool he was sitting on. He'd meant to do something about the weak leg days ago but hadn't gotten around to it and, in fact, had forgotten all about it. The stool wobbled and the wet claw slipped out of the tongs.

Without thinking he grabbed for it with his hand and a moment later was staring at the claw, embedded deep in the palm of his right hand, the small bit of ancient meat hanging from the wound like a limp flag. Even as he watched, blood welled out from around the claw to run down the creases of his palm and drip onto the table top.

Too late, he remembered the other reasons why medical labs would be interested in the claw.

"You don't agree," the reporter said to Austin, his pen poised above his notepad.

Austin pulled on his beard and thoughtfully shook his head.

"I guess I don't believe in bolts out of the blue. There have been at least eight mass extinctions, the last one about ten thousand years ago that wiped out the mammoths, the mastodons, the saber-tooths, the giant camels, and a dozen other species. I haven't read any theories that postulated a meteorite was responsible for that one."

Paschelke managed a nervous smile.

"We have our professional differences. Any good research institution does and this museum is also a research institution."

"So why'd they die?" the reporter persisted. "I mean, the dinosaurs, not the others."

"I guess I don't buy the premise to begin with," Austin said. "If you believe in the theory, you have to believe they all died within a matter of months. Actually, the extinction was spread over hundreds of thousands of years."

The reporter stopped writing.

"The meteorite," he said, curious. "There wasn't any?"

Austin shrugged.

"Could have been. If it was, it was just the last straw as far as the few remaining dinosaurs were concerned."

"The sea animals," the reporter frowned. "Professor Paschelke says that many of them died out as well."

Austin shook his head in disagreement.

"Not because of the meteorite. Most of them lived in shallow seas and when the continents rose, the seas drained off and they lost their habitat—they couldn't live in the colder waters of the oceans."

The reporter folded up his notebook.

"Well, I thank you, gentlemen. I think I've got more than enough."

"There were other reasons, too," Austin added tentatively.

The reporter paused, then opened his notebook again. Paschelke groaned to himself. Harry wasn't going to leave not-so-well enough alone.

"Once the seas drained off," Austin continued, "land bridges were established and animals from the different continents mixed—mammals and dinosaurs crossed over to North America from Asia and vice versa. That was at the end of the Cretaceous and could have resulted in a lot of extinctions."

The reporter looked puzzled.

"I don't get it. How did that cause extinctions?"

"It's one of the theories," Paschelke said before Austin could answer. If he didn't say something now, the reporter would think he was wedded to one theory and actually he was a good deal more open-minded than that. At least, it would be politic to appear that way in print.

"It's actually a disease theory. Animals in one area have certain diseases that they've grown relatively immune to, then they travel to another area and the new population of animals is suddenly exposed to diseases to which they have no immunity at all. After the seas had drained and the land bridges opened up, it probably worked both ways. Dinosaurs from North America spread diseases to those in Asia and vice versa."

"Any examples?" the reporter asked.

"Sure," Austin interrupted with just a trace of bitterness, and Paschelke remembered that Harry was part Navajo. "When the first settlers came to America, they brought smallpox with them and an estimated fifteen million Indians died from it because they had no immunity. Cortes never conquered the Aztecs—smallpox did."

The reporter looked thoughtful.

"You're trying to tell me the dinosaurs were killed by plague?"

Austin smiled. "Now you've got it. Maybe they had fleas on them that spread it or maybe they had viral diseases, a dinosaur version of AIDS, or maybe it was something bacterial."

"Interesting thought," the reporter said. The photographer had packed up by now and they were both ready to leave. "Any idea when the next mass extinction will come along?"

Austin hesitated. "You're living in one," he said slowly. "In the last three hundred years more species have died off than at any time since the late Cretaceous."

Another scribble in his notebook and the reporter turned to go, almost bumping into Reid Locke, who, with a red-stained handkerchief wrapped around his hand, was hurrying toward the glass doors.

It was Austin who noticed the handkerchief and said, "Hey, Reid, what'd you do to your hand?"

A small incident in time that nobody would think about until later—but not much later. It was Austin who unwrapped the handkerchief to inspect Locke's profusely bleeding wound; he wasn't bothered by the blood that dripped on his own hand. He handed the handkerchief to Paschelke to hold while he went to the storeroom to get some clean cloth to wrap the hand. Paschelke got some of the blood on his suit and even though he held the handkerchief gingerly, a little of the blood smeared on his fingers.

They bound Locke's palm with clean cloth, dropped the sopping, bloody handkerchief into a waste bin, then shook hands with both the reporter and the photographer as they left. Unknown to both, small flecks of blood were transferred from Austin and Paschelke to their own hands.

Later that week, Paschelke's wife handled his suit and sent it to the cleaner's, who handled it once more before passing it on to the workers in the shop.

Reid Locke got home and told his wife he had to visit his brother across state. He didn't know what to do. By the next day, Austin and Paschelke would have found the pieces of amber and the bloody claw where he had hidden them in a drawer, wrapped in muslin.

The story came out in the Sunday paper and the museum was swamped with visitors. Paschelke wasn't feeling well and suspected that, with clogged sinuses and the sniffles, he was coming down with a viral infection. But he acted as host for the dignitaries who showed up, stared in awe at the ultrasaurus rearing overhead, then shook his hand and went back to a hundred different cities and museums across the nation.

Austin fought his own rising fever and toward the end of the week, had to excuse himself from talking to the kids who toured the bone room in droves. But, as usual, he patted them on the shoulder as they left.

That following week, the reporter got a new assignment in Los Angeles to chronicle the closing of what had been an aircraft plant vital to Defense. He met with the heads of the union and various plant officials, embarrassing himself when he suddenly sneezed and failed to cover his mouth while talking to them.

The highway patrol found Reid Locke dead in his car near Vegas, his face contorted with agony and with black, ugly sores on his skin. Oddly, when they moved him, the nails fell off the ends of his fingers. None of the patrolmen wore gloves or masks and neither did the ambulance workers who handled the body.

Two days later the reporter checked into the hospital and three days after that he died, his nurses now wearing masks and gloves because none of the doctors had been able to identify the disease. But before that, none of them had taken any contagion precautions.

By this time, of course, both Professors Paschelke and Austin had died. They had never found the bits of amber and bloody claw in the bone room.

Æons went by and a new race evolved to fill the evolutionary niche that had suddenly been deserted. Cities rose and fell, science progressed as science always does, and eventually a researcher discovered the thin layer of mud that was the boundary between the Quaternary and their own geological period. It was heavy in iron and was found in scattered parts of the globe and dated back to approximately fifty million years before. The most popular theory was that the layer had been the result of a huge meteorite colliding with the earth, since meteorites were heavy with iron.

And it would also explain the huge mass extinction that occurred then. Below the boundary layer, the earth was thick with fossils, especially those of primates, while above it there were none. But the primates weren't the only ones. Countless numbers of other species had vanished as well, including much vegetation and sea life. There had been evidence of mass extinctions before, of course, but never one of this size and scope.

They called it "the period of the greatest dying."

REVENANTS

by Judith Tarr

Judith Tarr is a best-selling fantasy novelist.

Janie wanted to pet the pterodactyl.

"Here's the auk," I said. "Look how soft his feathers are. Look at the dodo, isn't he funny? Don't you want to give the quagga a carrot?"

Janie wouldn't even dignify that with disgust. It was the pterodactyl or nothing.

Janie is four. At four, *all or nothing* isn't a philosophy, it's universal law. A very intelligent four can argue that this is the Greater Metro Revenants' Zoo, yes? And this is the room where they keep the ones that can be petted, yes? So why can't a person pet the pterodactyl?

No use explaining that everything else was inoculated and immunized and sterilized and rendered safe for children to handle. Everything but the pterodactyl. They'd just made it, and it was supposed to be pettable when they were done, but not yet. There'd been plenty of controversy about putting it on display so soon, but public outcry won out over scientific common sense. So the thing was on display, but behind neoglas inlaid with the injunction: *No, I'm Not Ready Yet. Look, But Don't Touch.*

Janie reads. I should know. It's one of the chief points of debate between her father and me. She could read the warning as well as I could. "So why can't I touch? I want to *touch!*"

She was fast winding up to a tantrum. I could stop it now and risk an injunction for public child abuse, or wait till it became a nuisance and we were both shuffled off the premises.

Inside its enclosure, the pterodactyl stretched its

wings and opened its beak and hissed. Neoglas is new, about as new as revenants; it's one-way to sound as well as sight. The pterodactyl couldn't see us or hear us, which was lucky for Janie. I wished we couldn't see or hear it, either.

It wasn't particularly ugly, just strange. One whole faction of paleontologists had been thrown out into the cold when the thing came out of its vat warm-blooded and covered with soft silvery-white fur. Without the fur it would have been a leathery lizardlike thing with batwings. With the fur it looked like a white bat with a peculiar, half-avian, half-saurian head, and extremely convincing talons.

Janie's fixation and the thing's furriness notwithstanding, it didn't look very pettable. Its eyes were a disturbing shade of red, with pinpoint pupils. I wondered if it was hungry, or if it wanted to stretch its wings and fly.

Janie had stopped whining. She was going to howl next.

Something bellowed in the bowels of the building. Janie's mouth snapped shut.

"There," I said. "Look what you did."

If that got me cited, let it. It cut off Janie's howl before it started.

"They've got something big down there," somebody said.

"Probably the aurochs," said somebody else. "Mammoths trumpet like elephants."

"Maybe it's a *T. Rex*," said a kid's voice.

"They don't have one of those yet," said the one who knew it all. "They'd need a bigger enclosure than they can afford to build, with a stronger perimeter field. So they're bringing back later things, because they're smaller."

"But if they've got the mammoths—"

"Mammoths don't have teeth as long as your arm. They don't *eat* people."

Janie's eyes were as big as they can get. I got her out of there before she decided she wanted to howl after all.

*   *   *

Ice cream distracted her. So did a pony ride in the zoo's park—the pony was a Merychippus, a handsome little dun that looked perfectly ponylike except for the pair of vestigial toes flanking each of its hoofs. By the time we picked up our picnic and headed for the tables by the mammoths' pit, I was starting to breathe almost normally.

If you haven't got your kid license yet, you can only imagine you know what it's like to take the qualifying exam. Studying for it is hell, and the practicum's a raving bitch. Then when you pass and get the kid, six times out of ten you and your SO are so done for you split, and you get into a whole new brand of bureaucratic balls-up: the custody war.

This was Marco's year to have Janie. It coincided with his decision to take his statutory change-of-lifestyle, which wouldn't have been quite so bad if he hadn't decided to become an Atavist. I appealed, of course. How could any public office, even the Bureau of Family Values, consign a four-year-old child to the life of an Ice Age hunter?

BFV could, and did. *Healthy* was one of the words it used. *Back to basics. Good for growing minds.* And, as the caseworker pointed out to me, it wasn't as if the Atavists really lived as they did in the Ice Age. There weren't any major predators in the preserve. My nightmares of sabertoothed cats and direwolves and charging mammoths were just that, nightmares. Even the Atavists' League couldn't afford the price of a revenant, let alone a whole ecology full of them.

So what was I doing taking Janie to the revenants' zoo on my monthly visiting day? Maybe I thought it would be a harmless way to spend the day, and she could go back and tell her father that I'd shown her what real atavisms looked like, and he'd get the message while I got points for culturally relevant entertainment of child during custodial visit. I got her back in nine months, but only if I demonstrated that I was still fit to keep her. If I blew it on points, Marco kept her. And she grew up wearing deerskins, with a bone through her nose.

To be strictly fair, she hadn't come out of the preserve this morning looking like a savage. Her hair was
longer, and somebody had cornrowed it—not Marco,
he didn't have the patience for anything that persnick-
ety. She was wearing pants I'd bought for her, and a
shirt with a hologram on it, one of the Lascaux cave
paintings. She'd been clean when she started, too. Ice
Age didn't mean Dirt Age, Marco was fond of pointing out.

I couldn't even complain that she was different. She
hadn't forgotten about cars and buses and taxis. The
city didn't make her whimper and cower. Whatever
she was living on in the preserve, she wasn't turning
up her nose at ice cream or fruit juice or, goddess
forbid, chocolate.

The trouble was, I *wanted* her to be different. I
wanted grounds to get her back permanently. If she'd
started grunting and rooting for grubs, I'd have been
on the net to BFV so fast, the phosphors would have
been spinning.

No such luck. The first visiting day, she'd cried
when she left Marco, and cried when she left me. The
second, she'd said a cool good-bye to Marco and an
equally cool one to me. This time, the third, she'd
kissed Marco good-bye and taken my hand and said,
"I want to ride a pony."

"They don't have those in the Ice Age?" I'd asked
Marco.

He wouldn't give me the pleasure of looking annoyed. "We're domesticating a few, but not for the
kids, yet. Give us time."

Time was all he had, I thought of saying but didn't.

Now here we were, doting mother and loving
daughter, carrying a picnic basket through the park to
the best place of all, right up over the mammoths' pit.
There wasn't anybody at the table I'd had my eye on,
which I decided to take as an omen. We spread out
our picnic, everything Janie liked best, peanut-butter-
and-banana sandwiches and chocolate soymilk and
green cheese puffs and her favorite edible thing of all,
pink marshmallow bunnies. I figured when I packed

the basket that I'd lose points on Healthy Nutrition and gain them on Allowable Indulgences.

Janie ate half of her sandwich, drank three swallows of her milk, ate one cheese puff and the tail of a marshmallow bunny, and said, "I want to pet the pterodactyl."

My blood sugar was in the stratosphere—I'd be eating broccoli for a week to compensate—but it kept me from flipping out a flat negative. I decided to try being reasonable. Sometimes it even works. "Why do you want to pet the pterodactyl?"

"I want to," said Janie.

"Why?" I asked again.

"I could pet the auk. I could pet the baby mammoth. I want to pet the pterodactyl."

"The pterodactyl's not ready to be petted yet," I said. "It might bite."

"It won't bite me," said Janie. "I want to pet it."

"Would it help," I asked, "if I bought you a toy pterodactyl? Then you can pet that."

"I want the real one," said Janie. She was getting that look again, like a thunderstorm about to break.

"You can't have it," I said. "Does Daddy let you have anything you want when you're in his cave?"

"We don't live in a cave," said Janie. "We live in a longhouse. He lets me pet the pterodactyl."

"Daddy has a pterodactyl?"

She nodded solemnly.

Lying, I thought. Incipient pathology. Grounds for appeal?

Not yet, unfortunately. "Then you can pet yours when you get home. Eat your sandwich. Do you want more milk?"

"No, thank you," said Janie politely. When I kept my eye trained on her, she picked the bananas out of her sandwich and ate those, and fed the bread and peanut butter to the pigeons that had been lining up since we headed toward the table.

The mammoths moved around in their pit. They had their own Ice Age habitat, complete with miniature glacier. While Janie fed the pigeons, I watched an enormous female mammoth show a relatively tiny baby how to suck water into its trunk and give itself a bath. The mother looked like an ambulatory fur rug. The baby wasn't much different from a very hairy newborn elephant.

Janie fed the last bit of her sandwich to the greediest pigeon. "May we pet the pterodactyl now?"

"No," I said. "Watch the mammoths. They're real Ice Age animals. Real hunters would hunt them to feed the tribe."

"Daddy killed a bear," said Janie. "I like deer better. May I pet the pterodactyl?"

"No," I said.

Thinking about Marco killing a bear effectively killed my appetite. And I still had to get through the afternoon. Janie was fixated, there wasn't any doubt about it. I gave up on the rest of the zoo after she threw a fit in the raptors' habitat, and took her home till it was time to head back to the preserve.

The caseworker was waiting for us. It was the female version this time, in mode six: pleasant but strict. "You're back early," it said from the wallscreen.

"Certainly," I said through clenched teeth. "Quality time, you know. Best spent at home in familiar surroundings, without external distractions."

Quoting the book never did any good with caseworkers. Human or AI, they all had the same level of cynicism programmed in. I was fairly sure this one was an AI. Its lip curled faintly. It didn't say anything as I changed Janie's shirt—substituting one I'd bought for her, with Lunar Habitat III on it—and asked her what she wanted to do.

"Pet the pterodactyl," she said.

"Her new *idée fixe*," I told the wallscreen. Janie was digging in the toy chest. I had her model farm all ready, but she wanted the dinosaur set. No guesses as to what she was looking for.

"This signifies something," the wallscreen said, frowning.

"No kidding," I said, just as Janie threw the whole

bag of plastic monsters on the floor and started to bawl.

"No pterodactyl. *No pterodactyl!*"

"Regression," the wall diagnosed. "Separation trauma. Acid indigestion."

Under cover of siren shrieks and fatuous declarations, I found the plastic pterodactyl. It was a retro version, the leathery lizard. Janie hit it out of my hand.

"'You should attempt to affirm the parental bond," the wall advised. "Her craving for soft white wings represents a yearning for the missing mother figure."

"Marco's got a whole clan marriage," I said—all right, I snapped, at fair volume, to get above Janie's roaring. "At last count she had half a dozen mother surrogates and a platoon of aunts and cousins."

"None of whom is her mother," said the wall.

That did it. "So give her back to me!" I yelled.

Janie shut up. So did the wall. AIs don't look nonplussed, but they get a look when they shift programs: a total and inhuman blankness.

When it came back to life it was in a new mode: Bureaucratically Stern. "Regulations prohibit—"

"Want," said Janie. "Pterodactyl."

"All right," I said. "You want, you get."

She didn't light up all at once. She knew about broken promises. Marco had broken plenty. So had I.

"The revenant labeled *pterodactyl* is off limits to—" the wall intoned. I shut it off.

I had about six and a half minutes before it could key the override and come back on. That would be enough. What I needed to do, I do for a living, after all. I logged onto the net, triple-time, and hit the requisite nodes as fast as they came up. The headset needed modification, but Janie's records were still on file from three months ago.

Marco would pitch a fit. Atavists aren't just back-to-the-cave cultists. They're back-to-the-natural-brain ideologues, too.

"Back to the natural brawn," I muttered as I made the last couple of adjustments. I'd promised Marco I wouldn't log Janie on or plug her in while she was in his custody. I hadn't signed anything. Nothing in the rules said I had to deny her what she wanted because her father had a kink about virtual-reality headsets.

Real reality hadn't been cooperating, had it? "There," I said to Janie. "Put on the headset and say 'Pterodactyl.' "

One thing about kids. Real's real, and virtual's real, too, if they want it bad enough. Janie got to pet her pterodactyl.

The wall came back on while she was online. This time I got a human. I think. "Ten points off for shutting down the AI," he said. "Twenty on for ingenuity. Five off for the fit your ex-SO is going to throw when he finds out how you solved the problem."

"But he gets ten off for failure to consider the needs of the child," I said. Then: "Wait a minute. You're not supposed to have a sense of humor."

"Sorry," said the caseworker. He didn't sound very sincere.

We watched Janie. She was smiling in the headset, and her hands were making stroking motions.

"She's happy," the caseworker observed.

"And I'm not?"

"Did I say that?" asked the caseworker.

"Thanks," I said, "but I can play my own head games. Am I supposed to be happy that my ex is a mighty mammoth hunter manqué and my daughter spends her life in a wooden firetrap? If he'd gone off and worked on a farm in Antarctica or something equally ordinary, I'd live with it. So what did he do? He turned into Grunt the Barbarian."

"I don't find your daughter particularly barbaric," the caseworker said. "Particularly for a small child."

"So she's been coached," I snarled. "Tonight at precisely 1900 hours she goes back to the preserve. She takes off her nice clothes, she puts on furs if she puts on anything, she has a nice dinner of raw bear tongue."

"Have you considered that your hostility may be affecting her responses?" the caseworker asked.

I hit the off switch, but he was ready with the override.

"You could reflect," he said, "that the child's father is concerned for her health when she leaves the preserve on these visits. She breathes city air, she eats city food, and she lays herself open to city violence."

"A wounded bear isn't violent?"

"It's a matter of degree," he said. "From the viewpoint of an Atavist, that is. I have to preserve neutrality."

"So why are you taking his side?" I demanded.

"Because you can't conceive of anyone's being neutral," said the caseworker. "If you leave in twenty minutes, you'll just make the shuttle to the preserve."

"What if I don't?"

Caseworkers don't do rhetorical questions. "Forty points. Cancellation of next month's visiting privileges."

I hate it when a human being gets rational.

We were at the gate on the dot of 1900 hours. You'd expect something rustic for the entry to the Atavists' preserve, wouldn't you, unstripped logs or rough-hewn stone. This was just a gate between two concrete blockhouses, with a wall stretching off to either side. The preserve was a couple of miles past that, through a kind of no-man's-land. It was huge, and it was complete wilderness, except where the Atavists lived.

That wasn't too close to the wall. Marco had to swallow his principles once a month and take the underground shuttle that ran the circuit of the preserve. He was always on time, coming and going. Ice Age hunters might live in an eternal now, but Marco was a lawyer before he filed for change of lifestyle. Scheduled down to the millisecond.

I wish I could say he was dirty and hairy and smelly. He did smell like leather, but it was well tanned, and so was he. He swore he shaved with a flint razor; he had a couple of artistic nicks for proof. He looked healthy, fit, and disgustingly happy.

Janie ran to him and hugged him. I stood there feeling empty. She was babbling ninety to the dozen, all about pterodactyls and mammoths and chocolate ice cream.

"Chocolate," sighed Marco. "I do miss chocolate."

"You know what you can do about it," I said.

Even before we split, I couldn't talk normally around Marco. Everything I said came out sharp or whiny or both. Now wasn't any different.

"You're looking pale," he said. "Are you all right?"

"Yes, I'm all right!"

That's the other thing. Looking at him always makes me want to cry.

"Caitlin," he said, "you could get a month's admission on Janie's account. You must have that much time accumulated, at the rate you don't use vacations."

He tried that every time. He'd tried to get me to move into the preserve with him in the first place, and never mind that the divorce had been final for a year.

I can't say I didn't look at his bronzed muscles (skin cancer city, I reminded myself) and his air of complete satisfaction, and wonder, just for a nanosecond, if . . .

"No, thanks," I said. "I hate raw bear." I swallowed. "Good-bye, Janie. See you next month."

Janie pulled loose from Marco and ran to hug me. I thought of holding on and running, but I was supposed to be civilized, wasn't I? I kissed her and said, "Be good."

"Good-bye," said Janie. "Thank you for the pterodactyl."

The shuttle was waiting. Marco glanced at it but didn't say anything. It was Janie who got hold of his hand and pulled him away. She was talking about pterodactyls again: big beaks, strong talons, soft fur. Nothing about red eyes or hunger, or yearning to fly out of its cage.

"Next month," I said to the shuttle as it pulled away, "I'm taking you to the Space Museum."

She'd like that. She'd forget about things that should have been dead for the past few million years. She'd look where I wanted to look: ahead, instead of back.

"No more pterodactyls," I said. "No more revenants."

ONE GIANT STEP

by John E. Stith

John E. Stith is a Nebula nominee and the author of half a dozen hard science fiction novels.

A huge cylindrical image formed suddenly in the morning mist, then vanished just as quickly. Tree branches cast three-dimensional shadows in the mist. In the thick, blued rays, tiny insects danced over the luxuriant, green-and-yellow ground cover. The cacophony of animal noises diminished for a second.

As the sounds began to swell to their original volume, the image reappeared in the air, first as insubstantial as a mirage, then solidifying instantly with a clap of thunder. Bellows and howls came from every direction.

The object, a huge featureless canister half as tall as the nearest tree, materialized far enough above the ground that when it fell to earth, the powerful shock tricked some of the local wildlife into earthquake-avoidance mode, and sudden flurries of activity spread out in concentric rings, as if the large form had dropped into a lake instead of crashing into a jungle.

A sharp *click* came from somewhere inside the canister, and a vertical line appeared on the dull-gray surface. With a *hiss* a curved door slid aside into the curved wall.

A broad snout protruded from the opening, and two large dark eyes blinked. A huge green, clawed foot extended from the doorway and sank into the dense ground cover and fertile black soil, forming a deep footprint.

"That's one small step for a reptile, one giant step for Reptilia." The creature's voice was deep and gravelly, almost a modulated roar.

"Can you not find something even more pretentious to say?" came a softer but even deeper-pitched voice from farther inside the canister. "And will you hurry up and get out of the way, Bal? I want to see what it looks like out there."

"Oh, don't lay an egg, Ektor." Bal extended her other foot from the canister, and it sank into the ground beside her first foot. Together, her feet crushed almost half a square meter of the local vegetation. She moved away from the canister until there was room for Ektor to reach the doorway, and one huge foot splashed into a small puddle teeming with life.

Bal stood almost three meters high, her spiked tail sticking out the tail-hole of her blue Tonsar Chronocorps uniform.

Ektor stepped lightly down from the canister. He was almost as tall as Bal, but was much thinner, massing only half what Bal did. He had no tail, and his skull was wider than Bal's. When he walked away from the canister, he took gentle steps, and the ground didn't shake much at all.

At the opening in the canister appeared a third body, also dressed in blue, but wearing only shorts, since the spikes on his back made a shirt impractical.

"Millions of years into the past," Plort said in a hushed, throaty voice. "Absolutely incredible." His two large black eyes blinked as he scanned the horizon, and he belched. A white dueling scar showed against his rough hide. "Ektor, you're a genius."

Ektor snorted gently, making a sound like someone pulling one foot from sucking mud. *And you're an idiot,* he thought.

Bal turned full circle and looked back at Ektor. "Plort's right. I was impressed with the one-century run, but somehow I didn't really think we could go back this far. You really are a genius, Ektor. Your name will go down in history. What an opportunity."

Ektor dragged a huge case from the interior of the time machine. "Let us not be too quick to assume we are in the target time period. I admit it does look like I imagined it might, but we could have missed by millions of years." With his stubby arms he tilted the case onto its back. Short claws flicked open the latches, and Ektor withdrew a number of instruments.

As Bal and Plort scanned the horizon with binoculars, Ektor set up an air analyzer, then took water samples from a nearby pool. A flying insect with gossamer wings buzzed around Ektor's head. He quickly made sure his companions were looking elsewhere, then flicked out his tongue and grabbed the insect. Mmm, good. He liked it when they were crunchy.

As Ektor worked, Plort set up a cylindrical force field to keep their ancient ancestors from straying too close to the time machine. Ektor and his companions were smaller and less massive than some of the local inhabitants, and Ektor was convinced the team members were also slower and less violent than the locals. Plort did the job competently and without having to ask questions, so Ektor didn't feel it necessary to repeat his constant objection that Plort should not have been selected for the mission solely because he was Bal's brother-in-law.

Ektor finished his preparations and let the automated mechanisms start their work. "We should have the results in a few hours," he said. "The oxygen level is high enough that so far things look good."

"I still say we should have come at night so we could just take a quick look at the stars and verify the date," said Plort.

"And I still say this is safer," Bal said, managing to summon images of government safety organizations and top-heavy bureaucracy. And what Bal said was what mattered.

"Indeed," Ektor said, as he nodded at the far side of the force field, where a reptile massing far more than the three of them put together was drawing sparks from the energy barrier. The creature's long neck was topped with a head no larger than Ektor's, but its eyes held the vacant look of the very young and the very dumb. "We came millions of years. It's not going to hurt us to wait a little longer."

Plort belched. "Well, I'm going to extend the force field some more. I feel too hemmed in."

Ektor glanced at the first few readings generated by the equipment, then went back to the canister and withdrew another large box.

"I swear to mud and sand," Bal said. "You brought enough stuff for a month's visit."

"It is all necessary, I assure you." Ektor didn't slow down; he just kept unpacking more and more equipment. He placed five shiny cylinders on the ground and withdrew a locked container from within a large box.

"You're not going to lose anything back here?" asked Bal. "I'm still nervous about the possibility of generating some change."

"Do not worry about it. I have got everything under control." Ektor felt something squish under his foot. He picked up his foot and inspected the underside. Yuck. He had squashed a small lizard, smearing yellow-green guts all over. Ektor wiped his foot on a nearby broad-leaf bush. He took another look, then shook his foot to get rid of the goo clinging to his claws.

Ektor looked up just in time to see a huge flying reptile crash into the force field exactly like a bird crashing into a window, but this creature had a wingspan of ten to fifteen meters. The reptile crashed to the ground outside the force field, its neck broken.

The mangled body quickly attracted a food fight among the local carnivores, who trumpeted and snorted as they fought over the body and then hooted in surprise when they were shocked by the force field.

Ektor continued his experiments. Bal and Plort wandered around the enclave in so many overlapping paths that by the time dusk arrived they had trampled nearly everything shorter than their hips.

Plort examined the first constellations visible. "Oh, look at the Egg Layer. It's all wrong, twisted."

Ektor confirmed the locations of several key stars, then sighed heavily. "Everything fits. We are where we expected to be. Sixty-five million years into the past.. All the other tests say the same thing."

"I still can't get over it. This is just incredible," said Bal. Her voice tightened suddenly. "Ektor, what do you have there?"

"Rhetorical, right? Sorry, Bal, Plort. You know what it is. It is a Farn and Wessel five centimeter."

"Watch where you point that thing," said Plort. "You could damage the time machine."

"Precisely. Stand aside, please."

"What the Saturn is going on?" asked Bal. "Are you crazy?"

"Oh, I hope not." Ektor laughed a bitter laugh. "I really hope not. Now move aside."

Bal stayed right where she was. "No."

"I can shoot right through you. And I will." Ektor waved the gun muzzle.

"What's going on?"

"Move aside and I will tell you."

Bal finally moved to one side, and Plort moved to the opposite side. Ektor had no doubt that they would split wider and wider until he couldn't focus on both of them.

"Stop right there, or I'll kill you." Ektor aimed between them, pulled the trigger, and ten rounds of ammo hurtled into the doorway of the time machine, where the bullets proceeded to ricochet around until they perforated most of the hardware. The machine would never leave this time period.

"Mother of Mars," said Bal. "We'll never get home!"

"True. But actually it is even worse than that," Ektor said. "By the time I am finished, there will not be a home to go back to." He pressed a button and rockets shot upward from each of the five cylinders he'd positioned earlier in the day. The five exhaust plumes rose high into the night, easily clearing the top of the force field.

"What are you talking about?" cried Bal. "What are you doing?"

"I am doing what I have to do," Ektor said, tears

blurring his vision. "I am making sure reptiles don't have the chance to evolve after all. One of those rockets will drift back to Earth with an explosive force powerful enough to kick up dirt sufficient to cause a nuclear winter. Another rocket will release an airborne immuno-contraceptive virus designed to make most female reptiles immune to the sperm of the male. The third rocket carries—"

"You're killing our own ancestors?" said Bal. "You're mad! Stop this while you still can, I command you."

"It is already too late," said Ektor.

"But why?" asked Plort. "For Saturn's sake, why?"

"Because there is just no other way. Reptiles were not meant to rule the Earth. Look at us. Look at our lives. Look at what we have done. We do not deserve to live. Let some other species take over. They could not possibly do as bad as we have."

"We haven't done that bad," said Bal. "We've got atomic energy, time travel—"

"We have not done that bad?" Ektor raised his voice in angry disbelief. "We have not done that bad? What a wonderful epitaph. In our race for control and self-perpetuation, we have slaughtered how many species? Thousands? Tens of thousands? Where are the otter, the chimpanzee, the tiger, and all the others? Dead. Just because we wanted a better view for a house, or more space for a factory. We live every day with the threat of nuclear holocaust, and we choke on our own pollution. We are a race filled with bigotry. The spikes think the scales are inferior; the flatnoses think they are better than the four-claws."

Ektor took a breath and tried to calm himself. "It is just all so insane."

Bal shifted to one foot, then the other. "But with the time machine we can change all that."

"Exactly right!" said Ektor. "Why do you think I worked so hard on this?"

Plort edged farther from the time machine. "So you're prepared for genocide? You want to kill all the reptiles now alive?"

"How is that any worse than what we have done already? Right now they are just dumb animals, just like the spotted owl, the ape, the elephant, just like the thousands of species we have exterminated in the glorious name of progress. It seems fitting, actually."

"Drop the gun, Ektor," said Bal. "You're delusional. You're sick."

"Oh, no, I do not think so. For the first time in my life I feel genuine optimism. Nothing can bring back what we once were. The Earth will get a second chance, a chance for some other species to rise to the top. And in my soul I know there will be a species who deserves to inherit the Earth. I have a dream, and in my dream I see an intelligent species living at peace with the Earth, taking just enough to survive in happiness, giving back whatever it takes to preserve this garden of beauty."

"This is crazy, Ektor!" Bal shouted as a rocket exploded in the night sky.

Ektor smiled sadly as he aimed his weapon at Plort and began to squeeze the trigger. "That is what I have been trying to say."

As Ektor turned the gun on himself, the sounds of the first shots were still echoing in the clearing.

A shiny form suddenly exploded into view in the morning mist. The pyramid-shaped vessel sprouted a multitude of antennae of various lengths and orientations. Eight shock-absorbing legs damped the motion as the craft fell to earth.

One triangular surface pivoted outward from the base and landed point-first on the spongy ground. The first traveler out of the vessel was an eighty-kilo cockroach. Sunlight glinted off its shiny black carapace. The creature's useless vestigial wings drooped like flags in still air.

The cockroach sniffed once, then said, "That's one small step for an insect . . ."

LAST RIGHTS

by Mercedes Lackey and Larry Dixon

Mercedes Lackey is a best-selling author; Larry Dixon is a successful artist and part-time science fiction writer.

Two men and a woman huddled in the wet bushes surrounding the GenTech Engineering facility in Los Lobos, California. Across the darkened expanse of expensive GenTech Grasite lay their goal; the Gen-Tech Large Animal Development Project. It was "Grasite," not "grass"; this first product of GenTech's research was a plant that was drought-resistant, seldom needed mowing, and remained green even when dry; perfect for Southern California. Sadly, it also attracted grasshoppers who seemed to be fooled by its verdant appearance; they would remain on a Grasite lawn, hordes of them, trying valiantly to extract nourishment from something the texture and consistency of Astroturf, all during the worst droughts. Anyone holding a garden party in Hollywood had better plan on scheduling CritterVac to come in and sweep the premises clean or his guests would find every step they took crunching into a dozen insects, lending the soiree all the elegance of the wrath of Moses.

But Grasite was not the target tonight; these three had no argument with gene-tailored plant life. In fact, they strongly supported many of GenTech's products—RealSkin, which reacted to allergens and irritants exactly the way human skin did, or Steak'N'Taters, a tuber with the consistency and taste of a cross between beef and baked potato. But all three of them were outraged by this assault upon helpless animals that GenTech was perpetrating in their new development lab.

Mary Lang, Howard Emory, and Ken Jacobs were

self-styled "guerrillas" in defense of helpless beasties everywhere; charter members of Persons In Defense of Animo-beings; P.I.D.A. for short. There was nothing they would not do to secure the rights of exploited and abused animals. This year alone they, personally, had already chalked up the release of several hundred prisoner-rats from a lab in Lisle, Illinois. It was too bad about the mutated bubonic plague spreading through Chicago afterward, but as Ken said, people had choices, the rats didn't. Tonight, they were after bigger game.

DinoSaurians. Patent Pending.

Real, living, breathing dinosaurs—slated to become P.O.Z.s (Prisoners of Zoos) the world over. And all because some corporate MBA on the Board of the San Diego Zoo had seen the attendance numbers soar when the Dunn traveling animated dinosaur exhibit had been booked there for a month. He had put that together with the discovery that common chickens and other creatures could be regressed to their saurian ancestors—the pioneering work had already been done on the eohippus and aurochs—and had seen a gold mine waiting for both the zoos and GenTech.

"How could they do this to me?" Mary whined. "They had such a promising record! I was going to ask them for a corporate donation! And now, *this*—"

"Money," Ken hissed. "They're all money-grubbing bastards, who don't care if they sell poor animals into a life of penal servitude. Just wait; next thing you'll be seeing is DinoBurgers."

Howard winced, and pulled the collar of his unbleached cotton jacket higher. "So, what have we got?" he asked. "What's the plan?"

Ken consulted the layout of the facility and the outdoor pens. It had been ridiculously easy to get them; for all the furor over the DinoSaurians, there was remarkably little security on this facility. Only signs, hundreds of them, warning of "Dangerous animals." Ridiculous. As if members of P.I.D.A. would be taken in by such blatant nonsense! There was no such thing as a dangerous animal; only an animal forced to act outside of its peaceful nature. "There are only three Dino-animopersons at the moment, and if we can release all three of them, it will represent such a huge loss to GenTech that I doubt they'll ever want to create more. There's a BrontoSaurian here—" He pointed at a tiny pen on the far northern corner of the map. "It's inside a special pen with heavy-duty electric fences and alarms around it, so that will be your target, Howard. You're the alarms expert."

Howard looked over Ken's shoulder, and winced again. "That pen isn't even big enough for a horse to move around in!" he exclaimed. "This is inhuman! It's veal calves all over again!"

Ken tilted the map toward Mary. "There's something here called a 'Dinonychus' that's supposed to be going to the San Diego zoo. It looks like they've put it in some kind of a bare corral. You worked with turning loose the rodeo horses and bulls last year, so you take this one, Mary."

Mary Lang nodded, and tried not to show her relief. The corral didn't look too difficult to get into, and from the plans, all she'd have to do would be to open the corral gate and the animal would run for freedom. "Very active" was the note photocopied along with the map. That was fine; the rodeo horses hadn't wanted to leave their pens, and it had taken *forever* to get them to move. And she'd gotten horse crap all over her expensive synthetic suede pants.

"That leaves the Triceratops in the big pasture to me." Ken folded the map once they had all memorized the way in. "Meet you here in an hour. Those poor exploited victims of corporate humanocentrism are already halfway to freedom. We'll show the corporate fat cats that they can't live off the misery of tortured, helpless animals!"

Howard had never seen so many alarms and electric shock devices in his life. He thought at first that they were meant to keep people out—but all the detectors pointed inward, not outward, so they had all been intended to keep this pathetic BrontoSaurian trapped inside his little box.

Howard's blood pressure rose by at least ten points when he saw the victim; they were keeping it inside a bare concrete pen, with no educational toys, nothing to look at, no variation in its environment at all. It looked like the way they used to pen "killer" elephants in the bad old days; the only difference was that this BrontoSaurian wasn't chained by one ankle. There was barely enough room for the creature to turn around; no room at all for it to lie down. There was nothing else in the pen but a huge pile of green vegetation at one end and an equally large pile of droppings at the other.

Good God, he thought, appalled, *Don't they even clean the cage?*

As he watched, the BrontoSaurian dropped its tiny head, curved its long, flexible neck, and helped itself to a mouthful of greenery. As the head rose, jaws chewing placidly, another barrel of droppings added itself to the pile from the other end of the beast.

The BrontoSaurian seemed to be perfect for making fertilizer, if nothing else.

Well, soon he would be fertilizing the acreage of the Los Lobos National Park, free and happy, and the memory of this dank, cramped prison would be a thing of the past.

Howard disabled the last of the alarms and shock fences, pulled open the gates, and stepped aside, proudly waiting for the magnificent creature to take its first steps into freedom.

The magnificent creature dropped its head, curved its neck, and helped itself to another mouthful of greenery. As the head rose, jaws chewing placidly, it took no note of the open gates just past its nose.

"Come on, big boy!" Howard shouted, waving at it.

It ignored him.

He dared to venture into the pen.

It continued to ignore him. Periodically it would take another mouthful and drop a pile, but except for that, it could just as well have been one of the mechanical dinosaurs it was supposed to replace.

Howard spent the next half hour trying, with diminishing patience, to get the BrontoSaurian to leave. It didn't even *look* at him, or the open door, or anything at all except the pile of juicy banana leaves and green hay in front of it. Finally, Howard couldn't take it any longer.

His blood pressure rising even higher, he seized the electric cattle prod on the back wall, and let the stupid beast have a good one, right in the backside.

As soon as he jolted the poor thing, his conscience struck him a blow that was nearly as hard. He dropped the prod as if it had shocked *him,* and wrapped his arms around the beast's huge leg, babbling apologies.

Approximately one minute later, while Howard was still crying into the leathery skin of the Bronto's leg, it noticed that it had been stung. Irritating, but irritation was easy to avoid. It shifted its weight, as it had been taught, and stepped a single pace sideways.

Its left hind foot met a little resistance, and something made a shrieking sound—but there had been something shrieking for some time, and it ignored the sound as it had all the rest. After all, the food was still here.

Presently, it finished the pile of food before it and waited patiently. There was a buzzing noise, and a hole opened in the wall a little to its right. That was the signal to shift around, which it did.

A new load of fresh vegetation dropped down with a rattle and a dull thud, as the automatic cleaning system flushed the pile of droppings and the rather flat mortal remains of her savior Howard down into the sewage system.

Mary approached the corral carefully, on the alert for guards and prepared to act like a stupid, lost bimbo if she were sighted. But there were no guards; only a high metal fence of welded slats, centered with a similar gate. There was something stirring restlessly inside the corral; she couldn't see what it was, for the slats were set too close together. But as she neared the gate, she heard it pacing back and forth in a way that made her heart ache.

Poor thing—it needed to run loose! How could these monsters keep a wild, noble creature like this penned up in such an unnaturally barren environment?

There were alarms on the gate and on the fence; she didn't have Howard's expertise in dealing with such things, but these were easy, even a child could have taken them off-line. As she worked, she talked to the poor beast trapped on the other side of the gate, and it paused in its pacing at the sound of her voice.

"Hang in there, baby," she crooned to it. "There's a whole big National Park on the other side of the lab fence. As soon as we get you loose, we'll take that big BrontoSaurian through it, and that will leave a hole big enough for a hundred animopersons to run through! Then you'll be free! You'll be able to play in the sunshine, and roll in the grass—eat all the flowers you want—we'll make sure they never catch you, don't you worry."

The beast drew nearer, until she felt the warmth of its breath on her coat sleeve as she worked. It snuffled a little, and she wrinkled her nose at the smell.

Poor thing! What were they feeding it, anyway? Didn't they ever give it a chance to bathe? Her resentment grew as it sniffed at the gap between the metal slats. Why, it was lonely! The poor thing was as lonely as some of those rodeo horses had been! Didn't anyone ever come to pet and play with it?

Finally she disabled the last of the alarms. The creature inside the corral seemed to sense her excitement and anticipation as she worked at the lock on the gate. She heard it shifting its weight from foot to foot in a kind of dance that reminded her of her pet parakeet when he'd wanted out of his cage, before she'd grown wiser and freed it into the abundant outdoors.

"Don't worry, little fellow," she crooned at it. "I'll have you out of here in no time—"

With a feeling of complete triumph, she popped the lock, flipped open the hasp on the gate, and swung it wide, eager for the first sight of her newly freed friend.

The first thing she saw was a huge-headed lizard, about six feet tall, that stood on two legs, balancing itself with its tail. It was poised to leap through the gate.

The last thing she saw was a grinning mouth like a beartrap, full of sharp, carnivorous teeth, closing over her head.

Hank threw his rope over a chair in the employee lounge and sank into the one next to it, feeling sweat cool all over his body. He pulled his hat down over his eyes. This had not been the most disastrous morning of his life, but it was right up there. Somehow the Dino had gotten into Gertie's pen—and whoever had left the gate open last night was going to catch hell. The little carnivore couldn't hurt the Bronto, but he had already eaten all the Dobermans that were supposed to be guarding the complex, and he was perfectly ready to add a lab tech or lab hand to the menu. You couldn't trank the Saurians; their metabolism was too weird. You couldn't drive a Dino; there wasn't anything he was afraid of. The only safe way to handle the little bastard was to get two ropes on him and haul him along, a technique Hank had learned roping rhinos in Africa. It had taken him and Buford half the morning to get the Dino roped and hauled back to his corral. They'd had to work on foot since none of the horses would come anywhere near the Dino. All he needed was one more thing—

"Hank!" someone yelled from the door.

"What, dammit?" Hank Sayer snapped. "I'm tired! Unless you've got the chowderhead that left Dino and Gertie's pens open—"

"They weren't *left* open, they were opened last night," said the tech, his voice betraying both anger and excitement. "Some animal-rights yoyos got in last night, the security guys found them on one of the tapes. *And* the cleanup crews found what was left of the two of them in the pit under Gertie's pen and just inside Dino's doghouse!"

That was more than enough to make Hank sit up and push his hat back. "What the hell—how come—"

The tech sighed. "These bozos think every animal is just like the bunny-wunnies they had as kids. I don't think one of them has been closer to a real bull than videotape. They sure as hell didn't research the Saurians, else they'd have known the Dino's a land-shark, and it takes Gertie a full minute to process any sensation and act on it. We found what was left of the cattle prod in the pit."

Hank pushed his hat back on this head and scratched his chin. "Holy shit. So the bozos just got in the way of Gertie after they shocked her, and opened Dino's pen to let him out?"

"After disabling the alarm and popping the locks," the tech agreed. "Shoot, Dino must have had fifteen or twenty minutes to get a good whiff and recognize fresh meat—"

"He must've thought the pizza truck had arrived—" Suddenly another thought occurred to him. "Man, we've got three Saurians in here. Did anybody think to check Tricky's pen?"

Alarm filled the tech's face. "I don't think so—"

"Well, come *on*, then," Hank yelled, grabbing his lariat and shooting for the door like Dino leaping for a side of beef. "Call it in and meet me there!"

Tricky's pen was the largest, more of an enclosure than a pen; it had been the home of their herd of aurochs before the St. Louis zoo had taken delivery. Tricky was perfectly placid, so long as you stayed on your side of the fence. Triceratops, it seemed, had a very strong territorial instinct. Or at least, the Gen-Tech reproductions did. It was completely safe to come within three feet of the fence. Just don't come any closer. . . .

Hank saw at a glance that the alarms and cameras had been disabled here, too. And the gate stood closed—but it wasn't locked anymore.

Tricky was nowhere in sight.

"He wouldn't go outside the fence," Hank muttered to himself, scanning the pasture, his brow furrowed with worry. "Not unless someone dragged him—"

"Listen!" the tech panted. Hank held his breath, and strained his ears.

"*Help!*" came a thin, faint voice, from beyond the start of the trees shading the back half of Tricky's enclosure. "*Help!*"

"Oh, boy." Hank grinned, and peered in the direction of the shouts. "This time we got one."

Sure enough, just through the trees, he could make out the huge brown bulk of the Triceratops standing in what Hank recognized as a belligerent aggression-pose. The limbs of the tree moved a little, shaking beneath the weight of whoever Tricky had treed.

"*Help!*" came the faint, pathetic cry.

"Reckon he didn't read the sign," said Buford, ambling up with both their horses, and indicating the sign posted on the fence that read, "If you cross this field, do it in 9.9 seconds; Tricky the Triceratops does it in 10."

"Reckon not," Hank agreed, taking the reins of Smoky from his old pal and swinging into the saddle. He looked over at the tech, who hastened to hold open the gate for both of them. "You'd better go get Security, the cops, the medics, and the lawyers in that order," he said, and the tech nodded.

Hank looked back into the enclosure. Tricky hadn't moved.

"Reckon that 'un's the lucky'un," Buford said, sending Pete through the gate at a sedate walk.

"Oh, I dunno," Hank replied, as Smoky followed, just as eager for a good roping and riding session as Hank wasn't. Smoky was an overachiever; best horse Hank had ever partnered, but a definite workaholic.

"Why you say that?" Buford asked.

Hank shook his head. "Simple enough. Gettin' treed by Tricky's gonna be the best part of his day. By the time the lawyers get done with 'im—well, I reckon he's likely to wish Gertie'd stepped on him, too. They ain't gonna leave him anything but shredded underwear. If he thought Tricky was bad—"

"Uh *huh*," Buford agreed, his weathered face splitting with a malicious grin. Both of them had been top rodeo riders before the animal-rights activists succeeded in truncating the rodeo circuit. They'd been lucky to get this job. "You know, I reckon we had oughta take our time about this. Exercise'd do Tricky some good."

Hank laughed, and held Smoky to a walk. "Buford, old pal, I reckon you're readin' my mind. You don't suppose the damn fools hurt Tricky, do ya?"

Faint and far, came a snort; Hank could just barely make out Tricky as he backed up a little and charged the tree. A thud carried across the enclosure, and the tree shook.

"Naw, I think Tricky's healthy as always."

"*Help!*" came the wail from the leaves. Hank pulled Smoky up just a little more.

And grinned fit to split his face.

This wasn't the best day of his life, but damn if it wasn't right up there.

AFTER THE COMET

by Bill Fawcett

Bill Fawcett is a successful novelist, short story writer, editor and anthologist.

The great beast took satisfaction in the surge of his muscles as he led the herd across the bleak plain. Each massive step rumbled through the earth, echoing the near-constant thunder in the low clouds above. The herd always stepped hard, the sheer power of their presence driving away any smaller carnivores that might threaten those born recently. Nothing would deter the larger meat eaters. To deal with those every adult was equipped with three long horns and a strong tail.

The need for food tinged every thought. They were all hungry. The herd leader's shared awareness was tinged with the pain of an empty belly and the tortured strain of the older and weaker members trying to keep up with the others. Still he had no choice but to maintain the grueling pace. The leader ignored their discomfort. Already they had slowed and another day without food would mean the loss of too many of those who trailed behind him.

He led the group and if they had a language, or names, he would have been called leader or hunter. Though as the first walker of the giant beasts he sought only plants they might feast on. Hunter was the largest of the behemoth plant-eaters. Men, not to be born for millions of years, would call his species triceratops. But men needed labels, and had to speak because to Hunter and his kin, they would seem painfully deaf. The great beasts had no need for speech, for they touched each other's minds and thus had no need for intermediate labels.

Deep within their shared memory was the image of a valley located not far ahead. In the remembrance it was green and lush with succulent plants. It was not really the three-horned mountain of muscle and determination that remembered the place, but he reveled in the image. The shared memory was one of their best, so clear and strong that the herd leader could almost feel his belly distended and his mouth full of moist, thick leaves. This was a sensation he had never really known in his own lifetime.

So Hunter shared the memory of the lush valley and the others trailed after him. This was necessary as the plain they were crossing was nearly bare. All they had found to eat was the bark of otherwise barren trees. Yesterday one of the small ones had fallen, too weak to continue the migration, and they had stood waiting until his presence had left their minds. It had taken most of the short, cold day and there had been no food. Now, if they were to lose no more of their dwindling numbers, they had to find food soon.

The sky in the memory of the green valley was a bright blue. This was quite different from the gray and brown clouds he had known all of his life. There had been a bright warmth overhead during the day, instead of the soft red glow Hunter knew. And the herd he saw grazing in the memory was many times the size of those who remained.

Sometimes the memories served. But they also could hurt and Hunter knew a longing for times he had never seen. For times when they ate every day and times when there were places at the end of migration where all the herd could be happy. Behind him the triceratops heard an old mare's longing bellow. Her cry of need was tinged darker by the herd leader's knowledge that she could not survive many more seasons of inadequate food and skin-cracking cold.

They entered the valley late in the day. All were too tired to even moan their disappointment of the poverty of the meal they could make off the stunted plants and drying bark they found there. The memory of the time when the valley had contained enough plants that they could pass the cold season in it without hunger faded a bit farther as the current reality overwhelmed it. In a few more generations the happy time would be a vague mystery and after that forgotten or ignored.

Just a little bitterly, Hunter was glad. To know of such comfort, but to never be able to touch it was its own kind of hunger. The rumbling ache of his belly was hunger enough. He didn't need any other kind. Disconsolate, the giant dinosaur wandered among the low trees, filling his mouth with the leaves of some, leaving more for those that followed. There was no method to his path. This place had been the end of the journey his ancestors had known for so many millions of seasons. Here there was supposed to be enough to carry them until the days began to lengthen. Yet now little remained. The instincts that had served them so well over the aeons were failing and Hunter's mind was reluctant to accept that tomorrow they would be forced to move on into unknown lands.

Most were already weak and a few of his herd might even refuse to go on. They would prefer to follow the old paths, though those meant certain starvation. Even if they shared some of their thoughts and feelings, each of the herd was also different. Hunter would not have thought of himself as an innovator, but he was. His type was encouraged by the harsh conditions the dinosaurs now faced. As much as anything, it would be his willingness to continue the migration, and the others' habit of following the herd leader, that might give them a chance for surviving the coming cold season. Dimly the herd leader knew this, but amid the hunger gained no satisfaction from his own importance.

The clouds cleared slightly toward sunset, though it had been like twilight beneath the dust-filled clouds most of the day. The storm had cleared much of the dust which had settled into the lower air and the evening was almost bright. It had rained almost every afternoon Hunter had been alive. It was, to him, the way things were. Different from the older memories, but to be simply accepted as something he could not change. That day the water had come in sheets and, except for the chill it carried, the great dinosaurs had welcomed how it sluiced the itchy dust off their hides. Some of the herd clumped together, sharing their warmth and preparing for the night. Hunter stayed apart on a slight rise in the ground, fulfilling his role as guardian and leader by watching for any threat. There was no way for anything to sneak up without being seen in the nearly empty valley, but they took no chances. The great carnivores were desperate, too, as their hunger drove them into attacking with reckless abandon.

Though the darkness grew deeper, not one herd member was tempted to sleep. All were exhausted, but for the next few precious moments they would unite in the pattern. Only a few young males would remain apart, ready to sound the alarm should any danger appear. All others huddled even more closely in expectation of the sharing.

The pattern was not a thing. It had no physical presence at all. Still, it was the center of the herd's existence. The phenomenon was similar to the great ballad first begun by the several species of whales at this time. These ballads may even be vague continuations of other patterns. The pattern was the magic that held the herd together; that which taught each member how to best survive. It was many things, including their guide, source of pride, and giver of continuity.

This pattern was a mental construct built slowly, over millions of years, by the herd. Most likely it did not really exist. Certainly it had no physical form. It contained the memories, past attitudes, and even recollections of all that had added to the success of the herd for uncounted millennia. This collage of racial memories was an intricate weave of all the ancestors of these triceratops had done or learned. Those pathways which were often visited appeared as thick strands; to most they appeared to be glowing brightly. Those areas which were unused would fade and become thin ghosts that only hinted of almost remembered battles and warmer days. The herd summoned from within themselves this vision each night before resting. Sometimes they added their own successes, other times simply finding solace in the sheer beauty of the intricate mental construct. Too often lately they'd been forced to turn to the construct for guidance. Rarely was there the tale of a success added for later generations to treasure and learn from. Occasionally they had met other herds whose minds were able to touch with their own and the pattern grew with a surge of new ideas. But it had been a long time since that had happened. They had not met another herd of triceratops since Hunter had taken over as first walker. Tonight the herd had little to add to this racial memory other than the grim reality of their dwindling numbers and starvation.

There had been a time when the pattern was the product of thousands of minds. The memory of that glory still lingered, both encouraging and taunting the herd. In those millennia each thread had glowed with power and hundreds of memories were summoned every night. The Hunter often feared that someday the herd would become too small to maintain this vast reservoir of memories. Already distant corners of the pattern had been lost as the herd grew smaller. Those lost were likely memories too distant or unimportant to be kept by the lesser numbers. But the herd leader would never know and the stress of sheer survival dulled his curiosity.

It was easiest for Hunter, who considered himself unimaginative, to see the pattern as a glowing shape hovering over the herd. Each pathway shimmering with its own color and brightness. As leader in their annual migration he understood paths and needed to recognize often traveled ways. This made following familiar routes through the pattern easy for him.

The temptation to return to the memory of that lush valley for the short time they would have the strength to hold the image was great, but Hunter resisted. They needed something different. Some memory he could use to encourage the others to follow him further now that they had reached the bleak end to their familiar route. Something that gave them hope of better pastures and safer lands. It was likely that any promise he found would be as ephemeral as their memory of this once-green valley, but he didn't care. The herd needed to maintain its numbers to survive. He had to get even the most reluctant to overcome habit and continue.

In a distant corner, Hunter found the memory he needed. It was from a past even farther gone than the happy valley. The threat had been ice, and early snows that killed the plants. This had forced that herd leader to change the entire pattern of migration. Survival had meant moving away from the snow, rather than into it. Only after almost countless generations had passed was the herd able to return to the ancient route. Now it was the same. Once more Hunter understood the cold had returned, though now it had also brought dust-filled skies that wilted the plants before they could grow.

Hunter pulled the memory to the front of the pattern and held it for the herd to examine. He felt confident now. Doing something new was frightening and finding he was repeating even a rare part of the pattern was reassuring. In the front of his mind the triceratops bellowed. It was the cry often used by young bucks to challenge his lead position and choice of mates, a demand for attention which could not be ignored. Then he led them through the memory. The memory had hinted at better times in distant places. It promised a return to the time of full bellies and warm sunlight. Tomorrow he would lead them onward and all would follow.

The herd trailed out winding across the mountains. They'd already lost two of the older members on the march. That had worried Hunter. It also concerned him that this small loss had hurt so badly. The pattern was filled with memories of times when the herd had grown so large small portions had been driven away to start new herds. In those times a hundred young might be driven off to form a new herd and nothing lost. Now this herd was so pitifully small that even a few deaths stung them all and even threatened the pattern.

Beyond their valley there had been hills and then mountains. Not massive craggy peaks, but gentler slopes except where deep ravines had been cut by the incessant rain. As they climbed higher, the sky had changed from soft brown to a brighter shade of gray and they all were happier spending their days in this wan sunlight despite the colder nights. The slopes were covered by leafless trees that were still green, though occasionally blotched yellow. All had eaten enough, though there was little strength to be found in these always green trees.

The bitter foliage of the trees had restored some of their strength and Hunter allowed himself the luxury of thinking of the future. On the second night he had detected the smell of joy beginning to emanate from one of the females. It was the one with a bright spot around her lightly colored eyes. She was already one of his favorites. The arising of the mating scent had been a rare occasion since the dark skies came. It rarely appeared when they were hungry and this had been the normal situation for all of Hunter's life. He had found himself almost uncontrollably excited. So also did many of the younger males.

Only one young buck dared challenge for the right to lead and breed. Hunter had beaten him before. But that had been two long marches ago and they were both weaker now. The younger male approached carefully. He waited until he was within a few steps before screeching his challenge. There was a feverish look in the young dinosaur's eyes that worried Hunter. The hard times had made them all a little crazy. Combined with the drive of frustrated desire, this challenger might not show the restraint called for in such battles. Even worse, if this was the case Hunter might have to kill his opponent to save himself, a loss the herd could hardly afford.

Just before they drove at each other Hunter wondered if he would be better off losing. Then this young, strong male would have to choose the path and he could simply follow. But the scent of the bright-eyed female goaded him and he answered the challenge with a deep-throated roar of his own.

The herd had stopped to rest in a slight widening of the path, an area too narrow and empty to call a valley, but wide enough for four or five triceratops to walk abreast. The sides sloped steeply and were covered with damp moss. A few of the young were using the distraction of the challenge to hurriedly scrape into their mouths what moss they could gather before the larger dinosaurs forced them aside to get at the grazing themselves.

Hunter gazed at the slopes and realized that there would be no finesse to this battle. Moments later the young male lowered his head and rushed at him. Hunter responded with his own short charge and they met in a crash of horns against hard shields. With their heads protected by a thick, bony plate such meetings rarely caused damage. The only risk was that of an eye being torn open as an opponent's horn scraped past. But both males lowered their heads at the last instant and avoided that danger.

Locked together by the initial crash, the triceratops stood facing each other. Horns entangled, each pushed against the other with all his strength. To give ground risked being thrown off balance. Falling would expose their soft undersides to possibly serious injury.

Their feet tore into the soft ground until the pads caught painfully on the rocks below. Both of the multiton behemoths had also planted their tails against the ground for leverage.

Leg and shoulder muscles strained until Hunter's shoulders felt as if they were on fire. Small snappings inside the muscles promised morning pain no matter who won. Still he pushed, driven by instinct, desire, and pride.

Minutes passed, broken only by the occasional grunts of the fighters. Slowly Hunter realized that he was losing strength more quickly. Breaking the way for the herd and scouting ahead had taken a toll on his endurance. It was becoming harder to hold back the younger triceratops' assault. The younger male sensed this growing weakness and began to push even harder. This renewed surge was quickly using up Hunter's last reserves of strength.

Realizing that he had to do something or lose, Hunter shifted. It meant his opponent was able to take advantage of the change and began to force the older leader aside. But as he began to move, the herd leader tossed his head high.

The younger dinosaur's three horns scraped down across his shield. The edge of the one grazed across Hunter's left eye. Bellowing in rage and agony, the herd leader pushed forward with all his remaining strength. Now off balance himself, the young challenger crashed to the ground. His pale belly was exposed to the wrath of Hunter's horns.

Then the crooning of the herd began. Soothing Hunter and calming his challenger now that the dominance battle had ended. As always, they sang of the joy of unity and the need for all to join in the pattern. Had they continued longer, they might even have summoned the pattern again. Their message fought its way through the haze of Hunter's pain and rage. Hunter scraped the now frightened male's underside almost gently and turned away.

It was three days after the challenge that Hunter noticed the new presence in the pattern. It was a familiar, blurry awareness. It was the presence of his unborn spawn by the bright eyed female. The developing egg brought rejoicing to every member of the herd. They were taken by all as a sign that this new beginning was a good one. As a result, they followed Hunter more easily through the unknown hills. That night the herd luxuriated in the distant memories of

better times and, despite the pain in his eye, even
Hunter rested well.

They had passed over the top of the mountains and
all paths now led down. To beasts as great as the
triceratops, any slope was dangerous and any fall potentially fatal. For a long time they walked along the
side of a river that rushed below. While the moss and
plants that grew along the water's edge provided vital
energy, the slippery rocks and damp soil remained a
constant hazard. They lost another elderly male when
he ventured too close to the water's edge in search of
the succulent algae which grew in the calmer eddies
and pools. The aged triceratops' panicky call had
ended in a loud splash.

In calm waters he might have swum or waded to
safety. But the rushing waters pulled the old dinosaur
away from the shore and repeatedly crashed him into
rocks or against high walls. By the time the body had
drifted out of sight downstream, it was staining the
water red from a dozen internal and external wounds.
Still they continued cautiously along the bank. There
seemed no other route to the lands below.

The next day they almost lost Bright Eyes and her
unborn eggs as well. The river had flowed down this
mountain since it had been pushed up uncounted ages
earlier. At each turn, the waters had laid a deposit of
the pebbles and even smaller stones torn from the
rocks above. Over time some of these deposits were
themselves covered by larger rocks and then plants.
The river often tried to recapture them, undermining
the loose detritus and forming cliffs overhanging its
banks.

The light-eyed female had been moving cautiously
along the shore a few steps behind Hunter himself.
Her position was a tribute to the promise she carried
inside her. She didn't slip as had the elder lost earlier,
but rather the undermined sand and pebbles gave way
under her heavy tread. One instant she was moving
gamely downward. In the next, she found herself slip-

ping toward the same death she had witnessed the day before.

The female's cry stopped Hunter and stunned the rest of the herd. The pregnant triceratops was flailing against a landslide of small rocks beneath her feet as she began to slip slowly into the river. Hunter felt a rush inside himself similar to when he was challenged. Every instinct cried to him to attack, but there was no enemy. Only the continuing flow of small stones under the front legs of his recent mate, a flow that threatened to plunge her into the frothing water.

Hunter began to turn around and then stopped. There was one weapon he might use against this threat. The large dinosaur backed toward the struggling female and braced himself as well as he could. His horns were useless, but he swung his tail in a short arc and shoved it gently into her side.

Bright Eyes grunted in surprise as the tail hit. She struggled harder when she realized it provided the leverage she needed to regain a stable portion of the bank. She scrambled to firmer ground even as Hunter could feel the earth under his own feet beginning to shift.

When both were safely back, Hunter found himself unable to restrain a bellow of victory. The female and her precious eggs were safe. After that mishap every member of the herd stayed close to the mountain's wall and away from the river whenever possible.

They were most of the way down and approaching a brown, level plain that had been tantalizingly visible for the last day's trek when they came upon it. Hunter could smell the valley long before they reached it. The air was full of pollen and seeds. It gave the air a scent that he had never known before. It was the odor of healthily growing plants.

Hunter's left eye was healing slowly. The lack of food and his own general weakness inhibited the healing process, leaving a permanent dark scar across the cornea that made him nearly blind in that eye. It was a dangerous flaw for the herd leader to have, but after his near defeat Hunter was beginning to realize he would not rule this diminished herd much longer. Somehow there was little sadness in his realization.

The pleasant scent cut through the fatigue and pain from his eye and the old leader found himself moving more quickly than he thought he was capable of up a gentle slope toward the valley's entrance. Behind him the hopeful cries of the others rolled down the line as the breeze carried to them a promise of rich food.

The entrance to the valley itself was fairly wide. Aeons earlier this had been a caldera, but the volcanic rock had become rich soil. A portion of one side had collapsed, creating a curving arc of debris and scrub. As Hunter reached the top of the debris, the valley itself became visible. It was not large, but the plants grew in abundance. Here were more green plants than he had ever seen. Perhaps more than the *total* of all he had seen before. It resembled the memories of the green years in the pattern. Hunter's belly reacted to the expectation of feasting with a gurgling rumble.

The valley's lush vegetation came from an accident of nature. The side away from the sun rose high and blocked the cold mountain winds. Down that wall in a dozen separate waterfalls streamed the river they had followed earlier. the falls' spray gently misted across the entire valley. It gathered into a large pool near the farther wall and drained down the slope from there. The slope in the direction of the sun was low, and covered with yet more vegetation. The valley was high enough that many of the clouds still scudded below and much more sunlight fought its way through the dust-filled sky above. Well-watered, protected by the natural formations, and receiving extra light, thousands of plants thrived.

The valley was too small to sustain the herd for long, but its abundance would give them all renewed strength. The few weeks they could rest here would allow even the oldest members to regain their vigor. Then they could begin the trek to find green lands and blue skies. As the other members of the herd topped the rise, they also paused, to marvel at the view.

They had seen signs of other plant eaters on this side of the mountains, and briefly the triceratops wondered why those others had spared this valley. Surely all could not be as it seemed, though the succulent plants were no illusion. Hunter's warning growl almost came too late to prevent a rush into the valley below. But millennia of discipline held the rest of the herd until Hunter began to cautiously lead them down. As they approached, the thick leaves and tall grasses became even more tempting. A young male, barely beyond suckling age, dashed ahead but then hesitated when it heard Hunter's disapproving growl. Confused, it milled about until its mother caught up as the herd passed it by.

They were almost among the plants when it sprang. The reason no other grazers had feasted in the valley became instantly and dangerously apparent. The giant carnivore rushed at the herd, his jaws open and tail stretched straight behind him. Normally the tyrannosaurus hunted on the open plains. There he could use the speed given by his two great legs to run down his prey. But finding enough game in the bleak valleys below to satisfy his voracious need had become nearly impossible. Perhaps he had pursued some potential victim up the mountain and into this valley. Whatever brought him here, the giant meat eater had soon found he was in the entrance of something that brought his prey to him.

The tyrannosaurus loomed large and its muscles had the firm look of a carnivore that had gorged well and often. It was soon obvious that any dinosaur hoping to feast on the valley's abundance had become the meat eater's meal instead. The killer moved quickly up the gentle slope with powerful, confident strides.

The tyrannosaurus came from their right, angling toward the herd from where he had waited, hidden in the thick foliage. He stood twice Hunter's height, though he was slightly less massive than the lead triceratops. The meat eater's rows of sharp teeth

gleamed in the sunlight and his thick talons tore up
the earth as he dashed forward on his hind legs. As
he neared, the predator emitted a roar that froze most
of the herd in terror.

Hunter could see the monster searching over the
herd and choosing a first victim. Once the T-rex's
black eyes locked on Bright Eyes, it looked no further. Heavy with eggs she was soon to lay, the female
was clearly vulnerable and also one of the largest dinosaurs in the herd. He would feast on her flesh for a
week.

Answering with his own roared challenge, Hunter
turned to face the threat. Moving at many times his
speed, the killer swerved away and an instant later
hovered over the gravid female. That terrified triceratops flinched at the fall of the saliva dripping from
those massive jaws and this saved her from the rapid
slash of the monster's clawed foot. Rather than tearing
out her throat, the claws merely nicked one shoulder.

Screaming more in fear than pain, she backed away.
Hunter answered her call with a bellowed challenge
of his own. He had begun to move. While slow, his
strength made his approach a powerful threat. The rex
had no choice but to turn and face him. The tyrannosaurus began to circle, working carefully to avoid the
long horns that were Hunter's best weapon. For a few
seconds they simply stood facing each other. Neither
moved as their eyes locked. There was no bravado.
No real thought or even awareness of the drama of
their clash. Both knew at a visceral level that only one
would live. The other would feast.

Hunter knew also that if he died, so might the herd.
Leaderless and terrified, the others would scatter. This
bounty would be lost and their remnants hunted by
the nimbler predator across the mountainside.

The carnivore was faster and moved first. He tried
to circle behind Hunter. If he could plunge his jaws
into the triceratops' shoulder, vital arteries would be
severed and the fight soon over. The tyrannosaurus'
feet scrambled among the stones and low growths as

it circled. Hunter moved more slowly, but managed to keep his horns facing those slavering jaws.

Without warning, the predator changed direction and dashed in on the side of the surprised triceratops. Unable to swing his horns to bear in time, the grass eater continued to circle away and swung his tail around in as high an arc as it could manage. Two tons of tail smashed into the thick chest of the charging rex and threw him back until his own tail stopped the fall.

Just as quickly, the tyrannosaurus slashed out with his now upraised feet. The titanic strength of those legs drove the talons easily through the triceratops' dense hide. The foot-long claws tore free gouges of flesh from the triceratops as Hunter instinctively pulled away from the pain. The cries of both dinosaurs rang across the small valley and down the mountain onto the dismal plains below.

Hunter hurried forward, even though this meant his back was to the killer. This carried him out of reach before the claws could strike again. Blood welled from his torn side, but he was still able to move. The tyrannosaurus, too, was hurt, one of his spindly upper arms dangling at an odd angle. There was a moment of shuffling silence and then the sound of their renewed challenges again echoed off the tall cliff face.

Twice more the carnivore tried to dash in on the wounded triceratops. Both times Hunter was able to turn in time to face the new danger. Each time his opponent stopped just short of his sharp horns. On the third rush Hunter changed tactics, running forward as he turned to face the T-rex's charge.

This time he scored, driving a horn deep into one of the legs. The quicker carnivore was able to pull away, but now both dinosaurs left great pools of blood as they circled in the gray dust.

On one level Hunter knew he hurt. There was pain where his side had been torn open almost to his lungs. He also knew that blood flowed easily from the deep wounds and he would soon weaken. On another level he knew only the need to destroy this enemy. This lone creature would mean the destruction of the herd and the end of the pattern. He drew strength from the memories of victories others of his race had gained over these great predators. Cynically, as they circled, he realized why there were no memories of losing such battles. No loser had ever lived to add those memories to the pattern.

Twice more the tyrannosaurus nearly managed to close safely. Hunter charged again, but this time the killer was prepared and the attempt gained him a new wound where the massive jaws had snapped briefly closed on his shield top.

Still they continued. Hunter, working to keep the predator in the vision of his good eye, was soon forced to continue to back up the debris covered slope. Then the rex feigned a charge and the triceratops was forced to hurry backward. Rather than allowing escape, this slammed his bulk against a large boulder that lay on his blind side.

The killer took advantage of the dazed moment it took Hunter to understand what had happened. In two gigantic bounds it was on the stunned plant eater. The triceratops could not ignore this new pain as those massive jaws clamped into the muscle just behind his shield. There was no challenge in his next cry, just agony.

The jaw shifted and the triceratops felt his own bone and muscle tear inside that powerful grip. His vision narrowed and blackness threatened. Despair rose, even as the predator's jaws again ground deeper.

He was lost, but Hunter willed himself not to concede. Amazing even himself, the massive dinosaur began to sing the herd song. The rhythm was interrupted by grunts of pain, but the rumbling sound brought him a new clarity. Distantly there was almost an answer as another joined in his chant, or maybe it was just a memory summoned from the millions of such songs that had formed the pattern. This filled the wounded leader with a determination that his herd must survive. He could still fight back, even if his own death was now certain.

Hunter saw now that he and the rex were far up the shale and dirt slope. And the tyrannosaurus was on the downhill side, using both legs to pin him against the boulder which had disrupted his retreat.

Summoning a final surge of strength, Hunter placed a leg against that massive rock and shoved. Both combatants tumbled down the slope. Each time they tumbled the rex's grip loosened as more of Hunter's muscle tore away and the predator himself was smashed and battered. At least once, Hunter managed to drive his horn into the tyranosaurus' chest. They clawed each other twice before their fall pulled them apart. Before they had reached the bottom the triceratops was maimed, but free. Both dinosaurs slid to the bottom of the slope, just where the plants began. Hunter lay still, too badly hurt to rise. The predator was unmoving as well, the blood pouring from its mouth and nostrils telling of smashed organs and blood filled lungs.

Then the great killing beast rose again, used his still powerful legs to drive unsteadily forward. Once more he paused over Hunter, opened his jaws, and plunged those hundreds of jagged teeth into the herd leader's side.

Hunter met the challenge. As the jaw descended, he turned his head and the rex's momentum drove one horn deep into the predator's belly.

It takes a long time for the great beasts to die. Unable to rise, both lay dying even as the young male Hunter had beaten earlier led the herd past them and into the valley. Soon all the triceratops had entered and begun to gorge. It pleased Hunter that the herd would regain its strength and survive, at least for a while longer. Then as the world began to grow darker, all the gathered dinosaurs stopped eating this dearly bought feast.

As if night had come, even as the final darkness grew inside Hunter, they again gathered close together. Over his now labored breathing their former leader heard the song and then saw once more the pattern form. Even as the last of his life poured away below, he traveled along the golden threads to the memory of the greener times.

REX TREMANDAE MAJESTATIS

by Kathe Koja and Barry N. Malzberg

Kathe Koja is a best-selling horror novelist as well as a science fiction writer; Barry N. Malzberg, winner of the Campbell Memorial Award, has published more than ninety books and three hundred short stories in his career.

LEONA AND THE STEGOSAUR: Pinned beneath the beast and staring at the ceiling, pale mauve. Leona had painted it herself, hung the curtains, even trimmed the carpet on her hands and knees with a little retractable razor, cutting and cutting in a rhythm not unlike the motion of the bed, his brutish back, the hump and stutter of the sounds he made: like being hammered by a stegosaur, his prehistoric crouch and groan and she pushed at him, really pushed, shoved the beast and his befuddlement (did he take it as passion?), his dry gasp—what? what is it, *oh* and coming already, half-slack and half-straining. It was all she could do to lie still until it was over and as soon as it was she was pushing again, harder than ever, his inertia, her insistence and she was up, then, she was washing in the bathroom, scrubbing and scrubbing, washing it all away in the soothing heatless light of the shaded bulb.

And from the bedroom, stegosaur stripped of his scales and his passion, only a brute again, his call plaintive as a bark, an animal sound as ultimately heedless. *Shut up,* she wanted to call back, *shut up, you'll wake Darrell, he's a light sleeper, he's always been a light sleeper.* Even in his crib, tossing, forcing her to walk the floors, and now at nearly six he was still at times unable to sleep the night through. She had let him stay up extra late, instructed the babysitter whom she had driven home, and then returned (past the littered living room, the toys and crushed potato chips, the pile of pennies, score or spoor of some idiot game) to find him, her date, already naked in her bed. His hairy arms were crossed, his hairy back against her mauve pillows, the crest of his head, the little, bright eyes taking on the stegosaur's tint, and slowly he had seemed to waver to reptilian dimensions, Sonny Stegosaur, another character on her ex-husband's dinosaur cartoon show. "Hi, babe," the thing in the bed had said, inclining its head to peer at her lasciviously. A comet had wiped out the dinosaurs, or had it been an ice age, or was all of this an alien illusion and the dinosaurs possessed the planet to this moment? Waiting in her bed, demanding their procreative necessity, tiny brains and all.

"Hi, yourself," and she had stripped, more than a little irritated. He could have waited at least for her to get back; what if Darrell had wakened, wanted his mother, called for her and gotten—what? A hairy naked thing in Mother's bed. Jesus. Talk about a primal scene. Her body warm and slightly sweaty, it had not been a long time so much as a bad time. She helped the stegosaur don its gear for patrol and grunted and pushed as it hammered away and finished and, a simple brute again, walked naked to the bathroom past her cry of dismay. "Oh, you fool," she said but he didn't hear or pretended not to, his hand on the door, and said, *"Damn!"* so loud she shuddered. "My kid," she said. "He's—"

But her smooth dinosaur, her date, annoyed: "Hey, I stepped on something, all right?" He showed it in one hand, big hand dwarfing the object inside, a bright red plastic dinosaur, triceratops with one horn of bone now cracked off at the base. "It was on the floor," he said. "It's not like I tried to—"

Oh, you fool, but this time silently, head back against the mauve pillows, contemplating the shadows blue against the ceiling, the sound of bare feet across the carpet, the sound the springs made as the bed gave grudgingly against his entering weight, a sound her own more delicate body might have made, pink and damp and unsatisfied as if awaiting its own extinction: some cool mauve plain, Leona, at the beginning and the end of time.

He stank in the morning like a stegosaur, too.

BE PART OF THE ACTION WITH DINO DUDES: Darrell hummed to himself, the cereal box squared so she could not see his face, hummed and played with his food probably and didn't eat. He was a terrible eater, a bad sleeper: all her fault, of course, like the rest of it. Had to be her fault: divorce is never that of the child, dissolution and decay begun before he was, death before life, the wide plains of Montana stripped by the comet of all life, fungus in the outback stinking to the dawn in the empty time after the dinosaurs. Death before and after life and there was no sense starting it all up again, was there? The guilt and the terrors, the rage as mindless as the plunging meteor which might have exploded the ice caps, and that rage old, old like the bones found in archaeological digs and patiently and calmly assembled for the museums. Oh, yes: here is a horn and here is a toe and here is the long tumbled skeleton like a puzzle anyone could put together, even you with your dissatisfactions and bad luck and bad faith: see? Not so hard.

"Darrell," her firm, even voice, not mad. "Darrell, come on now, eat your cereal before it—"

"I am eating," from behind the box. Small plastic scratching sounds. The dribble of milk falling fountainlike from spoon to bowl. She felt like moving the box but did not, did not feel like arguing with him, maybe she had used it all up with his father. Who was in California now with his Saturday morning cartoon show, Davy Dinosaur and his friends Barry Brontosaurus, Tyrone Tyrannosaur, Sammy the Steg and the rest of them, Tony Triceratops gamboling in cheap jumpcut herky-jerky between commercials. "It pays damned good," he had said in that last phone call, defensive and arrogant all at once. "So it isn't *King*

Lear, so what? That's what you care about anyway, right? That it pays. The money. Child support."

"Dead things," she said into the receiver, "you are making heroes of dead things for little kids' eyes."

His cackle. "You always were a litterateur, Leona. Davy pays good. What do you want, *Anna Christie*? O'Neill died at sixty-five, he was a drunk, the booze and the tuberculosis got him. Shakespeare at fifty-two. Maybe you want Davy to become a poet?"

"What else" (closed eyes, turning from her son: shield him, here is the fire) "do you want to give? Dead things on cartoons? *Ugly* cartoons?"

"Give? To you, nothing. Nothing." Then, in a different voice, "Is Darry there?"

"Of course he's here. He lives here, doesn't he?"

"Yes. Yes he does. Put him on the phone and try not to listen in on the other line for once, all right? All right?"

"I don't listen," she wanted to say, but that was a lie. She had listened plenty, starting way back with his sneaky upstairs phone calls, calling his girlfriends from their bedroom, her bedroom, making appointments, her own guilt present like acid in the stomach but not guilty enough to stop. She wanted to know, she *had* to know what was going on. Knowledge was power. If Davy and Barry and Sammy Stegosaur had known the comet was coming, maybe they could have made plans, run for cover, or cleared the plains. Ever since she had learned about Davy and her ex's new assignment she had been obsessed with the dinosaurs. They had circled behind her eyes when she dozed, danced on cereal boxes, once had come to hump her (but she wouldn't repeat that). "Darrell," she said, holding out the telephone, "it's Daddy. Daddy Dinosaur for Darrell Dinosaur," she said and laughed. Her son stared at her. She had not tried that one again.

And how long ago had that phone call been? Four months? Six? Six, yes, it had been snowing, she had felt the unseen current of furnace air against her ankles as she talked, no snow and no furnaces in cartoon land, of course, and no little extras either although he had sent a box once, a big box marked with some studio's return address and inside all manner of paraphernalia from the new show. DINO DUDES ACTION on T-shirts and visors and a poster and some absurd sign-up kit, BE PART OF THE ACTION WITH DINO DUDES. And, of course, Darrell had wanted to sign up, send away, be part of the action but also, of course, it was ridiculously expensive and a membership had not been part of Daddy's package. She simply did not have the money. No way to explain that to her little triceratops, not adequately, and after some display of sullenness and temper he had seemed to forget about it and enjoying playing with the Dudes themselves, three-inch action figures, stegosaur, tyrannosaur, pterodactyl, triceratops with legs that really moved and jaws that really opened. And closed. But were incapable of sensible speech and did not know that they were doomed by forces so enormous as to reduce them to—well, to scrambling action figures for Saturday morning Harry the Hominid cartoon shows. Harry Hominid was the Davy Dinosaur of the fortieth millennium, Leona thought. When the ultimate comet came in on them, they would last embalmed for the smart creatures who would rise from the ash. This passed for sociological or futuristic thought in what had become—she was terrifically aware of this—a severely depressed and somewhat obsessive perspective.

Darrell was playing with one of them now behind the cereal box, itself advertising toys and gadgets, marketing junk, and her voice became a little sharper now, confronted as always by the things she could not afford. "Darrell, eat!" After all, it had been worse than stupid to spend all that money on the bedroom. The carpet had been on sale and the paint very cheap and she had reasoned since she could not move out of the house she might as well change her personal scenery, but that was ridiculous, you didn't erase ten years of screwing and fighting and crying with a couple coats of paint and new curtains. If she burned the house, if she ran a flamethrower through, that would change nothing. Like bones under soil it was always there, waiting for somebody to come along and dig it up. Put it on exhibit in some dusty Hall of the Marriages, late twentieth century division, adultery and deceit, retarded orgasm and terminal envy. In the case, under the blue fluorescence, the incomprehensible aliens of the fifth millennium looking at Leona Living or Dead in the Harry Hominid tank.

Something like her stegosaur last night, stumbling through the exhibit of her life and thundering and evacuating in the center; at least he had left before Darrell got up, small mercies and so on and so forth. "Darrell," sharper still, "eat your *cereal*," and his innocent secret revealed, pushing aside the box to show her the empty bowl, the triceratops balanced delicate and broken on his spoon.

"I did," he said. "I finished it all. I finished him."

"Yes, you did," she said. "Good for you, honey. You did a good job on the dangerous thing."

FORAGING CREATURES IN THE HALL OF SCIENCE: Tired. *Tired*. Leona, moving like an animal now, some horned and brutal triceratops ready to fall into a tar pit and die, not even needing the impact or the fire, ready to die all on its own. At least then she could take a break. Always something else to do but right now she just did not have the stamina—Darrell cross and crying from latchkey and nothing to fix for dinner. She needed to shop, she needed to fix good meals for him and not fast food crap night after night, but they were both hungry now and so it was pizza in front of the TV again, she still in her suit, cheap suit with a new stain on the jacket, she would have to drop it at the dry cleaners and there was another expense. Dry cleaners, grocery store, pick up Darrell from latchkey, and it was almost the end of the month again, time to pay latchkey again, did it ever end? Never? Was a natural disaster, the fire and the impact, the only way out for her? Did she need something so big and terrible that she could simply yield to it and give it up?

Volume too loud from the tape in the VCR, Darrell

laughing at something blowing up; cartoons were so violent, it figured that *he* would want to write for them. Imagine: a grown man writing words for Sammy Stegosaur, Tyrone Tyrannosaur, writing words for dead drawings of dead creatures to speak, it made a sick kind of sense for that one anyway. A pterodactyl, not one of those he had sent, lay perhaps an inch from the toe of her shoe, scuffed toe. Screw it. She flipped the pterodactyl forward as if she were a force of nature cleaning out Wyoming; it flew a surprising distance to land on Darrell's plate, paper plate, and he laughed. He thought she had done it on purpose. "Do it again, Mom, do it again." It was appealing; she was the comet, Darrell the forces of entropy, and the pterodactyl was—well, the pterodactyl stood for all the dinosaurs. Once beasts of the plains, now models of foraging creatures in the hall of science. "Mommy's tired," she said, wanted to say. "Mommy's too tired to do it again," but, of course, she did it anyway, tried it that is to say, tried to reproduce that perfect, stunning hit, once and twice and six times until finally her shoe went with it and crashed on the coffee table, knocking over Darrell's glass, grape Kool-Aid soaking darker than blood into the carpet, and he had laughed and she had not, unable to commit even a good act of entropy. If it had been up to her, the dinosaurs would have lurched their way from the Mesozoic to the Wall Street crash and completed their foraging on the floor of the Exchange. Dumb powerless Mommy and on the way back from the kitchen predictably pierced by another one, Barry Brontosaurus this time, that big two-brained creature which ate leaves and was too dumb to move. Darrell had hundreds of them it seemed, they were all over the place, her ex had certainly caught hold of some real merchandise here. How kids loved dinosaurs, and now a new cartoon series fully populated by them. The head of the thing stabbed into the flat ball of her one bare foot with astonishing brutality and, *Damn!*, shaking it loose, big blue splinter and Darrell's laughter gone, sitting stunned, scared, still beside the Kool-Aid, staring at her as she limped to kneel at the stain with a sponge and a towel. "It's okay, Darrell," she said. "Really, it was just a little accident." If I were Entropy, she thought, if there were a god named Entropy with a capital E I would have exterminated them all.

Something else blew up in the cartoon: Darrell laughed, his attention swinging from her now as she slopped and sponged. Another stain on her suit. Barry Brontosaur had ripped a hole in the heel of her pantyhose.

THE SLOW PROCESSION OF THE BEASTS: Her sleep that night uneasy, waking again and again, checking on Darrell until it was obvious (even to her) that the noises she heard were not, could not have been made by him: little boy sprawl beneath the big red blanket, careless crash of stuffed animals (only two of them, she noted, not dinosaurs) around his body like a wall, protection against missing fathers, against the pain of missing fathers, what? What was the difference? Go to sleep, Leona told herself, careful hand on his door, just go back to sleep. Give it up. At least the stegosaur is not here nor will come again; the dive-bomb wiped him off the Earth. Take what comfort you can.

But the noises continued, subtly, softly, the sly movement of beasts past her vision, rhythmless grumbling thump under, beneath, below; no basement here, cheap ranch house sitting on a cheaper foundation, just like her cheap little life sat on a foundation of latchkey and child support, just as the dinosaurs had streamed through the Plains States on sufferance, not abating but timed to the disaster which would surely come. If this had been California, they would all be out on their asses when the next quake hit. The dinosaurs must have been terrified when the flash had come, but then again were they smart enough to know terror? Was there some threshold beneath which you could not capture the sense of your life, and if she reached it herself would she know?

Oh, thump, thump, Leona; like subsonics, like the

sound your heart makes when you are terrified, pounding as if it would pound you to pieces the way it had for her in court, hands on her purse and still as an animal in a thicket as tyrannosaur rumbles by; she thought everyone in the courtroom could see the terror in her. Thump, thump, like bones moving in the darkness, that slow and insistent procession crawling and grinding, trying in vain to force reassembly where none could ever be possible. The scientists who knew about this stuff, she had taken a book out of the library when the cartoons had first come on— knowledge is power—said there were bones everywhere, all across the country. You could be sleeping over a giant cemetery and never know it, never guess unless the bones decided to reform, reanimate to reenact a different, less total ending, an ending in which disaster did not play such a prominent part.

Dinosaurs in the sun then, blinking and chewing, a quarter of a million tons of raw meat on the hoof and those alien eyes like the eyes of insects, compound eyes to see all sides of a problem. If they were smart enough to live and get so big, why were they dumb enough to have all died then, together? *Thump, thump,* and she thought through closed eyes she could see them, their shadows, the moving glyphs of their forms dark against the midnight wall. *Thump, thump,* and she felt like screaming: "Just be quiet, you're dead, shut up! I need to get up in the morning, I can't afford to lie down and die." But she did not say that or anything, she was Leona living as opposed to Davy Dinosaur Dead and she made no sound, did nothing but put the pillow over her head and let it ooze slowly into position, covering her ears, covering her sleepless and staring eyes. *It is coming,* she thought, *the comet is coming. It is plunging in the abysmal sky, small and deadly, toward the target and it will level everything. We shall all be changed, we shall be no more, Davy Dead and Leona Living merged at last.*

LEONA AT THE GATES: In the morning she called her ex at the studio. He was difficult to find, difficult to procure, furious when at last the connection had been made. "Darry," he said, "something is wrong with Darry, that is the only thing it could be, you should never call me here, I told you—"

"The comet," she said. "The comet is coming. Davy and Sammy and Tyrone were doomed, and now it is coming for us." She felt exceedingly calm, reasonable, the night had been terrible beyond all telling, but in the morning she had woken to a sense of absolute purpose. Otherwise how could she have arranged to take off the week from work, how could she have so mildly, pleasantly, without urgency sent Darrell off on the bus? "I just want you to know," she said. "I see it in the sky, the portents. I see in the night that what came for Davy and Sammy is coming for us."

"Leona," he said. "I want you to listen to me. I want you to listen to everything I am saying. Call your mother immediately. Tell her to come over right now. I will call her, too, and speak to her after you do, but you call first. Where is Darry? Is he at school now?"

"He's on the plains," she said. "He is wandering through the trees, eating bark and minding his business with all the other little dinosaurs. What does he know? What do any of them know?" The absolute clarity of the thought assaulted her. "What did any of us know before the lights went out?" she said. She giggled. The stegosaur had been enormous in her bed, its tail flapping and flopping as it had backed its way into a randy and dangerous exercise. If the dinosaurs had all had stegosaur's persistence and force, they might have lasted, but while stegosaur randied into position his big brothers and little sisters ate leaves. "Your mother," he said, "call your mother right now. I'm going to make some calls, too." He put down the phone. She felt the thunder of his rooting and disappearing snout and then she backed away, slowly, from the instrument, tangling her feet in the toys on the floor but no longer oblivious, instead attuned. She felt the distant rays of the distant visitors congealing around her, felt the ultimate force of that conjoinment imposed.

THE MISTS OF ETERNITY: In the grasp of those who sought so desperately to understand her but could not, for all of their will, comprehend the truth, in the rasp of the soon-to-be-extinct, Leona saw all of them finally for what they were; gathered in the basilica of the planets on the far star, draped and anointed by the mists of eternity. Leona Living, the warrior queen of Harry Hominid, stood proudly in the cool and eternal aspic of her preservation, holding the spear that signaled her defense of the cities in which she had dwelt. *We came,* Leona Living's plaque would say, *we walked the jungles and the darkness of our Earth for a while like all of the other creatures, and then we departed. But we leave this, we leave that, we leave our perfect, replicated spoor through all of those spaces and when we, dead at last in the basilica, awaken we leave true and final testimony of our troubled, our grief-stricken but our not-inconsequential history.* Partnered by stegosaur, loomed by tyrannosaur, flickering in the ancient and ghastly light of the cartoons dragooned from vanished Earth and dying sun to that basilica, that testimony and testament Leona gave her own testimony to all the raves of the night, knowing from the heart of her own ascension that she gave difficult, and eternal, and pervading light. As had Tyrone Tyrannosaur. As had grunting and embalmed Sammy Stegosaur in her pulsing, gathering, human embrace.

THE SKULL'S TALE

by Katharine Kerr

Katharine Kerr is a best-selling fantasy novelist.

I was going along, bounding, mostly, though sometimes I stopped to rear up and wait, sniffing hill-smell and valley-smell. I was not hungry but on guard, searching out not food-smell but enemy-smell. None came, and I bounded on, slap, slap, slap on the hill ridge, though sometimes I stopped to squat and mark. As I said, I was on patrol. At hill crest stood my grandmother's stone, the hard shaft she had clawed from the earth over the many years of her long life, a claw of dirt here, one there each time she passed. My mother and her clutchsisters had pulled and pried and teased this stone upright. Dirt they had kicked round it, dirt they had stamped down, till the stone stands like a tree, our stone, upon our hill.

When I squatted to mark the stone, I smelled enemy stink. She had marked on the dirt round the stone. She had rubbed her cheeks upon the stone itself, leaving musk smell. Rage filled me. I marked over her mark, I rubbed over her rub. The rage abated, but anger remained. For a long time I bounded back and forth on the hill crest, smelling the wind, but she had gone away. I could not smell her stink, but I knew I would remember it. When I found her, there would be blood between us, me and the one who had dared mark my grandmother's stone.

I was going along, leaving the stone behind me, bounding downhill to the water valley. It was near the place known as Three Heaped Rocks that I heard the whistle of a Hookclaw. I stopped bounding and shuffled three times around the Rocks, keeping always to the motion of the Sun, as is proper; then I haunched

124

and let my hands dangle, claws in to show the Hookclaw I was not hungry. Whimpering under its breath,
it crawled out of the tangle-brush and came toward
me, blowing and bowing, its puny arms out, its bluish
clawed hands holding out a dead fur-thing, the gray
kind with four legs. Hookclaw bared its pointed teeth
as it bobbed its round head. When I took the fur-
thing as a pledge I would not kill, the creature sucked
in its breath, then sighed.

"Mighty Eater, Mother of Thousands!" it said. "Let
there be peace between us this one day."

"What do you want with me?"

"My herdmaster sent me, Mighty Eater. Something's happened, something very strange, something
painful to Hookclaw."

"And just how does this threefold importance concern me?"

"The Eaters are stronger, the Eaters are wiser, the
Eaters are bigger than Hookclaws."

I hunkered and tail-propped. The pitiful thing was
obviously too frightened to think at its full capacity,
small though that is at the best of times. I also tried
to keep my voice very soft and small for its tiny ears.

"Now think for a moment. Is this mysterious thing
trying to kill you?"

"My master is unsure, she is confused."

"Is it important that the Eaters are bigger and
stronger?"

It stared up with blank round eyes and thought for
a very long time about that question. Once it even
glanced furtively at its three fingers and seemed to be
trying to count on them.

"It is important, it is very important, it is most
important."

"And why is it important?"

It wove its fingers together in front of its face and
moaned. For a moment I considered the possibility
that perhaps the Hookclaws were laying a trap, that
perhaps at last they had found a spark of courage in
their miserable livers and were going to fight against
those that harvested them. I considered it until I

looked again at the small and scaled creature writhing before me. Its long ringed tail thrashed and slapped the dirt. The glands in its armpits were sending out fear-smell in noxious drifts.

"There is another one," it said at last. "She bounds on your lands."

"Ah."

At last, things came clear. Too many harvesters, and there would be no Hookclaws.

"Don't eat me! Please, don't eat the bearer of bad news!"

And thus, its fear. I bit off the head of the dead fur-thing and handed the body to the Hookclaw to give to its master as a token. It is part of the pact between us, that once we share a kill, we will not eat the being who holds the other part. My own portion, the head, I put safely into my belt-pack.

"Now go to your master and tell her that the Eater known as Lilas Rock-shaper is on patrol."

With a little screech that might have been either gratitude or simple relief at getting gone, it ran away, striding on its two legs down to the river below in the valley. I watched until it was too small to see clearly, then marked our meeting place, went round the rocks, marked again, and started after.

I was going along, shuffling more than bounding on the steep slope, and I was keeping my head well up to catch all the smells that wind might bring me. Since it was hot, they were many and strong: richness of crushed dust, sharpness of purple flower-grass and sweetness of lavender flower-grass; Hookclaw juiciness and the dry husk smell of fur-things, more Hookclaws, many more, meaty and succulent and very far away; Grasseaters, not so meaty, but an acceptable blood-stink, and with that nice summer overtone of fat, too; and, finally, clean-running water. Ah, is there anything so lovely as the smell of water in the summer's heat? I drank and drank, filling myself for my patrol.

Every smell seemed somehow stronger, richer, clearer, standing out each from the other as if I already knew deep in the pit of my stomach that this day was a marker-day, destined to stand out in the long Telling of Days. And yet, I knew only that a Hookclaw had overcome its fear and asked the help of the Eaters—a rare occurrence, certainly, but not unknown.

Finally I reached the bottom of the slope, and the easy going along the bank of the river. By then I was hungry, but I was mindful of the pledge I had taken and the token I had given. I paused, soaking up the light of the Sun, head cocked, waiting, opening my mouth to let the smells filter into the sensing-slit at the back of my throat, for the nose-smells were so rich there by the river that it was hard to untangle them. Finally I picked up what I wanted: a Digger burrow, and not far. I bounded, leaning forward, head low, until my eyes saw the dark gash in the ground. I bent and clawed, scooping up dirt, two handfuls, many handfuls, and at last two squealing Diggers. Since they have no speech, I ate them alive, as is tastiest. Then I shuffled to the river and washed the blood from my face and hands, because I did not want to frighten the Hookclaws who had asked for my help. Although their noses are poor, they can see blood and know its meaning.

I was going along, heading for the river place known as Splendor of the Moon at her Widest, though sometimes I stopped to squat and mark, for I was still on patrol, the red stones and the white thongs hung round my neck, the scent of my clutchsisters on my scales. I smelled clean-running water under bright Sun, low water and rich mud, oily with living things, and the juiciness of Hookclaws, thick swarming camps of delight, many warm tasty Hookclaws, across the river. The bony Diggers had filled my stomach but not fully pleased my mouth, yet I was mindful of my pledge and my token. You are my friends, my clutchsisters, my sleeping-companions, you have heard me speak this way before, so you will not spit or bare your fangs at me when I say that I regretted that the

Hookclaws have speech, that they are speaking things
with words and names.

Besides, I had enemy stink in my mind, and they
had seen my enemy. As I bounded by the riverbank
(neck arched, head high, tail curled over my back)
always did I keep my nose alive and open, searching
for her scent. I came to Splendor of the Moon at
her Widest, wreathed round with the sweet scent of
Hookclaws and the bitter crushing of the purple long-
grass and the green tube trees. As I was arriving, I
saw the two standing stones and the lying stone between them, and on the lying stone I saw as I grew
closer still the cleft that my grandmother herself chis-
eled out to mark the coming of the turning toward
winter. If, when you hunker on the grass and look
through the crack she made there, you can see the
Sun rising straight ahead, then you know that the time
of cold wind is coming, when the fur-things burrow
and sleep, and the Hookclaws begin their trudge
southward, where we must follow them.

But that day I did not hunker down on the grass to
admire the work of my grandmother's hands, for I
smelled again the enemy stink, her mark upon the
tube trees, her cheeks upon the stone itself. My rage
consumed me; I threw back my head; I boomed from
my throat, like thunder all up and down the river
valley.

And far far away I heard her, booming in answer.

I smelled her stink, too, a whisper on the wind.

I bounded, I went along, I did not stop to mark.
Down the river valley I bounded, up the far hill crest
I shuffled, along the crest I bounded again. Down the
hill I bounded so fast and high that at times it seemed
I would leave the ground like one of the Flapwings
and sail the winds. Stronger and stronger her foul
stench became, my enemy closer and closer to my
mouth. By the spring we call Scraped Stone I saw her,
hunkering, waiting among tube trees, her leg raised,
her foot thrumming on the ground. Fool. She was
young yet and small.

I stopped bounding and walked straight toward her.

When she saw me, she let her jaws open, but not far in only a small defiance. Now she could see me as well as smell me. Now she could see my size. When I slapped my tail once upon the ground, she stopped her thrumming and crouched, somewhere between the blood posture and the hatchling posture, so that I could not tell what she intended to do.

"Who are you?" I said.

"My name is my name and not for you to know."

I let my jaws open wide, very wide. For a long moment we looked into one another's eyes. I felt my eyes become Sun rays, hot and golden, boring into her eyes like the claws of a mighty Sun. For a long time she let those claws pierce her, so long that I felt admiration in my liver for the creature, just a tiny egg of it that might or might not hatch. All at once she slumped into the hatchling pose, laying her head upon the ground so that I could have snapped her neck with one bite. For a moment I let her feel fear, just as a lesson. When she trembled, I spoke.

"What is your name?"

"I am Ger, but I have earned no second name."

"Why do you mark upon my stones?"

"My mother's mate has filled me with eggs. I must flee her. I must find a spot to nest."

"You may not nest here. When will you lay?"

"Soon." She considered me, looking up with one glittering eye, as if she contemplated saying an untrue thing. At length her head slumped a little farther. "But not so soon that I will die if I find no nest."

"Then you must go along. You may not nest among my stones and the stones of my herd."

She said nothing, but closed her eyes, waiting perhaps for my bite. Instead I circled her three times, going in the direction of the Sun as is right and proper. After the third circle was finished I marked upon her, once for contempt, once to show that I had met with her and dealt with her. As I said, I was on patrol. For the patrol and for the sake of the guard I drew blood, but it was claw blood, not mouth blood. I took three red drops from her neck, then withdrew my claw and shuffled round to face her.

"You must go along," I said.

"I will go along." Slowly she raised her head, watching me with both eyes. "May I raise further?"

"You may raise."

With a grunt, she haunched, shaking her neck and head, but she opened her mouth only as wide as was necessary for the speaking.

"Which way must I go?" she said. "I will leave your stones as soon as I can, but which way must I go?"

"You must head toward the place where the Sun sets. Soon you will be beyond our stones. I warn you. Return this way, and you will die. I spare you only for the sake of the eggs you carry."

"For the sake of the eggs, I thank you."

I boomed and slapped my tail. I did not want her to know that I had spared her for the courage she had shown in meeting my eyes.

"If you return," I said, "my clutchsisters and I will rip your body open and pull out the eggs from within you, and we will crush them, each and every one."

"So I know you will do. It is proper and right. I thank you for your mercy to one who carries eggs."

And so she went along, bounding toward the place where the Sun sets every night, bounding fast and faster, till I feared for the eggs within her. Yet did I follow, bounding more slowly, ensuring that she would keep going along, until we reached the place known as Stone of a Thousand Scratches, the flat slab that lies on the top of the hill of the fern trees. There among the ferns I stopped, for it is the last of our stones. I marked, I haunched. I waited, tail-propped, until I could see her no more as she bounded down the hill of the fern trees. Again I waited, until her stink became very small, a half-heard whisper on the wind.

Only then did I leave, going along toward the place where the Sun rises every morning. Now have I met with you, my clutchsisters, here on the hill crest at our grandmother's stone. I was on guard. This is my tale of my guard. May you think that the tale is good and that I did right when as I spared the Hookclaw, I spared Ger, one young and yet to lay her first clutch.

I am Lilas Rock-shaper. I will lay the head of the fur-thing at the base of this stone to mark my mercy. When the tiny Eaters with Six Legs have cleaned the skin and meat from its skull, we will know that the tale of Lilas and Ger has passed into the Telling of Days. It will be the mark between us, the white skull of the Hookclaw's token.

CUTTING DOWN FRED

by Dean Wesley Smith

Dean Wesley Smith is not only a successful author, but also the editor and publisher of Pulphouse.

I tried to make love under Fred for the first time on a warm October evening two years ago. It was right in the middle of Big John's annual Halloween bash, the very same party that keeps three square city blocks up all night. My current girlfriend, Annie, was in one of her moods, none of which I ever figured out. So when I suggested, after six very fast and hot dances, that we go somewhere cool, take off some costumes, and really get hot, she laughed and said she would love to. But she wanted to go somewhere new. She said she was tired of my apartment and "those old squeaky bed springs." She wanted to be daring. "Really live," was the way I think she put it. So we ended up under Fred.

We left the party with a wave at Big John and headed downtown. I was wearing my Buckey the Space Pirate costume, with the white tights, white cape, lace shirt, saber, and plumed white hat. Most people thought I looked like one of the Three Musketeers, but what the hell did they know about space pirates, anyway?

Annie had on her Queen of the Alien Warlords costume made up of black tights, high black boots, and lots of chains over a very open-necked blouse. On her head she wore this three-foot-tall jeweled headdress that gave the entire costume a feeling of power. The only problem was that she kept forgetting to duck when going through doors.

I didn't exactly know what Annie had in mind when she said "daring," but I figured Russell Park might fit. And it was close by. I didn't feel like walking too far dressed as Buckey, especially in this part of the city.

Russell Park was the second oldest park in the city. I'd been there a few times, mostly passing through. It was one of those places where old people sat around on the benches and watched the young mothers ignore their children. It measured half a block wide, a block long, and was filled with benches, small patches of grass, and big old oak trees. But it didn't smell much like a park because there just wasn't enough green to hold back the smells of the city.

We ended up under one of the biggest trees in the park, tucked off in one corner, near a hedge and a wooden bench that looked like no one had sat on it since the First World War. There I hoped we would have the least chance of being seen, yet give Annie the thrill she needed.

To say Annie was thrilled would have been putting it lightly. She liked the idea of making love out in the open. In the two months we'd gone out she said we'd never done anything this much "fun."

"My dear Queen Annie," I said, taking my plumed hat off and bowing deeply at the waist while sweeping the hat along the grass. "Will this place of repose suit a lady of your stature?" She always loved it when I went formal on her.

"You have done well, faithful servant," she said, smiling. Then she reached up, took off her headdress, and sat it against the base of the tree. Then the chains came over her head, then the blouse. She was working on taking off the tights before I had enough common sense to start getting undressed, too.

She was totally nude and lying on the grass by the time I had gotten my boots and saber off. So instead of finishing undressing, I went to work, kissing that soft skin, starting at her right ear and working my way down. I was doing my best to not miss a spot on that beautiful body, when this deep voice came out of nowhere.

"There was a young lady from Hunt
whose body could take a small punt.
Her mother said, 'Annie,
It matches your fanny,
Which never was that of a runt.' "

I thought my heart was going to explode right out
of my chest. I expected to look up and see a police-
man standing there with a big nightstick, slapping it
into his palm as he smiled down at us. We were going
to end up in jail. I just knew it. Mom would never
understand.

So from between Annie's legs I glanced quickly
around. No one. At least in sight.

"What did you mean by that?" Annie said, pushing
me away and sitting up. "That seemed like a pretty
crude thing to say, especially when you were doing what
you were doing. And just what the hell is a punt?"

"I didn't—"

"It's a flat-bottomed boat that is propelled by
thrusts from a pole," the voice said.

Annie glanced quickly around, then stood up and
stared down at me, hands on her hips. "I don't think
I like you any more," she said and pulled on her black
tights.

"But I didn't say anything," I pleaded.

"Then who did," she asked. "And you know, if you
were any bigger than a pencil, you wouldn't think I
was so large."

"A pencil?" I said. "But—"

She pulled her blouse on quickly, grabbed the chains
and headdress, and stormed off with me still there on
the grass trying to get my boots back on. "But—
But— But—" I said over and over as she disappeared
through an opening in the hedge.

"There was a young fellow of Buckingham
Wrote a treatise on girls and on fucking them.
A learned Parsee
Taught him Gamahuchee,
So he added a chapter on sucking them."

"Who's there?" I quickly turned around, but couldn't see anyone. The deep baritone voice sounded like it had come from right beside me. "Come out, damn you!" I pulled on my boots and grabbed my saber and checked behind the trunk of the old tree, then in the hedges, and then in the branches of the tree itself. No one. In fact, the entire little park looked completely deserted.

"Aren't you even curious," the voice asked. Again it sounded as if it was coming from right beside my head. I spun around, then checked my shirt for hidden microphones someone might have slipped in at the party. Nothing.

"All right," I said. "I give up. What's the joke?"

"Oh, no joke," the voice said. "But I wonder if you are curious as to what Gamahuchee means. Most people would be."

"Who's talking?" I shouted at the dimly lit park. This was getting damned annoying. It was going to take me a week to calm Annie down, if she would even talk to me again.

"I'll tell you who I am if you first ask me what Gamahuchee means."

"Oh, for hell's sake." I checked once more in the limbs of the tree, in the hedge, and around the trunk. Just one old oak tree. No one anywhere near. Finally, I gave up and sat down. "All right, what the hell does Gamahuchee mean?"

"No one is really sure," the voice said.

"Great," I said. "You—"

"But it is thought to have a Japanese derivation, and in the context of the limerick, it refers to oragenitalism. Or, in more current terminology, oral sex."

"I could have figured out as much," I said. "If I really gave a shit. Now would you please tell me who the hell you are? And where you are so you can laugh and I can kill you?"

"I am the tree you now repose under. I refer to myself as Fred. I am sure you would not like to hear the story of how I came to acquire that name, even though it *is* quite interesting."

"You're right," I said, looking up into the thick green leaves of the tree. "I wouldn't. And I don't buy this for a minute. Where's the speaker hidden?"

"I am really the tree," the voice said, sadly. "Why don't you believe me? Dressed as you are, I had hoped you at least would believe me."

"Well, I don't!" I shouted up into the tree. "And there's not a damned thing wrong with how I'm dressed." I felt immediately stupid for shouting. Somewhere, someone was laughing their fool head off and I was playing along. I stood and headed for the entrance to the park. A joke was a joke. But Buckey the Space Pirate had let this one go too far.

By the next afternoon no one had come up to me and laughed at how much they had got me. And Annie didn't show one sign of talking to me no matter how much I pounded on her door. The only way she was going to ever speak to me again was if I proved to her that it wasn't me who had accused her of being able to do strange things with boats. If I uncovered whoever the joker was, I could prove to her it wasn't me. So that evening I found myself back down at the park under the old tree.

"You look much more normal for these times dressed as you are today," the voice said as I walked up. I had on a T-shirt and Levis. "Would you like to hear another limerick?"

"Whoever you are," I said as calmly as I could. "Please show yourself."

"I am showing myself. I'm shading you from the sun. What more do you want? Don't you like my limericks? I have one I made up for a young couple back thirty, maybe forty years ago. I was much smaller then and they were one of the first who used my shelter for the purpose that you were using it for yesterday. I feel it is one of my best limericks. And by the way, my name is Fred."

"Fred. Sure. You told me." I moved slowly around the tree trying to humor the voice while spotting exactly where the speaker was hidden. "You know you could have at least waited until we finished. And I'm not buying this talking tree line. I know someone's behind all this and when I find out who, I— I—"

"Do what you like," the voice said. "I won't be around much longer for you to believe or not believe."

"Sure." I searched through some high grass near a sprinkler head. "You're just going to pull up roots and walk away. Right?"

"Hardly," Fred said.

"All right, then," I said and went back to searching the trunk, feeling for any loose bark. "Why don't you tell me, for starters, how you can talk. Some witch cast a spell over you or something?"

"I suppose it could be called magic," Fred said. "But I prefer to think of it as the miracle of life. Actually, us trees are much more intelligent than you humans think and have very long memories."

"Sure. Sure. All from the miracle of life." I said, as sarcastically as I could make my voice sound. "So how'd that get you a voice?"

"I don't actually know. I don't actually have vocal cords as you do, but I can project my thoughts to make humans hear the thoughts as a voice. You see, ninety-seven years ago, a sailor visited a brothel here in this fine city. The man used a prophylactic. It was disposed of in the alley outside of the brothel and a very young girl found it a short time later. She took an acorn from my mother, put it in the sperm and planted the entire thing here. The young girl watered me carefully for the first two years until she died, run over by a wagon right in front of me. Poor child. Of course, there was nothing I could have done."

I had kept looking the entire time he had been talking and still hadn't found one hint of any speaker, microphone, or wiring. The voice seemed to come from everywhere around the tree and inside my head at the same time. "You don't really expect me to believe that?" I said.

"You asked," Fred said. "Would you like to hear another limerick? I know all of the good old ones."

"Not just yet." I had come to the realization that this stunt was so well done that I was going to get nowhere unless I played along. Eventually whoever was behind it would slip up. "Say, why don't you tell me how you came to do limericks?"

"If you stood in one place for almost a hundred years, you'd do limericks, too."

With that I granted he had a point. I studied the tree for a foothold. The speaker was probably hidden in the limbs somewhere and I was going to have to climb up there to find it. Best thing to do was keep humoring the voice while being quiet while climbing the tree. "What's this about you not having much longer?"

"Tomorrow, to be exact," Fred said. "That's why I decided to talk to you. Do you realize that I have only talked to seven people in almost one hundred years. I look back and find that fact most amazing."

"What's going to happen?" I picked my way carefully up the bark like a rock climber going up a sheer face. Finally I got my arms around the lowest limb and pulled myself up.

"See the stakes in the grass?" Fred said. "The ones with the orange ribbons on them?"

I looked back down through the branches. "Sure." They were scattered across this corner of the park. I hadn't noticed them last night with Annie.

"I overheard workmen talking about widening the road. I'm scheduled for the chain saws tomorrow."

"You're kidding?" I finished checking out the limb I was on and climbed higher where I could see the stakes better. They did show a pattern that looked like the street was going to be wider right through the big tree.

"I am afraid I am not kidding," Fred said, his voice almost too faint for me to hear. Then he got suddenly louder. "But, that is life. Or death. And please do be careful. I've had fifteen children and three adults fall out of my limbs. It is always so painful an occurrence. Actually, the first person who fell out of my limbs was killed by a dinosaur. It was a very sad experience since his wife was standing nearby in the park at the time and never really understood what happened."

"A what?"

"A dinosaur. Actually a pterosaur angry that he was there. You know that pterosaurs were large flying reptiles that . . ."

"Now you have gone too far. First you expect me to believe you are a talking tree and then you expect me to believe that you have been around since the dinosaurs. There were no men during that time. That much I remember from grade school. And you said you were not even a hundred years old."

"You are quite right," Fred said. "But we oak trees have family memories that go back, for lack of a better way of putting it, to our roots, which incidentally, were in the early Cretaceous Period in this part of the world."

"Fine," I said, glancing down at the ground below, wondering when the funny farm wagon was going to come and take me away for talking to myself in a tree.

"I can tell you do not believe me."

"No shit," I said. "I am still looking for the microphone so I can get this joke over."

"Please hold onto a limb and I will take you back. Do you have a favorite dinosaur you would like to see?"

"Yeah, sure," I said and started down. "And next you will be telling me I can ride a triceratops if I want."

Fred laughed softly. "Not hardly, but I can certainly show you why you *wouldn't* want to ride one."

Around me the air suddenly shimmered and the branches of the oak seemed to move and sway, as if there was a slight earthquake shaking the roots. I grabbed tight around a limb and held on as I was suddenly hit by a wave of hot and very humid air that smelled of swamp and fresh greenery.

Below me there was a crashing of brush and again the tree shook. Through the shaking leaves I could see that the city was gone. There was nothing except trees and brush. And below me was the ugliest, most scarred-up triceratops I could ever imagine.

"Hold on," the voice of Fred inside my head said as the dinosaur bumped into the tree and then started using it to scratch itself. I thought I was on a ride at a carnival.

The dinosaur stepped back, then bumped the tree and I bounced among the limbs. Then the triceratops backed off, looked at the tree, and hit it again.

As I held on for dear life, I heard Fred's voice in my head. "See why you wouldn't want to ride one?"

Somehow, as the dinosaur took aim once more on the base of the tree I managed to scream, "Get me out of here!"

And I was back in the tree in the park.

A tree that wasn't moving.

I looked slowly around to make sure that I was where I seemed to be, then carefully pulled my fingers out of the grooves they had dug into the bark.

"Pretty amazing beasts, weren't they?"

I took a deep shuddering breath and let it out. "How did you do that?"

"How do you walk around and drink water without roots? It is just a part of what we are. We can move our conscious minds back and forth through our ancestors and through time. I guess it makes up for not being able to move in real time. You didn't actually leave the park, but I took your mind back with mine. Fun, huh? Now, would you like to hear another limerick? I have one about a dinosaur."

"No. Thanks." I gave one more quick look to make sure the city was where it should be and there was no triceratops lurking behind the hedge, then climbed down. Once I was back on the ground I walked quickly around the tree, than sat down.

"You seem upset," Fred said.

"That ride you gave me was really something. I am not saying that I believe you, but can you take me to any time at all?"

"Sure," Fred said. "And to almost any place as long

as the oak at the location is, as we say, in my family tree."

I groaned.

"Sorry," Fred said. "But," his voice suddenly sounded sad. "I am afraid that today will be the last day for you to experience any other time, so we should make the best of it."

I climbed back to my feet and walked along the line of stakes in the grass. They did start at the corner and go inside the edge of the tree. "Just for the sake of argument," I said, "is there something I can do for you? I doubt that I could stop the street from being widened, but—"

"Oh, my dear man," Fred said quickly. "It is so kind of you to ask. I was hoping you would. I have studied the problem at some length and I feel the only solution would be to repeat the process from which I came."

"What?" I asked. I had lost whatever Fred was talking about halfway through.

"In other words," Fred said, "get a rubber, ejaculate into it, put one of my seeds in the resulting solution, and plant it. Very simple, really."

"No way! You must think I was born yesterday?" Now at least I was starting to see the joke. I didn't know how they had pulled off the voice and the dinosaur shtick, but someone was having a great laugh on this one and I wasn't going to play along anymore.

"I'm afraid I do not know when you were born," Fred said. "But I got here by exactly the method I told you. I have watched it happening. I have studied the event many times and I fear it may be my only chance for survival."

"Sure." I made one more quick check of the tree, then studied the stakes. I had to admit it was sure one elaborate gag. And it looked like the only way I was going to get to the prankster was by going along and getting it over with. Then I could prove to Annie that I didn't say anything and get back on her "good" side.

"All right," I said. "I'll bring back the part of the

deal you need from me. Where will I find a seed from you?"

"I will drop an acorn that is ready to sprout," Fred said. "And thank you."

"No problem," I said. I made one more quick check around the area of Fred to make sure no one was hiding in the bushes laughing their fool heads off, then headed for Annie's house in hopes of her giving me a helping hand. She still wouldn't talk to me or even let me explain what I was trying to do. Not that I really blamed her. So I went back to my place and did it myself. I was back at the tree in an hour.

I checked quickly around to make sure no one was watching, then held the rubber up. "Here you go."

An acorn hit the grass right at my feet. I picked it up, looked at it, then stuck it inside the rubber. "Got any place special you think I should plant it?" I asked, checking the area of the branches it fell from to make sure there was no one sitting up there.

"Anywhere that will be safe," Fred said.

"I'll be back tomorrow morning early." As I headed for the park gate, I heard Fred start into a limerick about a girl from Troy.

I took my "package" to Mom's house in the suburbs and planted it off to one side in her backyard. She didn't care. As far as she was concerned, I was always doing strange things. And she hadn't even seen me in my Buckey the Space Pirate costume.

I staked out where I planted the seed. I told Mom it was a special seed for an exotic tree and needed really special care. She liked that.

I made it back to the park by ten the next morning, but I was way too late. The old tree was in a hundred pieces piled in neat stacks. I watched while the workmen used chain saws on what was left, but I couldn't take it for very long. Even though I knew the entire thing had just been a joke, I couldn't shake the feeling of pain and sadness coming from that wood.

I never did get back with Annie. She wouldn't have anything to do with me. And no one ever came forward and laughed at me about jacking off into a rubber and then planting it. If it was a practical joke, or a hidden camera stunt, I never found out about it. Seems to me that I would have, too. I don't understand why someone would go to all that trouble without pulling the final "gotcha."

Since I never uncovered the joke, every time I visited Mom I found myself checking the spot where I had planted the tree. Nothing. Over the winter I pretty much forgot about it.

It wasn't until the following May, while I was mowing Mom's lawn, that I almost ran over the little oak tree. I spent an entire hour cleaning the weeds and grass away from it, then putting up a solid, two-foot-high wire fence around it. It felt kind of funny to know that my sperm had worked as fertilizer for a tree.

I checked back on the little tree all through that summer and fall, telling myself I was crazy each time I did, but yet doing it anyhow. It became one of those little obsessions a person has that they can't explain. I sure in hell made no attempt to tell anyone. Mom loved it. Said she'd never had so much help with the yard.

It wasn't until the following May that something finally happened. I was carefully mowing around the now almost four-foot-tall baby oak tree when I heard this high, childlike voice. At first I thought it was something going wrong with the mower, but after I turned the engine off, I heard:

> "A bather whose clothing was strewed
> By waves that left her quite nude,
> Saw a man come along
> And unless I am wrong
> You expect this line to be crude."

I sat down hard on the grass. I couldn't believe it. I was either going completely crazy, or it had worked. I had actually planted a tree with my sperm that grew and could talk. No way. That was just too stupid. Just like before, it was either a joke or I had imagined it.

"You know," the little voice said from what seemed like the direction of the little tree. "I have this strange desire to do things to a woman dressed in a costume."

I lay down on the grass with my face real close to the small trunk of the tree. "Fred?"

"Hi, Dad," the little tree said. "You want to hear a limerick? Or maybe go see a dinosaur?"

SHADOW OF A CHANGE

by Michelle M. Sagara

Michelle Sagara has sold four fantasy novels, and was a 1992 Campbell Award nominee.

She didn't know when it started.

One morning, she had simply been April Stephens, part of the typing pool at a large, sedate computer firm. She caught the same bus every morning at 7:30, arrived at work every morning at 8:15 (give or take a few minutes for traffic), and made her way to her desk, coffee in hand, at exactly 8:30. She wore neutral colors, neutral styles, and a very conservative bob; she wore sensible shoes, ate healthy food, and lived a very quiet life.

Sometimes, on the bus on the way home, when traffic stalled in the misnamed rush hour, she would gaze out the window and try to remember if this was what she had wanted out of life. Eavesdropping on the fluttering conversations that changed daily, she would catch a spark of something bright and shiny and new in the hushed whispers or excited chattering, that made her yearn, for a moment, for someone else's youth.

Home was a simple affair; she lived in the two story, two bedroom home that she had inherited when her mother had passed away. Her father, long gone from even memory, had not survived her second year, but his picture hung over the mantle of the fake fireplace. She dusted that mantle, oiling its dark, rich wood, with a particular care to detail; it was one of the few things in the house that she thought beautiful.

Certainly she did not consider herself so.

She had one or two friends, made in grade school, whom she had anchored a part of herself to, and she kept in contact with them by the use of the phone and a judicious letter here and there, although they all lived in the same city. She rarely went out, and rarely invited anyone in; it was stressful, not to know how to behave, what to say, or how to entertain. Easier was simply this: to enter in through the side door of her home, lock it behind her back, drop her bags by the side of the umbrella rack, and sag against the wall. She added tea to her daily routine; she watched television. She did not live an unhappy life.

She should have known something was wrong when she missed the bus on a Monday morning in early spring. The snow had started its second melt of the season, and her rubbers, filthy with mud and crusted with dried salt, made squishy, awful protests as she ran, briefcase tailing her like exhaust, to the bus stop in time to see the great, red rectangle pull away.

In six years of work, she had not once missed the bus. Unsettled, she clutched her briefcase to her chest and held it there, as if it were a shield. The next bus came, and she caught that easily enough; fumbled in her pocket for her bus pass, and then stumbled to a seat.

The drive to work, across the muddied water left by melting snow, was not restful either; she rocked back and forth, against the lurch and halt of the bus's motion, while she tried to remember the dream that had anchored her so thoroughly to sleep that she had slept late, missed breakfast, and then been late for the first event of her morning.

She missed her morning coffee, but made it to her desk in time for an orderly 8:30. But the day had an edge to it that even a large lunch and a whole pot of tea at its end couldn't dull. When she went to bed that evening, she made certain that the alarm was set just a little early; made certain that it was across the room, rather than beside her bed.

But the darkness held her in. When she managed to open her eyes in the morning, the light through the sheers told her that the claxon of the alarm had been going on for at least fifteen minutes. She struggled with blankets, tossed them off, and then tried to stand.

I'm sick, she thought, as the room spun. Her knees hurt, and her elbows; her focus came strangely, as if she were looking through convex glass. Holding the side of the bed, she stood. She had to shut off the alarm clock before the bells shattered the insides of her skull.

She made it, although her fingers felt thick and wide and she had to struggle—every movement came at some effort, as if movement itself were foreign—to hit the small switch that would stall the bells.

They stopped, and the silence that descended, rich with sunbeams and the blue of a clear, morning sky, felt hollow. She barely noticed the time. Breakfast. Food. She stumbled out the door and down the stairs, clinging to the banister.

That morning, she was also late for work.

April half-walked, half-crawled, through the side door of her house at the end of the day. She dropped her bag in the wrong spot, left her coat on, and plunked herself down on the couch. She wanted to sleep, but the light in the room was too bright; with an exhausted snarl, she stood up, yanked the blinds closed, shut off the lights, and then returned to the couch.

There, in the silence and the blessed shadow, she listened to the heavy rasp of her breath. Wondering what she was sick with. Wondering where she had got it, and how long it would take to go away.

That night, when she finally managed to leave the couch and the living room, she dreamed of shadows and darkness and hunger.

"April, are you all right?" Susan Lundstrom, the oldest member of the typing pool and therefore the one with the unspoken seniority, made a place for herself at the cafeteria table, settling down with her tray, her purse, and the ashtray that she'd moved from the smoking section.

April nodded, distracted.

"Well, if you don't mind my saying so, you look a little green. Are you sure you're okay?" When April failed to hear her, Susan leaned forward, casting a shadow over the wood veneer surface.

"I'm fine," April said. She straightened out her shoulders and picked up her sandwich. "I just didn't sleep well last night."

"Have it your way," was the cheerful reply. But the voice lost some of its lightness. "April? April?"

April Stephens was staring at the two slices of white bread and the tomato, cheese, and lettuce between them as if they were asphalt. She tried to bite it all, even tried to chew it, and at last stood up, muttering her apologies around a mouthful of food that she could not swallow.

She found the washroom, trying to tuck the food beneath her tongue so that no one would notice, and quickly swung into a cubicle. There, she got rid of it. And the soup that had preceded it.

Shuddering, her stomach rolling beneath her flesh, she wiped her mouth with the back of her hand, stood, and made her way to the sink. The mirror, with someone's fingerprints at the lower edge, showed her the tired and strained face of a very upset woman. She breathed deeply, breathed again, and then straightened out her glasses.

Come on, April. It's not like you've never been sick before.

But it was like she'd never been sick.

Coming home by bus, with a stop at the supermarket, became a fog of dizziness, hunger, and nausea. She wasn't certain when she got off the bus; wasn't certain when she entered the supermarket; couldn't remember what she'd bought there. All she remembered was the *now* of the moment; the past and the future faded around her as if the present were the only island on which she could stand.

The only time she panicked was when she couldn't remember having paid, but a quick count of her money assured her that she'd certainly spent some of it.

Dinner was quickly prepared; she turned on the television, settled uncomfortably back against the couch, propped her legs up on the coffee table and started to eat. She tried to keep track of what was on the television—she thought it was the news—but the picture kept rotating like a warped record. Annoyed, she played with the remote, but it brought no relief— only a surge of new colors, different distortions.

Snarling, she turned her full attention to her food.

Which she didn't remember cooking, because she hadn't. She stopped chewing as she realized that her mouth was full of something cold and wet; looked down to see that her fingers had all but disappeared into what was left of a slab of beef. Blood and warming fat greased her nails as she dropped the meat. She ran to the sink, bent over it, and spit out everything that she hadn't already swallowed.

Then, choking, she slid down the side of the cupboard in front of the sink, curled her knees up under her chin, and began to cry.

She didn't notice that as she did, she was licking her fingers clean.

She knew her work wasn't up to standard in the following week. Susan knew it. Alexis knew it. Kelly knew it. None of them said a word, although Susan continued to ask after her health. Susan even did her best to see that the workload was less evenly distributed than usual; if April hadn't felt too ashamed, she would have been grateful.

But she did have to do typing work, and the work that she did get assigned was expected to have a certain quality to it. Until now, April had always been certain that everything that left her desk with her initials on it was as perfect as anyone could make it. That was gone. Her fingers felt sluggish and heavy; the keypad of the word processor was suddenly tiny and incomprehensible. She had to *look* at the keys; her fingers had forgotten years of instinctive movement.

Stephen Hawthorne was the first person to bring back a complaint. He didn't, of course, carry it directly to her; he had to go to the head of the typing pool to let his displeasure be known. But April heard him shouting in his high, nasal voice. She hated it; had she not been afraid of drawing more attention to herself, she'd have plugged her ears.

He came back three times that day, and at the end of the day, Susan was exhausted enough to call April to the front of the room, where Stephen Hawthorne stood, angrily tapping the floor with his perfect black shoes.

"Ms. Stephens?" He asked, in that clipped, nasal voice.

"Yes?" She kept her own as steady and as low as possible.

"What is your excuse for *this*? I need this report for a *client;* this is not a normal interoffice scribble. Look at *this*—did you even run it through a spellchecker?"

She nodded obsequiously, hoping that it would be enough to send him away. But he kept on and on and on until at last she grabbed the report and curled it in trembling hands. She couldn't—wouldn't—listen to another word.

"I'll fix the goddamned report and have it on your desk in the morning. Is there anything else or do you expect me to sit here and listen to you whine for the rest of the day?"

She had the satisfaction of watching all of the blood rush to his face before she turned and marched smartly back to her desk. She half-expected him to follow her, but he didn't. Which was a pity.

At the end of the day, only this memory stayed with her; all others vanished into the haze of her encroaching disease. Perhaps tomorrow she would do the unthinkable. Perhaps tomorrow she would miss her first day of work.

*   *   *

When she got home, she walked into the kitchen, turned the oven on, pulled her dinner out of the little Safeway bag, and walked into the living room. The windows remained shuttered against the end of the day; the television remained dull, faceless glass. She didn't want the noise, or the mix of noises. She felt nauseated, but beneath the nausea was hunger. She ate.

This time she paid careful attention to what she was eating, fascinated by it, detached from its reality. The meat in her mouth was cold and grisly; it tasted slightly rank, too old. But it was food; real food; she could chew it slowly and then swallow it. It was almost good. Only when she had finished eating did she remember to turn off the oven.

In bed, the lights dimmed, the clock set, she cried; the tears silent and bewildered, with no force and no anger behind them.

In the morning she saw the first clear sign, the whisper of a real change. Her skin was darker, harder. She thought at first that her fingertips themselves were somehow callused; nothing felt right to the touch—not the bedsheets, not her clothing, not the meat that she ate in the morning.

She looked at herself, carefully, in the mirror. Her face was the same shape, but it, too, was darker. She opened her mouth and her teeth were sharp.

The doctor. She had to call the doctor.

She ran back to her bedroom, leafed through the phone book, found the number and then picked up the phone. Jabbing awkwardly at the impossibly small buttons, she managed to hit the right sequence of numbers—on the ninth try.

"Doctor Kennedy's office, may I help you?"

"I'd like to make an appointment to see Dr. Kennedy," April said, her voice throaty and deep with the early morning. "It's an—an emergency." She wasn't used to making this much of a fuss, and her voice broke on the last word.

The sound of flapping pages could be heard before

the receptionist's voice returned to the receiver. "There's an appointment for tomorrow at 11:30, if you're available then."

Tomorrow. April Stephens shook her head.

"Hello?"

"I'll—it's not important."

She lied, of course. It was important; she knew it. So important, in fact, that she phoned Susan to carefully explain that she would be coming in later in the day. She dressed carelessly and grabbed a purse—not her briefcase—before she flew out of the house in search of a bus.

The bus, hot and crowded, was oppressive. She was aware of every stranger's gaze, and wondered if they were looking at her because she looked like a circus freak. She covered her teeth more prominently with her lips, pressing them into a tight, whitened line. She also pulled up the collar of her long jacket, and tried skulking beneath its line. It wasn't comfortable.

Transferring helped somewhat; the air, cool and crisp, refreshed her. For a moment she felt almost human. Then the second bus came, and once again she was crushed into a tiny, rectangular space with far too many people and far too little air. She wanted to scream, bit her lip instead, and instantly regretted it.

But the hospital, thankfully, loomed up ahead with its twin smokestacks. She could leave this bus, and these people, and find solace in the emergency room there. They could tell her what was happening. They could help.

Before she crossed the street, she was hit by a wave of nausea. Her knees bent; her arms stiffened and drew up. Everything twisted, converging and separating in a mindless, dizzying pattern.

She managed to remember where she was; where she had to go. Forcing herself to her feet, she crossed the street. She couldn't understand why the cars screeched out in wide circles around her; couldn't understand why they were honking so loudly. Someone rolled down a window and waved a fist in the air; his words were lost to her comprehension, but his meaning was perfectly clear.

April Stephens opened her mouth and *roared*.

The roar lengthened into a terrified scream. With halting, awkward steps, she loped up the long stretch of road toward the emergency ward of the hospital.

It shouldn't have been crowded at this time in the morning; she was certain it shouldn't be so crowded. But she hadn't been to a hospital since she was eight years old and skateboards were a necessity of life, and she didn't remember clearly.

"Miss? May I help you?"

It took a minute to realize that the person sitting behind the desk was talking to her, and another minute to realize that he expected her to come to him. She walked across the floor, once again too aware of the eyes of the people in the waiting room. Her hesitance grew as she awkwardly took the chair in front of the young man and his computer terminal.

He asked her questions. Had she been here before. Did she have her Health Card with her. Did she know her family doctor. She answered them curtly, impatiently. Finally, after filling out line by line of trivial information he actually *looked* at her.

"What exactly is the nature of your problem?"

She blinked, confused.

"What's wrong?"

"I'm—I'm changing," she replied.

The young man raised a pale brow. "Changing, ma'am?"

"My skin is harder and my teeth are funny and I can't eat properly."

If he noticed that her voice was going up an octave, his expression didn't give him away. He carefully and neatly input all of her information and then watched the computer screen for a minute. "That'll be all, Ms. Stephens. If you'd care to take a seat, a doctor will be with you as soon as possible."

"When? When is that?"

"Just as soon as possible," came the firm reply. It did not allow for any other question.

The chair that she chose was as far away from anyone else as she could possibly make it. She wanted to curl her legs up beneath her chin, but they felt awkward and heavy, and she wasn't sure they would fit on the small edge of the chair. There were magazines, all at least a month old, in messy piles on a small table beside her. She picked one up. Politics.

But politics was better than change. She forced herself to read article after article while she tried to remember who all the names and faces in the little pictures belonged to.

At last, they called her name. They had to call it three times, as if her conscious mind, slumbering in an uneasy state, refused to recognize it as her own. She rose stiffly, kept her lips firmly shut, and followed the young man in the green nightshirt. He pushed his way out of the waiting room, through a thick, wide door which creaked as it swung on its hinges. He was obviously used to patients who walked slowly, for his step was measured, and he glanced over his shoulder often.

She followed him, glancing from side to side in bewilderment. Within this new set of rooms and curtained vestibules was another set of chairs, another wait. Still, the chemical, medicinal smell of the inner room reassured her; she was close to help now, she was certain of it. She sat.

Five minutes passed, at least it felt like five minutes; she was certain that that's what the round clock on the wall said. Big hand, little hand, hand that moved quickly. Her head hurt; her stomach rumbled and twisted painfully. She doubled over, clutching her sides. Crying, or trying not to cry. After a while, there was no difference.

Someone was ushered into the room with great care. They put him beside her. She knew this because there was something about his *smell* that was familiar, almost tantalizing. Out of the corner of her eye, she glanced in his direction, hoping that he wouldn't notice, half-embarrassed.

She forgot it, though. His arm, bandaged somehow, was a deep, bright red. His face was white, but his forehead was cut, and a little rivulet of blood ran, like a tiny brook, between the crevices of his wrinkled forehead.

"I'm all right, miss," the man said, as he drew back from her probing fingers. "Just had a little disagreement, s'all."

April nodded, hypnotized. She looked at her fingers, at the blood on their tips, and then raised them slowly to her mouth. She didn't notice when the patient blanched and moved four seats away.

"Well, then, what seems to be the problem, Ms. Stephens?"

She opened her mouth suddenly, pulling her lips over her pronounced teeth.

"Throat problem, is it?" He reached for a wooden stick. "Let me see it, then." He reached for her chin, and then frowned as she pulled away. "Feels like you've got yourself a case of eczema there, ma'am." He paused, ran his hands over his eyes, and then blinked. It had been a long shift, and he was almost, thank God, off. Interning was a rite of passage so stressful it was impossible to imagine it from the relative safety of medical school.

She watched him with her wide, unblinking eyes. He could see the fear in them, but their intensity made him uncomfortable. "I'm changing, Doctor," she whispered, and her voice was a rasp. "I don't know what's wrong."

He could tell, from the thick puffiness of her lids, that she'd probably been crying. Now, now, he thought, glancing furtively at his watch. Two cardiac arrests, two very serious knife wounds and a host of stitches on three hours of sleep left him very little room for sympathy, very little strength to comfort.

"It's nothing," he said brusquely. "You're probably under some sort of stress, and you're obviously eating or wearing something you're allergic to. Here, I'll give you a shot of Atarax, and I'll give you a prescription for the skin itself." She started to speak, and he held up his hand to ward the words. "Don't worry about it, Ms. Stephens. Happens all the time." Standing, and trying very hard not to yawn or show his fatigue, the young intern went in search of the section nurse.

April Stephens sat alone in the curtained vestibule, with the little lights flashing in her eyes. All of the words she wanted to say backed up in her throat; she choked on them, shaking. She wanted to believe the doctor—doctors knew what they were doing, didn't they?—she did her best. She took deep breaths.

She was almost relieved to see the nurse, who proved to be a matronly woman, not a young, almost teenaged-faced girl. "You're Ms. April Stephens?" The nurse asked, as she set aside a clipboard. "Good. Here, then. You might want to bend over—this is a muscle shot, and it'll hurt your arm like hell."

April shook her head mutely, but offered her left arm instead of her right one. The nurse shrugged, took the offered arm, and readied the needle.

Just a single shot, April thought, repeating the words like a mantra, a prayer. Just a single shot. It happens to everyone.

She was heartbroken, but not at all surprised, when the needle snapped before it penetrated her skin. The nurse, flustered now, disappeared, but April Stephens didn't wait for her return. There were too many odd smells in this hospital now, and chief among them was the lingering scent of blood beneath her nails.

She didn't go to work; she couldn't. When she got home, the mirror showed her that her skin was indeed of the consistency to break—snap, really—the thin, hard spine of a doctor's needle. Her head hurt, her stomach ached, and the taste of a wounded man's blood lingered in her mouth. She stumbled to the kitchen, yanked the fridge door open, and watched it fall off its hinges with a crash.

Her hands were clumsy as they pulled the packages

out of the fridge. Molding lettuce and cucumbers that had almost liquified she tossed to the side and forgot; she didn't even spare them more than an instinctive shudder of disgust. She ate what she could, but it wasn't enough; she knew it.

She knew what she wanted. She bit her tongue, and her tongue bled; she growled and whimpered.

This isn't happening. This can't be happening.

But she had never been in control of her life and its changes, and although she felt despair and horror, she felt no surprise.

That night, she woke up in the open drive of her house, the upturned throat of a limp cat between her jaws. She felt good for at least two seconds, and then her mind caught up with her body and she began to choke. She was changed, she knew it; she could see, in the soothing moonlight, the shadow of a thick tail at her back.

She didn't bury the cat; indeed, until she got into the house, she would have sworn that she had thrown it aside in either fear or disgust. But she hadn't; its warm, sticky body remained with her, as if it were steel and she, a strong magnet. In the dim light of the inner house, she recognized the slack face of the cat—it was Duffy, from two houses down. A young cat.

She had killed it. She was eating it. She couldn't make herself stop.

No. No, she wasn't this. She wasn't doing this, it wasn't real. Bones snapped against the second row of her sharp teeth.

With a cry that was feral, worse than feral, she threw the cat away and ran down, down into the darkness. The steps were hard to take, too close together and too tiny for her feet. Gravity started what determination had finished; she felt the ground shake as she hit it with her full weight. Standing, she could just make out the large, round metal dome of her ancient furnace. Wooden joists scraped against her head; she heard the unpleasant, hard sound of something meeting wood.

She thought she must be crying, and opened her lips to moan; instead, she growled, a sound so low and so gravelly it reminded her of a car tearing down an unpaved drive. Silence descended as she clamped her jaw shut. Her teeth clicked sharply.

She would stay in the darkness, in the cool damp shadows. Wait here, without light to show her the changes, without a mirror to reflect how out of control she had become. There were no living things, there were no other people; if she could be still and sleep, everything would pass into dream.

Her lids grew heavy. Her forehead fell forward slightly, although she had no desire to do anything but stand as sleep began to wash over her.

This was fine. This was what she wanted. Just sleep. Escape. A place where the changing didn't matter.

"Hello?"

In the darkness, the word was hard and sharp and clear. It was followed by light, something that, like the word, was almost crystalline in its clarity.

"Hello? I'm here to read the gas meter. Door was open, and I thought I'd come in. Hello?"

Sound and light were followed by scent, the moving of shadow, the presence of warmth.

"Hello?" The light stopped bouncing, and suddenly became a spear, a straight beam shearing into the unwary eye.

She *roared* in anger, and the sound of her voice killed the little words completely. Joists creaked as she stood; she lifted her head and felt them snap against the column of her spine. Her tail hit poured cement, her claws left a trail in the ground. In the darkness, she could not see herself, could barely see the thing that made noise and light.

And she knew what she wanted. Her nostrils were full of the scent of fear and life. The fear was no longer hers. She had slept, she knew, and in waking, the dream of ages was pulled from her mind, the sight of smallness lifted from her vision. This was what she was, what she had been, what she would be.

Hungry, she took one step, and then another. The little creature turned to flee, moving quickly, breathing loudly. She liked it, this sudden spurt of movement. It felt natural to follow it; felt natural to take it out of the world with a crunch of jaws and a swing of the head.

In the darkness, April Stephens fed, tearing flesh off bone with a tongue that would grate against metal. Then, not quite satisfied, she reared up again, pushing past thick layers of plaster and old wood. She had had enough of the darkness; now it was time for the jungle, the light, and the hunt to follow.

April Stephens had never been in control of her life or the things that changed it and shaped it. But she had never been so free as this: She neither knew that she had no control, nor cared. She strode out, primitive, great, old—a thing of memory, a dream of children, a walking death.

Her roar filled a slumbering suburbia with its life and its breath. Soon, all of the dreamers would wake to her call, and she would hunt again.

WISE ONE'S TALE

by Josepha Sherman

Josepha Sherman is a fantasy and science fiction novelist who is also an editor for one of the major sf publishers.

Wise One crinkled up her eyes in a smile, folding her leathery wings more neatly against her lean body. Let the adults scorn her stories, she who was the oldest of the Winged Hunters. The young ones, the winglings, still came. She watched as they struggled up to her cliff, dragging a small Sweet-Meat Prey among them. They hadn't even taken a taste of their kill, tempting though that might have been!

The winglings settled down on the ledge, crouching politely just out of beak-reach. They warily pushed the Sweet-Meat Prey toward her with their own small beaks. Wise One waited just the proper length of time to make them respect her strength of will, then devoured the kill, wing-claws holding it in place, toothed beak easily tearing aside the tough hide. When she had eaten her fill, Wise One drew back, inviting the winglings, mind-to-mind, *"Join me."* When all were finished, and one of the winglings had neatly tossed the remains over the cliff, Wise One added, *"Why have you come?"*

The winglings wriggled. *"A story,"* they pleaded. *"Give us a story."*

So! The young *were* still interested in the past. *"What story do you wish?"*

The smallest of the winglings, too young to have a use-name yet, snapped his sharp-toothed little beak with excitement. *"Tell us about us!"* he cried. *"Tell us about the Winged Hunters and—and how we got our wings."*

"Stupid eggling," one of the females taunted. *"We have always had wings!"*

"Have not!"

"Have too!"

"Stop that!" Wise One snapped. *"The smallest is right. Once, long ago, we did not fly, but crawled upon the ground."* She glanced about, seeing horror in the young, fierce eyes. *"We crawled,"* Wise One continued, *"eating only the smallest, feeblest of prey, in danger from the whole world of fanged and taloned ones. So it would have remained, so we would have been prey instead of hunters, had it not been for one known as Quick Trickster."*

"Quick Trickster?" a wingling wondered. *"But that isn't an honorable name!"*

"Listen to his tale," Wise One said sharply. *"Then tell me if he is not worth our remembering."* She paused to be sure she had each wingling's full attention, then clacked her beak in approval. *"The tale begins . . ."*

Quick Trickster (said Wise One) was hardly the largest or the greatest of his kin. No, he was so small and weak the merest Plant-Eater could have crushed him with a swipe of its tail. But Quick Trickster's mind was a swift hunter, always finding new, clever ideas, so clever he could trick a Sharp-Fanged Tyrant out of its prey. Maybe some of the kin claimed trickery wasn't an honorable thing, but Quick Trickster didn't care.

"It's this crawling on the ground that's no proper way to live!" he insisted. "Not for me, not for my kin."

But what could be done about it? Quick Trickster glanced up at the free, open sky. How wonderful to be up there above the mud, soaring, streaking down on prey like the fire that comes from the storm!

A daring idea came to him. Off Quick Trickster went into the Fiery Mountains. Up and up he climbed, over rock so hot it scorched his claws, through ashy clouds that made him cough. But he never flinched, for he was hunting Fire Being, god of gods. He dared hunt her, sly little Quick Trickster, he alone of all the kin.

At last he reached the peak of Fire Being's mountain. Panting, his talons torn and broken, his leathery hide scratched and scorched, Quick Trickster looked around at all the rugged rock, feeling fire rumbling far below his claws. He was afraid, all alone up there with the emptiness. But he called out bravely enough:

"Fire Being! I have come to speak with you!"

Fire Being rose out of the rock, tall and hot and terrible, glowing so brightly with her inner heat, the heat of the molten rock, Quick Trickster could hardly bear to look at her. "Who has come?" she asked, her voice the crackling of flame. Quick Trickster answered as cheerfully as he could:

"Why, it is I, Quick Trickster!"

Fire Being's hot eyes stared at him. "I see only a small crawling thing. What do you want of me, small crawler?"

"Only a tiny, tiny thing, Fire Being. Something that would take the barest claw-swipe of your power."

"What do you want?"

"Wings. Wings for me and all my kin. Please, Fire Being," Quick Trickster pleaded, "are we not your children? Yes! Should we be left to crawl like prey when we have the teeth and claws of hunters? No!"

"Do you dare tell *me* what is right and wrong?" Fire Being thundered. "Go, crawler! Prove to me you are a hero, and perhaps I shall not burn you to ash."

"What would you have me do?" Quick Trickster asked, though his heart was pounding like a frightened little Plant-Runner's.

"Bring me the claw of a Giant Wader, the spike of an Armored Browser, and the claw of a Sharp-Fanged Tyrant. Then perhaps I shall grant your wish. Now, *go!*"

Quick Trickster hurried to the shore of a great lake and looked things over. All at once he clacked his beak together as an idea came to his cunning mind. Giant Waders, as everyone knows, are swift swimmers, but they are big and slow of thought. There in the lake browsed a herd of Giant Waders.

"Hey!" Quick Trickster called to one of them. "Fat, stupid prey!"

The Giant Wader only blinked.

"Fat, stupid prey, I say! No, no, you are too stupid even for prey! You are too stupid even to mate with females!"

The Giant Wader rumbled, deep in his long, long neck.

"Stupid, useless thing, I say!" Quick Trickster taunted. "Your females won't let you near them! You mate with *logs*, stupid thing, with ugly, rotten *logs!*"

This was too much even for a Giant Wader to bear. He charged. In the water, he was faster than any, but Quick Trickster stood on land, at the edge of mud. The Giant Wader surged ashore—too angry for his slow brain to realize the danger—and fell deeply into the mud. Quick Trickster, too small and light to sink in that mud, raced forward and neatly clipped off one of Giant Wader's claws with his teeth. Hastily he stuck the claw into his own neck skin to hold it safe, then raced off before the Giant Wader could pull free. Now for the Armored Browser!

Quick Trickster found one grazing near a thicket of thick-leaved trees, idly swinging its heavy, spike-ended tail as it ate. "Look out!" Quick Trickster yelled. "Sharp-Fanged Tyrant, there, behind you!"

The startled Armored Browser lashed out with its tail—and snared it in the thicket. Quick Trickster hastily snipped off the end of one of its spikes with his teeth, then darted away before the Armored Browser could pull free. Sticking the spike next to the claw, Quick Trickster said, "I'd better hunt up a Sharp-Fanged Tyrant in a hurry, before my neck gets too sore!"

But even though Sharp-Fanged Tyrants aren't very clever—not half as clever as Quick Trickster—they are still deadly hunters. Quick Trickster looked up as the mighty Tyrant towered over him on its powerful hind legs, and trembled so hard he was afraid the claw and spike would pop from his hide.

But he shouted boldly, "Hey, old Fangs, slow Fangs, can't catch me!"

The Sharp-Fanged Tyrant heard this taunt, caught the scent of Quick Trickster, and came lumbering forward, gathering speed as it came: too much speed! To his horror, Quick Trickster realized he was in danger of getting eaten! He dodged and darted this way and that—and suddenly ran out of land altogether. Desperately, Quick Trickster scrabbled for a grip. His claws caught in cracks in the cliff and held. But the Sharp-Fanged Tyrant, racing too swiftly to stop, came plunging past and knocked Quick Trickster right off! Together they plunged into the valley below. The Sharp-Fanged Tyrant smashed on the rocks. But Quick Trickster landed on top of the creature, and so, bruised and breathless, he lived. Gasping, he snipped off one of the Sharp-Fanged Tyrant's terrible claws, then started wearily back up Fire Being's mountain.

She was waiting at the peak, her hot eyes blazing. "You have failed!" she roared.

"No!" Quick Trickster gasped. Hastily, he pulled the two claws and one spike from his neck skin, trying not to wince. "You told me to bring you the claws of Giant Wader and Sharp-Fanged Tyrant and the spike of Armored Browser, and here they are."

"I told you to prove yourself a hero," Fire Being said. "But have you done that? No! You have won the prizes by trickery, not heroism."

Quick Trickster trembled beneath her rage, so hot it burned at his skin and choked his lungs. But he insisted, "Your pardon, but to me that *is* heroism! I am not big and strong like some Sharp-Fanged Tyrant. Had I tried to act like one, I would have died!"

"Do you dare argue with me?" the god roared.

Quick Trickster shrank back. But he continued as bravely as he could, "Well, maybe you think I've failed you, and maybe I have, in your eyes at least. But don't make my kin suffer because of me. Let them, at least, have wings."

"What would you do for them?" Fire Being asked. "Would you die?"

Quick Trickster gasped. "I didn't mean—"

"You defiant little crawler, come here. Look!"

Far below them boiled a red sea of rock such as is sometimes spewed forth from the mountains. "I s–see it," Quick Trickster said.

"End your shame!" Fire Being roared. "For the sake of your kin, *jump!*"

Poor Quick Trickster! For once his clever mind could find no way out. "So be it," he said. "Only let my kin have wings."

And with that, he jumped. But he didn't fall! All at once Quick Trickster felt the skin between forelimbs and body stretch and change. All at once he found himself soaring up on brand-new wings!

"You have won those wings for yourself and your kin," Fire Being said. "I agree: There is more than one type of heroism. Now, begone!"

And her terrible, hot eyes glowed with approval.

Wise One stretched stiffly. The last of the winglings were gone, chattering together over what she had told them. But then the old Winged Hunter froze as Strong Leader, fierce ruler of the kin, came out of hiding.

"You were listening?" Wise One asked. *"Why?"*

"I was curious. You don't really believe that old tale of Quick Trickster, do you?"

Wise One stirred restlessly. *"Who can say what happened so long ago? But the winglings believe, and that is enough."*

"Why fill their heads with such foolishness?"

"Agh, Strong Leader, don't you see? This tale, all the old tales, are the property of our kin. Whether or not they are true, whether or not you think them important today, they are ours. They make us what we are."

"Nonsense." For a moment, Strong Leader's sharp teeth glinted in his open beak. Wise One looked at that hint of menace and sighed.

"Would you kill me? I am the only one who knows all our stories. Would you have them be lost?"

"*I—No.*"

"*A kin must have its stories, Strong Leader. Ha, you know that as well as I, for you fold your wings and settle back down. You know that once our stories are forgotten, our past is lost. And without a past, there can be no future.*" Wise One crinkled her eyes in a wry smile. "*Why, without our stories, the ones after us would think us nothing more than—than so many mindless beasts!*"

CURREN'S SONG

by Laura Resnick

Laura Resnick has sold more than a dozen romance novels and some fifteen science fiction stories, and was a nominee for the 1992 Campbell Award.

In the sixth century A.D., Saint Columba left Ireland and ventured into Scotland where he preached to the Picts, whose warriors were covered with blue tattoos or body dye. According to the saint's biographer, he saved a swimmer from the Loch Ness Monster by ordering it away. This so impressed Brude, the local king, that he and his people converted to Christianity.

One theory about the Loch Ness Monster is that a small herd of plesiosaurs have survived in that isolated environment—like the coelacanth, some thirty of which have been caught in the South Atlantic despite prior belief that they had been extinct for seventy million years.

The sky was gray, a wet, mourning color that did not change from dawn till dusk. A misty rain fell softly upon the steep green hills, its rhythm soothing and hypnotic. The steady, gentle sound comforted Curren's wounded spirit as he crept beneath the sheltering branches of a clump of fir trees overlooking the loch, the great inland sea which split the land like a deep wound.

Curren sat on the damp ground and hugged his knees, gritting his teeth and refusing to cry as he stared at the black surface of the water. He was too old for tears, he told himself.

Why had the gods cursed him with their visions? What sort of life was this for a boy about to become a man? To be forever an outsider, forever different, forever apart from his own people. Laughed at by some, shunned by others, ridiculed or feared since his birth, each day of his life brought a fresh, piercing pain.

This morning he had done it again, had spoken when he should have kept silent. He could never separate the things everyone knew and saw from the things that he alone knew and saw, and so he was forever alienating everyone around him.

He had, of course, known it would rain today. He had seen the soft, watery sky in his mind, had heard the gentle drumming of the rain many hours before its arrival. Old Daron had also known it would rain today, and he had told everyone. No one seemed to find it strange that the gruff, gnarled old man knew when the weather would turn. Yet everyone had looked at Curren with contempt when he had once told them the moon would hide the sun in the middle of the day; and when it had happened, only his position as the king's nephew had kept the people from burning him alive as a demon.

Curren didn't understand why Daron knew about the coming of the rain but not the changing of the sky, or why Daron's knowledge was accepted and his own was not. He didn't understand why no one minded when a flat-bellied woman suddenly knew she carried a baby inside her, while he himself was loathed for knowing the color of the glowing mist which surrounded each person. Why was it normal for a woman to know in the summer that she would bear a child at winter's end, while it was considered evil for him to know whether the child would live or die?

So this morning, out of respect, hoping to please, Curren had told Brude, the king himself, to prepare for the visitor who was coming from across the water. How was he to know that no one else knew about the big, dark man whose long journey brought him at last to their village by midday? Why did old Daron see the coming of the rain but not the coming of the man? Why was Daron's vision good and Curren's bad?

But Curren had not run from the village and come to hide under the trees because of the way the king glared at him, the way the women shied away from him, or the way the other boys whispered about him. No, today he had run away because of the way the stranger had pointed at him, cried out to the crowd that he must be cleansed, and ordered him to accept a new god.

Columba was the stranger's name, and Curren hated him already. In shame and anger, he had run from the village and come here, to the only place in which he was never lonely. For it was here that he heard the silent songs from beneath the water, here that he had friends.

"Curren?"

He flinched, turning suddenly at the sound of the wholly human whisper. It was an intrusion upon the welcome which rose out of the murky loch and curled around him.

"Curren? Are you here? Please answer."

"Aithne," he said, surprised. He hadn't known she would come. Would someone else have known? Was he as strange in what he *didn't* know as he was in what he *did* know? "I'm here."

She came toward him through the descending mist, her red-brown hair gleaming with droplets of water, her cheeks shiny with rain, her dark lashes sticking wetly together. She was his age, and almost a woman. She was, he noticed suddenly, ripening quickly. She smiled when their eyes met, then sat down beside him. "I've looked everywhere for you."

"Why?"

"So you wouldn't be alone."

"I'm not alone here."

Aithne's head turned sharply, looking around. "Oh? Who else is here?"

"They are."

She blinked at him. "They who?"

"*They* are. Don't you hear them?"

She shook her head, studying him warily. He flushed and cursed himself silently as he realized he had done it again. She couldn't hear the silent songs, the ancient stories, the aching welcome of the lonely voices in the loch. She couldn't hear, and she would be disgusted because he could. How could he have known? He knew she heard water kelpies in the dark, even though he didn't, for she had told him so when they were much younger. But now she couldn't hear the watery sighs which rolled around them.

He looked away, afraid and ashamed. If only he could learn which visions were allowed and which weren't, then he could pretend to be like everyone else and hide the visions which made them all hate him.

"I don't hear anyone," she said.

"It doesn't matter," he said gruffly.

She was silent for a long moment before asking hesitantly, "Why did you run away?"

He shrugged, not looking at her.

"I wish you had stayed," she said, her voice as soft and soothing as the rain. "You were right. I wanted them to admit that you were right. Again."

Curren glanced at her bashfully. Encouraged, Aithne continued, "A stranger came from across the sea, just as you said. They should see that you're blessed, not cursed."

"I don't feel blessed," he answered bitterly.

"That's because of the way they treat you. But I think you're blessed. I think your mother was seduced by one of the gods, and he gave you some of his powers. How else could you see colors around my skin that no one else can see? How else could you know about things before they happen, and hear what no one else hears?"

He felt like crying again, and it confused him. "Aren't you . . . afraid of me?" he asked thickly.

"No." The touch of her hand on his was cool, yet it made him burn deep inside. "No, I'm not afraid."

He looked into her eyes. Green, they were, green like the rain-drenched hills, like sprouting leaves, like moss on a rock. "I'm glad," he said at last.

Her fingers tightened over his. After a while, she said, "Tell me what you hear."

"It's not important."

"Yes, it is," she insisted. "I want to know things. Things that no one else knows, that only you and I will know."

He shyly laced his fingers with hers. "There are living things in the loch," he began.

"Salmon, eels—"

"More than that," he interrupted. "This is like . . . a clan."

Aithne frowned at the opaque water far below them. "No clan could live in the water."

"These aren't people."

"Then what are they?"

"I'm not sure. They're . . . like monsters, I suppose."

Her eyes widened. "Monsters?" Her voice quavered slightly.

"They look like, oh, like things you see sometimes in paintings left by the Old Ones. They're big, bigger than anything you've ever seen, with long necks, flat heads, and bodies like giant serpents. They have long tails, wide backs with humps, and thick gray skin with deep lines and furrows. They have no arms or legs, just big fins." Aithne looked so horrified he stopped speaking.

"You've *seen* them?"

"Only in my mind."

She glanced fearfully at the loch. "I thought . . . I thought it was just a story they told children to keep them away from the water. So they wouldn't drown."

"No. They're real."

"And they eat virgins," she breathed in terror.

"No. Just fish."

"How can you be sure?" she asked doubtfully.

"They talk to me."

"Why?"

"*Why?*"

"Yes. Why do monsters in the loch talk to you?"

He had never even wondered about it before. He shrugged at last and said, "Perhaps because I can hear them."

Curren stayed away from the village as much as he could now that Columba was living there. The priest harassed, pursued, even frightened him. Columba claimed Curren's visions were evil and must be expelled from his soul. This could only be done, the big man said, if Curren accepted the new faith, the new god.

"The story makes no sense," Curren told Aithne when she joined him beneath the clump of fir trees where they often met now. "His god was killed by Romans. Our grandfathers' grandfathers drove the Romans away, but Columba worships a god who let the Romans kill him. Some god." It felt good to sneer at someone else for a change.

"It's a strange story," Aithne admitted. "But he says many across the sea believe it. He says there is even a village on Iona where they make more priests."

"Like him?"

She nodded. "You didn't know?"

He shook his head. "No. But I believe it. I can see Columba's god chasing away the gods who live here now."

"But you said he's a weak god. He let the Romans—"

"It doesn't matter what *I* think of Columba's god. Others will turn to him. Many others." He looked down at the blue tattoos on his body. More would be added soon, when he was old enough for battle. "Columba wants us to stop painting ourselves. He says it goes against his god's wishes."

"Brude will never agree to that," Aithne said with certainty. "Our men will always be painted."

"No," Curren said, for he saw it. "Not always. Some day, their skin will be plain."

Aithne was distressed enough by this information to want to change the subject. "Let's not talk about the priest anymore. Tell me instead about the monsters in the loch."

"You believe me?" he asked.

"Of course I do." She looked at the opaque surface of the inland sea. "If anyone could hear them, it's you."

He felt an absurd pleasure where he might have felt shame. If Aithne admired it, then the knowledge must be good, a thing of pride. "There are many of them."

"Ten?"

"More."

"A hundred?"

"Less."

She sighed. "Where do they come from?"

"Once, long ago, they came from the open sea."

"Why did they come here?"

"They came in search of food. It was plentiful, and they stayed and mated here. But the path to the sea filled up over many years. Sand and silt blocked their way until, one day, they became prisoners of the inland sea and could never again leave."

"Was this in the time of the Romans?"

"Before that."

"The time of the Old Ones?"

"Before that."

She frowned. "There was nothing before that."

"Oh, no, Aithne, there was a great deal before that." Curren closed his eyes, swaying as he listened to the songs and turned them into words for her benefit. "There were giants in the earth. Great creatures whose footsteps shook the mountains and made new valleys, whose weight could sink an island, whose reach extended into the sunset. They roamed the earth and the seas. They were the rulers, the kings, the first true conquerors."

"Were they . . . were they beautiful or ugly?"

"Beautiful?" Curren's head tilted back, the images flying behind his closed eyelids. Strange, terrifying, devouring creatures of immense power. "They looked like gods of the underworld," he croaked, the words harder to push out of his throat as the dreams enveloped him.

"Curren!" Aithne gripped his hand, frightened by his manner, his descriptions.

"They weren't evil," he murmured dreamily. "Nor were they good. They knew the hunt, the chase, the kill. They knew the taste of plants and trees and water; they swallowed whole forests, whole rivers in their hunger."

"Where are they now?" she asked. "I mean, what happened to the rest of them?"

The songs which came in answer to Curren's searching mind were sad, so sad. The mournful, watery echo of the memories broke his heart as it wailed over and over in loss, in loneliness, in sorrow and bewilderment.

Where are they? Where are they?

"Dead," he sighed, "all dead. Dead for longer than this hillside has been green. They died so long ago."

"How?" Aithne asked. "How could such great creatures simply die off?"

"Everything changed, changed and turned and became something else." Curren saw the disaster, felt the fear, heard the terrified howling of a billion sunsets past. "The earth shook, the skies grew dark. Wind and water swept the land for endless years, destroying everything."

Aithne looked down at the depthless water which legend said was deeper than the open sea beyond the hills. "But *they* survived."

"Yes." In his heart he was singing with them now, learning their songs, tumbling into the murky water to share their sorrows.

"All the others are gone, except for them?"

"Gone, gone," Curren wept. "All gone, but we remain. For all eternity, we remain, alone in this strange world."

"Curren, stop." She shook his arm, frightened for him.

"We do not belong here," he cried. "This place is so strange. Who are these creatures, these hunters?

What is the burning, orange magic that they bring with them?"

"Curren!"

"Alone. Oh, we are so *alone* here." He wept, his heart broken beyond bearing, recognizing the only loneliness in the world which matched his own. To be so different. To never, ever belong. Forever apart. "Oh, so alone . . ."

"Curren!" Truly terrified now of this power that had taken hold of him, she struck him with all her might. His head snapped sideways, and his eyes flew open. With bewildered eyes and a tear-streaked face, he sat gazing at her, blinking as if awakened from sleep in the middle of the night. Aithne knelt at his side and cradled his face between her hands. "Are you well?"

"I . . . Yes."

He looked so very young and helpless now, so different from the angry, black-haired, fire-eyed boy who stalked around the hills and the glens with the solitary pride of a king. Afraid for him, afraid of what those ancient creatures in the loch might have done to him, she took his hand and pulled him to his feet. With a fearful glance at the water, she said, "This is an evil place. We must go home."

Curren looked away. "All right." She didn't understand, he realized. She believed him, but she could never really know what it was to be like him. But *they* knew.

Aithne found him at the water's edge often after that, sitting a little closer to the flat, murky waves each time, as if gradually approaching the creatures who called to him from below. And each time, it was a little harder to coax him away, to bring him back to the village, where Columba's new god was taking root and starting to change their world, as the world of the great monsters had once been changed so thoroughly.

"Columba has said he would like you to be at the

ceremony this evening," she told Curren one day, trying to pull his gaze away from the water.

"What has he planned for tonight?" Curren asked distractedly, attuned to the beckoning voices in the water.

"Some kind of ritual. It involves water and accepting the new god," Aithne answered vaguely, wishing she could wipe that dreamy look off his face.

"I know why he wants me." Curren's voice was rich with contempt. "If he can silence the voices and blind my visions, he'll be able to make everyone believe that his god is more powerful than any of the old gods, even the demons."

"Curren . . ." She bit her lip, aware that this was dangerous territory. "Don't you *want* the voices to stop?"

His face clouded. But he sounded more weary than angry when he said, "Go away, Aithne."

"No!"

"Go home."

"No! I want to stay with you."

"No, you want to make me like the others. Why don't you just settle for one of them?"

"No, I want you to be only like yourself. But I'm afraid for you, Curren! I have been ever since *they* started calling you to them." She waved toward the water. "You think I don't know how they're tempting you? You wear the look on your face that my father wears before he mates with my mother. You wear the look of a man who wants to marry! But *what* will you marry, Curren?"

"Be quiet!"

"An ancient monster from a dead race of creatures that belonged to a world that disappeared long before the Old Ones built the stone circles?"

"Go away!"

"Curren! This is madness!"

He hit her. She had never thought he would do such a thing. No matter how his eyes glittered when he looked at his brothers or the king, they had always been soft when he looked at her. His hands, his voice, his smile had always been so gentle. But now he struck her with a fury that knocked her to the ground. She put a hand to her bloodied lips and turned away from him, curling herself into a little ball. She had never loved before, would never love again. How could he not see the gifts she offered him? What did he hear that drew him away from her?

She lay there for a long time, unwilling to leave him, unable to look at him. Finally, when the sun had passed over her shoulder and cheek and had begun to die softly against her back, she heard him gasp, a sound of mingled fear and joy. As she rolled to face him, he scrambled to his feet and stood staring out over the water.

"Curren?"

His whole body was rigid with tension, his gaze fixed in the distance, his expression alight with wonder. "They've come for me."

"What?" Terror made her bones liquid as she clumsily struggled to her knees and squinted into the distance to see what held his gaze. *"No!"*

The creature was as big as Curren's description. Its neck alone was as long as two full grown men, and the body which stretched out behind it, though mostly hidden by water, was much larger than any boat or building Aithne had ever seen.

"No! Curren, come away!" she urged, horrified into motion. He resisted her insistent tugging and stood transfixed as the monster peered at them across the water.

Though the creature's head appeared small and flat from this distance, Aithne guessed that it was easily twice her size. The eyes were like slits, and Aithne could see no warmth or welcome in them, despite the excitement which vibrated throughout Curren's body as she tried to drag him away.

"They want me, they want me," he murmured ecstatically. "They *know*."

"No, you mustn't, you mustn't!" she babbled, chilled anew as she realized his intent. "Curren, please!"

"Let me go!"

The creature began to swim slowly toward them, its long tail propelling it with lazy, powerful strokes. The great body undulated with hideous grace, neither fish nor serpent, yet reminiscent of both. Aithne shook violently as tears of helpless fear spilled down her cheeks. She swore to all the gods above and below that she would not let this thing have Curren, and she held her ground. But when the monster looked directly at her, its flat, expressionless eyes revealing nothing, Aithne forgot everything but her blind terror, and she turned and ran.

She never remembered climbing the hill, tearing her garments against the clinging branches, or screaming for help. She remembered nothing between the moment she fled the ancient monster and the moment she found herself in Columba's arms, sobbing with anguish and begging him to save Curren.

"My god is more powerful than this monster in the loch," Columba promised Brude and his men.

"Save him! Stop talking and save him!" Aithne cried.

"And will you come to the one true god, then?" Columba asked. "Will *he*?"

"Yes! I promise! I *promise*. Only save him!"

They rushed forward in a great mass of rattling weapons and war cries, swooping down the hill and toward the water's edge. Columba led them, weaponless, his exultation plain to see, bearing his faith as his only banner.

Where Curren had stood a few minutes ago, now only his clothing remained, an untidy heap from which his footprints led to the water.

"There!" Aithne screamed, seeing him swimming through the water, eagerly approaching the creature who waited silently for him. "There! Stop him!"

The men looked to Brude for an order, their voices gruff with terror, their eyes wide with shock. No one there had ever expected to see the beast of legend with which they threatened their children and grandchildren.

"There is nothing in heaven or earth more powerful than the love of Jesus Christ!" Columba cried, climbing onto a rock and raising his arms toward the sky.

"Help him!" Aithne screamed, certain the beast would devour Curren at any moment.

"God Almighty, I call upon You and Your son!" Columba shouted to the empty skies.

Aithne sank to her knees, hating Columba, hating them all.

With grand, sweeping gestures, Columba pointed directly at the enormous, undulating creature, drawing the gaze of its flat, staring eyes. "Touch not that man! Go no further!"

"Talk will not help," Aithne snarled.

"Quiet!" Brude ordered her.

The monster stared. Its undulation slowed, then ceased. Aithne's next breath burned her lungs.

"Quick! Go back!" Columba cried, his voice booming around the hills and across the water.

"Please . . ." Aithne whispered. "Please," she begged the new god, the god who had died at the hands of the Romans. "Please, I will worship you forever."

The monster seemed to sink deeper into the water.

"Wait!" Curren screamed, his exhausted voice carrying faintly on the wind.

"Touch not that man!" Columba exhorted.

"It's . . . It's going away," Brude said slowly, his tone throbbing with disbelief.

"No! Wait!" Curren cried, his voice raw with anger and despair.

"Go back to the bottom of the darkness from which you came!" Columba cried. "Go!"

They would never agree on who the monster was looking at—Columba or Curren—when it finally sank, silently and completely, back into the opaque depths of the loch. A series of ripples on the surface marked the creature's passing, and then the loch looked normal, as it always had, with no trace of the struggle which had just taken place there or of the ancient secrets which had briefly revealed themselves to this new world.

Only Curren remained, his cries assailing Aithne's ears with their rage and desolation, his arms beating angrily against the water, sending up showers of spray that glistened in the dying sunlight.

It was Columba who swam out to save him, to haul him in against his will, dragging him back to shore after exhaustion had put an end to his violent struggles. Curren lay unconscious and half dead as Columba prayed over him, anointing him in the name of the new god. Aithne saw the expression on Brude's face as he looked down at the boy's motionless form, and she knew that he would have preferred to let his nephew drown that day. But Columba was not about to relinquish his first convert among Brude's people.

The priests who had held sway in Brude's kingdom began to lose their power that day, and it was not long before Brude himself accepted Columba's god and joined in the foreign priest's strange water ritual. Aithne and Curren married when the time was right and their bodies had ripened, and, as she had promised, they, too, joined the new faith.

Now a quiet young man and an obedient warrior, Curren bore the pain of his new tattoos to please Brude, just as he bore the water ritual to please Columba. Most of all, though, he bore his loneliness to please Aithne. How could she know that the pleasures of the flesh she so enjoyed, the pleasures which had left Curren's seed in her belly, were as nothing compared to the remembered pleasure of the silent songs which had reached out from the loch to dance in his head?

The songs were gone now, as were the visions. They had disappeared with his rebirth at Columba's hands, disappeared with the horrifyingly beautiful creature who had slid into the darkness without him, leaving him behind to forever bear this strange new world in utter solitude.

Sometimes, when his king did not need him, when his wife would not miss him, he slipped away for a while, to hide beneath a clump of fir trees and gaze at the flat, opaque waters of the loch.

Somewhere down there, somewhere so deep that no one could find them, they lived and died, they ate and mated, and they waited, waited for another who could hear their song. They had waited millennia for him, and he wondered, with a heart made raw with longing, if they were now doomed to wait for all eternity.

WHILST SLEPT THE SAUROPOD

by Nicholas A. DiChario

*Nicholas A. DiChario is a relatively new writer; this is his
sixth professional sale.*

In the little town of Sleepy Mountain, a town named
for the massive range of hills and rocks and trees beside which it lay, where time was measured in seasons
passed, where farmers tilled their fields with mules
and muscle and sweat and plowshares, where the
townsfolk bought and sold the local wares every seventh sunrise at open markets at the village square . . .
there once came a terrible earthquake.

The people, in their fear, gathered their families in
horse carts and rode to the village square, where the
young maiden who taught at the schoolhouse tolled
the bell twenty times to signal an emergency.

"There is nothing to fear!" she cried. "The earth
is shifting. Our ancestors have written of it in the
ancient records. Let us all stay together, out in the
open, so that if the buildings and trees collapse all will
be safe."

And in answer to their deepest, darkest fears, a
great fissure split the earth, and Sleepy Mountain, the
great mountain that had stood beside them for generations, began to shake and crumble.

Those who held their ground, those who did not
break and run for the false protection of the forest,
were the first to see the mountain shed its skin of dirt
and shale and pine and oak and wildflowers, the first
to see the dinosaur unveiled, its four huge legs as thick
and rigid as marble gods, its long neck rising up and

curling out over the land, its sleepy eyes blinking like two giant suns surprised by the dawn.

For those people frozen in fear in the village square, there was time enough to see all of this before the huge plumes of dust and ash from the fallen mountain billowed into the sky, casting what remained of the village—its shattered farm houses, its terrified horses and mules and sheep and goats and cows, its few holds of grain and fruits and vegetables—into utter blackness.

In the days of unnatural darkness following the fall of Sleepy Mountain, the young teacher tended the wounded, calmed the frightened, and enlisted the skills and services of those who otherwise might have remained frozen in terror, so that many more survived than not.

When the skies cleared, the towering beast remained as the mountain it once was, occasionally stretching its long neck to feed on what had survived of the treetops far to the north, occasionally shifting the weight of its giant tail up under its colossal rump.

Each night the townsfolk huddled uneasily in the village square, speaking their fears, arguing what course of action to follow.

"We must leave this place," said the farmers. Their crops had been ruined, their livestock destroyed. "The process of turning the soil and reseeding will bear no wheat or maize or squash or apples for many seasons. We haven't enough meats or fruits or vegetables stored to feed us all. Surely we will starve."

"We're afraid of the monster," cried the children. "What if it wants to eat us or step on us?" (In truth, all of the villagers were afraid of this.)

"But we have lived here all our lives," said the millers and weavers and carpenters. "Our ancestors are buried here. We know no other place, no other life."

It was the mayor, a portly fellow, much respected for appointing the young schoolteacher, who said, "Who knows what dangers lurk deeper in the forest. Who is to say there aren't more of these beasts out roaming the hills? Are we not industrious? Can we not use the fallen trees to rebuild? Can we not become hunters and gatherers until the crops are replanted? Surely you have seen the foxes and deer running terrified through the woods. Not all animals have perished."

"So we will become scavengers!" said the old people, proud and angry. They did not want to leave their homes, but they wanted life to go on unchanged, as it always had in Sleepy Mountain.

In the end, it was the schoolteacher to whom they listened. "Let us wait," she said. "I may find some clue to this beast in the ancient records." So she searched through her razed schoolhouse and unearthed the volumes of notes written by the earliest inhabitants of Sleepy Mountain, and spent hours reading for clues concerning the monster that had slept so peacefully beneath Sleepy Mountain until the terrible earthquake had wakened it.

She found more than clues. The first inhabitants of the village had written all about the huge beast, and other beasts like it. Dinosaurs, they were called—terrible lizards. "Some had hides like armor, and horns and tusks," she told the people. "Some, called tyrannosaurs, were carnivores and walked erect. Others, pterosaurs, soared through the air, giant birds of prey as big as houses. I believe our dinosaur is a sauropod, the largest of all the dinosaurs, but a harmless planteater."

"How did it get to be so big?" they asked.

"According to the ancient records, a dinosaur doesn't stop growing when it reaches adulthood, but continues to grow throughout its entire life. This one has had a very long life. It appears to be ten times larger than anything our ancestors wrote about."

"It won't attack us?"

"It probably doesn't even know we're here."

"Is it safe to stay in Sleepy Mountain?"

"It's a risk. The dinosaur means us no harm, but nothing can stop it from hurting us unintentionally."

In the end, the townsfolk decided it might be more

dangerous to move to unfamiliar lands than to rebuild their lives in Sleepy Mountain, so they settled in and constructed new homes and planted new fields and hollowed new wells and hunted for food, for they saw that life would go on, though a great many tasks lay ahead.

In the winter, when the snows fell, the giant sauropod didn't stir. Many thought the harsh temperatures might kill it, but when the ice thawed and the valleys turned green and lush with spring, the dinosaur stretched its long neck and fed from the treetops to the north, as if it hadn't even noticed the long spell of winter.

It had to happen sooner or later: The children, their curiosity conquering their fear, went to investigate the beast, secretly at first so as not to suffer the wrath of their parents, and then with more courage as they saw no harm would come to them. They played at the toes of the dinosaur and climbed its rough and pebbled skin, its natural crevices supplying footholds and handholds just right for scaling.

Not long afterward, the adults ventured forth, at first to watch the children, afraid the little ones might be crushed by some sudden movement should the dinosaur shift its weight or lean toward the north for food, but soon they learned the dinosaur was incapable of sudden movement. When the monster was ready to shift, its mountainous body shivered and the earth trembled and later, much later, hours or in some instances a full day or two, its tremendous girth would rise up and just as easily settle down, as if it hadn't moved at all. But, of course, it had. Often to do nothing more than defecate a ton of waste. The stench was so awful it choked the inhabitants of Sleepy Mountain until their eyes watered and their throats burned. Steam would rise up over the town and its surrounding valleys, and then a cry of joy would echo through the hills as the farmers rushed to the dinosaur with their horse carts and wheelbarrows and shovels to mine the huge mounds of excrement with which they fertilized their fields. In short order, their maize and squash and wheat and apples grew back taller and stronger than ever.

When the mayor died, he was the first to be buried at the foot of the dinosaur. Some years later, when the teacher passed away, she was buried beside the mayor for the townsfolk believed the two had secretly loved each other for many years.

Eventually a generation perished, and a new one took its place, and the townsfolk led a life of such peace and plentitude in the little town of Sleepy Mountain that they forgot all about the terrible earthquake and the unnatural darkness—even though the schoolteacher had documented the event in unfailing detail in the ancient records—and they forgot all about a time when the dinosaur was not a dinosaur at all, but a mountain named Sleepy.

But all things must change.

One day, when the townsfolk were thinking of harvests and festivals, of the golden sun and the sleek rains of summer, the dinosaur rose up on its huge legs, and instead of stretching its long neck to the north to feed in the forest, or defecating in the field, it took one step away from the town, and then another, and another, barely lifting its gigantic legs, splitting and snapping and crunching the northern forest from which it had so long been feeding.

The townsfolk stood in silent horror as the beast tromped away.

"What are we to do without the dinosaur?" said the farmers. "How will we fertilize our fields?"

The children cried because they were so fond of the giant beast and would no longer be able to play upon it. The elderly people were angry because life would not go on as it always had.

"We must not be alarmed," said the new schoolteacher. "I have been reading the ancient records, and our ancestors lived happy and fruitful lives long before they knew of the dinosaur's existence. We, too, shall survive."

But the townsfolk were not so easily convinced.

"Perhaps we should follow the monster," they argued. "It might lead us to more plentiful lands."

In the end it was the mayor who came forward with a compromise. "The dinosaur's way will be easy to follow. I propose we send scouts to track the beast until it comes to its resting place, and then these scouts will report on the condition of the soil and the plentitude of wild game."

The townsfolk agreed. Scouts were selected that very day, and sent to track the sauropod.

The people waited.

"It's a miracle!" the scouts proclaimed. "The dinosaur traveled north to the shore of a huge body of water from which it drank. The water was so vast we could not see from one end to the other! The land was rich and fertile, the wild game plentiful, and we saw strange white birds that fed upon the fish, and other odd beasts that swam in the water and flopped upon the shore to bask in the sun. And the most amazing thing of all," said the scouts, "large vessels that floated upon the waters! Carrying men from one shore to the other! Another town, or two, or three exist, maybe more!"

It did not take long for news to spread amongst the inhabitants of Sleepy Mountain. Before the mayor could don his coat and hat and confer with the young teacher, the villagers had begun to gather at the village square to discuss their next course of action. But the teacher came out and calmed the people. "Let me talk with the scouts," she said, "and I will gather all of the information from the ancient records and we will have a meeting in the town hall two nights hence."

The townsfolk agreed.

"All of you have probably heard most of what the scouts have reported to me," began the teacher, speaking to the villagers who had crowded shoulder to shoulder into the town hall. "I am here to tell you that all they have seen is confirmed by our ancestors."

The people shouted and clapped with joy.

The young teacher waited for them to quiet. "Our forebears documented the vast body of water and the sea birds that feed upon the fish and the strange animals that sun themselves on shore, even the great ships that carry people from one shore to another. All of this and more has been recorded."

"We must go!" shouted the townsfolk. "We must visit these people and bring them gifts of friendship and discover how they live!"

"Wait!" said the teacher. "There is something more I must tell you." She waited until the crowd fell silent so all would hear. "It was amongst the earliest entries in the ancient books that I found the writings about these other lands and people. This concerns me. Why would our ancestors, having learned of such wonderful things, leave them behind and return to live in seclusion here in Sleepy Mountain? I am afraid they discovered something that was not altogether wonderful, and turned away from the outside world for a reason. I'm not convinced it is safe for us to explore these new regions of the world."

The crowd murmured and shuffled and nodded.

Then the mayor stood. "In the ancient records, was there any mention of violence or hostility or persecution that might have led our people to remain hidden?"

The teacher shook her head. "Not that I have found, but there must have been something to—"

"And these vessels that float upon the water. Do our ancestors tell us how to build them?"

"Yes, but—"

"Then I propose this," said the mayor. "Let us build one of these water vessels, and let us send a small party over to visit these villages across the sea. We shall go in peace, bearing gifts, and if we are welcomed by the strangers, and they seem like peaceful and kind people, then we can open our town to them, and they to us, and we can all prosper from the union."

The townsfolk thought this a wonderful idea. They

cheered and whistled and shook hands. The meeting was adjourned, plans set in motion. The carpenters built a marvelous ship, and on a bright cool morning the ship was launched to sea.

Even the teacher was impressed by their discoveries in the new land. They met people of different colors and religions and languages, who wore strange and wonderful clothing. They discovered incredible machines and devices about which the ancient records only hinted: Carts that rode across the land without horses, plows without mules, machines that could count, clocks that kept perfect time, and huge buildings made of steel and glass. The young teacher had expected to see many strange and wonderful things, but not even she was fully prepared for this.

"They are such knowledgeable and intelligent people," she told the mayor, as she studied one of the huge maps of the new world.

"They push a lot of buttons," he replied, unusually grim.

"Their inventions are marvelous!"

"They hardly notice us."

"They are busy. They have so many things happening all at once. Look at all of the people here from other towns and villages who have traveled from so far away. Just look at this map! We didn't know any of these places existed. We didn't even know we lived on an island, for God's sake, an island so small we're not even a speck on their world. Do you really expect anyone here to take notice of us?"

The mayor shrugged. "I suppose not."

"There is so much to see, so much to learn. A new life awaits Sleepy Mountain!"

"Are you sure we want this new life?"

"How can we turn our backs on it?"

Change came swiftly to Sleepy Mountain. There were many firsts: The first foreigner to visit their little town; the first trade ships; the first food and clothing from foreign lands; the first gold and silver; the first clocks; the first banks; the first inventions and technologies that would eventually make their lives so much easier.

But there were many other firsts as well: The first deaths at sea; the first foreign diseases; the first crimes; the first taxations; the first war.

"We have no interest in this war!" complained the people. "Why should we fight?"

The mayor and the teacher, who were much older now, didn't want their people to fight any more than did their fellow townsfolk, but they recognized the need to protect themselves. "If our friends across the water are threatened," said the mayor, "then we are also threatened." And the teacher said, "We must support our friends in their struggle, as they would support us in ours."

"We had no struggles when we had no friends," said the people, but because they trusted and respected the mayor and the teacher who had opened the world to them, they sent many of their young men to fight, and buried many sons before their time, and the bell in the tower, which had never been tolled more than twenty times, learned to toll twenty-one times, in honor of the soldiers and sailors who had fallen in battle.

The mayor died shortly after the town changed its name to Royal Cove. This came long after he had retired. The commercial travel industry had been calling Sleepy Mountain, Royal Cove for many years, named after the large hotel built upon the waterfront, and the town voted that the name, already recognized by the other port towns, would serve them well.

The not-so-young teacher attended the mayor's funeral. She wept that day not only for the mayor, whom she had secretly loved for many years, but because she remembered a time when the entire township would have come to pay its respects at the funeral of one of its own. True, the town had grown large over the years. People seemed very busy. Many had moved away with their families to live in the new world, and many others had taken their places. Countless unfamiliar faces roamed the streets. Still, the mayor had been a great man. Now he was dead.

Shortly thereafter, the schoolteacher also died.

One day, the schoolteacher's daughter, Emma (a teacher herself) came across the ancient records tucked away in a dusty chest, amongst some of her mother's old things. She sat down to browse the entries. Most of them dated back long before her mother was born. She read about Sleepy Mountain—the vast and beautiful mountain that once graced the landscape. She read about the day the great earthquake unveiled the sleeping dinosaur, and how so many people had died that day, and how her ancestors' world had changed. She read about the dinosaur's path north to the sea, the first ship, and her mother's journey to the new world.

At first she thought mention of the dinosaur strange, then it began to trouble her. She was a teacher, and all of the experts from the North wrote that the dinosaurs were prehistoric beasts. They cited bone and fossil samples and other discoveries to prove it. And yet her mother had written about the great dinosaur only fifty or sixty years ago. Was her mother crazy? Were her ancestors crazy?

She showed her husband the ancient records, but he thought them the silly scribblings of a senile old fool. "My mother was not senile," said Emma.

"Are you sure?"

"Some of these writings date back centuries. Our ancestors recorded much of this information."

"We don't need to look at dusty old books anymore," he concluded. "And I don't want you spreading nutty stories around town." Emma's husband was a lawyer with political aspirations. "Our culture has progressed beyond the rumblings of our primitive ancestors. Let them rest in peace."

She showed the ancient records to some of the other teachers, and they were equally unimpressed. "We have purchased these beautiful new books from the North," they argued, "where very intelligent professors of archaeology, paleontology, and taxonomy have spent their lives collecting data on the dinosaurs. The dinosaurs all died aeons ago. Besides, if our parents had seen a dinosaur, don't you think that at least *one* person of that generation other than your mother would have said something or written something about it?"

"Don't you see?" Emma said. "That's why the dinosaur is still alive. It has survived for thousands of years. How? Why? It eats, it shits, it drinks from the sea, and then it sleeps unnoticed for centuries. And what do we do? We forget it ever existed. It *makes* us forget. Somehow."

But they all looked at Emma as if she were crazy, and she knew, then, that she would have to find out for herself.

So one weekend she told her husband and children she needed to get away by herself for a while, and she reserved a room at the Royal Cove Seaside Hotel, near the last area, according to her mother's writings, the dinosaur had been seen by the scouts.

Emma made note of certain natural landmarks as she walked the hills, and searched for unusual bends and breaks in the wooded mountain range. To the southwest she spotted a long, wide valley that might have been cut out of the forest by the giant sauropod. She expected much evidence of the dinosaur's passing to be camouflaged by natural growth, but she also knew that even after so many years other clues would remain—trees, for instance, hundreds of years old, uprooted, cracked in half, tipped over, alongside deep indentations in the earth, and crushed granite. Yes, she was certain she had found the dinosaur's trail. But how far had the beast traveled?

She returned to the hotel, sent a message to her family that she would be involved in a research project for a few weeks, and spent all of her money on food and supplies and a small tent. She was an excellent outdoorswoman who taught a course in forest survival at the school, and she knew what berries to pick and what barks and plants were safe to eat.

Emma tracked the sauropod relentlessly. Its path started west, turned south, and then eventually wound back toward the east. Then the trail, which at first had been so clearly marked, began to blend with the surrounding woodlands. The broken trees became less evident. Fewer unnatural breaks appeared in the earth. Was this a natural valley she'd been following for the last few miles, or the valley of the dinosaur? Did the ancient beast have the ability to mask even the physical evidence of its passing?

Eventually she came to a dead stop. There seemed to be no more clues. What would she do if the dinosaur was lost forever? What would she do if it never existed? Could she admit that her mother and her ancestors had been crazy all along? Why had she even bothered to track the beast? Something inside her drove her on, some instinct she did not fully understand. She pitched her tent in a shallow clearing and gathered sticks for a camp fire.

That's when she realized she was not alone.

Emma glanced up and saw the dinosaur.

She didn't *see* it, at first. It was more of a feeling, an emptiness of the heart, a shallowness of breath, a cold feeling spreading along her skin, an image that shimmered in her mind like a mirage. Yet the dinosaur was there, she knew it was there. She held her breath and fixed her gaze upon it until the image became clear, became more than a massive range of hills and rocks and trees, she held her gaze upon the mountain until it became a dinosaur.

So big, so camouflaged by the flora was the monstrous beast, she had completely missed it. But there it lay, already buried beneath layers of dirt and rock and foliage, already disappearing. Emma sat on the damp leaves and broken branches and stared at the marvelous creature—its gigantic flank, its massive head, its impossibly long neck and towering legs—so huge, so solid, so still, the dinosaur had become all but a mountain again. Sleepy Mountain.

She stared at it for hours. Then she touched it, tracing exposed portions of its gray pebbled skin with her trembling fingers. "How long have you lived?" she whispered to the dinosaur. "Is there no end to your life? No death? No time?" She knelt beside the beast and tried to get a sense of its being, tried to tell it she was there. "You are not alone," said Emma. "You will never be alone. We will all come home . . . my people . . . the way it was in the beginning . . . the way it was always meant to be."

Just as the dinosaur had come home. After it had drunk from the endless sea, it had turned around and returned to its familiar resting place as silently and inconspicuously as the shadow it had learned to become for the sake of its own survival—too large to be seen or noticed, like the Earth, like the sky.

When Emma returned to town she asked her husband if he wouldn't mind moving west, where she had found some wonderful land upon which to build. She felt so exhausted from the hustle and bustle of Royal Cove, she told him, that she needed the solitude of a country retreat. He was against it at first, but when she showed him the little piece of land she had selected near the mountain he was hooked, although he couldn't say exactly why.

Eventually, tired of Royal Cove and its breakneck pace, more people moved out of the big city and settled in the little town named Sleepy Mountain. Years later, when the Royal Cove Seaside Hotel closed, those who remained in the city suffered from the drop in tourism, the loss of trade, and a terrible recession. Many moved their families to larger, more prosperous port towns. In time, people from foreign lands stopped visiting Royal Cove, and the outside world forgot that the small port town had ever existed.

Meanwhile, the people of Sleepy Mountain tilled their fields with mules and muscle and sweat and plowshares, and drew water from deep rich wells. They bought and sold the local wares every seventh sunrise at open markets in the village square. Time was measured in seasons passed.

Whilst slept the sauropod.

REX

by David Gerrold

David Gerrold is a best-selling novelist, as well as a success-ful television writer, and the creator of Star Trek's "tribbles."

"Daddy! The tyrannosaur is loose again! He jumped the fence."

Jonathan Filltree replied with a single word, one which he didn't want his eight-year-old daughter to hear. He punched the *save* key on his keyboard, kicked back his chair, and headed toward the base-ment stairs with obvious annoyance. He resented these constant interruptions in the flow of his work.

"Hurry, Daddy!" Jill shouted again from the base-ment door. "He's chasing the stegosaurs! He's gonna get Steggy!"

"I warned you this was going to happen—" Filltree said angrily, grabbing the long-handled net off the wall. "No! Wait here," he snapped.

"That's not fair!" cried Jill, following him down the bare wooden stairs. "I didn't know he was going to get this big!"

"He's a meat-eater. The stegosaurs and the apato-saurs and all the others look like lunch to him. Get back upstairs, Jill!"

Filltree stopped at the bottom and looked slowly around the basement that his wife had demanded he convert into a miniature dinosaur kingdom for their spoiled daughter. Hot yellow lights bathed the cellar in a prehistoric ambience. A carboniferous smell per-meated everything. He wrinkled his nose in distaste. For some reason, it was worse than usual.

The immediate problem was obvious. Most of the six-inch stegosaurs had retreated to the high slopes that butted up against the north wall, where they milled about nervously. Their bright yellow and orange colors made them easy to see. Quickly, he counted. All three of the calves and their mother were okay; so were the other two females; but they were all cheeping in distress. He spotted Fred and Cyril, but Steggy was not with the others. The two remaining males were emitting rasping peeps of agitation; and they kept making angry charging motions downslope.

Filltree followed the direction of their agitation. "Damn!" he said, spotting the two-foot-high tyrannosaur. Rex was ripping long strips of flesh off the side of the fallen Steggy and gulping them hungrily down. Already he was streaked with blood. His long tail lashed furiously in the air, acting as a counterweight as he bent to his kill. He ripped and tore, then rose up on his haunches, glancing around quickly and checking for danger with sharp birdlike motions. He jerked his head upward to gulp the latest bloody gobbet deeper into his mouth, then gulped a second time to swallow it. He grunted and roared, then lowered his whole body forward to again bury his muzzle deep in gore.

"Oh, Daddy! He's killed Steggy!"

"I told you to wait upstairs! A tyrannosaur can be dangerous when he's feeding!"

"But he's killed Steggy!"

"Well, I'm sorry. There's nothing to do now but wait until he finishes and goes torpid." Filltree put the net down, leaning it against the edge of the table. The entire room was filled with an elaborate waist-high miniature landscape, through which an improbable mix of Cretaceous and Jurassic creatures prowled. The glass fences at the edges of the tables were all at least thirty-six inches high, and mildly electrified to keep the various creatures safely enclosed. Until they'd added Rex to the huge terrarium, they'd had one of the finest collections in Westchester, with over a hundred dinos prowling through the miniature forests. And every spring, the new births among the various herbivores usually added five to ten adorable little calves to their herds.

Now, the ranks of their menagerie had been reduced to only a few light-footed stegosaurs, some lumbering apatosaurs, two armored ankylosaurs, the belligerent triceratops herd, and the chirruping hadrosaurs. Most of those had survived only because their favorite grazing grounds were at one end of the huge U-shaped environment, and Rex's corral was all the way around at the opposite end. Rex wandered around the herbivore grounds only until he found something to attack. Like most of the mini-dinos, Rex didn't have a lot of gray matter to work with; he almost always attacked the first moving object he saw. In the six months since his installation in what Filltree had once believed was a secure corral, Rex had more than decimated the population of the Pleasant Avenue Dinosaur Zoo. He was now escaping regularly once or twice a week.

Slowly, Filltree worked his way around the table to the corral, examining all the fences carefully to see where and how the tyrannosaur might have broken through the barriers. He had thought for sure that the thirty-inch high rock-surfaced polyfoam bricks he had installed last week would finally keep the carnivore from escaping again to terrorize the more placid herbivores. Obviously, he had been wrong.

Filltree frowned as he studied the thick blockade. It had not been broken through in any place, nor had the tyrant-lizard dug a hole underneath it. The rocks were not chewed, but they were badly scratched in several places. Filltree leaned across the table for a closer look. "Mm," he said.

"What is it, Daddy? Tell me!" Jill demanded impatiently.

He pointed. The sides and tops of the bricks were sharply gouged. Rex had leapt up onto the top of the wall, surveyed the opposite side, and leapt down to feed. Judging from the numerous marks carved into the surface, today's outing was clearly not the first. "See. Rex can leap the fence. And that probably explains the mysterious disappearance of the last coelophysis too. This is getting ridiculous, Jill. I can't afford this anymore. We're going to have to find a new home for Rex."

"Daddy, no!" Jill abruptly became belligerent. "Rexie is part of our family!"

"Rexie is eating up all the other dinosaurs, Jill. That's not very familylike."

"We can buy new ones."

"No, we can't. Dinosaurs cost money, and I'm not buying any new animals until we get rid of him. I'm sorry, kiddo; but I told you this wasn't going to work."

"Daddy, pleeeaase! Rexie is my favorite!"

Jonathan Filltree took his daughter by the hand and led her back around to where Rexie was still gorging himself on the now unrecognizable remains of the much smaller stegosaur. "Look, Jill. This is going to keep happening, sweetheart. Rexie is getting too big for us to keep. It's all that fresh beef that you and Mommy keep feeding him. Remember what the dinosaur-doctor said? It accelerates his growth. But you didn't listen. Now, none of the other dinosaurs can escape him or even fight back. It isn't fair to them. And it isn't fair to Rexie either to keep him in a place where he won't be happy."

That last part was a complete fabrication on his part, and Filltree knew it even as he spoke it. If Rexie was capable of happiness, then he was probably very happy to be living in a place where he was the only carnivore and all of the prey animals were too small to resist his attacks. According to the genetic specifications, however, Rexie and the other mini-dinosaurs would have had to borrow the synapses necessary to complete a thought. Calling them stupid would have been a compliment.

"But—but, you can't! He'll miss me!"

Filltree sighed with exhaustion. He already knew how this argument was going to end. Jill would go to Mommy, and Mommy would promise to talk to Daddy. And then Mommy would sulk for two weeks

REX   199

because Daddy wanted her to break a promise to their
darling little girl. And finally, he'd give in just to get
a little peace and quiet again so he could get some
work done. But he had to try anyway. He dropped to
one knee in front of his daughter and put his hands
on her shoulders. "We'll find a good place for him,
Jilly, I promise." And even as he said it, he knew it
was a promise he'd never be able to keep.

He knew he wouldn't be able to sell Rex. He'd seen
the ads in the Recycler. There was no market for tyrant-
lizards anymore—of any size. And Rexie was more
than two feet high, and rapidly approaching the legal
maximum of 36 inches. Rexie required ten pounds of
fresh meat a week; he'd only eat dry kibble when the
alternative was starvation. They still had half a bag of
Purina Dinosaur Chow left from when they'd first
bought him. The dinosaur would go for almost a week
without eating before he'd touch the stuff, and even
then he'd only pick at it.

Nor did Filltree think he'd even be able to give the
creature away. The zoo didn't want any more tyrannosaurs, of *any* size. They were expensive to feed and
they already had over a hundred of the little monsters,
spitting and hissing and roaring—and occasionally devouring the smaller of their brethren.

At one time it had been fashionable to own your
own miniature T. Rex; but the fad had passed, the
tyrant-lizards had literally outgrown their welcome,
the price of meat had risen again (due to the Brazilian
droughts), and a lot of people—wearying of the smells
and the bother—had finally dropped their pets off at
the zoo or turned them over to the animal shelters.
Because they were protected under the Artificial Species Act, the cost of putting a mini-dino down was
almost prohibitive. Some thoughtless individuals had
tried abandoning their hungry dinosaurs in the wild,
not realizing that the animals were genetically trace-
able. The fines, according to the newspaper reports,
had been astonishing.

"I promise you, Jilly, we'll find a place for Rexie

where he'll be happy and we can visit him every week, okay?

Jill shook his hands off, folded her arms in front of her, and turned away. "No!" she decided. "You're not giving Rexie away! He's my dinosaur. I picked him out and you said I could have him."

Filltree gave up. He turned back to the diorama. Rexie had stopped gorging himself and was now standing torpidly near his kill. Filltree grabbed the metal-mesh net and quickly brought it down over the dinosaur. Rexie struggled in the mesh, but not wildly. Filltree had learned a long time ago to wait until the tyrant-king had finished eating before trying to return him to his corral. He swung the net across the table, taking care to hold the dinosaur well away from him and as high as he could. Jill tried to reach up to grab the handle of the net, and instinctively he yanked it up out of her reach—but for just a moment, the temptation flickered across his mind to let her actually grab Rexie. Then he'd see how much she loved the little monster.

But if he did, he'd never hear the end of it, he knew that—and besides, there was the danger that the mini-dino might actually do some serious damage. So he ignored Jill's yelps of protest and returned Rexie to his own kingdom. Temporarily at least. Then he went back and scooped up the bloody remains of poor Steggy and wordlessly tossed that into Rexie's domain as well.

"Aren't we going to have a funeral for Steggy?"

"No, we're not. We've had enough funerals. All it does is annoy the tyrannosaur. Let Rexie have his meal. It'll keep him from jumping the fence for another week or two. Maybe. I hope. Come on. I told you to stay upstairs. And you didn't listen. Just for that, no dessert—"

"I'm gonna tell Mommy!"

"You do that," he sighed tiredly, following her up the stairs, realizing that of all the animals in the house, the one he resented most was the one who was supposed to know better. She was eight and a half years old—and at that age, they were supposed to be almost human, weren't they? He felt exhausted. He knew he wasn't going to get any more work done today. Not after Jilly finished crying to Mommy about Daddy threatening to get rid of poor little Rexie. "Rexie didn't mean to do anything wrong," he mimed to himself. "He was hungry because Daddy forgot to feed him last night."

Filltree both hated and envied Rexie. Jill gave all her attention and affection to the dinosaur, speaking to her father only when demanding something else for her menagerie. Filltree scowled. Mommy was another one—she paid more attention to preparing the little tyrant's meals than to his. The dinosaur got fresh beef or lamb three times a week. He got soy-burgers.

For a long while, he'd been considering the idea of a separation—maybe even a divorce. He'd even gone so far as to log onto CompuServe's legal forum and crunch the numbers on the network's divorce-judgment simulator. Although CIS refused to guarantee the accuracy of its legal software, lest they expose themselves to numerous lawsuits, the divorce-judgment simulator used the same Judicial Engine as the Federal Divorce Court, and was unofficially rated ninety percent accurate in its extrapolations.

All he wanted was a tiny little condo somewhere up in the hills, a place where he could sit and work and stare out the window in peace without having to think about tyrants, either the two-foot kind or the three-foot kind. Tyrant-lizards, tyrant children—the only difference he could see was that the tyrant-lizard only ate your heart out once and then it was done.

According to CompuServe, he could afford the condo; that wasn't the problem. *Unfortunately,* also according to CompuServe's Judicial Engine he could not afford the simultaneous maintenance of Joyce and Jill. The simulator gave him several options, none of them workable from his point of view. A divorce would give him freedom, but it would be prohibitively expensive. A separation would give him peace and quiet, but it wouldn't give him freedom—and he'd still have to keep up the payments on Joyce's and Jill's various expensive habits.

Grunting in annoyance, he pulled the heavy carry cage out of the garage and lugged it awkwardly back down the basement stairs. Jilly followed him the whole way, whining and crying. He slipped easily into his robot-daddy mode, disconnecting his emotions and refusing to respond to even her most provocative assaults. "I don't love you anymore. You promised me. I'm not your daughter anymore. I'm gonna tell Mommy. I don't like you. You can go to hell."

"Don't tempt me. I might enjoy the change," he muttered in reply to the last remark.

Back downstairs, Filltree discovered that Rexie had not only finished his meal; he was already standing on top of the rock barrier again, lashing his tail furiously and studying the realm beyond. He looked like he was preparing to return to his hunting. At the opposite end of the room, the stegosaurs were mooing agitatedly.

Rexie spotted Filltree and his daughter. He turned sharply to glare across the intervening distance, cocking his head with birdlike motions to study them first with one baleful black eye, then the other. Perhaps it was just the shape of his head, but his expression seemed ominous and calculating. The creature's eyes were filled with hatred for the soft pink mammals who restricted him, as well as insatiable hunger for the taste of human flesh. Filltree wondered why he'd ever wanted a tyrannosaur in the first place. Rexie hissed in defiance, arching his neck forward and opening his mouth wide to reveal ranks of knife-sharp little teeth.

Filltree frowned. Was it his imagination or had the little tyrannosaur grown another six inches in the last six minutes? The creature seemed a lot bigger than he remembered him being. Of course, he'd been so angry at the little monster that he hadn't really looked at him closely for a while.

"He's awfully big. Have you been feeding him again?" he demanded of his daughter.

"No!" Jill said, indignantly. "We've only been giving him leftovers. Mommy said it's silly to waste food."

"In addition to his regular meals?"

"But, Daddy, we can't let him *starve*—"

"He's in no danger of starving. No wonder he's gotten so voracious. You've accelerated his appetite as well as his growth. I told you not to do that. Well . . . it's over now. We should have done this a long time ago." Filltree picked up the net and brought it around slowly, approaching Rexie from his blind side, taking great care not to alarm the tyrant king. The thing was getting large enough to be dangerous.

Rexie hissed and bit at the net, but did not try to run. Tyrannosaurs did not have it in their behavior to run. They attacked. They ate. If they couldn't do one, they did the other. If they couldn't do either, they waited until they could do one or the other. The creatures had the single-mindedness of lawyers.

Working quickly, Filltree caught Rexie in the net and swung him up and over the glass fence of the terrarium. He lowered the dinosaur into the open carry cage, turned the net over in one swift movement to tumble the creature out, lifted it away, and kicked the lid shut. He latched it rapidly before Rexie could begin bumping and thumping at it with his head. Jill watched, wide-eyed and resentful. She had stopped crying, but she still wore her cranky-face.

"What are you going to do with him?" she demanded.

"Well, he's going to spend tonight in the service porch where it's warm. Tomorrow, I'm going to take him to . . . the dinosaur farm, where he'll be a lot happier." To the animal shelter, where they'll put him down . . . for a hefty fee.

"What dinosaur farm? I never heard of any dinosaur farm."

"Oh, it's brand new. It's in . . . Florida. It's for dinosaurs like Rexie who've gotten too big to live in Connecticut. I'll put him on an airplane and send him straight to Florida. And we can visit him next year when we go to Disney World, okay?"

"You're lying," Jill accused, but there was an edge of uncertainty in her tone. "When are we going to Disney World?"

"When you learn to stop whining. Probably when you're forty or fifty." Filltree grunted as he lifted the carry cage from behind. He could feel its center of gravity shifting in his arms as Rexie paced unhappily within, hissing and spitting and complaining loudly about being confined. Jill complained in unison. *Neither* of the little tyrants were happy.

Somehow Filltree got the heavy box up the stairs and into the service porch. "He'll be fine there till tomorrow, Jill." In an uncharacteristic act of concession, he said, "You can feed him all the leftovers you want tonight. The harm has already been done. And you can say good-bye to him tomorrow before you go to school, okay?"

Jill grumped. "You're not fair!" she accused. She stomped loudly out of the service porch and upstairs to her bedroom for a four-hour sulk, during which time she would gather her strength for the daughter of all tantrums. Filltree waited until after he heard the slam of her door, then exhaled loudly, making a horsey sound with his lips. Considering the amount of agida produced, he wondered if he'd locked up the right animal.

Dinner was the usual resentful tableau. The servitors wheeled in, laid food on the table, waited respectfully, wheeled back, then removed the plates again. His wife glared across the soup at him. His daughter pouted over the salad. Not a word was said during the fish course. Instead of meat, there was soy-burger in silence again. Filltree had decided not to speak at all if he could possibly avoid it. Joyce couldn't start chewing at him if he didn't give her an opportunity.

Idly, he wondered how much meat it would take to accelerate Rexie's growth to six feet tall. The idea of Rexie stripping the flesh from Joyce's bones and gulping it hungrily down gave him an odd thrill of pleasure.

"What are you smiling about?" Joyce demanded abruptly.

"I wasn't smiling—" he said, startled at having been caught daydreaming.

"Don't lie to me. I *saw* you!"

"I'm sorry, dear. It must have been a gas pain. You know how soy-burger disagrees with me."

He realized too late his mistake. Now that the conversational gauntlet had been flung, picked up, and flung back, Joyce was free to expand the realm of the discussion into any area she chose.

She chose. "You're being very cruel and unfair, you know that," she accused. "Your daughter loves that animal. It's her *favorite*."

Filltree considered the obvious response: "That animal gets more hamburger than I do. I'm the breadwinner in this family. I'd like to be treated as well as Rexie." He decided against it; that way lay domestic violence and an expensive reconciliation trip to Jamaica. At the very least. Instead, he nodded and agreed with her. "You're right. It is cruel and unfair. And, yes, I know how much Jill loves Rexie." He tasted the green beans. They were underdone. Joyce had readjusted the servitors again.

"Well, I don't see why we can't rebuild the terrarium."

"It isn't the terrarium," Filltree pointed out quietly. "It's Rexie. He's been accelerated. Nothing we do is going to contain him anymore." He resisted the temptation to remind her that he had warned her about this very possibility. "If he gets any bigger, he's going to start being a hazard. I don't think we should take the risk, do you?" He inclined his head meaningfully in Jill's direction.

Joyce looked thwarted. Jonathan had hit her with an argument she couldn't refute. She pretended to concede the point while she considered her next move. Perhaps it was just the shape of her new coiffure, but her expression seemed ominous and calculating. Filltree wondered why he'd ever wanted to marry her in the first place.

His wife patted the tinted hairs at the back of her neck and smiled gently. "Well, I don't know how you intend to make it up to your daughter . . . but I hope you have something appropriate figured out." Both she and Jill looked at him expectantly.

Filltree met their gazes directly. He returned her plastic smile with one of equal authenticity. "Gee, I can't think of anything to take Rexie's place."

Joyce tightened her lips ever so delicately. "Well, I can. And I'm sure Jill can, too, can't you, sweetheart . . . ?" Joyce looked at Jill. Jill smiled. They both looked to Daddy again.

So. That was it. Filltree recognized the ploy. Retreat on one battlefield, only to gain on another. Jamaica appeared inescapable. He considered his options. Option. Dead end. "You've already made the booking, haven't you?" His artificial smile widened even more artificially.

"I see," his wife said curtly. "Is that what you think of me . . . ?" He recognized the tone immediately. If he said anything at all—*anything*—she would escalate to tactical nukes within three sentences. The *worst* thing he could say would be, "Now, sweetheart—"

Instead, he opened his mouth and said, "We can't go, in any case. I have research to do in Denver." This time, he amazed even himself. Denver? Where had *that* idea come from? "I'll be gone for a month. Maybe two. At least. I'm sorry if this ruins your plans, dear. I would have told you sooner, but I was hoping I wouldn't have to go. Unfortunately, I just heard this afternoon that no one else is available for this job." He spread his hands wide in a gesture of helplessness.

Joyce's mouth tightened almost to invisibility, then reformed itself in a deliberate smile. "I see," she said, in a voice like sugared acid. She refused to lose her temper in front of Jill. It was a bad role model, she insisted. She had declared that eight years ago, and in the past five, Jonathan Filltree had amused himself endlessly by seeing how close to the edge he could push her before she toppled over into incoherence. Tonight—with Denver—he had scored a grand-slam home run, knocking it all the way out of the park and bringing in all three runners on base. "We'll talk about this later," she said with finality, her way of admitting that she was outflanked and that she had no choice but to retreat and regroup her energies while she reconnoitered the terrain. She would be back. But for the moment, the conversation was temporarily suspended.

"I'll be up late," Filltree said genially. "I have a report to finish. And I have to pack tonight, too." He took a healthy bite of soy-burger. It was suddenly delicious.

Joyce excused herself to escort Jill upstairs to get her ready for bed. "But, Mommy, don't I get dessert . . ." the child wailed.

"Not while your Daddy is acting like this—"

Jonathan Filltree spent the rest of the evening, working quietly, almost enjoying himself, anticipating what it would be like to have a little quiet in the house without the regular interruption of Rexie's intolerable predations. If only he could get rid of Jill and Joyce as easily.

Filltree wondered if he should sleep on the couch in his office tonight, but then decided that would be the same as admitting a) that there had been a battle, and b) he had lost. He would not concede Joyce one inch of territory. Before heading upstairs, he took a look in at Rexie.

The tyrannosaur was worrying at the left side wall of the carry cage, scratching at it with first one foot, then the other, trying to carve an opening for itself. It bumped its head ferociously against the side; already the thick polymoid surface was deformed and even a little cracked. Filltree squatted down to get a closer look at the box, running his hands over the strained material. He decided that the damage inflicted was not sufficient to be worrisome; the carry cage would hold together for one more day. And one more day was all he needed.

He headed upstairs to bed, smiling to himself. It was a small victory, but a victory nonetheless. The knowledge that he'd be paying for it for months to come didn't detract from the satisfaction he took in knowing that he'd finally held the line on something. Today, Rexie; tomorrow, the soy-burger.

He was awakened by screaming—unfamiliar and agonized. Something was crashing through the kitchen. He heard the clattering of utensils. Joyce was sitting up in bed beside him, screaming herself, and clawing at his arm. "Do something!" she cried.

"Stay here!" he ordered. "See to Jill!" Wearing only his silk boxers, and carrying a cracked hockey stick as his weapon, he went charging down the stairs. The screaming was getting worse.

A male voice was raging, "Goddammit! Get it off of me! Help! Help! Anyone!" This was followed by the sound of someone battering at something hard with something heavy. High-pitched shrieks of reptilian rage punctuated the blows.

Filltree burst through the kitchen door to see a man rolling back and forth across the floor—a youngish-looking man, skinny and dirty, in bloody T-shirt and blue jeans. Rexie had his mouth firmly attached to the burglar's right arm. He hung on with ferocious determination, even as the intruder swung and battered the creature at the floor, the walls, the stove. Again and again. The screaming went on and on. Filltree didn't know whether to strike at the burglar or at the dinosaur. The man had been bitten severely on both legs, and across his stomach as well. A ragged strip of flesh hung open. His shirt was soaked with blood. Gobbets of red were flying everywhere; the kitchen was spattered like an explosion.

The man saw Filltree then. "Get your goddamn dinosaur off of me!" he demanded angrily, as if it were Filltree's fault that he had been attacked.

That decided Filltree. He began striking the man with the hockey stick, battering him ineffectively about the head and shoulders. That didn't work. He couldn't get in close enough. He grabbed a frying pan and whanged the hapless robber sideways across the forehead. The man grunted in surprise, then slumped to the floor with a groan, no longer able to defend himself against Rexie's predaceous assault. The tyrant-lizard began feeding. He ripped off a long strip of flesh from the fallen robber's arm. The man tried to resist, he flailed weakly, but he had neither strength nor consciousness. The dinosaur was undeterred. Rexie fed unchecked.

Behind him, Joyce was screaming. Jill was shrieking, "Do something! Daddy, he's hurting Rexie!"

Filltree's humanity reasserted itself then. He had to stop the beast before it killed the hapless man; but he couldn't get to the net. It was still in the service porch—and he couldn't get past Rex. The creature hissed and spit at him. It lashed its tail angrily, as if daring Filltree to make the attempt. As if saying, "This kill is mine!"

Filltree held out the frying pan in front of him, swinging it back and forth like a shield. The small tyrant-king followed it with its baleful black eyes. Still roaring its defiance, it snapped and bit at the frying pan. Its teeth slid helplessly off the shining metal surface. Filltree whacked the creature hard. It blinked, stunned. He swung the frying pan again and reflexively, the dinosaur stepped back; but as the utensil swept past, it stepped right back in, biting and snapping. Filltree recognized the behavior. The beast was acting as if it were in a fight with another predator over its kill.

Filltree swung harder and more directly, this time not to drive the creature back, but to actually hit it and hurt it badly. Rexie leapt backward, shrieking in fury. Filltree stepped in quickly, brandishing the frying pan, triumphantly driving the two-foot dinosaur back and back toward the service porch. As soon as Rexie was safely in the confines of the service porch, screaming in the middle of the broken remains of the carry cage, Filltree slammed the door shut and latched it— something went thump from the other side. The noise was punctuated with a series of angry cries. The door thumped a second time and then a third. Filltree waited, frying pan at the ready. . . .

At last, Rexie's frantic screeching ebbed. Instead, there began a slow steady scratching at the bottom of the door.

When Filltree turned around again, two uniformed police officers were relievedly reholstering their pistols. He hadn't even heard them come in. "Is that your dinosaur, sir?"

Shaken, Filltree managed to nod.

"Y'know, there are laws against letting carnivores that size run free," said the older one.

"We'd have shot him if you hadn't been in the way," said the younger officer.

For a moment, Filltree felt a pang of regret. He looked at the fallen burglar. There was blood flowing freely all over the floor. The man had rolled over on his side, clutching his stomach, but he was motionless now, and very very pale. "Is he going to make it?"

The older officer was bending to examine the robber. "It depends on the speed of the ambulance."

The younger cop took Filltree aside; she lowered her voice to a whisper. "You want to hope he doesn't make it. If he lives, he could file a very nasty lawsuit against you. We'll tell the driver to take his time getting to the E.R. . . ."

He looked at the woman in surprise. She nodded knowingly. "You don't need any more trouble. I think we can wrap this one up tonight." She glanced around the room. "It looks to me like the burglar tried to steal your dinosaur. But the cage didn't hold and the creature attacked him. Is that what happened?"

Filltree realized the woman was trying to do him a favor. He nodded in hasty agreement. "Yes, exactly."

"That's a mini-rex, right?" she asked, glancing meaningfully at the door.

"Uh-huh."

"Lousy pets. Great guard animals. Do yourself a favor. If you're going to leave him running loose at night, get yourself a permit. It won't cost you too much, and it'll protect you against a lawsuit if anyone else tries something stupid."

"Oh, yes. I'll take care of that first thing in the morning, thank you."

"Good. Your wife and kid know to be careful? Those rexies can't tell the difference between friend and foe, you know—"

"Oh, yes. They know to be *very* careful."

Later, after the police had left, after he had calmed down Joyce and Jill, after he had cleaned up the kitchen, after he had had a chance to think, Jonathan Filltree thoughtfully climbed the stairs again.

"I've made a decision," he said to his shaken wife and tearful daughter. They were huddled together in the master bedroom. "We're going to keep Rexie. If I'm going to be in Denver for two months, then you're going to need every protection possible."

"Do you really mean that, Daddy?"

Filltree nodded. "It just isn't fair for me to go away and leave you and Mommy undefended. I'm going to convert the service porch into a big dinosaur kennel, just for Rexie. Good and strong. And you can feed him all the leftovers you want."

"Really?"

"It's a reward," Filltree explained, "because Rexie did such a good job of protecting us tonight. We should give him lots and lots of hamburger, too, because that's his favorite. But you have to promise me something, Jill—"

"I will."

"You must *never* open the kennel door without Mommy's permission, do you understand?"

"I won't," Jill promised insincerely.

Turning back to Joyce, Filltree added, "I promise, I'll finish up my work in Denver as quickly as possible. But if they need me to stay longer, will that be okay with you?"

Joyce shook her head. "I want you to get that thing out of the house tonight."

"No, dear—" Filltree insisted. "Rexie's a member of our family now. He's earned his place at the table." He climbed into bed next to his wife and patted her gently on the arm, all the time thinking about the high price of meat and what a bargain it represented.

THE PANGAEAN PRINCIPLE

by Jack Nimersheim

Jack Nimersheim is the author of more than twenty nonfiction books and a dozen science fiction stories.

"To know yourself, you must be willing to learn from others."

How often had Pietor Sinkovich heard these words, growing up in Talinn? More times than he could possibly recall. His father repeated them almost daily, as if they were a mantra. He even inscribed them on a wooden plaque, presented to his only son the day Pietor graduated from the University of Leningrad. The elder Sinkovich favored the older name, the one from before the dissolution of the Soviet Union. To say Pietor had been educated in a school called St. Petersburg made it sound as if his son held some useless theological degree, rather than the Doctorate in Biogenetics for which he had strived so diligently, for so long.

Today, twenty years later and nearly a decade after his father's death, Pietor still treasured the unpretentious gift. It was one of his most prized possessions. Hanging on the wall, the crude, hand-carved plaque provided a stark contrast to the sterile medical equipment and modern electronic paraphernalia that threatened to crowd him out of his own laboratory. He sought inspiration in the unassuming words, words that provided eloquent testimony to their own veracity, whenever a particularly vexing problem threatened to frustrate his research.

Pietor Sinkovich was staring at the plaque, contemplating a father's simple wisdom, when the lab door swung quietly open.

"Earth to Dr. Frankenstein. Earth to *the* Dr. Frankenstein. Is the mad scientist accepting unannounced visitors at this time?"

"What? Oh, hello, little one. I'm sorry. I did not hear you come in."

"I'm sure you didn't, Father. You had that blissfully preoccupied look on your face. Let me guess. You were gazing out across the millennia again, weren't you?"

"Guilty as charged, pumpkin. But only slightly. I journeyed back a mere eighty million years or so, this time."

"Dreaming of the dinosaurs again, eh? That's my daddy. Let others recall with fondness obscure periods euphemistically referred to as the 'good old days.' The great Dr. Pietor Sinkovich operates on a much grander time scale. He reserves his nostalgia for the entire Mesozoic era."

The source of this affectionate ridicule was Pietor's *most* prized possession, although Katrina Sinkovich would protest vehemently against being described in such a manner. At seventeen—a bright and beautiful young woman who each day became more and more a mirror image of the mother who had died giving her life—Katrina considered herself no one's property, not even her father's. *Especially* not her father's. She deeply loved the kind and gentle man who had raised her, to be sure. Like any teenager, however, Katrina also cherished the freedom of adolescence, without realizing that this freedom was largely illusory.

"And a glorious age it was, little one, that time of the thunder lizards."

"I know, Father, I know. Allow me to continue, please. I've sat through this lecture so many times, I can repeat it by heart.

" 'For over one hundred and fifty million years the dinosaurs dominated our world. Their size was immense, their numbers legion. And their footsteps echoed across three geological periods—the Triassic, the Jurassic and the Cretaceous—collectively referred to as the Mesozoic era.'

" 'From an evolutionary perspective, few creatures, before or since, rival the success of these magnificent beasts. Compared to the dinosaur, humanity itself is little more than a brief footnote in the annals of Earth's history.'

"How was that, Father? Did I get it right?"

"You certainly did, Katrina. Although you chose to omit some very critical details."

"I know I did, Father. But I'm afraid you'll have to settle for the abridged version today. I just dropped by to say hello and to let you know that I'll probably be late for dinner this evening."

"And why might that be?" Pietor asked, although he already suspected the reason.

"I'm meeting Nikolai at the library in fifteen minutes. He's promised to help me study for my math exam."

"Ah, the handsome Nikolai. That makes the third night this week the two of you have seen each other. And here it is, only Thursday. You realize, of course, that I'm quite jealous of this young man who monopolizes so much of my daughter's time, these days."

"Grievance noted, Father. But I trust *you* realize that you have no one to blame but yourself. It was you, after all, who introduced the two of us."

"That I did, didn't I? And for perhaps the first time in my life, I fear I may have acted impulsively, without giving sufficient consideration to the consequences of my deed. Unfortunately, it's a little late to indulge in self-recrimination now, isn't it?" Pietor smiled and winked at Katrina, a subtle assurance that he was only teasing.

In truth, Pietor liked Nikolai Vostov. And he could not help but notice how happy his daughter seemed to be, since she and Nikolai had started seeing each other seriously.

"Well, child, you had best be on your way. I'd hate to make you late for your, ahem, studies. As for dinner, don't feel too badly about that, Katrina. My own responsibilities promise to keep me working long into the evening. To be honest, I spent much of the day trying to figure out how to diplomatically inform you that *you* were going to have to dine alone tonight. I'm relieved to hear that my concerns were unnecessary.

"I'll tell you what. Why don't you and Nikolai go out and grab a bite to eat together—after you've completed your work at the library, of course? My treat. Consider it a father's attempt to atone for the guilt he feels over abandoning his young daughter to spend the evening with a bunch of old dinosaur bones."

"Why, thank you, kind sir." Katrina grinned and curtsied as she accepted the money her father offered her. Enough of the little girl survived within her to display such childlike behavior from time to time. "And, Father, try not to work too late tonight, please. You've been looking awfully tired lately. I worry about you."

"I'll be fine. You just concentrate on passing that math exam tomorrow. Now, scoot."

Katrina's observation had been correct. Her father was tired. Exhausted would be an even more appropriate word to describe the way he felt. His fatigue, however, was unavoidable. For two decades, Pietor had enjoyed the luxury of pursuing his research in a slow and deliberate manner. An unexpected discovery changed all of this. He still remembered the phone call that forced him to shift his pet project into overdrive.

"Pietor! Are you sitting down?"

"Rashad? Is that you? It's been so long since we last spoke, I almost didn't recognize your voice. How have you been?"

"Forget the small talk, Pietor. There'll be plenty of time for such pleasantries, later. Right now, I have some wonderful news to tell you."

Rashad Kirmann was the last person Pietor would have expected to hear, breathless and excited on the other end of the line, when he picked up the telephone. Exuberance was not an attribute one normally assigned to the noted paleontologist. Cold. Stoic.

Somber. Impassive. Each of these and a dozen other, similar adjectives were used to describe Rashad in the numerous articles and profiles that had been written about his professional accomplishments. This particular afternoon, however, Kirmann sounded downright euphoric.

"Calm down, Rashad. You sound as if you're ready to burst."

"Indeed, I am, Pietor. As you will be, once you hear what I have to tell you."

"Well, then, do so quickly, old friend, before you succumb to a heart attack."

"We have DNA, Pietor!"

"I hate to burst your bubble, Rashad, but a couple of Noble Laureates named Crick and Watson beat you to that little discovery by more than half a century. I'm surprised you missed it. It was in all the journals."

"Don't be a wiseass, Pietor. Obviously, I wasn't referring to human DNA. I happen to have in my laboratory several amazingly well preserved dinosaur bones that, if one can trust the preliminary results of our tests, may contain a viable sample of DNA. My guess is they belonged to a seismosaur, based on the photographs I've seen of other, larger fossils recovered from the dig at which my team unearthed them.

"Now, are you at all interested in hearing more about this miraculous find, or would you rather continue trading puerile banter back and forth for the duration of our conversation—which, I can assure you, won't last very long, if such is your intent?"

The two men talked for over three hours. Theirs was a serious discussion concerning a potentially extraordinary discovery, one that presented to Pietor Sinkovich a professional and personal opportunity about which, prior to now, he had only been able to fantasize. By the time he hung up the phone, Pietor's own euphoria matched, perhaps even surpassed, that of his friend and colleague.

The first time Pietor Sinkovich examined the small vials containing the various bone samples forwarded to him by Rashad Kirmann, his mind wandered back to a lecture given by one of his college professors. In it, the professor compared the joys of scientific discovery with a fad embraced by American youth, early in the previous century.

Turning over one of the vials in his hand, he tried to visualize these young people, half a world away, contemplating a jar of . . . what was it called? Ovaltine. Yes, that was it. Pietor could imagine their youthful exuberance as, sifting through the fine powder, their tiny fingers finally found the coveted prize, a Captain Midnight decoder ring. Oh, in that moment, the enigmas they must have aspired to uncover, the mysteries these young children undoubtedly hoped to solve!

Pietor experienced a similar exhilaration, now.

Kirmann informed him that additional tests had established an even higher probability that the bone fragments did, indeed, contain deoxyribonucleic acid. DNA. And not just any DNA. Preserved DNA from a dinosaur! A coded message of life transmitted through history.

No. More than this. If, indeed, the genetic blueprint of a seismosaur lay trapped within these ancient remains, Pietor was holding a biological thread that stretched across a span of time so vast, so immense, its other end was anchored in an epoch that *preceded* history. Exposing the secrets entangled within the deceptively unsophisticated double helix of this biological thread would reveal previously unknown information about grand and magnificent creatures that last wandered the Earth tens-of-millions of years in the past.

And if he could do that . . .

No, Pietor admonished himself. Successful scientific inquiry relied on precise procedures. The most fundamental of these was to establish and maintain strict priorities. It was not prudent to anticipate what *might* be accomplished beyond your immediate task, before that task was itself completed. Evaluate, then extrapolate, based on the results of your objective analysis.

First things first. And the first thing Pietor had to

do was determine exactly what he was dealing with. There would be plenty of time later to speculate on the wondrous things that could be possible, using the genetic tools fate may have placed within his grasp.

Kirmann's decision to contact Pietor Sinkovich had not been based exclusively on their friendship. Among his colleagues, the unassuming Russian was considered one of the world's preeminent biogeneticists. Given the number of bright stars illuminating this relatively new and highly specialized field of scientific research, such kudos represented no small accomplishment. Although a naturally modest man, Pietor recognized the honor inherent in the recognition of one's peers. There were times, however, when he questioned whether his abilities matched his reputation.

Case in point: the weeks immediately following Rashad's call. The proverbial needle in a haystack would shine forth like a beacon at midnight, compared to a single, elusive strand of DNA embedded within a fossilized bone. Ferreting out this genetic chimera was a tedious and time-consuming process. Pietor had to constantly remind himself that the speed with which he was making progress—or, to be more precise, the lack thereof—was dictated by the complexity of the challenge confronting him, rather than any absence of skills on his part.

He began by extracting several minute core samples from a number of the bone slivers. After grinding these samples into a fine powder, each was given a bath. This cleansing did not involve anything as mundane as soap and water. Rather, Pietor used a special acid mixture that, although it was corrosive enough to break down the minerals in each sample, preserved any organic materials it might contain. "Tough on dirt, but gentle on your hands . . . or any other living matter, for that matter," Pietor would quip, whenever he was asked to describe the process.

This acid bath transformed the pulverized bone chips into gelatinous puddles of chemical soup. Pietor then passed what remained of each sample through a series of special filters he jokingly referred to as his "Soup-er Sieve." These filters were designed to extract large particles, leaving behind a highly distilled liquid in which Pietor might possibly—and, he had to keep cautioning himself, only possibly—discover a biological Holy Grail, the search for which had preoccupied much of his adult life.

Pietor honored his pledge to proceed methodically right up until the afternoon a complex combination of chemical dyes revealed the existence of viable DNA within one of the liquefied bone fragments. The instant this telltale stain appeared, his focus shifted from discovery to dreams.

The announcement captured the world's imagination. Within a single week, the proud duo of Kirmann and Sinkovich graced the covers of *Time*, *Newsweek*, and *Discover*. The following month a comprehensive if somewhat clinical account of their achievement, complete with exhaustive descriptions of the exact procedures used to unearth, identify, and isolate the tiny DNA sample, appeared in the prestigious scientific journal, *Nature*.

Pietor accepted his sudden fame gracefully. Whenever possible, however, he deferred to Kirmann on those occasions when opportunities arose to bask in the glow of public acclaim.

Let Rashad enjoy this brief moment in the limelight; and, indeed, the normally reserved paleontologist seemed to be doing exactly that. Living within the shadow of his associate suited Pietor just fine. He still faced months, possibly years, of experimentation. Each minute he did not have to waste satiating the public's seemingly endless curiosity freed up an additional minute for his own research, which he now pursued with renewed fervor.

Pietor reacted sharply to the sound of the opening door. This being the weekend, he did not expect any visitors—or unwelcome interruptions, to put it more bluntly.

"What? Who? Oh, it's you, Katrina."

"Oh, Daddy," his daughter sighed, glancing around the laboratory. One look told her everything she needed to know.

The air in the room was stale, laden with the odor of constant occupation. Assorted burettes, flasks, and petri dishes, the contents of which Katrina could only speculate about, challenged half-empty food containers for space on the desk, tables, and countertops. It was obvious that her father had been working virtually around the clock, stopping only long enough each night to catch a few hours of sleep on a cot he had set up in one corner of the room.

Katrina walked over to this makeshift bed and smoothed out the rumpled sheets, picked up the crumpled feather pillow. "Oh, Daddy," she sighed a second time, hugging the pillow to her chest and burying her face within it.

"What do you want, child?" Pietor asked brusquely.

When she looked up, Katrina was weeping. She dabbed her eyes with a corner of the pillowcase. "I want to talk, Father. I want to talk about you. About me. About you and me. About me and Nikolai."

"Can't this wait until I get home? I'm very busy here."

"You're always busy, these days. And you're always here. Take today, for example. Did you know it's Saturday?"

"Of course I do, child. I haven't forgotten how to read a calendar."

"No, I'm sure you haven't. But do you remember what Saturday this is?"

Irritated, Pietor closed his eyes and drew a deep breath. He tried to recall what his daughter might be referring to. The look on his face communicated clearly his inability to do so.

"You, Nikolai, and I were supposed to take the train to Talinn today. I purchased our tickets weeks ago. I even reminded you about it Wednesday morning—which, you probably don't realize, is the last time I saw you.

"Well, this morning the two of us went to the station, positive that you would be there. We waited until our train departed. That was two hours ago. Damn it, Daddy! I can't believe that you forgot."

"You watch your tongue, young lady. No daughter of mine uses language like that."

"How would you know? You haven't been home often enough these past few months to have any idea *what* I do."

She was right, of course. Since isolating the DNA uncovered by Kirmann's team, Pietor had dedicated almost every waking hour to his research. He left the lab only rarely. But didn't what he was trying to accomplish justify such sacrifices? Especially now, when success seemed so near.

"You just don't understand, Katrina. What I'm working on here is important, more important than anything else I've done in my entire life. Surely, you and Nikolai can think of some other way to occupy your weekend. Here. This should cover the cost of whatever the two of you decide to do."

Katrina did not take the money from her father's outstretched hand. Nor did she acknowledge his offer in any way. Instead, she walked in silence toward the door. When the young woman did finally speak—her back to the room, one hand already reaching for the doorknob—her voice was indifferent, almost a monotone.

"There's something I have to tell you, Daddy. Don't worry. I'll do so quickly. After all, I wouldn't want to interrupt your precious experiments." Opening the door, Katrina turned around to face her father. There were no longer tears in her eyes. Like her voice, they also lacked any emotion. "Last night, Nikolai asked me to marry him. We were hoping to discuss our plans with you this weekend, during the train ride to Talinn. Since you obviously don't have time to concern yourself with such mundane matters, however, I'll simply inform you that I have decided to accept his proposal.

"And now, Father, I'll leave. Don't worry. I won't bother you again."

A pneumatic hiss, the sound of the laboratory door closing slowly behind her, punctuated Katrina's parting words. Pietor wanted to go after his daughter. He started to, until he remembered the group of cultures he'd prepared earlier that day. They required his immediate attention.

He could always talk to Katrina later, after she'd calmed down. Right now, he had to analyze the results of several critical tests. If they were what he expected, dinosaurs would wander the Earth once again.

And beyond that? This close to success, it was impossible to ignore the possibilities.

Pietor returned home three days later, exhausted but elated. He was also confident that, once he told Katrina what he had achieved, she would forgive him his uncharacteristic selfishness of the past several months. Then he and his daughter—and her new fiancé, of course—would reschedule their trip to Talinn.

Together, they would travel to the city in which Pietor had spent his youth, the city in which Katrina was born. On the train, the two young lovers would inform Pietor of their desire to wed and, after the appropriate amount of hesitation and feigned uncertainty, he would consent.

Once they arrived in Talinn, they would visit the small cemetery containing the graves of his wife and father. There, Pietor would tell Nikolai about the family into which he would soon be welcomed. He would tell Katrina everything he remembered about the woman she resembled so closely that, at times as his daughter was growing up, it had been impossible for Pietor to look at her without considering what might have been, if only things had turned out differently. He would tell them both about an uneducated yet wise man who raised his son and then helped raise a granddaughter, after his daughter-in-law's unexpected death left Pietor alone with a newborn child—a responsibility for which the then young biogeneticist found himself sorely unprepared.

Together, they would laugh. They would cry. They would experience emotions impossible to convey with a single word. And then, when he felt the time was appropriate, Pietor would tell Katrina and Nikolai of his accomplishment. He would explain how, as a direct result of the startling discoveries he'd made while working with Kirmann's DNA samples, these marvelous people, this wonderful family, would soon be more than just a memory.

Only after he returned to St. Petersburg—having shared an amazing secret for a short while with his daughter and the man she loved—only then would Pietor once again don the scientist's frock and reveal his latest triumph to the rest of the world.

"Katrina!" Pietor shouted, as he burst through the door of the apartment. "Katrina, come quickly! We have such wonderful plans to make!"

Pterodactyls in flight suits. Tyrannosaurs in tweed. Surreal and serendipitous images merged into one another like slides on a carousel—changing too rapidly to be perceived clearly, remaining visible just long enough to register on your subconscious. His father slogging through a primeval swamp, naked, knee-deep in the mud and muck. Maria, his wife, screaming in pain. Then, an instant later, weeping with joy as she clutched an infant to her breast.

The child lay motionless. It did not appear to be breathing. Smiling, Maria extended her arms, slowly, tenderly, offering the infant to some unseen observer of this macabre tableau. Suddenly, inexplicably, the tiny body began to dissolve—individual cells breaking off, seeping through his wife's outstretched hands like grains of sand slipping through an hourglass. When Maria saw what was happening, she began to laugh. An instant later, she screamed.

Pietor awoke with a start. He had fallen asleep at the desk, his head resting on his arms. No lights were on in the laboratory. Pietor was alone in the darkness.

Outside, it was snowing. A damp, oppressive snow. The kind of snow to which people quietly acquiesce, seeking temporary sanctuary in a warm and cordial place. Their home. A church. The neighborhood tavern. Anywhere they were not forced to confront the elements. Anyplace they could share their forced hibernation with friends or, if necessary, only acquaintances.

The thick, white shroud muffled the familiar din of civilization. Even echoes, their vibrations effectively muted by the dense and frigid air, did not disturb the silence that had descended over St. Petersburg.

Pietor would have been sitting in his laboratory, alone, even if the city were not under Nature's siege. He had nowhere else to go.

A handwritten note lay on the desk in front of him. He did not need to see Katrina's words to know what they said. Pietor had read them so many times since finding the envelope addressed to him on the kitchen table, they were branded into his memory.

Dear Father,

I wish I didn't have to write this, but I must. I have moved out of the house to live with Nikolai. We still plan to marry, probably in the spring, but I could not stay here until then, not with the way things are. I don't think you realize how much you've changed in the past few months, since you and Dr. Kirmann announced your discovery. I can no longer watch what you're doing to yourself, to me, and to everyone else around you.

Once, you were passionate about your work. I respected that. And I loved and respected you in large part because of your dedication.

Lately, however, you've become obsessed with your research. This new attitude, I hate. And I realize that I have to get away from here before I end up hating you also.

Do you remember how resentful Granddaddy became, just before he died? I do, even though I was very young then, only seven or so. This was in the waning days of the Great Empire, as he called it.

I recall asking you once why Granddaddy seemed so bitter. You explained to me, in your patient way, that he was unwilling to accept the changes happening around him. Instead, you told me, Granddaddy wanted things to stay the way they were, the way that, in his mind, they had always been. "If your grandfather would treasure the past but live in the present," you told me, "he would be a much happier man." In the end, I believe this bitterness and unhappiness contributed to his death.

I have helped you collate enough of your notes to understand what it is you're trying to accomplish. I know that you hope to resurrect the seismosaur by replicating and reproducing its DNA. This seems, on the surface, to be a wonderful achievement. I also believe, however, that I've figured out your ultimate goal. I know about the cell samples you took from Granddaddy and, yes, even my mother, before they died. If you are attempting what I suspect, then you're making the same mistake Granddaddy did.

Please, Father, recall your own words, before it's too late. I don't want what happened to him to happen to you. I love you too much to watch that.

Today disappears with the fulfillment of its own promises. In this way, the present surrenders itself to the future. And once today becomes yesterday, it is gone. Forever.

It cannot be recaptured. It cannot return.

I don't know if any of this will make any sense to you. I can only pray that it does. If it does, you know where to find me.

Katrina

The Earth had changed dramatically in the sixty-five million years or so that had passed since thunder lizards last wandered the planet. Gone was Pangaea, the single, monolithic land mass upon which the dinosaurs originally evolved. Plate tectonics had slowly but inexorably divided it, subdivided it, and then subdivided it yet again, into seven distinct continents, until it was, quite literally, a new and different world.

The arrival of *Homo sapiens* on the scene accelerated this process. Unable to leave nature to its own
devices, humanity had etched additional and artificial
divisions into the Earth's surface. Provinces now existed within regions, which existed within nations,
which existed within the countries that arbitrarily par-
titioned the planet.

Where did a 160-foot, Brontosauruslike creature
from a primitive era fit within this geological and political Chinese puzzle box? Surely, the alterations humanity had made to the Earth would overshadow even
this mammoth beast, in much the same way he once
towered over nascent mammals with whom the dinosaurs had shared a primeval planet—ironically, the ancient ancestors of a humanity that had displaced him.

The dinosaurs once dominated the world, to be
sure. And yet, Pietor was forced to admit, the world
over which they ruled no longer existed. Their present, in the words of his daughter, had surrendered
itself to the future.

It was relatively easy to detect change across such
a vast time period. And, as Katrina was so fond of
pointing out, Pietor tended to perceive things on a
grand scale. But could his daughter be correct in her
other assumption, as well? Was it possible that the
same principle also applied at the more personal,
human level?

The world of his father no longer existed. Like Pangaea before it, the monolithic empire under which
he'd lived his entire life had split asunder. It had been
divided, subdivided, and subdivided yet again, into
numerous, smaller nations, not all of which recognized
the sovereignty of the others. Border skirmishes and
internal civil strife still erupted constantly—pitting
friend against friend, neighbor against neighbor and,
in some cases, brother against brother.

What kind of man would his father be, Pietor had
to wonder, reborn into such a world? How might he
develop, amidst such madness? Surely, whoever
evolved from the few strands of DNA Pietor had

available as a template would not be the same person he had known and loved.

And what of Maria, Pietor's wife, Katrina's mother? How many times had he imagined a life that might have been, had she survived? And yet, wasn't Maria, like his father, a human amalgam of unique experiences—culminating, and then ending, with the birth of a daughter Pietor loved more than life itself? Mammals did not flourish until the dinosaurs disappeared. One could not prosper, until the other passed away. Was it possible that, in some curious way he could not hope to comprehend, Maria's death served a similar purpose?

So many questions. So much uncertainty. Searching his own soul, Pietor could find no answers, at least, not with the degree of certitude his current decision demanded. He needed counsel. He needed someone to analyze the potential consequences of his planned actions from a perspective other than his own.

Grabbing his coat off the back of the chair, Pietor picked up Katrina's note, folded it carefully, and placed it in the pocket. Surely, his daughter and her fiancé would be home on a night as inclement as this one. As he opened the laboratory door, light from the hallway spilled into the darkened room, briefly illuminating a small, hand-carved plaque on the opposite wall.

"To know yourself, you must be willing to learn from others."

Tonight, the wisdom contained in his father's epithet would once again transcend the generations.

ON TIPTOE

by Beth Meacham

Beth Meacham is a Hugo-nominated science fiction editor, as well as a successful short story writer.

I was walking in Lower Manhattan on a Sunday morning with my old roommate, Alice, who was visiting New York for the first time. Alice is the kind of person who has an excessively romantic notion of what the city is like, drawn from novels and old movies, and she had insisted on seeing the Big Apple from top to bottom. Our tour had focused on famous buildings, and Alice had photographed every gargoyle and bit of incidental architectural sculpture she could find. Alice is a fan of the bizarre; she has a knack for spotting statuary three stories up. She noticed everything: the carved cornerstones, the gargoyles, the wrought-iron manhole covers.

"This city is too much," she was saying. "It's a museum of art displayed in the midst of garbage. The people who live here don't even notice what's around them." She turned her sharp blue eyes on me, and frowned. It's something to be frowned at by a tall blonde Valkyrie from the upper Midwest. I felt guilt. I had become one of the oblivious.

I made an effort, and noticed a shadow pass across the gray stone facade of the building across the street. At the same moment, Alice whipped her head around so fast that the end of her long braid hit me in the eye.

"What the hell was that?" she asked, rather more loudly than necessary in the quiet, deserted streets.

"Just a shadow across the sun. Keep it down, okay?" I asked a little anxiously. "We don't want to attract the attention of the street people down here."

"It was not a shadow across the sun. It was a *thing*."

"What kind of thing?" I asked. "Did you see a rat or something moving along the gutter?" She'd probably seen something moving in the street while I was looking at shadows.

"Not unless you have rats the size of elephants around here." Alice peered intently at the building, squinting up her eyes and nose, tilting her head back and forth. "I don't know what it was. I can't see anything now, but I'd swear that something really big moved right along there—" she pointed at the front of the office building, lifted her camera and quickly shot a couple of frames— "and then stopped at the corner and disappeared."

We stood and stared at the corner. Nothing happened.

"Alice," I said, "let's get out of here."

"I saw something."

"I believe you," I said reassuringly. "We were going to go up to the Museum of Natural History, and here's the subway entrance. Let's go."

"I saw it." One of Alice's most endearing traits was her steadfast honesty. It had gotten us into trouble more times than I could remember over the ten years we'd known each other. As I pulled her down the stairs to the train, I wondered what she'd really seen.

We got up to 81st Street and into the museum just in time to catch a lecture-tour of the dinosaurs. If there was one thing Alice loved more than lamps in the shape of gilded Victorian cherubs, it was dinosaurs. The tour leader, a member of the museum research staff, was a young man, not unattractive with his long, lanky body and curly, shoulder-length red hair. His name was Matt, and he and Alice hit it off. He joined us for coffee after the tour was over.

Matt was saying, "—and there was quite a scandal when the artists doing the new mural made all the dinosaurs gray."

"Why did they do that?" Alice asked.

"Because it's traditional?" I ventured.

"Because that's what people expect." Matt turned

to explain it to me. "Dinosaurs probably had as much color variation as modern lizards do. My post-grad work was on some samples of fossilized skin that the museum found out in New Mexico. The cell structure I saw there hints that many dinosaurs were very brightly colored, with strong markings that varied within species, not just between species." Matt loved his work, you could tell.

"Wow." Alice sat back in her chair. "You mean they could have been like those iridescent blue and green lizards you see in the tropics?"

"Or bright red, or orange and white spotted, like today's Gila monsters. Forget the dull, gray, scientific dinosaurs of yesteryear." Matt was working hard to impress Alice, and she was willing to be impressed. I leaned in as a thought occurred to me.

"Could they have had color-changing skin, like chameleons?" I asked.

"Sure! Why not?" Then the grin faded a little as he thought about it. "Why not, indeed? It would make a lot of sense for the smaller ones during the end of the Triassic Period, when the big carnivores were around."

"Sure would be a survival trait," I said.

A silence fell. Alice looked very thoughtful, always a dangerous sign.

The next morning we got up late and took Alice's rolls of film to be developed-while-we-waited. These little conveniences of city life gave her a thrill. We drank coffee and ate bagels from the deli on the corner, and talked about what she wanted to see today. I didn't have to be at work till evening, since I was on the late shift at the club that week.

"Hey, lady!" The man in the photo lab came around the counter from the back room. His white cotton lab coat had "GLENN" embroidered on the pocket, and he was wearing rubber gloves. He looked back and forth between us, expectantly. Wondering which one of us could properly be called "Lady," I suppose. We were both dressed in jeans and oversized sweaters, boots and leather jackets, and looked a lot like the students we had been five years before. Alice raised her eyebrows, and not surprisingly he fixed on her.

"You an artist?" he asked.

"Of course," Alice replied promptly.

"Do you want all these negatives printed?"

"Why do you ask?" Alice wanted to know. "Why wouldn't I want them printed?"

"Well, a bunch of them have weird shadows and distortions and stuff on them. Normally I wouldn't print those—a lot of film these days is damaged, you know—but since you've got a lot of statues and stuff I thought you might have meant some of the lighting effects. So I thought I'd ask." He trailed off. Alice was staring at him with those big blue eyes of hers.

"Oh, please print them all. I'm just learning about photography, and I need to see what I've done wrong, you know." She looked suddenly as if she might cry. He waved his hands in an attempt to comfort her without touching her.

"That's all right. I'll print them all, and I won't charge you for the funny ones. Maybe you'd like to have lunch with me, and I'll explain what I think happened?"

"Oh, that would be wonderful. Thanks so much." She smiled at him.

"Alice," I said. "Don't forget that we have matinee tickets."

We waited while Glenn finished printing the pictures, which only took about five more minutes. He had a kind of automatic machine thing that ran long strips of photo paper through the developing solutions and then out through a cutter. I hadn't known they could do that. Alice paid for most of the pictures, and then we went back to my apartment.

"We do not have matinee tickets," she said. I explained about the dangers of unknown male predators in New York, and suggested that she might want to be a little more careful in accepting invitations from strangers. She just stared at me and sighed. "You live in a much more dangerous world than I do," she said.

We made more coffee, and then laid out the photos on my little dining table. They were great pictures—close-ups of carvings and brickwork, distance shots of turrets and pyramid-like rooflines. I hadn't realized what a Gothic city I was living in. But about every tenth picture had an unexpected shadow, or a distortion on one side or another of the thing Alice had been photographing. The distortions made the walls look as if they curved in and out of true in a random way. The shot Alice had taken on Wall Street Sunday morning, of the wall where she thought she'd seen something, had a distortion right in the middle.

"That's a shame," I said. "Where'd you buy this film? Maybe we can get you a refund. Or do you think it's your lens—is there something wrong with it?"

"If there was something wrong with the lens, all the pictures would be messed up the same way," Alice replied. "It might be the film, I suppose." She bent over the bad pictures. "You don't have a magnifying glass, do you? And some tracing paper?"

By mid-afternoon she had traced the distortions on all the pictures, and had a pile of flimsy drawings in front of her. I was getting more than a little bored.

"Alice, are we going to do anything today, or are we going to just hang out here till I have to go to work?" I was waiting tables and helping the sound man at a club on the east side. The tips were pretty good, and six more months of apprenticeship on the mixing board would get me licensed and into the union. It was more fun than working as an assistant at a PR company, which had been my last job until my boss was fired and the staff "scaled back." And it beat unemployment all to hell.

"When do you have to leave?" she asked.

"I have to be there by 5:30," I said, a little exasperated. "In two hours. I told you."

"Oh, okay. Come look at these, would you?"

I looked. She had a lot of curving lines on the paper: long arching curves; sinuous curves; some sharp angles; and a couple things that looked like the outlines of gargoyle heads. I pointed at those.

"Those practice tracings?"

"No," she said. "Those are the outlines of the distortions on these two pictures." She held up a couple of pictures of a carved doorway that had distortion patterns around the edges.

"That's really weird," I said. "What do you think it is?"

"Dinosaurs," she said.

She called Matt, at the Natural History Museum, and asked him to have dinner with her that night while I was working. I wasn't surprised that she had his phone number, but I thought she was a little too eager to share this new idea of hers with him. He, of course, wasn't busy.

"He's going to think you're crazy," I told her. "And, of course, you are."

"I'm perfectly sane. And I'll show him the pictures. It's not like I had this idea out of the blue based on nothing. Not like *your* idea that the poor man at the photo shop this morning was some sort of sex maniac." She had me there. If I argued any more we'd be having a fight, so I went into the bedroom and slammed the door.

I had just changed into my work uniform when Alice knocked on the door and came in. The uniform is tight jeans, black cowboy boots, and a black satin shirt that I wore halfway unbuttoned with nothing underneath. Alice grinned at me.

"If you walk around dressed like that, it's no wonder you have to worry about maniacs." She came around behind and brushed my hair for me, which was a nice way to apologize. Then it was time for me to go.

The club was loud and busy that night—the band onstage was really good for a change, the customers were drinking plenty, and I had an extra two hundred dollars in my pocket by midnight to pay for the handprints on my butt.

Someone grabbed my arm, and I whirled around to slap whoever it was away. Alice jumped back, startled. Matt was standing right behind her, and had to put his arm around her waist to keep both of them from falling down.

"What the hell are you doing here?" I shouted over the noise.

"Hi, nice to see you again, too," Matt replied at the top of his lungs. He was quick, I'll give him that. Alice turned in his arm and smiled at him, and he got that dazed look on his face again.

She said something to me that I couldn't quite make out, so I led them off the floor backstage, waving Jake off when the bouncer moved to intercept. The dressing room was relatively quiet.

"We're going to go downtown and try to get some more pictures of the dinosaurs," Alice said, pointing at the big canvas bag Matt had over one shoulder.

"Tonight?"

"Yeah. Want to come with us? I told Matt you'd be interested in helping."

I walked up real close to him. He blinked, but kept his eyes on my face. "Are you nuts?" I said.

So we ended up down in lower Manhattan, just the three of us and Alice's camera and tripod, and a motion sensor shutter and strobe flash that Matt had borrowed from the ornithology lab. It was crazy. I said so, several times, until Alice finally told me to shut up or go home. Matt wasn't any help at all. He agreed with me that this was nuts, but he said that there was no scientific data to eliminate the hypothesis that chameleon dinosaurs might have survived, and besides Alice was too pretty to be allowed to wander around the canyons of Wall Street alone at night. I did get the distinct impression that he wouldn't mind if she wandered around with just him for company.

They set the camera up at the corner where we'd seen whateveritwas, then faded back into a doorway to wait. No matter how much room I tried to make, Alice ended up practically sitting in Matt's lap. She said that she would bear the hardship.

Time passed slowly. It never really gets dark in Manhattan, what with all the lights that stay on all night long, but it got pretty damn dark and quiet that night along Rector Street. I kept expecting the flash to be set off by some bum picking up garbage, but nothing happened. There was no one there, maybe no one for blocks around. It was eerie. I'd lived in New York for years, and had gotten used to the idea that it was a city that never slept, that no matter what time it was, there were people around, working, playing, preying on the hapless. But Wall Street at 2:30 a.m. on a Monday morning was quieter than Dayton, Ohio ever got.

I heard the faint rumble of the subway, a few blocks away, and then the flash gun on the camera started firing and the shutter whirring, and in the space of about thirty seconds there was a surprising amount of thudding from the street and a squeal from Alice.

Then silence fell again. I started to get up, but Matt's hand landed heavily on my shoulder, holding me down. One of them whispered, "Wait."

I strained my eyes to see what was going on, but I couldn't make out anything but the dark shadows cast by the intermittently working streetlight down the block from where we sat. There were a lot of shadows. I had just closed my eyes again and leaned back to doze a little, when all hell broke loose once more. The flash gun strobed, the shutter clicked, the automatic film advance whirred, and a subway train rumbled by, shaking the street.

When it was over, Matt and Alice stood up and stretched. Alice reached a hand down to help me to my feet, and hugged me when I was standing.

"Oh, we did it, we did it!" she said.

"Did what?" I asked, feeling put out. "Seduced a beautiful young man in a doorway?" She looked hurt. Well, I didn't mean it. I stroked her shoulder and said I was sorry.

We straggled back to my apartment, and Matt got a few hours of sleep before he had to leave for work at 8:00. Alice made him a pot of coffee, and he made her promise to bring the developed pictures to his office as soon as she had them.

We went back to the same photo place, and Glenn

developed the rolls of film. Alice leaned over the
counter while he was working, and asked him to
please be sure to print them all, because she was test-
ing the film for defects and needed to see everything.
He smiled kind of shyly, and told her that if she ordered them now he could give her enlargements for
the same price as the regular prints.

"An unadvertised special," he said.

"Oh, that would be just wonderful!" Alice's eyes
were shining.

"What time is your plane tomorrow?" I asked
loudly, just as Glenn opened his mouth to say something more.

She took the big envelope of photos and shoved it
into her shoulder bag without letting me see them.
"We should wait till we get to Matt's office. He has
a right to see them at the same time we do—he was
there, after all. And *he* believes me."

"I believe you think it's true, Alice. I just don't
believe there are invisible dinosaurs living in
Manhattan."

"They're not invisible. You saw the pictures—
they're camouflaged." Clearly the argument was not
over. "These pictures," and she patted her bag, "will
show you the truth. I know we caught some moving
last night."

"Alice, if there were dinosaurs still alive, wouldn't
someone have noticed by now?" I swung around the
corner post and down the stairs to the subway. Alice
was right behind me.

"People *have* noticed them before—or at least the
photo labs have noticed them. Remember that Glenn
said they got a lot of distorted film, but didn't print
those pictures? Those are pictures of dinosaurs! I bet
every person taking pictures in Manhattan has a photo
of a dinosaur. If people here weren't so oblivious to
everything going on around them it would have been
discovered long ago!"

A woman across the subway platform turned away
from us and put her head down real close to her book.

"Alice, keep it down."

"Anyway," she went on, ignoring me, "since everyone believes that the dinosaurs all became extinct, nobody ever thought to look for living ones. Especially," she said, looking around the shadowy station thoughtfully, "since they're so hard to see."

The train came, and we got on. I tried not to stare at the dark corners.

Matt's office was really just an old metal desk and a light in the corner of a cavernous, dark, dusty room filled with shelves and boxes that had old rocks and bones sticking out of them. As we came in, I looked through an empty space in a set of tall shelves and caught a glimpse of Matt's startled face as he shoved something into his desk drawer. But he was grinning like a puppy when we came around the corner and Alice kissed him. We found chairs—an old broken-down easy chair with the stuffing spilling out of holes in the arms for Alice and a low metal stool for me, and pulled them up to the desk. Alice pulled the envelope of pictures out of her bag, and laid them out.

I couldn't see the pictures from where I sat. Alice pointed. "Look at that! Just look at it!" Matt bent over beside her, their heads almost touching, staring at the pictures.

"It could be," he said. "It's hard to see—there's no really distinct line."

"Here, look at this one." Alice interrupted. "See, crossing the street? Look!" she demanded and held it out to me.

Although we had used color film, the photo looked like a black and white. The strobing flash gun had created stark bars of light and shadow in the gray concrete and granite canyons of Wall Street, with only black darkness like the roof of a cave above. The picture showed a narrow street, with the corner of a building intruding on one side. It looked like a building. I glanced up, puzzled, and Alice pointed to one side of the photo.

"There! Right there. It's crossing the street."

There was a dark shape there, to be sure. Big and

squarish; and you could see that it had something holding it up off the street at each corner.

"Alice, that looks like a dumpster to me. You know, the ones with the wheels?"

She shook her head at me. "There weren't any dumpsters in that street before we took the pictures, or when we were leaving. I turned the flashlight that way to see what the street looked like." There was a note of triumph in her voice.

I looked again. I shook my head.

"It's there," Alice insisted. "Look. You can see the tail curving around here." She pointed at a low mass of something along the side of the street. "It must be moving fast, because this is the only picture in the sequence that shows it in the street."

Matt reached over and took the picture from her, and I stood up and walked over to the window behind his desk. The window looked out over one of the garden courts of the museum—a beautiful view, with no dinosaurs in it. I was surprised that he didn't turn his desk to look out the window, instead of inward toward the bones and shelves and long dark corridors of the storeroom. When I turned around he was reaching into his desk drawer for something, a magnifying glass or a pencil. Over his shoulder, in the drawer, I could see a photograph of a pretty dark-haired woman holding a redheaded child that looked just like Matt. He closed the drawer on their faces.

Alice and Matt traced out all the dinosaurs they could find in the pictures—Alice admitted it was hard to see them, because of the chameleon effect. Matt said that probably they'd evolved the ability to match the color of rocks as the forests and marshes gave way to desert. But Alice was looking at a photo when he said that, and couldn't see the grin on his face.

Finally, Matt said, "It's going to take some time for me to get the data sorted out so I can write this up for publication. We'll have to keep it a secret till then. But it'll be big. Really big." Alice was glowing with enthusiasm as she hugged him.

"We'll have to spend a lot of time together working on it, won't we?" she said.

"Mmmm. Starting tomorrow. I've got meetings tonight, but how about an early dinner tomorrow night?"

Alice smiled up at him; he looked down at her with a goofy grin on his face.

"Alice, your plane leaves at nine o'clock tomorrow morning," I reminded her. She winked at me over his shoulder.

She left the pictures there when we went out for lunch.

On our way home after lunch I asked her what she thought of Matt. I was beginning to get really worried about him and his intentions. It was one thing to have a mad fling with a beautiful young man, and quite another to get involved with a married man. But Alice didn't want to hear about it.

"You're just being jealous because he's my partner in the Dinosaur Quest. You won't even admit they're real!" She whirled and peered down the stairs at me. "Why don't you just admit that that was a dinosaur tiptoeing across the street last night?"

"Tiptoeing?" I was too astonished to shout it as loudly as I felt like. Which was just as well, since there's a hell of an echo in that stairwell. I live in a fourth floor walk-up, so I spent a lot of time on the stairs. "Dinosaurs thud, they crash, they move ponderously. They don't *tiptoe*."

"That one last night was tiptoeing. You saw how its feet narrowed down to a point." I sat down on a stair to listen. Alice was about to Explain Something.

"See, I could understand how dinosaurs could survive in a city like this just standing still, since their skin would blend in with the walls so well. And when most New Yorkers notice a big, hulking thing they think it's a dumpster, just like you did. But I couldn't figure out how the dinosaurs could move around. I mean, there's always a chance that someone would see them, and then it'd be all over. And nobody ever *has* seen them, at least not and talked about it. Of course, there are all those stories about drunks seeing pink elephants." She was digressing, always a danger when she had an idea.

"Movements, Alice."

"Yes. You know, a really drunk person, a derelict, you know, probably wouldn't know the difference between an elephant and a dinosaur, would he?"

"Probably not."

"Anyway, when I saw that picture I realized that they must move really really fast between concealments, to minimize the chance for discovery. And I got to thinking—there's proof that people have seen them before."

"What proof is that?" She was having a brainstorm, even more dangerous than an idea.

"You know those old cartoons where the cat tiptoes really fast between trees or telephone poles, and then disappears behind a pole about half the size it is? I bet that cartoonist saw the dinosaurs."

That gave me pause. I remembered one cartoon like that with an elephant doing the tiptoeing. What if she was right?

Alice reached down, grabbed my hands, and pulled me to my feet. "Let's get going," she said. "I have to pack, and we still need to get back to that junk store that had the lamps. I wonder if they'll ship the big one to me?"

"You're still planning on leaving town tomorrow? What about dinner with Matt?"

"I can't afford to blow off the ticket. Besides, he'll be a good reason for me to come back sooner to visit you again. I'll call him and explain everything."

"I wish I thought you knew what you were doing," I said.

But she just laughed at my worries and suggested Chinese take-out for her last night. That was another of the things she found amazing about New York.

Matt didn't answer the next morning when she tried to call him before we left for the airport. During the cab ride to LaGuardia, she spun out fantasies of how the world would react to their unprecedented discov-

ery of surviving dinosaurs, how the media would cover
it, what the books and magazine covers would look
like. She'd been thinking about it overnight, I could
tell. She finally made me promise to call Matt when
I got back home from seeing her off.

I stashed his phone number in my address book
when I got back. I wasn't going to call him just yet.
I didn't know if Matt was the kind of guy who made
a practice of seducing out-of-town girls even though
he was married, or if he was just an innocent victim
of Alice's charm, but either way he was leading her
on. He didn't believe in Alice's dinosaurs any more
than I did. There wouldn't be any scientific revelation.
But I couldn't convince her of that. For the moment
Alice was as enthused about Matt as she was about
the invisible dinosaurs. God only knew how long it
would last. All I could do was stand by, like always,
and pick up the pieces afterward.

One thing I'd learned over the years was that when
Alice and a young man broke up, the young man was
always in more pieces than Alice was. And Matt's
pieces were going to be a pleasure to put back together again.

BETRAYAL

by Susan Casper

Susan Casper is a science fiction writer, anthologist, and the wife of Gardner Dozois.

There was no music that morning. Usually he heard it when he set out in the boat. Music in the sad sweet faces of the boys who sat on the edge of the pier, holding their willow rods out to the water, open safety pins inviting unwary catfish home for dinner. Music, too, in the slap and swish of water against his boat, the counterpoint of dipping oars, the heavy staccato of crickets on the bank, and the trilling of morning birds. But on that morning the sounds were all noise. There was no peace in him. He was setting out, once again, to betray an old friend and his heart was hard and bitter with the rightness of it all.

Eldon had been a happy man for most of his life. The kind of happiness that came from having every-thing he needed and not really wanting for more. Somehow he never questioned that she had been re-sponsible. At least, not until now. He had rowed out the morning he met her, angry and confused, with some vague notion of having his boat dashed against the rocks. Thirteen he was. A lonely boy without many friends, he was in trouble at home and not sure why. There had been a note from school accusing him of stealing, but he hadn't taken anything. How angry his parents were, his denials falling on them like rain on the rocks, but he'd show them. When his body washed up on the shore, they'd be sorry. So he left the motor lifeless and rowed the little craft down to the inlet and out to sea, stopping once or twice to throw a line overboard and reel in his catch. It had taken most of the day and the beaches were deserted when he turned and headed past them out to the rocks glowing gold where the sun splashed against their tips.

He found the cave by accident. Half asleep with anger and exhaustion, his boat just drifted inside, into the cool darkness. By the time his eyes opened he was well inside. He'd never known darkness that black before. It was almost as if the sun had turned itself off and all the lights of the town, like the stars in the sky had simply vanished in the night. There was an odor, too. Not the brackish smell of standing water. Oh, that was there, too, but mixed in with it, almost covering it over, was something else. Something somehow musty yet not unpleasant. For a moment it comforted him, but the shadows refused to lift and let in the light, and suddenly he was afraid, his urge to die vanished like the sun itself. He could laugh about it now, what a silly kid he had been, yet even now he could remember how tight every muscle in his body had been with his eyes squeezed shut, waiting to adjust to the dark. Then, after a bit, he could just make out the opening, a softer gray against all the blackness. Then something cut the water between himself and the light. He couldn't really see it, but it arced for just a moment and disappeared with a splash that echoed like a crash of cymbals.

It should have frightened him, but somehow it set him at ease. It was that smell he supposed. Somehow it set his mind reeling with images of mythical beasts and magical places and wishes granted. "Please," he said in a voice so large and resounding that he might have been twenty feet tall, "please make them believe me. Help me out of this mess and I promise I'll never tell anyone about you." He wasn't sure why he said it, or who or what he was speaking to, but he didn't feel silly at all. The moment the words had passed his lips, he felt the fear melt right out of his body. Then, as if to somehow prove his good faith, he tossed his meager catch into the water. Something broke the surface again, this time brushing against the boat and heading it toward the opening. By the time he was out in the sunlight he had turned his motor on and headed for home.

Somehow, as he charged back up to the pier as fast as his boat would take him, he became more and more convinced that he had run into some sort of magical creature, and events at home seemed to bear him out. It was late when he arrived at the house, but far from the anger he expected, his parents seemed truly glad to see him. As for the theft, they'd caught the boy who'd done it. The very boy who'd turned Eldon in.

He went back the next weekend. Under power this time and leaving early in the morning, he managed to arrive while the sun was still high in the east and the sailing boats docked at the inlet still quietly moored to their little bobbing jewels of red and green and blue and yellow. The sky was as blue as any he'd ever seen, with soft sunlit clouds painting cotton dioramas in the sky. It took him a while to find the cave. Blocked from outside view by a shelf of rock, it was visible only once he was actually upon it, and it was obvious, even from here, that no amount of sunlight would ever penetrate into the dark interior. But Eldon had anticipated that problem, bringing a torch and a lantern along. He headed, cautiously, for the inside.

The cave was vast. So large, in fact, that his powerful torch wouldn't penetrate to rock in some directions. It was noisy, too. Much noisier than he remembered. Every sound echoed and amplified over and over again between the rocks and the sea. Even the light slapping of water against the sides of his boat resembled the roar of an avalanche. Nor had he been able to see the colors on his last visit, but now they took his breath away. Everywhere, oil-slicked rainbows that played on the rocks around him. Of that strange smell there was no trace now. No trace either, of the creature he'd seen break water. Still, it was peaceful there. The world might have been light-years away instead of right outside. He took out his lunch and ate it, and then he read by the light of his lantern until it was late afternoon.

She wasn't there the next time he went, or the time

after that, and he began to wonder if he'd ever really seen her at all. Still, the cave was peace itself and Eldon continued to go there whenever the world was too much with him. It was four months before he saw the beast again.

He was reading *Cyrano* when the creature next broke water. He still had that copy of the play, its pages smeared where the ink had run as the beast splashed water on her dive. She was like nothing he'd ever seen before, though it took quite a while before he'd seen enough to feel really comfortable with her features. She was about the size and general shape of one of the smaller whales, a little larger than a beluga, a little smaller than a killer, but that tail and face had never belonged in the whale family. More, she resembled a giant eel, yet in a strange way was much more beautiful than any eel he'd ever seen. She seemed to show no fear of him, and he talked to her softly, again promising not to reveal her secret and throwing her bits of food, most of which she ignored. He named her Roxanne.

Hoping against hope that she really was the mythical beast, he was determined to learn what he could about her. He searched the library at school all week until he found a creature that she resembled. Then he checked again. The mosasaur was supposed to be extinct, but there was little doubt, even from the dissimilarities of the re-creations that this was her family. Her coloring was blue, rather than the brownish-green of the creature in the picture. Her face was somewhat broader and there were fleshy bits that hung down under her chin, but this had to be her. Nothing else even came close.

For the next twenty-five years he kept her secret, though his visits grew less and less frequent. He owned a hardware store now, though it would never make him rich. He'd married his beautiful Mary and together they'd had a son, and even from them he kept the secret that was his alone. And every summer Sunday that he could get away, he spent in the cave. He had a bigger boat now, with running lights that let him see her well, and for her part she seemed to enjoy his visits. Why it was almost as if she knew he was coming, for she was there almost every time he showed up, and though he might be imagining it, she even seemed glad to see him, sporting around and jumping as his boat pulled through the opening. Mary respected his reclusive time. Often, he thought she suspected him of having a lover, and perhaps in a way it was true, for she never asked him anything about those times alone, and always seemed serenely happy to have him home again.

It was the year that the boy started college that things began to change. Expenses were piling up and business wasn't as good as it had been. Malls had opened nearby with big chain stores and discount prices and even on small town streets, homeless people could be seen sleeping under rags in doorways, in cardboard boxes in the park. Even at home money grew tighter. Again he asked Roxanne for help, but this time she couldn't or wouldn't do anything for him. Not that he still believed. Not really. Mary was forced to find work and eventually the store failed altogether. He watched in tears as the goods were sold at auction, thinking of his wife's meager earnings, his son's unfinished education, and he knew right then that there was only one asset left to him.

"I have no choice," he told her as he lifted the camera to his eye with fingers that shook and a heart that was almost ready to falter. But, after all, it had been her own fault. Hadn't he kept faith with her all these years. Where was the luck she had promised. As she leapt up to meet him, his finger stabbed down on the button. Again, and again, and again. He had no food for her this time, and he left without saying good-bye.

He sold the photos. It didn't make him a millionaire, but it was enough to buy a franchise from one of the larger hardware chains. Mary still had to work, but his son could finish school somewhere inexpensive. Now the cave was closed to him. The scientists came. They came by the truckload, settling once and for all the question of where the new state aquarium would be built. Within a very short time it stood tall and shining on top of the cliffs with escalators running down to the cave. The opening they blocked off with bright metal fences, locking Roxanne inside, and along the walls they built a walkway for tourists to stand and gape at the wonderful beast. It was silly to move her when they could study her best where she was. Eldon could only see her through thick, scratched-up glass at $6.00 a visit. He didn't come very often. He couldn't bear to see her that way, swimming listlessly around in a circle. No longer did she splash and play. Too much light. Too much attention.

Things were not going well at home either. He fought with Mary. It seemed that they fought about everything now, more and more often, until finally she left. He wasn't even sure he was sorry. Even work no longer gave him pleasure. Running the store was a chore. No longer were his customers the same friendly neighbors he'd sold to for years, content to wait while he held conversations, gladly willing to overlook a mistaken order, so long as he made it right in the end. These were strangers, impatient and always willing to start a row. He wasn't very good at it, and eventually even that was gone. Damn! It wasn't fair. He was the one who found something interesting, important. He should have had fame, glory, yet he received no credit for it at all. It was those doctors who wound up on talk shows, who wrote the articles in the papers and magazines. It was the big journalist photos that appeared now, his own grainy snapshots long forgotten.

Even the town was different now. The quiet bird songs replaced by hoards of gabbling tourists. Little shops dotting Main Street selling mosasaur T-shirts and little stuffed toys. Nor had he ever gotten the notoriety that he felt was his due. He was the one who found her. He was the one who told the world. Now he was the one who was going to do something about it.

Mooring his boat alongside the fence that now blocked the opening, he climbed the chain-link fence and jumped down to the platform at the side. There were no guards along here. No reason to post them. He ran into no one as he found the door to the now walled-in tank and slipped inside. No one could see him here in the deeper shadows, but somehow Roxanne seemed to know he was there. She slipped off her lethargy like a cloak and made a giant leap out of the water in his direction. He waited until she was close enough, then, raising his rifle, he fired right into her bright blue eye.

She made not a sound, but fell to the water with an uncustomary splash and lay there lifeless, a red pool spreading from her head. He could hear them all heading toward him now, but he didn't care. He threw the rifle into the water and raised his arms.

"I did it!" he shouted triumphantly. "It was me."

'SAUR SPOT

by Kevin O'Donnell, Jr.

Kevin O'Donnell is the author of more than half a dozen well-received science fiction novels.

Cockroaches clustered around the small tin on the kitchen floor, scraping carapaces while they jostled for position.

Gideon Cope let his reading glasses slide to the end of his nose. He peered at the chitinous scrum. Not so many years ago, the patrons of his library had crowded around the checkout desk in just such a manner, all of them equally eager to carry off bits and scraps of nourishment. "His library." He always thought of it as his, for all that it belonged to the people of New York City.

He frowned at the molded plastic device in his hands that had killed his library, then silently berated himself for indulging in sentimentality. The days of real books, bound of paper pressed upon with ink, had passed, and his time with them. No sense in lamenting the lost.

"Mary Ann," he said, in a mild voice almost but not entirely devoid of annoyance, "Mary Ann, the roaches want more poison; they've nearly finished this serving."

"Oh, dear," said his wife, a plump lady with pink cheeks and disarrayed white curls. She set down her scissors, and slid the bonsai juniper she had been grooming to the center of the dinner table. "That was the last of it. I'll have to go next door and borrow some. Be a love and add it to the shopping list, will you?"

Gideon shut off his book and levered himself out of his armchair. "We need a 'saur."

249

"Giddy's all-purpose solution." She grinned at him. In that moment she became again the beautiful botany major he had married thirty-seven years ago. "What we *need* is a boric acid permit."

"I don't know why they won't take our word for it."

"People do lie, you know." She opened the front closet and exchanged her bedroom slippers for a pair of sensible walking shoes.

"About not having children? Two seconds on a computer—"

"Now, dear, children don't always stay with their parents. So the Child Welfare Agency has to come out and inspect the premises in person. And since some people refuse to register their pets, the Toxic Substances Bureau insists on a search by Animal Protective Services before it will issue the permit."

"All this just for the right to scatter a little boric acid on the floor and kill the roaches. When I was a boy—"

"Yes, dear. But times have changed. I can't buy pesticides for the bonsai, either, and the scale's eating them alive." She waved her hand at the miniature plants that lined the windowsills, and huddled under grow lights suspended over almost every flat surface. Nearly five hundred tiny works of living art crowded the apartment; they gave the air a moist, earthy tang. "I explained that this is my livelihood, but it doesn't do any good. We've filed our application. All we can do is wait."

"What's the average wait now, two years? Mary Ann, we need a 'saur."

"Oh, Giddy." There was fondness in her voice, but fatigue, too. "We've been through this a million times. I won't have one of those cold, slimy creatures in the house, rooting through my plants."

"I believe you're confusing 'saurs with earthworms again, my love."

She blinked thoughtfully. "Perhaps I am. But I won't have one of those in the house, either." She gestured to the PDA—the Personal Digital Assistant—that sat on the counter visible through the open kitchen door. "Will you add 'roach poison' to the shopping list, please?"

"I will, I will." Arthritic knees aching, he edged around a three-tier display stand full of azaleas dwarfed in the *mame* style. "The Marshes have a Tee Rex."

"The Marshes have a yard, dear." She glanced into the mirror that hung beside the front door, and finger-fluffed her curls. "And you should hear Louise complain about it. Always underfoot, she says. It sharpens its claws on the living room sofa, makes stinky messes in odd corners of the house, and just the other day, while she was calling Fairfield to dinner, Othie jumped up on the table and stole Fairfield's steak." She shook a finger at her husband. "And you know how well-done Fairfield wants his steaks. No, I won't have that here."

"You prefer roaches?" He flicked on the PDA and brought up the shopping list. In shaky block letters, he scrawled "ROACH POISON" across the slate, and added the "insert" mark. The PDA processed a moment, and converted his uncertain hand to crisp LCD letters.

"They're not *that* much trouble. As long as I keep them supplied with poison, they stay out of the cupboards. And they don't bother my bonsai at all. A 'saur, though—can you imagine the damage?"

"But wouldn't you rather be rid of them?"

"That's impossible, dear; you know that. Roaches have been around longer than humans—longer than dinosaurs, for that matter—and they'll be around long after we're gone. We just have to learn to coexist." She pursed her lips. "Although I *do* wish the EPA would hurry up and authorize that new stuff from Mitsusanto. They say it's had wonderful results in Tokyo."

"But—"

"Really, Gideon." She came over to him and straightened his shirt collar. "I understand what it is to want something you can't have. For me, it's been

horses ever since—" She sighed. "Well. That's neither
here nor there. But be honest with me—aren't you
just using this as an excuse to get a 'saur? If the
roaches truly bothered you, you would have let me
bring home those banana spiders."

Gideon shuddered. "I have a visceral reaction—a
bad one—to spiders that span an area the size of my
palm, and leap about on legs as thick as my fingers."

"They're not really, you know. It only looks that
way because they're so hairy. And you *do* have slen-
der fingers, dear."

"No spiders," he said flatly.

"And no 'saurs, either." She gave him a sweet
smile, and went next door to borrow a cup of roach
poison.

Dinosaurs had fascinated Gideon Cope all his life.
He could not remember a time when he had not
known of them, had not dreamed of them. On the
very day of his birth, his uncle Joshua Mantell, his
mother's older brother, had arrived at the hospital
bearing a stuffed plush triceratops considerably larger
than the infant Gideon. For the next twelve or thirteen years, he had simply not been able to sleep without Toppy cuddled in his arms.

Of course, Toppy had rather distorted his image of
dinosaurs. He had to smile at the recollection of his
horror, when, at age four, he had discovered for the
first time that the real ones had had skins like the
outside of suitcases.

For the first fifty-five years of his life, he had made
do with daydreams and representations. But then the
biotechnicians had found the way to sequence fossilized DNA, to replicate it in their test tubes, and to
let the dinosaurs roar again. A savvy marketing company then convinced the biotekkies to manufacture
clones identical to the originals in all respects save
size. In a matter of weeks, pet 'saurs were quite the
rage.

He had wanted one so badly that sometimes his
teeth hurt from unrequited desire. But Mary Ann

would not permit one in the house. So he played with the neighbors' 'saurs, wandered through the zoo, leafed through the remaining illustrated volumes in the reference stacks, and wished. . . .

Early the next morning, an air-raid siren awakened Gideon. He sat up in bed more quickly than he had done in years. His eyes flew open. His shocked ears adjusted. He realized then that the "siren" had been Mary Ann, screaming.

She, too, had sat up. Almost silent, now, she had horror on her face, and a crackly brown paste on her fingers. When she tried to speak, nothing came out except a panting gasping, "Ah—ah—ah—ah—"

"Mary Ann, what is it, what's wrong?" He worked his left arm behind her waist and pulled her into a tight hug. "It's all right," he said in a whisper. "I'm here, everything's all right, what's wrong?"

She sobbed into his shoulder.

Awkwardly, he rocked her from side to side, stroking her hair and shoulder with his right hand. The position put a terrible strain on his back. If he held it much longer, he'd be in agony all day long. Then he sighed. If he let go of her, she might go into hysterics again. He could put up with the pain.

After five or ten minutes, she calmed to the point where her sobs came softly, intermittently, interspersed with the occasional hiccup. "Giddy, oh, God, Giddy, it was so horrible." She clung to him tightly.

"What was, dear?"

"A roach." She trembled so violently that she nearly put his back into spasm. "I woke up, and this roach was—oh, God, Giddy, it was in my *mouth*."

His stomach lurched at the thought. "Oh, my poor Mary Ann. What an awful way to wake up. Poor, sweet Mary Ann—"

"Giddy—" She pulled out of his arms and looked at him through blood-shot, red-rimmed eyes. "Get the 'saur. Today. First thing. Before you go to work. Don't even drink your coffee. Just get the 'saur and bring it home."

*   *   *

The guy at the 'saur shop, a middle-aged black man with a shaved head and a silver goatee, put his elbows on the counter and regarded Gideon thoughtfully. "Cockroaches, huh?"

"Lots of them."

"You tried boric acid?"

"We're waiting for the permit."

"Hah! I know that routine. How big's your place?"

"Five rooms. Maybe nine hundred square feet."

"Okay, I got something for you. Coelophysis." He straightened up, and walked toward the far end of the store. "Just came in yesterday from Stanford Labs."

Frowning, Gideon followed. "Coelophysis, you say? That's late Triassic, isn't it?"

The guy looked back over his shoulder. "Been doing your homework?"

"Dinosaurs have been a . . . a passion of mine for a long time."

"But you're only getting one now? They've been on the market for five years."

"Well, my wife—" He shrugged.

"Ah." The man grinned. "We got to keep the ladies happy, now, don't we? 'Cause if we don't, somebody else will." Then he looked uncomfortable. "Hey, sorry, man, I wasn't thinking. If you're buying a 'saur now, then I guess you and your wife. . . ." He made a vague, uncertain gesture with his right hand. "Sorry."

"No, it's not like that. We're still together. Just, ah . . . she's changed her mind."

"Yeah? Hey, good for you. What'd you, sweet-talk her?"

"I wish." He shook his head. "She woke up with a roach in her mouth this morning."

"That'll do it every time." He stopped, and pulled on a pair of thick leather gloves. Then he opened a cage door, reached in, and took out a dappled-skinned creature a little smaller than his hand. "Here we go. Coelophysis, a coelurosaur from about two hundred million years ago."

The 'saur seized the shopkeeper's pinkie with its

delicate three-fingered hands, braced its long tail on his palm, and nibbled on his glove.

He winked at Gideon. "These guys are always hungry. Appetites with legs, that's what I call 'em."

"We have enough roaches to keep it fed for a year." He hesitated. "You're *sure* it will eat roaches?"

"Positive. That's what they raised it on. Some of the others, now—" he pointed to the next row of cages— "were brought up to eat ants and termites. The guys over there, mice. Got some Tee Rexes in the back that like rats so much, they make cats look like sissies. Sell a lot of them over to the projects."

"How big will it get?" asked Gideon.

"This is it, man. This is a full-grown adult." He stroked the 'saur's belly with the index finger of his free hand. "The original form ran to about six feet; they've got a few full-sized ones over at the Museum of Living History."

"I know. I go there every Saturday."

"Figured you might." He raised one eyebrow. "So. You want him?"

"It's a him?"

"Yup. Sterilized, though; you know the law."

"Yes. And I'll take it."

"Then you'll need this." From a rack on the counter, the shopkeeper took a small squeeze tube. "Before you touch him the first time, rub this on your hands—and have your wife rub it on hers, too. It won't exactly make him imprint on you, but it's the next best thing. It pretty much burns your scent into his tiny little brain. After that, he'll never bite you. And once he learns to associate your voice with your smell, you'll be able to start training him."

"Thank you." Gideon turned it over in his hands. The label read NO 'SAUR SORES. "Is this included in the price?"

"You bet." He reached under the counter, brought out a plastic pet carrier, and eased the Coelophysis into it. Then he closed the grilled door and latched it shut. "There you go. $499.95. $69.95 for the carrier. And $100 even for the license."

Gideon paid gladly, filled out the myriad registration forms on the shop's PDA, and hurried home.

"Please be careful with that, Gideon. It's not one of mine; it's the Peabodys'—they hired me to root-prune and repot it for them."

"Yes, love." Gideon moved the tray of Chinese elms to the windowsill, and set the carrier in the space the tray had occupied on the kitchen counter. Carefully, he unlatched the carrier door. Mary Ann stood well away, back to the wall and lotion-smeared hands held at throat level in an attitude nearly of prayer.

He winked at her. "I've decided to name him 'Barnum,' because he's a real circus." After dabbing a bit more of the cream on his palm, and massaging it in, he reached into the carrier, scooped out the 'saur, and put him on the counter.

Barnum stood erect immediately. His tail, fully half his six-inch body length, swished back and forth across the counter's tiles. He held his small arms up and close to his chest, as if mimicking Mary Ann's stance. He had a neck like a swan, and a long, thin head with dark eyes set on opposite sides. He cocked his head as a bird does, and regarded Gideon with apparent aplomb.

Gideon gestured triumphantly. "Well?"

Her eyes had widened. "Giddy, it's . . . it's ugly!"

"Ugly?" His heart sank. When he looked at his 'saur, he saw only sleek grace. He had so hoped that she would see it, too, that he had not let himself imagine her responding in any other way. He forced a smile. "Well, you know what they say about beauty and all. Come meet him."

She stepped hesitantly forward. "Is it safe?"

"Of course. That was the purpose of the lotion." Gently, he ran the tip of his index finger along the top of Barnum's skull, down his spine, and along his tail to the very end. The 'saur gave a small cheep. "Don't be afraid."

"But I am," she said plaintively.

He could hardly tell her that he had been speaking

to his 'saur. So he reached out, took her right hand, and drew it toward Barnum. "Let him sniff your fingers."

"Giddy, dear, it's not a dog."

"His nostrils are located in the same place, though."

Her hand quivered as she extended it the last few inches. Barnum pigeon-walked forward. Raising his arms, he grasped her forefinger in his three-fingered hands. She gasped.

Gideon touched her shoulder. "Shh. Stay perfectly still. No sudden moves, no loud noises."

"But, Giddy—"

Barnum opened his mouth wide. Many tiny teeth sparkled within.

"Oh, God, Giddy, it's going to—" She yanked her hand away and ran from the room.

Oh, damn, he thought, then rushed after her. "Mary Ann— "

"No." She turned her back to him. "I didn't realize how horrible it would look. Those beady little eyes, staring at my throat, not blinking, just watching my pulse throb—no, I won't have it!"

Her rejection so disappointed him that he could barely form a coherent sentence, but he had to talk now, before her opinion set like concrete. "Mary Ann, love, he won't hurt you. He'll just eat the roaches. You don't want to go through *that* again, do you?"

She shuddered so hard her teeth chattered. "Oh, God, no, but I can't—I won't be alone with it, Giddy. I will not! I'll go to the black market. I'll get boric acid there. I'll—"

"There, there." He came up close behind her and began to rub her shoulders slowly, gently. "You know how risky that is. If word gets out that you're using chemicals without a permit, will anybody buy your bonsai? And if the EPA catches you, they'll take all your plants. They'll test the soil for contamination. And if they find any—"

"Gideon, I know, but I just can't be alone with—"

"You don't have to be. I'll take him to work with

me. We'll lock him in the kitchen at night. That's when the roaches come out, anyway. And I'll keep him in his carrier when I'm not playing with him. Don't worry, dear. Everything will be all right."

She stayed silent for a long time. At last she drew a long breath. "Gideon, I trust you. It can stay. But. If it ever bites me, I will kill it. I will beat it to death with a hammer and use its bones for fertilizer. Do you understand me?"

"Yes, love, I do." He kissed the hair above her right ear. "But don't worry. He'll never bite you. You'll see."

Gideon spent the rest of the day at the library, doing what he had done every day since the city had closed it permanently. This time, at least, he had company.

First he filled a book cart with the contents of a random shelf. He rolled the cart to the scanning room. He closed the door tightly, opened the pet carrier, and left Barnum to emerge in his own time. Then he began to sell off New York City's cultural heritage.

He opened the top volume to the copyright page. Laying it facedown on the scanner, he pressed the QUERY button. Silently, he counted *One, two, three*—The screen displayed a flawless image of the page. The status line at the bottom of the screen read "Scan complete. Enter corrections? Y N"

He touched "N."

The status line read "Accessing LOCO database."

He yawned; the machine beeped. The status line read "Archive exists."

He nodded. After all these years, LOCO—Library of Congress Online—had an electronic copy of nearly every book ever published in the English language. Still, he never dared take that for granted.

Now he evaluated the physical condition of the book, and entered that information into the system. Whirring, the machine printed title, publication information, and a bar code on a plastic bag. Gideon slipped the volume into the bag, sealed it, and put it on the collection cart.

At day's end, the consignment service would swing by to take that cart, wheel it into a van, and drive it to a warehouse in Hoboken. There each book would sit until ordered by a collector, or a scholar, or even an ordinary reader who just refused to settle for anything but an ink-on-paper copy. The consignment service would ship the book to the buyer, and order its bank to credit New York City's account with fifty percent of the purchase price.

It was a very efficient system. LOCO augmented its archives, New York City turned a cash sink into a money tree, and Gideon Cope drew a steady paycheck.

Barnum pounced on his foot and slapped his shoelace. Gideon grabbed him gently. He lifted him to eye level. "You know something, my very young yet very old friend? I despise this job. I became a librarian because I loved books and wanted everyone to love them as much as I did. Now . . . now they're obsolete, and so am I. I'd quit in a minute if only—" Ah, the eternal "if only." If only every other library in America weren't dismantling itself, too. If only he had another skill which someone would pay him to exercise. If only he weren't just two years from a full pension. . . . "Nice to have you here, though. But leave my shoelaces alone, do you hear?"

Barnum cheeped, and wriggled in his hand.

"All right, all right." He bent over, and released his 'saur. "Check the corners. There should be some nice juicy spiders wandering around in them."

Gideon came home from work that night to find Mary Ann seated at the dining room table, dabbing at the branches of her prize Japanese maple with a cotton swab. "I'm home, love."

She looked up. Her eyes were red; her cheeks, wet. "It's infested. Again!"

"Oh, no." He set Barnum's carrying case on the table and slipped into the chair at Mary Ann's side.

The 'saur immediately stuck his head through the carrier's grilled door and examined the scene with apparent interest. "What's gotten to it now?"

"Scale." She touched the swab to a glossy brown bump on a branch. "Mealybugs." She stabbed a fuzzy white growth in the crotch of two twigs. "Aphids. Oh, damn the EPA! *Thirty-seven years* I've been caring for this. Your mother gave it to us as a wedding present. Now it's—I don't know if I can save it. I can't see all the bugs, I can't reach them, and I haven't got time to take care of this and four hundred ninety-nine others, too." She got abruptly to her feet. "I can't look at it any more. Put it back on the sill for me, will you please?" She headed for the bathroom. "We're going out to dinner tonight."

He never argued with that tone. "I'll set Barnum loose now, then. He was chasing shadows and dust balls at the library, so I'd guess he's hungry."

She opened the bathroom door a crack and looked out. "But as soon as we come home, it goes back in its cage and stays there until bedtime, is that clear?"

"Yes, love, perfectly clear."

Dinner was a disaster. The service was slow; the food, cold; the bill, large. A busboy bumped into Mary Ann as she was rising to leave, and splashed her with iced tea. On their way home, an EPA team selected them, allegedly at random, for a contraband chemical search. Then they returned to their building to find an "Out of Order" sign taped to the elevator.

"There is a bright side to all this." Gideon locked the door and helped her off with her coat.

"A bright side? To the most horrible day of my life?"

"Yes, love." He almost patted her bottom, but realized just in time what a mistake that would be. So he rested his hand on her shoulder instead. "The bright side is—tomorrow *has* to be better."

She made a sound more of acknowledgment than of amusement. "Be a dear and put some water on, please. I have to get out of this dress."

"Ah, you're going to slip into something comfortable, eh?"

"Gideon."

"Sorry." He hung up her coat. "I'll get the water going."

"And put that *thing* back in its cage."

"Yes, dear."

He opened the kitchen door cautiously, just in case Barnum waited on the other side to burst through. The last thing Mary Ann needed right then was a 'saur scampering through her house.

He slipped into the kitchen, looked around—and froze.

Barnum was standing on the sink, his back to the door. His tail swung from side to side. His hands and head were buried in the canopy of the bonsai Japanese maple. Something was crunching between his teeth.

Gideon could have screamed. Of all the things that could possibly have gone wrong at that time and place, this had to be the worst. Mary Ann would explode if she found Barnum eating her plant. And even as he thought that, despair washed over him, for he realized she would explode anyway. She would see the damage the instant she entered the kitchen.

Gideon crossed the room. Barnum pulled his head out of the Japanese maple and twitched it sideways. Apparently Gideon's presence did not alarm him, for he opened his jaws and popped whatever he had in his hand into his mouth. With a high quick chirp, he leaned back into the bonsai.

Gideon reached for his 'saur—

And Mary Ann walked in. "What the *hell* is that monster doing?"

Gideon spun. "Now, before you get angry—"

She pushed past him as though he didn't exist. She raised her fist high.

Barnum brought his head back into view, cocked it to stare at her, and brought his hand to his mouth.

A puzzled frown wrinkled her forehead. She squinted at the Japanese maple. She peered hard at Barnum's tiny hand. Then, slowly, her eyes widened.

"He's eating the scale." She sounded stunned. "And the mealybugs, too."

"He is?" It took Gideon a moment to assimilate that. "I mean, of course, he is. He's a carnivore. And he's just the right size to pluck those bugs out of places that you can't get to." He paused a beat. "Still mad at him?"

"I—" She shook her head.

"All right, I'll put him away, now." He reached out for Barnum—

"Wait."

"Pardon?"

She touched Barnum's shoulder with her index finger. The 'saur's head whipped about. He fixed one dark eye on her. His jaws gaped.

Then his tongue came out, touched the end of her finger, and licked it three times.

The corners of her lips turned up the barest fraction of an inch.

Barnum closed his mouth, leaned sideways, and began to rub his head against the side of her finger.

Gideon smiled. "I think he likes you, Mary Ann."

"Do you now?" she said softly. "Do you really?"

But she wasn't looking at her husband as she spoke.

PTERI

by Lea Hernandez

*Lea Hernandez is a successful comic book artist and writer;
this is her third science fiction story.*

Hi. I'm Gelesse Sampson. Thanks for visiting my
shop. Have a seat. Tea? Is it made with lizard's eyes?
What kind of witch do you think I am? Nobody in his
right mind would drink something like that anyway.
I have Orange Zinger and Wild Forest Blackberry.
Orange? Good.

Careful, it's hot. Now, what—Pardon? I don't *look*
much like a witch? Hmm. If you're used to the
scarves, bells, and hoop earrings, pseudo-empath
type, I don't suppose I do. My left ear *is* double-
pierced, and I did the second one myself.

But you didn't come to listen to me tell you about
how I mutilated myself when I was stoned, did you?
What do you need? Something to cheer your home?
Something to cheer you? For you. You haven't been
able to write or paint for weeks, and you want something to help.

Oh, dear. I don't have anything to help you with
that. Wait, don't go. Look, no good witch will take
your money, give you a charm, or a bunch of flowers,
or whatever, and promise you that it will bring back
your painting and writing. Nobody's talent for creating
works that way.

Why don't I tell you about Pret? Who's Pret? I'll
hear about this later, I'm sure. Pret is my familiar.
Pret! Don't drop your tea, he's only a little pteri. A
dinosaur? Well, I suppose as much as you and I are
monkeys. A petite descendant of the mighty pterodactyls. He is pretty, isn't he? Vain, too. Show your

wings, Pret. All the colors of a rose. We almost didn't
find each other. Or, really, *I* almost didn't find *him*.

Would you like to hear about us? How much? Tell
you what: if what I tell you helps, you do a painting
of Pret. You noticed the pteris over in that corner,
didn't you? I made them. Why are the wings on the
papier-maché one broken? Are you ready to find out?

I've had what a friend called "pteris on the brain"
ever since I was a little girl, almost as long as I knew
I wanted to be a witch. I drew them, made them out
of clay, and jumped out of trees trying to fly like
them. I'd beg for dinosaur coloring books if there was
one page showing a pteri or pterodactyl. I lived for
them every second I wasn't living to be a witch. When
I found out that witches could have familiars, I knew
I would have a pteri, and from that day I lived to be
a witch *and* have a pteri. I just *knew* when I Called
my familiar, a pteri would come.

Wasn't I afraid I'd get a stego? I never thought
about it. The warlock you heard about that has a stego
Called one, believe me.

Why a pteri and not a cat or a fox or a unicorn?
Unicorns are for prissy girls who didn't get horses.
Really! Besides, by the time most witches or warlocks
are ready to Call their first familiar, they don't, um,
qualify any more. If they last that long, they usually
don't make it past the first serious boyfriend or
girlfriend.

Anyway, I ate, slept, breathed magic and pteris. To
this day, I don't think my parents understand this passion of mine. They *do* understand that the shop is a
success, and I'm happy, and that how much money I
make is *my* own business. You understand this, I can
tell.

When I was little, my parents would laugh when I
told them I would be a witch. Later, they said nothing.
Still later, my father made fun of me when I practiced
Craft, or tried to show him a new pteri I had sketched
or folded from a square of paper, and my mother
would sort of follow along. I don't think they meant

to be mean, they just had no idea what to do with a witch. I stopped sharing my dreams with my parents, and then with children my own age. Children can tell when you're ashamed of something, and it turns them into playground terrorists. I learned to keep my mouth shut. I took all the classes in the Craft I could, and drew pteris in my notebooks when I was supposed to be diagraming sentences.

By the time I was trying to earn a degree in Craft at a state school, I had become completely closed off. I still wanted to be a witch, and I was good at it when I *tried,* but something was missing.

I had lurched my way through most of my degree program and was well on my way to becoming a third-rate lifetime apprentice to a second-rate witch or warlock. Technically, I excelled, but hiding myself for years had made me frightened. Instead of being happy that I was finally with people with the same interests, I was bitter, surrounded by students who had never once in their lives heard someone suggest (or *insist*) that there was no future in being a witch.

The time finally came when I was supposed to Call my familiar. For a witch, this is like a final exam and graduation in one. The preparation for a Call proves that you know your Craft, and a Call answered shows that you're ready to practice it. A Call is also like blabbing on sodium pentothal. You find out who you are.

I spent months dipping rose-scented candles, studying the moon, and eating the right food. When I was finally ready, I had the span from a new moon to full moon to find my pteri.

I drew my circle and set my candles, and let my mind wander. I drifted back to when I was a teenager in middle school. I was walking next to a boy I had had a crush on, and I had decided to talk to him. He had brown hair that curled into a big cowlick over his left ear. When I started to talk, though, the only thing I could think of to say was about his hair. Men do not have a monopoly on unfortunate opening lines.

"You sure have funny-looking hair," I said.

"You sure have a funny-looking face," he answered, and stomped off to class. I knew I didn't have a chance, though, when he started dating a cheerleader named Felicity.

Crushing embarrassment and the memory of being utterly humiliated drove me back to the present. The candles had whiffed out.

On the next attempt, I tried to help myself focus by sculpting a little pteri, and dressing it up with a necklace of tiny paper roses. I drew the circle and set the candles once more, and, clutching the miniature pteri I had made, let my mind wander again.

This time, I remembered when I had made a papier-maché pteri for an art class. Yes, the one on the shelf. You took art classes in junior high, right? Remember all the jocks and nascent drug dealers who took those classes for the easy grade? Sort of a universal phenomenon.

I had made this pteri for an extra grade. I paid for the materials with carefully saved babysitting money and meager allowances and lunch money. The wings were the best part, made of silk I had dyed to show the changes of color from red to salmon to gold. I carried it into class, pleased by the commotion it caused among the other students.

Later in the class, I had to go to the bathroom. I didn't take the pteri with me because I had no reason to. When I came back, it was gone. Trying to act casual, I walked around the room. Maybe it was on the teacher's desk. Nope, not there. Behind someone's back? Nope. By the time I was to the other side of the room, I could see what had happened. It was under my desk. I walked back as slowly as I could stand to, and knelt to retrieve my pteri.

My *broken* pteri. The wings had been snapped, the twisted wires that were left stuck out like the ends of bones in a compound fracture.

"Who did this?" I stared at my classmates. Nobody looked any guiltier than the person standing next to him.

"It was an accident," one of the kids mumbled. "It fell."

It fell. It was all the explanation I would get until, months later, one of them told me the class bully had done it, because he could.

I fell for real, out of the trance for the second time. The candles had snuffed themselves again. I unfolded my hands. The little pteri was still there, unbroken. The roses were a little crushed from the pressure of my palms. I smoothed them carefully and cried.

Remember what I told you about a Call showing you what you're really like? I was finding out that I was nothing but a bundle of sour memories. I sulked during the day, and cried at night. My pissing and moaning drove my roommate in the dorm to sleeping on the lawn.

Out of compassion for my roommate, another student volunteered to talk to me. She was a journalism major, so I got right on my high horse, and explained my problem by alternating between being snotty because she wasn't in Craft, and abject self-pity. She didn't seem to listen too much, or notice that I was being patronizing. She picked up the pteri with the rose necklace.

"This yours?" she asked.

"Grumpf," I replied.

"I don't really understand your problem, then. If you can make beautiful things like this, then there must be something positive in you. You're just feeling sorry for yourself."

"Grumpf." I snatched the pteri away from her.

"You're the one who should be sleeping on the lawn, too."

She left quickly when I pretended I would put a curse on her. I didn't want her or anyone else to see me cry.

The moon was nearly full, and my candles much shorter than when I started. I knew if I didn't find my pteri soon, I would have to start the whole process again, and I wasn't sure I had the guts.

That night, I put lavender in my pillow to help me dream about my grief.

I dreamed I was in the clearing of a woods, at night, during a full moon. The trees were that secret green that only happens in the spring, leaves and trunks limned with a glowing white, shadowed with water-color indigo. In this clearing was an old-fashioned desk, (Yes, a *desk*. Come on, it was a *dream*.) not as old as the kind that had a desktop attached to the back, but the kind where the top opened.

I walked toward the desk. As I got closer, I could smell chalk dust, flowers, and the blue scent of fresh mimeograph copies. I squeezed myself into the little seat, and opened the desk. There was a sheaf of mimeo pages inside; grade-school reading lessons, spelling tests all marked with As, coloring pages. Under these was a bundle of seven dried roses, petals shaded from yellow to deep pink. And under the roses was a pteri made from construction paper. Is it the one on the shelf? Wait and see. It had a comically large head and feet, and a little stick was glued near the top point of the right wing. I had no idea what any of this meant, I just knew I felt, well, *good* somehow.

A fluting cry made me look up. Silhouetted against the pearly circle of the moon was a flight of pteris, dart-shaped heads and transparent wings. One would sing, then another, then another.

One. Good. Thing.

One. Good. Thing.

Re. Mem. Ber. One. Good. Thing.

A fluttering at the edges of my vision obscured the pteris and the moon, and I woke up. I was immediately stabbed with disappointment at not having the construction-paper pteri with me. I pushed that feeling away, and remembered the feel of the papers, and the incense of the dried roses.

One good thing.

I only had to remember one good thing.

* * *

The next night, I lit the candles, and tried not to notice just how short they had become. The waxy perfume of the smoke reminded me of the roses from my dream, and the world dropped away.

"You have to find roses that are small, and haven't opened yet."

I was twelve, and learning how to dry flowers. The person helping me was my sixth-grade teacher, Miss Goode. She was young, she didn't dress conservatively like the other teachers at school, she was a practicing witch, she liked me, and I worshiped her.

"Tie them in sevens with white string, and hang them someplace dry but not hot, and where the air can move all around them. Right by the window is good, don't you think?" She smiled at me. "I think you have a talent for this, Gelesse. Don't give up."

How could I give up? Miss Goode believed in me. She had seen that I didn't belong in the "slow learners" reading group. ("Slow" in my grade school was expectation code for "future juvenile delinquent." The kind of kid who would later break fabric wings because he could. I felt a wash of pity for him.)

She brought in books from the public library to supplement the school's meager cache. I didn't think much of the books about people swooping to the rescue on big fire-breathing dragons, since I knew that wyrms crawled most of the time, and nobody would want to sit on one. But I adored the books about punks and elves living together in cities on the edge of elflands, and the book about how a rock-and-roll band saved the world from evil faeries, and the story of a sailor-poet who returned to her lover after hundreds of years in space.

When the roses were dry, Miss Goode showed me how to bundle them with gypsophila for artists, and how to use the ones that broke. Petals for potpourri, stems soaked and bent to make wreaths for a kitchen. Nothing was a failure with her. I learned to make the best of everything. (How did I forget? I don't know.)

Once, the students in her class had an assignment to make paper animals for mobiles. I, of course, was making a pteri. Like the one hanging from the lamp over there. Tongue clenched between lips, I cut head, body, wings. Even though the pteri would fly from a string, I added feet big enough so that it could stand. When I looked away, another student sat on my pteri. I laughed and straightened out the bent wings. I went to the window and broke a twig off a bush, and glued it to the right wing, giving my pteri a magic staff to protect itself from further squashings.

Nothing was a failure. Straighten those wings and fly.

One. Good. Thing.
One. Good. Thing.
One! Good! Thing!
One good thing!
ONE GOOD THING!

I was back in my circle. Something was flapping at the edges of my sight, someone was singing One good thing! The candles were flaring incandescent, the points of the flames impossibly high, making the translucent fluttering petals glow red, salmon, gold. I threw out my right arm to clear away the colors, and delicate feet caught my hand. *One good thing!* There was an urgency to the song now, a request for acknowledgment.

"One good thing!" I cried, and promised to never forget again. The candles blazed one last time, and eclipsed to sparks, leaving me in the light of the full moon, the pteri clutching hand and shoulder, cooing *one good thing* as I laughed and wept.

Look, Pret, the mail came and there's a package that has the smell of our artist friend on it. Why is it so important that it's only been a week? The story about you and me always works because it's true, silly lizard. One good thing, my sweet. Here, you can have the string and the paper.

CHAMELEON

by Kristine Kathryn Rusch

Kristine Kathryn Rusch is a Campbell Award winner, a Hugo and Nebula nominee, and the editor of The Magazine of Fantasy and Science Fiction.

Wilhelmina crept inside Mrs. Anderson's room, and sat there, with the lights off. Outside the windows, snow fell in big white flakes, faster and faster, so fast that Willi couldn't see the teacher's parking lot just across the sidewalk. The chameleon paced in its little cage. The mama gerbil had her back to the cold, and the papa gerbil, in his own glass world, watched the snow as Willi did. The snake cage was open—the boa constrictor was still missing—and the mice were crowding their own cage in its absence. The rabbit sat on a table up front, nibbling on a carrot and staring at Willi with beady eyes.

Willi didn't mind. She felt safe here, in the humidity, with the smell of too many furry bodies. Even with the boa constrictor on the loose, popping out of the duct work, and scaring the principal as it had done the day before.

Everyone else was waiting out the storm in the auditorium. Willi hated the auditorium. She would rather wait here, with the animals.

The snow had started that morning, after gym. The principal made an announcement, saying it was too dangerous to drive. The radios had already announced that the parents should *not* try to pick up their kids. Everyone would spend the night at school, if they had to, and Mrs. Bates, the cook, would make them something extra special. Lucky she did at lunch, because the electricity went out just before math. The clock behind Willi's head still read 1:15.

Willi wasn't scared. She knew her mom would come anyway. A storm would never stop her mother.

The animals didn't seem frightened either. They liked the quiet, just like Willi did. She was glad to get away from stinky old Greg Matson, and weird Dougy Spencer. The kids hadn't stopped picking on her since she had come to school two months ago, just after Thanksgiving. They made fun of her clothes, and when she went into the bathroom and zapped herself into new ones, the kids stopped laughing and no longer even looked at her. Sometimes they called her a witch, and she couldn't even tell them to stop because that was what she was.

She brought her knees up against her chest. When she had told her mom about it all, her mom had said that Willi shouldn't want to be like the other kids. Willi didn't agree until a week later, when the teacher took them to the natural history museum, in the history of science building attached to the grade school. (Her mom had enrolled her in a university lab school, thinking that smart kids would be kinder than the dumb ones Willi had studied with in Kentucky.) The kids laughed and pointed at all the dead animals, stuffed and frozen in their glass cages. The bobcat had moth holes in its fur, and just beneath the surface, Willi could hear a faint whisper of memory, begging to go free. She wasn't powerful enough to free the bobcat, so she sat in front of the cage and cried.

And had been called Crybaby Witch ever since.

Outside the wind howled, and a bit of cold seeped in through the windowpanes. The rabbit's fur ruffled. Willi whispered a protect spell and blew it at all the animals. They looked up at her, as if in gratitude, and she blew them a kiss.

She wished she knew where the boa constrictor was. It had always been her favorite. She liked its long slimy length, the power in its straight body, the alien coldness in its black eyes. Maybe, if she used dust magic, she could find it.

She whipped the dust into little particles, and sent them searching, but the snake wasn't in Mrs. Anderson's room. Willi slipped out into the hall. Maybe the snake did travel the duct work like the principal said, and she would find it in someone else's classroom.

The hallway was dark, darker than she had ever seen it. The lockers stood like soldiers at the Air Force Base where she had lived with her daddy just before he died and her mother decided to stay for good. The window displays beside each classroom's door had lights glowing on the contents. The hearts Willi had painstakingly cut with scissors because her mom told her not to show her powers glowed redly. Something moved in the fifth grade's display case, and as she walked by, she saw the boa constrictor, its body flaking and dry, wrapped around a Peek-a-Boo doll.

It hadn't been eating school mice as Mrs. Anderson had said. It had gotten itself trapped. And it was dying.

Willi glanced up and down the hall. She didn't see anyone. In the distance, she could hear singing coming from the auditorium. They had been singing all afternoon in the fake generator lights, away from the storm. Willi thought that everyone would be hoarse by now. She saw someone cross the hall and disappear into the boys' room. She was as alone as she could be.

She ran back into Mrs. Anderson's room and got two mice, begging their forgiveness. She wasn't too fond of mice—they ate their babies, just like the papa gerbil did—and that made her mad, but she wasn't sure she wanted to kill them. But, as her mom would say, creatures ate each other. That was the way of the world.

Willi hurried back into the hall with the mice trapped in her pockets. She sat on the floor and raised her fingers, making a small turning motion. The thin silver lock guarding the display case clicked and the door swung open. The snake nearly fell out. Willi flattened her hands like a bed, and let the air carry the snake to her. She eased the snake down and put the mice in front of it. She made an invisible barrier so that the mice couldn't run away. The snake looked up at her, its cold cold eyes actually seeing her for the first time, and then it snapped a mouse between its oversized jaws.

Willi stood. She couldn't watch this.

Greg Matson stood behind her, his face white as the bunny's fur. "You *are* a witch," he whispered. "And I'm going to tell everybody that you stole the snake and you're killing mice."

"I did not!" she said. "It was dying!"

But he had already taken off, running down the hall, his Nikes slapping against the tile floor. She couldn't let him tell. She couldn't. The kids hated her bad enough. But if the teachers thought she'd messed with the snake, she would never go into Mrs. Anderson's room again.

Never see the rabbit again, never hold the chameleon and watch its personal magic. Never be safe.

Without thinking, she raised her hand and bid the air to tie Greg's feet. He tripped and skidded along the tile, finally landing outside the auditorium. He sat up and flopped his legs like a fish. Then he started screaming.

The principal burst out of the auditorium door, his short rotund frame crouching over Greg. Willi put a hand over her mouth. She had made it worse.

The snake had swallowed the second mouse and was slithering against the wall, trying to hide. Willi glanced around. The principal would see her. Anywhere she went, he would see her, and she had already used her magic quota for the day. She was trapped.

She turned and ran down the hall, past the doors to the gym, past the music room and into the narrow hallway where the grad students had their tiny offices. All the doors were shut and locked. They must have gone home before the snow hit.

The end of the hallway smelled of paint and formaldehyde. Willi burst through the double doors leading to the natural sciences building. She spun around the corner, and found herself face to face with a stuffed bear. She stifled a scream. The bear was so old, its fur had no whisperings at all. She ran past it and all the other dead animals, until she found the hall of the dinosaurs.

Her teacher, Mr. Hayes, hadn't taken them in there. He had pointed at the dinosaurs and laughed. "Those models," he had said, "were made in the 1950s, before I was born. They're out of date and wrong." But they had looked great to her, tall majestic beasts, with green skin and eyes as cold as the snake's.

She didn't hear anyone behind her. Her heart was pounding in her chest, and her breathing was coming hard. She hurried into the dinosaur room, and snuck around the big green dinosaur in the middle. The dinosaur had a long neck and a tiny head that was staring at the door. She touched its flank. The dinosaur was made of plaster of paris. It was cold and hard.

She sank on her knees and leaned against the dinosaur's leg, waiting for the principal to find her.

She didn't know how long she sat there, in the dust and the dry-smelling heat. No one had walked on this side of the dinosaur in a long time. Her tennis shoes had left patterned footprints on the floor. Her jeans were covered with a white and green powder. It took a moment before she realized that the dinosaur's legs were peeling.

Willi touched it, and more dust dropped onto her hand. She couldn't imagine being so old and out of date that no one even tended her. Poor dinosaur. She leaned her head on the plaster of paris, and listened, but heard no whisperings, no hope, no feeling of being trapped like she had gotten from the bobcat.

The dinosaur wasn't dead. It had never been alive.

Somehow that made her very sad. She brought her knees up to her chest and tucked her chin against them. Ice pelted the side of the building, sounding like rocks thrown against a concrete wall. No one had come after her yet. Maybe they hadn't seen where she had gone. She was used to her mother, whom no one could ever hide from.

Willi got up and dusted off her jeans. She wandered to the back of the dinosaur room. Other dinosaurs stood against the wall. A rounded one, with a big head, and an armor plated back, had lost all its covering on one side, revealing a mesh frame. The pterodactyl (her favorite and the only kind she had heard of) was missing one wing. Maybe Mr. Hayes hadn't brought them here because the dinosaurs were in such bad condition, not because they weren't up to date.

Maybe she would stay here forever. The dinosaurs didn't care who she was. They were different from all the dead animals, just like she was different from all the other children. Her mom said she had to blend in, learn how to get along with humans. But Willi didn't want to blend in. She wanted to save a snake without Greg Matson telling on her, and she wanted to talk to the rabbit without people thinking her crazy. She wanted to free what little life she had found in the bobcat, if she could only find a way.

Her mom made it look so easy. Everyone thought her mom was normal. They didn't know that she made dinner by pulling out the groceries they had bought for appearance's sake, snapping her fingers, and setting out serving trays. They didn't know that she changed her hair color without going to a beautician. They didn't know that she didn't work for a living because she had all the money she had earned on horse races since gambling became a craze in Atlantic City.

No one could put anything past her mom, but her mom could put stuff past them. That, her mother had said, was what Willi had to learn.

What Willi had failed to do this afternoon.

She sighed, and coughed as dust got into her lungs. No one would come for her. She would rot in this back room with all the non-dead dinosaurs. Half of her wanted to get found. Half of her wanted the principal to kick her out.

The other half wondered who would take care of the animals if he did.

She wandered back to her hiding spot and touched

the side of the dinosaur. This time she did hear whisperings, but like nothing she had ever heard before. Voices. Voices were trapped inside the dinosaur.

. . . is too. They get really big and they stomp all over everything and eat people . . .

. . . I'm going to get on its back and it'll take me away, like Danny and the Dinosaur . . .

. . . If only I was as big as you. Then they wouldn't hit me any more . . .

The voices were small, light. Children's voices.

. . . It is too real. You just can't see it. It comes out at night and watches us while we sleep. . . .

. . . and it was really hot, and all they got to do was eat and sleep, and hunt. . . .

. . . I don't know why I like 'em. I just think dinosaurs are cool. . . .

Willi moved her hand away. The dinosaur's head had turned just a little. It seemed to be smiling at her. What lived inside it were fantasies, beliefs, fears, and it held them dear. She leaned her head against its side.

"I'm sorry that you're flaking," she whispered. "If they let me come back tomorrow, I'll have enough magic to fix you."

The dinosaur's smile grew, and the voices swirled around her, almost too fast to catch. It took a few minutes for her to realize that some of the voices she was hearing were coming from the hall.

She let go of the dinosaur. The children's voices disappeared. Only two adult voices remained.

". . . saw her in the middle of the hallway, feeding the snake. We don't tolerate theft in this school, Mrs. Ramsey." The principal's nasal voice echoed. Willi ducked against the dinosaur's leg.

"Of course she fed it." The voice was her mother's. The tone was one of exasperation at a stupid human being. "The snake was dying. It must have been a hard choice for her. My daughter loves animals. She had to sacrifice mice to keep the snake alive."

"We don't know that the snake was dying, any more than we know that your daughter ran this far. This area is forbidden to children—"

"Mr. Caldwell, I have had just about enough of your prattle," her mother said. "I know my daughter's mind. If she's going to hide, she's going to hide well. And what I said about the snake is pure logic. You said it's been loose for a long time—a fact I find appalling—and I assume there are no mice or rats in this building, except for the ones in cages. Now, I don't know how long a boa constrictor can go without a meal, but it stands to reason that the thing would not be in good health."

They stopped outside the door. Willi saw their feet swirl the dust. Her mother was wearing her black cowboy boots with their four-inch heels. The principal had on his good leather shoes, the ones without the scuffs.

"I must be frank with you, Mrs. Ramsey. Ever since Willi came here, she has not fit in. She spooks the other children and she does strange things like she did this afternoon. I don't know what she said to Greg Matson, but he was so frightened that he couldn't move his legs for the longest time—"

"Mr. Caldwell, my daughter is brilliant and talented and unusual. I thought an experimental school like this one would be a haven for her, but you're like the other teachers in this country. You only care about making her normal. Well, she's not normal and she never will be. Perhaps you should concentrate on making the children better individuals instead of better clones." Her mother took a step into the room. "Willi?"

The yell was for show. Willi's mother knew where Willi was, and Willi knew better than to stay hidden. She snuck out around the side of the dinosaur, wishing it could protect her. But it could only listen and absorb her hopes and fears.

Her mother's hair frizzed in all directions, and her leather coat hadn't a speck of snow on it. The principal looked rumpled in his black suit.

Her mother said, "Willi, are you all right?"

Willi's hands were clenched in small fists. "I didn't mean to do anything wrong. The snake was just trapped, and I was trying to help it, and Greg Matson is so mean!"

"It's all right, honey. You're not coming back here." Her mother held out a leather-gloved hand. "Let's go."

"I must protest," the principal said. "There's a blizzard out there. You may have made it here safely, Mrs. Ramsey, but you'll never make it home, not with the child."

"Try me," Willi's mother said. They started down the hall, Willi's hand tightly wrapped in her mother's. "By the way, you might want to catch that snake. It's stalking Willi's favorite rabbit."

"How—?"

"No!" Willi shouted. She broke free. "Stop it, Mom. You've got to stop it." She ran down the hall, around the corners, past the bear, past the offices, past the rooms, until she reached Mrs. Anderson's. The snake had made its way under the desks to the table in the front. The rabbit was washing its face, all unaware. Willi scooped it up and hugged it to her chest, burying her face in its warm, musky fur.

"It won't get you," she whispered. "It won't."

She whirled and climbed on the table, leaning against the windows, against the swirl of depthless white. The rabbit trembled in her arms.

Her mother and the principal appeared at the door. The principal saw the snake, turned and hurried down the hall. "Willi," her mother said. "You're being silly."

"No, I'm not," she said. "This rabbit's just like me. Nobody likes it and nobody protects it."

"You protect it," her mother said as she came into the room, gingerly stepping over the snake. She stopped by the window and tapped the chameleon's cage. "You would do a better job if you became like this little fellow. Blending into your environment, but never losing track of who you are."

"That's what you yelled at him about."

"Mr. Caldwell?" Her mother smiled, making her entire face look no older than Willi's. "No, honey.

He wants all children to goose-step in place, to be the same creature. In the real world, snakes, rabbits, and mice all share the same plot of ground, but they have to be careful of each other." Her mother glanced around. "You're right. This is a very safe room. No wonder you like it here."

Willi leaned against the window. The glass was like ice against her back.

"Here, let's put that snake back so your rabbit is safe." Her mother clapped her fingers and the snake floated across the air. The lid on the cage came open, and the snake lowered into it, gently. Then the lid went back on.

Slowly Willi set the rabbit down. The rabbit scampered a few feet away, then huddled, as if it still wasn't over its fright.

"Let's go home, honey."

"No," Willi said. "They'll wonder how we did it."

"It's all right. You're not coming back."

This would be the fourth school she'd left in the past year, and the only one with animals. Willi glanced at her rabbit, at the chameleon, at the snake. The dinosaur in the next room needed her help, and the animals needed her protection. She didn't want to leave them, no matter how mean Greg Matson was.

When the snake had run away, it had nearly died.

"No," Willi said. "I want to stay."

"I thought you didn't like it here."

"I like some things," Willi said. She liked Mrs. Anderson and the animals. She even liked that back room, filled with dust and dinosaurs. She especially wanted to see the dinosaur again. "Maybe I've been too much like the rabbit. Maybe it's time to see what the chameleon can do."

Her mother smiled and hugged her. "Fitting in isn't what matters. Being true to yourself is. You're not a rabbit, honey."

She knew that. But she wasn't a chameleon either. She was a big green dinosaur, the kind that didn't exist by human standards, made of strange materials, and filled with fantasies, beliefs, and fears.

She put her arm around her mother, and they headed to the auditorium. They would stay. They would suffer through the singing and the cold food, and maybe Willi wouldn't fit in, maybe she wouldn't be normal, but maybe for a short time, in the dark, in the storm, the other kids would think she was one of them.

FELLOW PASSENGERS

by Barbara Delaplace

Barbara Delaplace is the author of more than twenty stories, and was a 1992 Campbell Award nominee.

So I'm a reporter for *The Blatant Inquirer*—you want to make something of it? It's steady dishonorable work and pays medium bucks. Lots of writers would be happy to be sitting in front of my word processor, believe me; the wages I get for the fictional "reality" I produce at *The Blat* (a little in-house joke there) is a lot better than what they make for their mid-list novels. Plus I don't have to pay for my caffeine—your basic drug of choice for any writer, whether she takes it hot and black or cold from a soda can. What more could a writer ask?

Well, sure, a little respect from my fellow journalists would be nice. You know, I was the first reporter on the scene that summer when the dinosaur first appeared from wherever (or maybe *when*ever—the scientists are still arguing about that one), but nobody noticed. Once the mainstream media picked up the story, who had time for a tabloid? Nobody's too happy about it winding up in the zoo, of course, but where else can you put a real live dinosaur? You just can't have it roaming free, no matter what those animal-rights idiots say. I don't want *anything* equipped with a manicure and dental work like that running around loose.

My covering the story made sense at the time (not that we had anything resembling a science reporter on staff, you understand). For one thing, nobody realized what we were going to be dealing with. I mean, who gives a damn about a bunch of cattle ranchers out in the boonies complaining about livestock losses? Happens all the time. That wasn't news.

Except that then they began to report sightings, too, of something that sounded like it belonged in one of those time travel stories. That *was* news. Or so my editor figured, the day he called me into his office.

"It's probably just some guy trying to make a fast buck from the tourists, but you may as well go check it out. We haven't had a good monster story in a month."

"It's a long drive out to the valley, boss. And all the company cars are in use right now." At least I hoped they were. "You know, it might take me a couple of days to get the whole story." I paused meaningfully.

He sighed. "Okay, okay, we'll pick up the tab for your mileage and motel." He emphasized the word "motel." "I don't want to find out *after* the fact that you've stayed at the local equivalent of the Waldorf again. Got the picture?"

I agreed there would be no undue waste of the paper's valuable money and got out of the office while I was still ahead. At least I'd get a couple of days or so in the fresh air, away from the city smog.

After a brief stopover at my townhouse to pick up my always-packed overnight bag, I headed up the valley toward ranch country. And it was beautiful country, too: lush fields surrounded by the ramparts of the mountains. It was hard to imagine there could be anything worse than an occasional cougar wandering down from higher country to stalk the herds pastured there.

But it turned out there was. The ranchers hadn't been exaggerating at all, as I found out when I visited the local feed store. ("Jim Logan, Owner and Operator," said the sign over the door.)

"Look, ma'am, this is no laughing matter, despite the way it may look to someone from the city," said the proprietor, a stocky gray-haired man. "I know one guy who's lost half a dozen head of cattle, and a few more that have lost two or three."

He was sincere and serious, so I responded in kind. "My editor figured it was someone trying to fake a monster appearance to draw tourists. Mind you," I smiled, "he's a city type like me. He doesn't know the area."

"He doesn't know *this* area, that's for sure. We're just working folks here. All the tourist trade is farther south. Why would a guy risk six months' profits for tourists who don't even know we exist?" Put that way, it made a lot of sense, I had to admit. "Besides," he continued, "I know the folks who've seen the thing. They're good reliable people, not the sort who yell 'wolf.' "

"Mr. Logan, do you suppose you could introduce me to a few of these people? Maybe someone who can show me some tracks? My editor likes pictures with his stories—you know the type." I grinned conspiratorially at him.

He grinned back. "Sure can. Tom!" he shouted to a weather-beaten man in denims who'd been browsing at the back of the store. "This lady's from one of the city newspapers; wants to find out about the stock killings." He turned back to me. "What was the name of your paper again?" Typical—our marketing department should work harder, I reflected.

Shortly after that I was being tossed around the passenger seat of Tom's pickup, clinging to armrest and dashboard as we barreled down the dirt road to his ranch. He was going to show me where he'd found the remains of one of his cattle, but as we bounced along, I decided he also harbored ambitions of becoming the local equivalent of Emerson Fitipaldi.

"You don't worry much about speeding tickets, do you?" I asked as we pulled up in a swirl of dust.

"No point in wasting time." He grinned at me as I climbed out of the cab on slightly unsteady legs. "Carcass's a bit of a walk from the main house," he said, pointing. "Do you good after all that sitting."

It was more than "a bit of a walk," but once we got there even my untrained eye could see the tracks around the body didn't belong to anything I could imagine. Huge, three-toed tracks. I studied one particularly clear print while focusing my camera. Didn't those marks in front of the outside toes suggest claws?

As for the body itself . . . well, I was sure our readers would love the black and white pictures, squealing in horrified fascination as they read the article to one another. Me, I had to gulp hard to keep down my lunch while snapping the scene in full color. It didn't seem to bother Tom much, though. He was upset about losing a valuable head of stock—I knew enough about beef prices to know that ranchers were having a very hard go of it right now—but he was happy to tell how he'd found the carcass two days earlier. "Nope, no sign of anything around," he said in answer to my questions. "I just stumbled over the body, but whatever killed it was gone."

"Aren't you a little nervous having something that can do that kind of damage roaming around?"

"Haven't seen anything around here yet that can stand up to this," he replied, patting the rifle he'd brought along.

I wasn't so sure. Whatever it was had made a hearty meal from the dead cow, but there was enough of the body left to see huge slashes ripping through the hide into the flesh beneath. What kind of thing could leave marks like that?

Tom drove me back to the feed store (breaking his previous land speed record in the process) and I thanked him for his help. "Always glad to help the press. When'll the story be printed?"

"It depends on my editor, but I hope it'll be in our next issue, on the stands next Monday."

"Well, I'll sure be looking for it. Say, what did you tell me your paper was called?" Mentally, I winced.

With Jim Logan's help, I tracked down and interviewed several other ranchers who'd lost cattle, though not as recently as Tom. None of them had ever seen tracks like these before, and all of them wanted it dead, whatever it was—the sooner the better.

I also talked to people who'd caught glimpses of the

creature. Jim had been right; they didn't strike me as the usual publicity-hungry loonies you tend to see in my job. And their descriptions agreed to a disturbing degree.

"It reminded me a little of one of those tyrannosaurus rexes, with all those teeth and walking on two legs. Only it was a lot smaller."

"All I saw was this big head with a lot of sharp teeth. No, I didn't wait around. I went into the house real quick. What d'you think I am, crazy?"

"It walked on its hind legs and had three claws on each foot. And let me tell you, the middle claw was enormous."

"Well, it sure looked like some kind of dinosaur to me. It had a long straight tail, and it walked upright. The rear feet had some kind of big spur poking up in front."

There was some speculation on where it had come from, and a lot of interest in when they'd see their names in the paper. ("What was it called again?") They, too, were anxious that it be killed.

I was getting uneasy. It was beginning to sound like there really *was* some sort of prehistoric creature wandering around here. *Something* out of the ordinary had killed those animals, no doubt about it. I thought about enormous claws and huge gashes in dead cows, and decided I didn't want to spend several days in the area doing research after all. The city seemed a lot more attractive than I would have believed possible earlier that day, and I headed home with a distinct feeling of relief.

The editor was pleased to see me back so soon; it saved him from another shouting match with the folks from finance. And he loved the story-complete-with-photos I produced, putting it on page one ("Cattle Killer Terrorizes Ranchers!").

We might have been there first, but we weren't there with the most. The city's major daily did a feature a day later. I guess one of the people I talked to *did* recognize the name of *The Blat* and decided he wanted his name in a newspaper with a higher circulation and a better reputation. It was the middle of summer and a slow news week, and they really played it up. They ran it at the bottom of page one complete with a sidebar interview with one of the university's paleontologists speculating on what kind of dinosaur it might be. (Something I should have thought of—I slipped up.) There was even an artist's sketch, which I studied closely. It fit the eyewitness descriptions to a T. Or maybe I should say to a "d," as in deinonychus, the breed the professor suggested. He said the name meant "terrible claw," and it was appropriate. Now I knew where those awful gashes had come from.

Of course, the radio and TV people picked the story up, and for a while there the feed store was News Central, there were so many reporters hanging around it.

My editor was annoyed. How the (expletive deleted) was he supposed to produce an (expletive deleted) tabloid when the (expletive deleted) mainstream press was doing *his* (expletive deleted) story, he roared at us during a staff meeting. I offered to go back and do some follow-ups, but he turned it down. Relieved, I didn't press the point. I didn't really want to go back there at all.

Well, it appeared some of the researchers at the Zoological Gardens didn't share my feelings, because they decided to have a go at capturing the beast. Or maybe some rancher called them and offered to lead them to it for a fee; the Gardens staff has always been conveniently vague on that point. Certainly they'd learned their lesson after the debacle two years ago over obtaining new killer whales for their aqua-park: they waited a few weeks until media interest died down before they went after it. The first the public knew was when they informed the press that with the help of a freshly slaughtered goat, a sturdy cage, and BCS ("Bring 'Em Back Alive") brand tranquilizer darts, their new deinonychus was safely ensconced in its new home in the zoo.

I went down to the Gardens to see it, along with what seemed like most of the city. Those witnesses—

and that artist—had been absolutely right. It *did* seem kind of small for a predatory dinosaur, after the reconstructions I'd seen of tyrannosaurus and allosaurus—it was only about eight feet long, and a lot of that was stiff, inflexible tail. But it was plenty big enough for my tastes: the large head had a very efficient-looking mouthful of sharp teeth, and there were equally efficient-looking talons on both front and back feet. The "terrible claw" that earned the creature its name was terrible indeed: it must have been a good five or six inches long, and it stood up from the middle toe on each hind foot. It never touched the ground and always looked razor-sharp.

Its color surprised me, but I guess I hadn't thought of dinosaurs as being anything but brown. This one, at least, was a deep vivid green, shading to warm yellow on the underparts. In the summer sunshine, it gleamed like burnished leather. There was a gay orange patch on the throat, which made me wonder if perhaps it had a throat sac that could inflate, the way some modern lizards do.

But what surprised me most of all was the aura of alien, watchful vitality it projected. It never stopped moving, and each movement was quick and purposeful. This was no dimly aware reptile wandering sluggishly through existence. When this creature looked at you (and it *did* look *at* you), you *knew* it was fully aware of what it saw: an enclosure, keeping it in. Prey, defenseless and frustratingly out of reach.

It made me shiver every time our eyes met. I was glad it wasn't free.

But in another part of my mind I wasn't glad. It always bothered me to see wolves, big cats, and the like in zoos. They should be out roaming free, the way they were meant to. I found myself feeling the same way about The Claw. (That was the nickname some news hound christened it with, and it was the name that stuck. At least it had more dignity than some of the others. I just couldn't see calling something as beautiful and terrible as that "Dinah, the Dinosaur.")

I wasn't the only one who didn't much like the idea

of it being in the zoo, although I didn't see we had much choice. But there were lots of people who had no doubt at all that The Claw should be freed. As the summer turned into fall, they began holding protests and rallies at the Gardens. I remember one demonstration in particular, organized by a group called Freedom for Animals, because I was there. On my own time, of course—protests aren't bizarre enough for *The Blat*.

There was a group of about thirty people milling around in front of the dinosaur pen, chanting and carrying signs that said things like "Free The Claw" and "Living In A Cage Isn't Living." (Not that it was *in* a cage—it was a large outdoor enclosure—but I suppose it's the sentiment that counts.) The leader was being interviewed by a TV reporter, easy to pick out because of the brilliant camera lights shining on them. And all this unaccustomed activity seemed to be affecting The Claw; it was moving restlessly around the enclosure, watching the crowd with predatory intensity. I edged away from the armor-glass windows, and closer to the camera crew so I could eavesdrop over the group's chanting.

"And you're demanding the Zoological Gardens set the dinosaur free, Mr. Nolan?" the reporter was saying.

"That's right," Mr. Nolan replied. "We feel it's cruel and inhumane to keep a noble creature like this imprisoned. It should be living the life nature intended it to live, hunting down its prey, not eating dead meat that someone has already butchered."

"But where should it be released? After all, it *is* a dangerous animal." The interviewer waved a hand toward the compound, where The Claw had stopped pacing and was crouched slightly, swaying back and forth.

"That's a typical human-centric view. To us, it's a threat simply because it killed a few cows—cows which are insignificant compared to this incredible creature. But in nature, there's always balance, with each species fitting into its niche in the ecosystem. If it were released into a national park, it would—"

Suddenly The Claw roared and charged toward the barrier with terrifying speed. (I guess the sight of all those potential dinners on the hoof unbalancing the local ecosystem was too much for it.) The protesters scattered, and I scattered right along with them. But it pulled up short of the windows set in the cement walls and glared at the panicky crowd. It roared again, then turned and stalked away, toward the rear of the enclosure. The rest of us tottered off with a good deal less dignity, wiping our collective brow.

After that, the zoo officials got a court injunction to prevent the demonstrators from gathering in front of The Claw's cage. Not surprisingly, the groups didn't put up more than a token protest. But they got more and more vociferous in their demands that the deinonychus be freed. Other people, like the ranchers, were just as adamant that it *not* be freed. After all, they pointed out, this animal was a dangerous killer. And all the time, the Gardens was drawing huge crowds—people were coming from all over the world to see it. Scientists were lining up hip-deep for the chance of a hundred lifetimes: to study a living dinosaur.

I don't know what the outcome of the whole debate might have been; the rhetoric was getting more strident on both sides. The animal rights groups were talking of taking the Gardens to court. The Gardens threatened to take The Claw off display. The groups retorted the Gardens would never do that—they were pulling in too much money from the record attendance. Zoo spokesmen responded that, yes, attendance was high, but their budget was in fine shape, and while they welcomed the crowds, the Gardens was concerned about the effect the cooling fall weather was having upon The Claw.

From what I could learn from my sources (don't ask; a reporter, even one from the lowly *Blat*, has friends in surprising places), that last was more than a PR ploy. The zoo really was concerned about the coming winter and wanted to construct a heated enclosure for the dinosaur to use if it felt the need. In fact, they did remove The Claw from its pen to temporary quarters in a nonpublic part of the zoo, in preparation for the renovations. Naturally the green-niks had a field day with that. So, I'm sorry to say, did *The Blat*: "Claw In Jeopardy: The *Real* Reason They're Covering Up!" Some days I wondered if there wasn't a better way to make a living.

It was planned as a temporary measure. And then Fate, in the form of graduate students Michael Thompson and James Warnecki, stepped in.

The Gardens are still tight-lipped about the whole thing, though they did admit that, as members of a bona fide research group studying at the zoo, the two had no problem obtaining entry into the grounds whenever they wished—including at night. And the temporary dinosaur quarters were a bit off the patrol's beaten track. Given a little time, I guess a hundred pounds of tranquilized deinonychus wouldn't have been too difficult for two men to handle. (Not that I'd have wanted one in the back of *my* pickup.)

All anyone knows for sure is that next morning, instead of a dinosaur, there was only a hand-lettered sign in the pen: "Liberty at last! Deinonychus Freedom Tour '93." Also a signed statement from the two grad students, proudly announcing their feat.

My editor was delighted and called me into his office. "There'll be panic. That means all sorts of rumors and false sightings. People will be dying to talk to the press. Bring me stories. Go." I went.

Of course, he was right. Animal rights groups were cheering. Nolan, the spokesman of Freedom For Animals, told me, "This is a blow against the unjust imprisoning of innocent animals for useless display to human beings. Now it's living a natural life, a life of freedom." When I asked if it was a good idea to have a dangerous predator loose heaven-knows-where, a possible danger to innocent bystanders, Nolan berated me for my unenlightened point of view.

Gardens officials were fuming and swearing judicial vengeance upon the perpetrators: "Thompson and

Warnecki will be prosecuted to the full extent of the law. They've done a disservice to our thousands of visitors, eager to see a one-of-a-kind animal. They've done a disservice to the many scientists visiting our facility, eager to learn all this animal can teach about a group that reigned supreme longer than any other on Earth. And they've done a grave disservice to The Claw itself. They claim to have freed it because they loved it and couldn't bear to see it cooped up in a cage—but they've freed it as winter is approaching, which a dinosaur is biologically unequipped to deal with. We fear they may have 'freed' it to die a lingering, unnecessary death from cold and starvation. What kind of concern for a fellow creature is that?"

Strictly off-the-record, a staffer told me they were also seriously worried that if there was any damage or injuries caused by The Claw, the zoo would be liable and lawsuits would follow.

City residents were scared to death they'd find one very hungry dinosaur lurking in their backyards. "I'm *sure* I saw it last night out by the garage," said one woman. "The police ought to be out there tracking it down." I refrained from asking how they could track a dinosaur when they had no idea whether it had been released in the city, the next county, or in another part of the country entirely. The latter, I found myself hoping fervently.

"What kind of idiots would let loose a dangerous animal like that?" one man asked me. I had every sympathy with him; I was edgy every time I walked near any cover large enough to hide a deinonychus.

The ranchers promised to shoot on sight anything with teeth that showed interest in a fresh beefsteak dinner. "We've lost enough stock as it is," Jim Logan, the feed store owner told me when I went up the valley to do interviews. (A day trip, believe me.) My friend Tom the Racing Rancher happened to be there and agreed with him. "I know a couple of folks who've already missed loan payments and the bank is ready to swoop in and foreclose. A bunch more are on the edge. We just can't *afford* to lose any more."

All of this kept me churning out stories as fast as I could type.

You know what finally happened. Thompson and Warnecki hadn't been complete fools; they'd released The Claw in the state forest, one of the largest in the country. But it didn't stay there for long. The zoo officials had been right: it wasn't comfortable in the increasingly cool weather, and started wandering, seeking a warmer place to live. There was also speculation by some that it was looking for more of its own kind, since deinonychus was a social dinosaur—it lived in small packs, the way wolves do. For some reason, that really got to me. It didn't occur to me that something as vicious looking as The Claw might be lonely, but I guess that's because of my human-centric thinking. The thought of that creature looking and looking, fruitlessly, for its fellows . . .

The Claw must have traveled pretty quickly, because it wasn't long before there were reports of sightings from towns south of the forest. As soon as more concrete evidence showed up—in the form of three-toed tracks and several dead sheep with big slashes on their bodies—the Gardens staff was ready. They packed up the cage, the tranquilizer gun, and a couple more slaughtered goats, and off they went.

You know what did the trick? A battery-powered heater. My source told me, "We just set it up on the off chance it might help keep The Claw near the carcass, once it had found it. Well, it ignored the bait completely—just curled up around the heater and basked there. We didn't have any trouble darting it."

So The Claw came back home. Well, to as much a home as it'll ever have. Did you know the last passenger pigeon that ever existed—they called her Martha—died in a zoo? I think about that when I go to the Gardens now.

After all the shouting, I find I agree with the eco-types: this isn't right. I watch it pace around the enclosure with that restless, frightening energy, and this isn't where it should be. But I don't know what else we can do for the last deinonychus. Where it *should* be no longer exists, hasn't existed for millions of years. The Earth has changed beyond measuring since then and it doesn't fit in anymore. It no longer belongs on the world that gave it birth. And it'll die alone, never again seeing another of its kind, just like Martha. The conclusion, the closing of a species.

I guess it'll only be free the day it dies and its spirit flees the prison of the flesh, to join those of the passenger pigeon, the saber-tooth cat, the woolly mammoth. Fellow passengers.

I know that this individual, particular extinction isn't my species' fault, but it makes me want to weep all the same. I've learned again a lesson I knew before, one I've known ever since I became a journalist: for some problems, there just aren't any satisfactory solutions.

Fly soon, fellow passenger.

THIRTEEN WAYS OF LOOKING AT A DINOSAUR

by Gregory Feeley

Gregory Feeley, who wrote The Oxygen Barons, *here offers a meditation—half fiction, half essay—on What Dinosaurs Mean to Us.*

1.

The dinosaur is a remarkably recent idea. Although humanity has been imagining dragons for millennia, the shaping events of our civilization—the Renaissance, the European discovery of the New World, the French and American Revolutions—all took place generations before the notion of an Earth once dominated by giant reptiles was proposed. The first dinosaur fossils were unearthed in the years following the Napoleonic Wars, and their significance emerged amid the upheavals of the Industrial Revolution. The word itself was only coined in 1841.

No one can say why the coiled and great-winged serpents of both Chinese and European antiquity have exerted such a tenacious hold on the human imagination. Jungians might suggest that memories of the Cretaceous' great dinosaurs have left some imprint on our collective unconscious, although this would require that great aquifer to have accumulated trickles since our days as tiny mammals scurrying between sauropods' legs. Carl Sagan speculates that humanity's dim view of dragons might derive from an instinctive fear of dinosaurs inherited from "manlike creatures who actually encountered Tyrannosaurus rex." If the fact that ancients in numerous cultures conjectured up great mythical reptiles while the bones of real ones lay beneath their feet is only a coincidence, it is a resonant one.

Having joined human culture late, dinosaurs have quickly established themselves as icons of remarkable versatility and durability. Dinosaurs have served as metaphors for a surprisingly wide range of phenomena (more on this later); they emblazon gas station signs, billboards, and magazine advertisements; their adventures fill comic books, cartoons, movies, and popular literature. Almost every male science fiction writer with a large body of published work has written a story about dinosaurs—but so has Michael Crichton, whose best-selling *Jurassic Park* was published by Alfred A. Knopf and shelved far from the science fiction section. No other prehistoric creature enjoys a remotely similar cachet.

The nineteenth century seems the natural age for dinosaurs. An expansive era fascinated with great powerful engines and the exploration of dark continents, the nineteenth century discovered that the Earth was hundreds of millions of years old; that buried strata contained evidence of early ages more astonishing than those described in the Bible. That the Earth left records of its past activities, which could be recovered and read, was a suitable and pleasing discovery to an age that did not know indeterminacy. Those enormous reptiles, who thrived and then gave way to fitter creatures, spoke eloquently to that era, which believed that superior specimens should naturally prosper and expand. Dinosaurs were practically Victorian.

But why does *our* century love dinosaurs?

2.

Noasaurus might be the deadliest predator to walk

the face of the Earth, but its eggs were being eaten by tiny mammals. Leona stared at the scattered shells incredulously. Rats, almost certainly: the Central Park Zoo was full of them. If Pest Control didn't keep vermin out of the Mesozoic Compound, these lizards would go extinct all over again.

Jack the Ripper (named in a contest by a Brooklyn third-grade class) was looking at her with speculative intelligence. The torpid indifference of the stegosaurs and diplodocus always lulled her, so the intensity of the noas' interest came as a shock. The tyrannosaur at the Berlin Zoological Gardens would actually snap his teeth at the spectators, prompting shrieks and shivery news clips.

The noasaurs scorned such wasted effort. Jack, who had noticed the observation panel near the nest, was invariably there when Leona checked the eggs, observing his observers. His willingness to meet her gaze was unnerving. Sixty-five million years lay in those centimeters of superplex paneling, and Leona was glad for every one of them.

And so on. The story would be set in an extension of Central Park carved from the decaying blocks north of 110th Street (an expedient I expect to see proposed someday), so that Harlem's scarred facades surround the dinosaur exhibit on three sides. The dinosaurs themselves were to have been resurrected through a technology that extracts genetic material from fossils, a plot device Crichton was not the first to use.

The rats infiltrating the zoo compound prove to be a secondary problem; the real conflict involves a gene-splicing kit taken from a visiting biochemist who had been mugged. It falls into the hands of a bright Harlem teenager, who uses it and the accompanying computer disks (which contain the genetic catalogs of all the saurians genotyped by the Massachusetts Institute of Technology) to cook up some dinosaurs of his own. Soon the refuse-strewn streets of upper Manhattan are overrun with cat-sized ornithischians, who eat rats, cockroaches, and garbage, and prove harder to eradicate than anticipated. In the end everyone settles down, dinosaur mesh over their windows, to wait for winter.

Such a story derives its motive power from the incongruity of its central image—dinosaurs on the streets of Manhattan. Additional interest can be generated by subplots: that noasaurus will have to escape, or at least threaten to; and any writer who cannot dramatize an urban family's morning encounter with a dinosaur in the bathroom should be drummed out of SFWA. But the arc of the story's trajectory, once begun in its early paragraphs, can be traced by an imaginative reader. A dinosaur set loose in a contemporary setting is a windup toy, Godzilla in prose. If we wish to understand the romance of the modern dinosaur, we must look elsewhere for its appeal.

3.

The plane banked sharply, and I looked out the window to see the payload billowing into a fine cloud as it spread over the herd. By the time it reached the ground the aerosol had dissipated into mist, but you could see the aetosaurs' heads turn as it settled over them. Great saurian snouts lifted into the air, and the charging beasts began to slow, as though puzzled by a sudden recollection.

Lisa clutched my arm. "Gil, I think it's working!"

I brought the Cub around for a second pass. The upraised reptilian heads, so inexpressive except when snarling, were cocking at odd angles, and a few of the larger males had begun to mill aimlessly. As we watched, a scuffle broke out among a group of younger ones. None of them took note of the plane.

"*Something's* happening," I said, not daring to hope.

Within seconds the momentum of the surge began to break up, like a storm wave crashing into invisible barriers. Several of the males were heeding their olfactory cues and attempting to mount the nearest females, which provoked a savage response. The females, baffled and irritated by the behavior around them, were glaring at each other suspiciously.

A half-grown cub, gender unknown, stood in a clearing staring at the behavior erupting around it with the frightened incomprehension of a child whose world is coming to an end. Despite my exhilaration, I could feel a moment's sympathy for the creature.

"Look," cried Lisa, pointing. "They're starting to turn back!"

She was right. At the trailing edge of the herd, some of the stragglers, evidently frustrated at the congestion in front of them, had turned around and were heading back the way they had come, straight toward the shimmering light on the horizon. Perhaps they were older adults, immune to the hormonal frenzy now convulsing their juniors.

"Now they're *all* turning around! Gil, we've done it!"

"*You've* done it, Buttercup," I replied. I was trying to keep excitement out of my voice. "If the entire herd goes back through the timegate, temporal equilibrium will be restored. Then the weather might return to normal."

She laughed, giddy with relief. "Who would have thought that a poetry-spouting bush pilot would prove decisive in repairing a breach in the spacetime continuum?"

"We are the unacknowledged legislators of mankind," I said. I depressed the autopilot switch and leaned toward her.

"Whoa, Gil! That stuff only works on reptiles."

"We're all dinosaurs on some level," I replied. "As the poet says:

> "*A man and a woman*
> *Are one.*
> *A man and a woman and a dinosaur*
> *Are one.*"

4.

But, of course, that isn't true. It is preadolescent
boys who like dinosaurs, just as preadolescent girls
may develop an interest in horses. A fascination with
dinosaurs, widespread as it is, remains skewed toward
young males, or males who were once young.

Girls want to ride horses, but boys want to *be* dinosaurs. Dragons may seem related to dinosaurs in popular culture, but the most beloved dragons around,
those of Anne McCaffrey's novels, are basically leather-
winged horses, ridden by humans dressed in boots and
jerkins who enjoy such telepathic rapport with their
mounts as the books' predominantly female audience
can only yearn for. The quintessential dinosaur-loving
kid, on the other hand, is the comic strip's Calvin,
who imagines his hometown in every sand castle he
tramples.

Dragons are often intelligent, and sometimes can
speak: small wonder that amity, even cooperation, can
be imagined between our kind and theirs. Dinosaurs
are, almost by definition, a primordial force: destruc-
tive, intractable. The one novel I know of to bring
together the two creatures, Roger Zelazny's *Road-
marks*, tellingly unites a female dragon with a male
dinosaur. ("He's not much on brains," she confides,
"but what a body!")

Perhaps the dinosaur's popularity derives from its
power as a symbol of boisterous male energies in a
post-chauvinist society. If so, it is an apter symbol
than Calvin perhaps appreciates. As even five-year-
olds know, dinosaurs stand for something else as well.

5.

An outline for a third dinosaur story:

A pair of seventh century Chinese alchemists are
alerted to a discovery at a quarry: the bones of an
unknown creature, embedded in limestone. The alchemists, who are under a commission from the emperor
to discover an elixir of immortality, recognize the

bones as reptilian. Reporting to the Imperial Court that the skeleton of a fabulous dragon has been discovered, they are able to pique the emperor's interest; and a crew of skilled artisans, carefully brushing away at the fragile find, is able to uncover the skeleton with minimal damage.

The reality of dragons is doubted by no one in T'ang China, but the alchemists, who are of a more empirical bent than most, have long noted that no one has ever reported seeing a dragon, and that paintings of them over the centuries differ crucially in matters of detail, in apparent conformity with changes in artistic fashion.

The alchemists soon grow obsessed with their skeleton. A broader excavation turns up two more sets of bones, both fragmentary and inferior to the first find, but also very different in size and morphology. The alchemists are confronted with what appear to be three different species of dragon, one of them quite small. The nearly complete skeleton, moreover, suggests, after patient sorting and assembly of its jumbled parts, a dragon with a tapering neck and an alarmingly small head. No wings are visible, and its massive rib cage suggests a hulking, plodding creature.

The pair undergoes a crisis of the spirit. While the emperor grows impatient at their lack of progress, each finds in his discoveries the seeds of his intellectual undoing. The younger alchemist, who scouts the mountains for likely deposits of cinnabar, is disconcerted by the layered depths at which the skeleton was found, which suggests that the world sits atop the dust of earlier ages, and that the sacred mountains may thus be less than eternal. Worse, he has observed bands of sediment bent like hairpins, intimating mutability in the foundations of the Earth; and recognizes that his dragon, so disturbingly shaped like a manatee, could have sustained its bulk only in flat wetlands.

The elder alchemist, learned in matters of pharmacology, has examined the teeth of the fabulous skeleton, and concluded uneasily that they strongly resemble the flat teeth of weed-chewing water buffalo.

Fossils of ferns and fishes have turned up in the limestone, which no dragons are thought to consume. And
a clutch of smashed eggs, long turned to stone but
plainly the shape of turtle eggs, hint bluntly at unceles-
tial means of propagation.

The two colleagues go on a tear, drinking themselves stuporous on Court wine and falling, after a
long melancholy discussion in which they express their
distinct misgivings, into soggy slumber. Acquainted
with each others' data, they share the same dream: of
grotesque waddling dragons that comport themselves
like lizards, lively in the sun but sluggish otherwise.
The sinuous neck that the alchemists have pondered
dips into marsh water, and the tiny head rises trailing
dripping fronds. Lizard-dragons of other shapes caper
on the shore, reptile tongues darting as they hunt insects and each other across sacred mountains that have
slumped into the concavities of a swamp.

When they wake, in late afternoon, their downfall
is complete. Functionaries from the Imperial pharma-
copoeia have confiscated the dragon bones and ground
them up into a powder, to rekindle the emperor's
waning sexual appetites. The alchemists are disgraced.
Weeping, they pack up their mortars and alembics,
bereft of past and future alike. Overhead, an archipel-
ago of clouds stretches across the sky like the recon-
structed skeleton, then slowly twists into an elongated
swirl, graceful, serene, and aloft.

What I like about this story probably constitutes its
major liability: the dinosaur exists only in the reader's
mind. One sees it only by stepping outside the charac-
ters' points of view; otherwise we have simply a historical short story (most uncommercial of forms), lacking
even a real dragon. By most criteria, the story would
better fit an anthology about alchemists.

This is my kind of dinosaur: a dinosaur of the mind,
as Macbeth might have put it. There is, let's face it,
no other kind.

6.

Nevertheless, dinosaurs stalk our fiction with increasing regularity; and most are native-grown. The remote Pacific island from which Godzilla (who, despite his fiery breath, is more dinosaur than dragon) hails is essentially the same Lost World that Conan Doyle and others imagined as a sanctuary for yesterday's monsters. Dinosaurs are found in Africa, South America, Loch Ness, on various islands, and at the Earth's core. Sometimes they are brought in through timegates or created in a laboratory, but writers retain a fondness for discovering their dinosaurs *in situ*, an expedient they pursue in this shrinking world to the limits of their ingenuity.

Is that it, perhaps? Do dinosaurs inhabit everyone's Land of Lost Content?

7.

Strong and enduring metaphors usually prove to suggest a number of things, many of them dissimilar or even antithetical to each other. The rising and setting of the sun has been likened for millennia to both the passage of seasons (which will recur in unending cycles) and the course of a man's life (which will not). High school students compare poems to note how the woods can be a symbol for life (Dante), death (Frost), familiarity (Wordsworth) and the unknown (Carroll). Critics have pondered for some years how the metaphor's arrow sign cannot be made to point in one direction only, a linguistic quandary far from most dinophiles' concerns.

The dinosaur's primary metaphorical burden has always been its most immediate attribute: that it is dead. Anything vanished from the Earth (or overdue for extinction) has somewhere been likened to a dinosaur: the outmoded automotive plants of Detroit are dinosaurs, as are disliked political parties, deadwood in upper management, and old farts impeding artistic movements. No opprobrium is usually attached: these fossils are simply old, their day long gone.

Interestingly, a few decades ago the obsolescence of dinosaurs held a distinct tinge of moral reproof. Dinosaurs had passed from the scene because they had *failed;* new conditions had arisen, to which the mighty creatures had neglected to adapt. This view of dinosaurs closely parallels Gibbon's popular view of the Roman Empire, and the Durants—middle-brow explainers of history and its tidy morals—may have been partly responsible for both. Books and magazine articles of the post-war years consistently portrayed dinosaurs as mighty creatures overcome by decadence, heedlessly enjoying their mastery of the Earth while the first snowflakes fell, or as enterprising mammals, full of get-up-and-go, ate their eggs.

This last view has come upon hard times itself, as evidence mounts that a planetary cataclysm—a meteor strike, or at least an eruption great enough to fill the upper atmosphere with ash—may have ended the Mesozoic era. The meteor theory, controversial for a decade, received what appears to be confirmation in August 1992 when the presumed site, long suspected to lie beneath the Yucatan Peninsula, was confirmed. Dinosaurs, it seems, vanished after a calamity that human civilization would be hard-pressed to survive.

Another trait that the dinosaur has been employed to suggest is stupidity. Those mammals were not just warm-blooded and quicker; they were *crafty,* and more than equal to knocking off those hulking but tiny-brained brutes.

This notion seems to derive from the concept, long taught in elementary schools, of evolution as progress: each new species was an advance upon the last, with man emerging at the end of a succession of steadily more upright habilenes the way a big American car, all fins and shiny valves, stood at the end of a progression of ever-improved vehicles starting with the horseless carriages.

While this conceit never had any scientific validity— yes, people knew in the 50's that the cockroach had been around for hundreds of millions of years longer than the dinosaurs, and promises to outlast humanity—it plainly suited the times, an era in which America had emerged as the undisputed world leader after a ruinous clash between old empires. Besides, its truth was self-evident: are not mammals smarter than reptiles?

To which the answer is: No, not necessarily. Dinosaurs, it turns out, were not especially stupid; they may not even have been cold-blooded. The walnut-brained saurischia (such as our poor alchemists found) may have been dull; but the more birdlike ornithischia, which included such daunting predators as deinonychus and velociraptor, were evidently quick-witted and even cunning.

And, of course, dinosaurs suggest savagery, an unforgiving Nature red in tooth and claw. But there were thousands of species of dinosaur (according to Peter Dodson, who estimates at least a thousand genera), as various in their habits as mammals are. Some species are even suspected of nurturing their young: out goes the image of neglected nests for those early mammals to find.

Turn a moment's thought to dinosaur as metaphor and the creatures' figurative power, strong as it is, breaks up like spectra, which shine prettily but convey little energy. Dodos were stupid (and are dead); saber-toothed tigers were savage; woolly mammoths vanished from the Earth owing to a manifest failure to adapt. Yet none of these creatures (save the dodo) possesses anything like the dinosaur's hold on our imagination.

8.

Some nights Marty was overcome with the desire to take Rex off the lot and walk it around outside. Stride past the security gate, rear up so that the cars on Santa Monica Boulevard could see the enormous teeth gleaming just under the sodium lights. Of course, studio security was terrific on this stage, as few knew better than he. But then he would realize that his knowledge of the successive layers of the system, which he had helped set up, peculiarly suited him to circumventing it, at least for a few hours. And the idea of a dinosaur joyride would stealthily take form.

Days were long and arduous. Marty was inside Rex by 5:30 each morning, and would often emerge only twice over the next twelve hours. Enough of the shots involved Rex stomping or clawing his way through the same routine, lasting only seconds and repeated through endless takes, that he sometimes wondered why they had wanted a human inside rather than an easily programmable micro that could follow the steps perfectly.

But then Kevin would frown at the choreography of some shot, and ask Marty (who could hear through earphones wired to pickups in the beast's own ears) to improvise a bit of footwork, or try for a touch of exasperation as Rex snarled and batted at a swooping copter. Then Marty would understand why he was sweltering inside a sixteen-foot mechanical dinosaur like a puppeteer swallowed by his creation. The terrible lizard would shuffle through a few steps; Kevin would frown and make a suggestion; and Marty, an itch beginning to form between his shoulder blades, would think: When I was twelve, I would have killed to be a dinosaur.

Maintenance on Rex took hours every night, and sometimes Marty stopped by after dinner to oblige the techs and take the beast through a test run. Sitting alone afterward, enjoying a cigarette in the vast dark space of the sound stage (No Smoking In This Dinosaur), Marty would find himself thinking of taking Rex out for a spin.

9.

Well, you can see where this story's heading, at least in the next scene or two. It's a dinosaur story, but it's postmodern—we see the artifice right out front. And the author doesn't have to try to make time travel sound plausible, or explain how a laboratory that had worked for years to breed a tyrannosaurus didn't make sure it had a strong enough cage.

And it promises that staple of all modern dinosaur stories: a tyrannosaur in the city, snapping at phone lines and stepping on sports cars. True, it's not a real one, but the populace won't know this, which allows for plenty of mayhem yet with a comic undertone. Marty, though an adept technician, will be in some ways quite the anti-dinosaur, which a subplot (involving his personal life) will demonstrate. And you can bet Rex is going to run into a twelve-year-old kid; this is Hollywood.

Such a story allows a fair amount of play for the author: Marty can be a schlemiel, or find in his Rex suit the path to self-realization: liberating the inner dinosaur. Stories about cutting loose have an unpredictable element: even the canny reader doesn't know whether it will ultimately be about returning to one's senses or letting go.

But even this story turns out to be about the end of an era. Film makers still use complex robots such as Rex because computer animation has not yet achieved sufficient power to fool the eye in sophisticated action scenes, but this will change. Full-scale models such as De Laurentiis' King Kong and the giant tyrannosaurs being used in the filming of *Jurassic Park* will become expensive and picturesque curiosities. Rex is a dinosaur in more ways than one, and I am sure that Marty knows it.

Is it possible to write a dinosaur story that doesn't turn out to be about obsolescence and extinction? Even a funny one?

10.

Cruikshank's Allosaurus

"A poet was to my father a sort of nondescript: yet whatever added grace to the Unitarian cause was to him welcome. He could hardly have been more surprised or pleased if our visitor had worn wings. Indeed, his thoughts had wings; and as the silken sounds rustled round our little wainscoted parlor, my father threw back his spectacles over his forehead, his white hairs mixing with its sanguine hue; and a smile of delight beamed across his rugged cordial face, to think that Truth had found a new ally in Fancy!"

—William Hazlitt
"My First Acquaintance with Poets"

Folks claim that the great monsters said to live in prehistoric times are bushwah, born of godless scientists with a theory and a jumble of old bones, but I don't take much stock in what people who boast of reading only the Good Book say. They insist that giants lived in those times, but not giant reptiles; yet I've seen the assembled skeletons arching across high museum spaces, and nobody has turned up the remains of a giant man yet. If there were giant men living then—and I believe there were, and are today—they were giants in some other sense, invisible to the senses of prosaic, mundane people.

During the long Sunday afternoons of August, I would drive out on the narrow roads that wound behind the San Gabriel Mountains to the tumbledown house where Erastus Cruikshank was building his allosaurus in the yard. Mrs. Cruikshank was standing on the porch, hands set reprovingly on her hips as she watched Cruikshank scurry over the half-covered framework like a small bird cleaning a crocodile's back. She would shake her head wearily, then see me and bring out a pitcher of lemonade and two tall glasses. We would talk a minute or two, and then I would carry the filled glasses across the expanse of unmowed lawn to the carriage house where the allosaur was taking shape outside its yawning, half-hinged doors.

"Great stuff, vegemite," Cruikshank would say when he noticed me standing beneath the edifice, the glasses held forth like an offering. "A kind of yeast extract; Australians spread it on their toast. They call it Marmite in New Zealand, although I couldn't tell you why. Responsible for the persistence of marsupials on the Australian continent, and you will note that both land masses have or had large, flightless birds. Also good for lubricating ball joints, which is why I buy it by the case. Hand up a jar, would you?''

I set down the glasses and pulled a jar from the box at my feet, but Cruikshank had already disappeared into an opening in the chest of the benignly smiling creature. Ratcheting sounds emerged, and a few bright ribbons of material like plastic shavings flew out the opening and fell twirling to the ground.

"Took him for a jaunt last night," said Cruikshank in a muffled voice. "Went over the next ridge, tramping through fields like some berserk combine. Would have left footprints to astound the populace had there been any rain in the past four months.''

Somebody sighed behind me, and I turned to see Mrs. Cruikshank, a long-suffering expression on her face, holding a plate of cookies. I took one with a commiserating look. Overhead, a series of clanks and squeaks emitted from the allosaurus, compelling Cruikshank to raise his voice.

"As it crested the rise, its saurian head was framed by the moon, a sight to curdle milk in the cow and put hens off their laying for a month. In fact, Allie crashed through Farmer Olmstead's henhouse while blundering around on the way back—a cloud covered the moon, and my controls won't really hold her once she gets disoriented and a bit panicky. Tore out one side of the house, sending birds flying like a cannonade.''

Mrs. C. and I exchanged glances. I knew she maintained faith in her husband, despite the mounting bills and occasional complaints from the zoning people, and it hurt to see her put through such trials.

Behind us, someone cleared his throat warningly. Cruikshank nattered on, oblivious, but his wife and I turned in surprise.

A red-faced man, wearing a flannel shirt and over-alls that appeared to be covered with feathers, stood glowering on the path. One hand clutched an open burlap sack, which was filled to bulging with what appeared to be limp white birds. . . .

11.

But satire is finally no escape, for it binds us to the author being satirized, his follies and preoccupations appearing in new guise like a reanimated hand. Though madcap and irreverent, parodies are by their nature retrospective, not prospective.

If dinosaurs appeal to young readers at the same time in their lives that they are most likely to become science fiction readers, they must contain some element of youthful, forward-looking vigor, must they not? Notwithstanding the undertones of desuetude and melancholy that one can invariably detect?

12.

Even dinosaurs that are actually aliens—not considered above, as they seem at best borderline cases—are invariably associated with loss and the extinction of hope. The sauropods who roar outside the Consul's porthole in the opening paragraph of Dan Simmons' *Hyperion* help set a scene which soon turns to sour disappointment, as the Consul departs unwillingly on a mission he expects not to survive. The brontosaurian bandersnatchi in Larry Niven's stories can make it in the interstellar economy of Known Space only by buying prostheses made by more capable species, which they pay for by selling the rights to hunt them. And when the dinosaurlike creatures are the dominant species of a planet, as in novels ranging from James Blish's *A Case of Conscience* to Robert Sawyer's *Far-Seer,* that planet is usually doomed.

13.

When I look into the mirror the next morning, scaly patches have begun to form on my chest and shoulders. I have trouble turning to see them, because my back feels stiff, as if strained and now taking time out to heal. Odd pains shoot down my legs, as though something is happening within.

Although I have little appetite, I force down the entire dietary regimen, high in proteins and calories, plus vile-tasting liquids rich in minerals. I know that if I cannot keep them down they will have to be given intravenously, and it will become increasingly difficult to punch through my thickening skin.

I look down at my genitals, which show no outward change. Soon they will begin to retract, as though I have been swimming in the ocean. This does not bother me.

I draw a hand through my hair, which brings away only a few loose strands. That will change. My clothing is already beginning to fit oddly, but there is no point in buying new garments. Soon I will not dress at all, and remain at home until the transformation is complete.

I sleep after eating, and wake feeling weak, as if I am convalescing. It is three days before I feel enough energy to go out, and I call a cab, feeling unequal to the task of driving.

Rascoe is in his yard, which has been expanded after they demolished the back rooms of his house. The remaining structure contains the walk-in freezer, the storage shed for the landscaping tools, and a small office for his caretaker. Rascoe has a special terminal set up outside for him, but I don't think he ever uses it.

I spent months talking through my decision with Rascoe, at a time when he was at roughly the stage where I am now. Seeing him go through the change has made it easier on me, but I find that I cannot tell him this. Rascoe glowers at me, perhaps without recognition.

"You seem happy," I tell him, and he cocks his head to get a better look at me. His tail lashes restively.

"I'm happy," I say, but the soul-searching I can recall inflicting on Rascoe seems remote and unnatural, like something once read in a book. I feel, if anything, more self-absorbed than before, but disinclined toward introspection.

"This may be our last real conversation," I say, but it occurs to me that our last real conversation may have been some time ago. I make a friendly gesture, a warm, mammalian act that even now feels a bit forced, and Rascoe growls.

We may get along better next year, when we will be members of the same species once more. Or perhaps not. I try to weigh the possibilities, but find the effort vexatious and irritating. I fumble the beeper from my pocket and summon a cab.

I sleep through the rest of the day, but wake in the middle of the night, feeling oddly at home. I amble outside, not bothering with the bathrobe. The yard has been stripped of its porch and rose garden, but a shallow pool was dug last week, and I accede to the urge to drink from it. The annuity to which I have converted my assets will not allow for an opulent lifestyle, but my needs will be modest. I look at the livestock chute, through which a young pig will be occasionally delivered.

A bright star is moving across the sky, part of the Satellite Defense system. "No meteor's gonna get us this time," I say aloud.

A warm breeze off Lake Erie stirs the leaves overhead, and I hear the air conditioner go on in the house across the street. It didn't used to be this warm in November, I think lazily.

Next door a chain clanks as the neighbor's setter, panting in the night, drags himself over to his water dish. "You're not going to make it," I tell him.

He whines anxiously, disturbed by my unfamiliar smell. I arch my neck, suppressing a mild impulse to snarl.

"It's good to be back."

EVOLVING CONSPIRACY

by Roger MacBride Allen

Roger MacBride Allen has written a number of well-received science fiction novels and short stories.

It *was* a dark and stormy night. That is the plain fact of the matter, and what's more, that piece of data played a central role in the events of the evening in question.

There was, however, nothing remarkable about Bueber paying a visit during bad weather. He always tended to show up during what he called "low-visibility conditions." He prided himself on being security-conscious. What the rest of us would call "paranoid."

Generally speaking, he didn't like coming to see me, because I live on a hilltop, off in the middle of the country. To my way of thinking, it was a nice, quiet place to live, but Bueber saw it as nothing more than a security nightmare. One man with a pair of binoculars could keep a precise catalog of who visited me at what time. Worse, I was the last house at the end of the road, and there was only one road that led to the small town where I lived. It would be child's play to button up and seal off my town in general, and my house in particular. In short, my house was, from his point of view, a severely insecure location.

To be honest about it, that was precisely why I bought the place in the first place. When I lived in the center of town, in the middle of a complex roadnet with many means of approach, in an apartment building with multiple exits and no good place for any imaginary opposition to set up observation posts, Bueber had shown up any time he wanted—usually at three in the morning. Being out in the middle of nowhere cut his visits down to a minimum.

Now, don't get me wrong, I enjoyed Bueber's visits. They were most stimulating. They were, however, the sort of thing best enjoyed in small, infrequent, doses.

Bueber was, nominally at least, a colleague of mine, that is to say a theologian, and a scholar. However, I would not be surprised to discover he had not cracked open a Bible in years, for his true avocation lay elsewhere. He specialized in finding the links, the connections, between things. Name any two events, mention any two people, give him ten minutes in his file room (plus another five either end to lock and unlock the doors to it) and he would be able to establish a connection between them.

He was, in short, the top conspiracy man in the country. He was the best there ever was at it, too—though some would say that was not necessarily a good thing.

He had proved, to his own satisfaction, at least, that there were no fewer than *eight* gunmen in Deally Plaza that day, working for at least three different—but interlocking—conspiracies. No fewer than six of them had instructions to "pretend to miss on purpose," for reasons so intricate they must be regarded as beyond the scope of the present text. He also established a clear link tying Oliver Stone to the subsequent, thirty-year cover-up plan—though even Bueber admits that one is somewhat speculative.

He has documents to show that Salvadore Allende was in the pay of the CIA. He has linked the Trilateral Commission to the Teamsters, and proved it was the Trilaterals—in league with rogue elements of the Interstate Commerce Commission—who caused Hoffa to disappear. However, contrary to popular rumor, Hoffa is *not* buried under the goal posts at the Meadowlands. It is his double buried there, a security agent hired by Clifford Irving to pretend to be Hoffa during the period in which the union leader was having round-the-clock secret meetings with Howard Hughes.

The substitution did not fool the Trilat-ICC conspirators, however. They took out *both* men, and buried the double in the football field in order to throw off the scent. They hired the same team that switched JFK's coffin during the flight from Dallas, and arranged for Hoffa to be doubled-up with another body in an existing grave, where no one would think of looking for it. Jimmy Hoffa is buried in Grant's Tomb. Bueber had documents demonstrating that the collapse of the Soviet Union was merely an unusually elaborate KGB misinformation operation. Once the West is lulled into what Bueber calls "a false sense of reality," Phase Two will be activated, and the resultant confrontation will make the Cuban Missile Crisis seem like a Swiss picnic.

Watergate, needless to say, was bungled *deliberately,* as a diversionary tactic, so as to insure that no one could ever believe that the Republican Party was capable of covert action. This allowed GOP special ops teams to act without fear of discovery when they staged the Munich Olympics attacks, and succeed in their goal of embarassing and radicalizing Yassar Arafat and thus derailing his attempts to infiltrate the United Jewish Appeal. As for the Iran-Contra affair, Bueber has the whole thing completely nailed down. Once the U.S. had infiltrated the CIA agents posing as Shiite Muslims into Lebanon and arranged for them to take the hostages in the first place, the stage was set for the supposed exchange of weapons to Iran. (In reality, the planes were full of surveillance equipment that Teheran traded to China in exchange for abandoned U.S. gear the Chinese had gotten from the Vietnamese. The Chinese later used the U.S. made, Iran-delivered surveillance gear to spy on the Tienamann Square demonstrators. Bush knew the spy gear was U.S. made, and so dared not stand up to the Chinese for fear of revealing this never-uncovered link to Iran-Contra.)

Meanwhile, the subsequent transfer of funds from Iran was to pay for ops in Nicaragua. Unfortunately, the units of the Sandinista army posing as Contras were in a temporary alliance of convenience with the Trilateral Commission and the Teamsters, faced off against the Centers for Disease Control in Atlanta.

By that time, CDC was on to the U.S. Army germ warfare project that had developed the AIDS virus and field-tested it in Africa some years before, and the Trilat-Sandinista-Contra (TSC for short) coalition did not want that uncovered, for fear of exposing the CIA connection to the Cuban military in Angola. (All three elements of TSC of course being CIA fronts.) TSC was therefore channeling the funds North's people provided into various Gay Rights groups, knowing the stronger those organizations were, the less likely CDC would risk the social unrest that would be caused by going public.

Bueber has a file three inches thick on the subject of the NSA project to recruit dentists to install receivers *and* transmitters in Ross Perot's teeth. Suffice it to say that the op was bungled, and many of the odd events Perot reported (Black Panthers plotting to kill him, the plot to wreck his daughter's wedding and so on) were the result of his receiving the audio portion of various old movies on UHF while asleep, a case of accidental subliminal suggestion.

For reasons that I have never gotten entirely clear, Bueber tended to come to me first with his discoveries. I have never dared ask why, for fear that he would regard the question as an attempt to investigate *him*.

The infuriating thing about his theories is that he always had *some* sort of evidence, however speculative or shaky or circumstantial, and he usually managed to set things up so that disproving his scenarios required proof of a negative. I never could prove, for example, that there *weren't* deep cover KGB agents so well hidden inside the U.S. Forest Service that no one could find them. So far as Bueber was concerned, if they were undetectable, that was merely proof they were well hidden. In any event, as of the night in question, Bueber had not come around for a while. I had been half-expecting him to show up as soon as the weather turned bad, rendering surveillance difficult. When the heavens opened up that night, I knew the odds were good for a visit, so I simply decided to sit up and wait for him.

When he arrived, I was reading in the library—with my back to the wall, facing the door. Bueber had taught me that much, but only by example. The first few times he showed up, he scared the hell out of me by materializing behind me.

This time I was ready for him, listening for him. So I heard the tiny, imperceptible click as he used his skeleton keys on the back door, the slight creak of the door as he came through, his near-silent tread down the hall. The library door opened without a sound, and Bueber was standing before me.

As has been said of another noted household intruder, he spoke not a word, but went straight to his work. Raising a finger to his lips as a signal for silence, he came into the room and carefully drew the door shut behind him.

He was a tall, very thin man, almost skeletal in appearance. He was naturally very pale, and his face was still cold and wet from the rain, making his skin seem even more transparent than usual. His hair, though at the moment hidden by his watch cap, was pale gray, and cropped close to his head. He was, needless to say, dressed completely in black.

He turned off the overhead lights, moved to the windows, looked outside while standing to one side of the glass, and then drew the blinds closed. He pulled a small device—a bug detector—from a clip on his Sam Browne belt and walked around the room, watching the gadget's display intently.

At last, he was satisfied. He shut off the detector, clipped it back onto his belt, then undid the belt. He sat down in the chair opposite me, setting the belt down on the floor. He pulled his watch cap off and tossed it on the side table.

"Hello, Deblick," he said, as if he had just come into the room in the most normal way possible. Of course, for Bueber, he *had* just come in in the normal way. At least, almost normal. I had learned to note his moods carefully over the years. That night, he seemed a bit nervous, a bit manic, a bit edgy, even for Bueber.

He was smiling, but there was no pleasure or happiness in the expression. It was closer to the look of madness than of joy. That much was clear in his eyes. They were open a bit *too* wide, shining a bit too brightly. His mouth was drawn back in a grin, but it was a skull's grin, the ghastly leering smile of rigor mortis.

"Hello, Bueber," I said, setting my book aside. "What brings you around tonight?" Bueber always liked to get right down to business.

"The big one," he said. "The grandfather, the one that ties it all together." He laughed, making a sound like a creaking gate. "The Grand Unified Conspiracy to end all Grand Unified Conspiracies."

"Again?" I asked.

"There is no need for sarcasm, Deblick," Bueber said coolly.

"My apologies," I said as solemnly as I could. It was often difficult to take Bueber as seriously as he wanted to be taken. Of course, if one *did* take him seriously, then the world was a much darker and more sinister place than most of us would care to believe. "I am always interested in your findings," I said. "Please do tell me what you have learned."

"Very well," he said, somewhat mollified. "But first, let me ask you a question. What do you regard as the greatest of all questions in the field of natural history?"

"*Natural* history? Isn't that outside your usual area of study?" I asked.

"Perhaps so. But that is as may be. Please indulge me. Answer my question."

I thought about it for a moment. "Origins, I suppose. The question of how we got here. How did life get here? How did humans get here?"

"But does not science have an answer?"

"Yes, of course, the theory of evolution. But, even ignoring the creationist ignoramuses, it is a theory that greatly troubles many in the religious community. It reduces the magnificent mystery of God's creation to a four-billion-year series of accidents. At best, it limits the divine spark of creation to an extremely limited role, and, in my opinion, is quite unsatisfactory in the way it deals with the development of human consciousness, to say nothing of the human soul. To extend the question back further, it seems to me that every nonreligious theory of cosmology ultimately requires a creationless creator, a profound failure of logic."

"Very good, Deblick, very good. You have hit the nail square on the head. It is completely preposterous to imagine all this—" he gestured around himself to indicate the universe at large— "was created by sheer chance. And it wasn't. He just wanted us to think it was."

"I beg your pardon?"

Bueber leaned in toward me, and the look in his eyes turned even wilder. "God is in on this one. God and the Cubans. I have Him dead to rights this time. I only have one piece of the story so far, but I'm going to have it all. Just you watch."

"What the devil are you talking about?" I demanded.

"The devil is precisely what I am talking about. The biggest cover-up of all time," he replied. "The effort to shield the great dinosaur fraud. Tell me, you're an educated man. When did the last of the dinosaurs die out?"

I shrugged. "A shade over sixty-five million years ago. The end of the Cretaeteous. No one knows quite why. There are a lot of theories. Maybe an asteroid struck the Earth and—"

"Ha! The magic asteroid theory! Really, Deblick, you are becoming far too predictable. But I should be fair. At first, I, too, accepted the single asteroid theory, despite all of its internal contradictions. Then I started looking into it. The *public* believes in the asteroid theory—but the scientists working in the field don't, though *they won't admit that in public*. They never address the most basic question: If the single asteroid theory is right, then why are there so many candidate craters? How many places could one rock hit."

"I thought they had found one in the Caribbean—" I began, but Bueber cut me off again.

"Check the literature! They've *never* agreed on where their precious struck. They used to say the evidence pointed to Iceland, or to a land strike, or to an impact in the Far East. How could one asteroid hit in four places? You would be amazed to learn the number of impact features that just happen to be the right age. Besides, do you know when the dinosaurs' population started to decline?"

"I'm no expert, but I assume that they died at the time of the asteroid—"

"Nonsense. Absolute nonsense. The dinosaurs were dying off long *before* the asteroid strike that was supposed to kill them. How do you explain *that*? They knew they were going to become extinct, so some of the species decided to beat the rush?"

Bueber was being more than usually confusing. "So what are you saying?" I asked. "That it wasn't an asteroid? Fine. What do *you* think killed the dinosaurs?"

"Simple. Nothing. *Nothing* killed the dinosaurs."

The room was silent, but for the ticking of the clock and the dull rumble of rain on the roof. I sat there, absolutely certain that Bueber had gone completely around the bend this time. "You mean the dinosaurs are still alive?" I asked, as gently as I could.

"I mean *there never were any dinosaurs to begin with*! All a fake, a dodge."

"Hold it. Wait a second," I protested, but Bueber was on a roll.

"All a fake," he repeated. "All of it, from start to finish. Bogus fossils salted into the rocks. Fake footprints. Planted evidence, everywhere."

"But who—how—what was—"

"God," Bueber said, with obvious satisfaction. "God did it all, in league with the Cubans. And I have the documents to prove it."

"But—" I started to protest, and got in the last word edgewise that I would manage for some time.

"Bishop Ussher was right," Bueber went on, the words pouring out of him. "Or at least he stole the credit from the monk who did the real work and got it right. The world *was* created in 4,004 B.C. *Everything* was created at that one time, the present-day world, and all the forged fossils and rock strata and so on, all at once." I tried to speak, but he lifted a warning finger to me and rushed on. "And before you can protest that the forgery job was too complex and complete, remember this is *God* we're talking about. God can do whatever he wants or else what's the point in being God? Except, of course, God *can't* do whatever he wants."

"What?"

Bueber laughed and shook his head. "Oh, God's good. Don't get me wrong. He's very, very good. But he is not perfect, not infallible. There's proof of *that* straight through everything I've uncovered. For starters, the fossil record is not all it could be. A very impressive job, yes, I grant you. But it failed. It did not do its job—or rather, did it too well."

I had almost given up trying to pretend I was following this. "What *was* its job, then?"

"To test our faith, of course. Religion is a matter of faith, and faith is meaningless, mindless, unless it is challenged and questioned. You should know that. You're a theologian. God *wanted* us to find the forged fossils, examine them, interpret them, derive from them the evidence of an extremely old Earth and the theory of evolution—and then reject all that because it didn't agree with scripture."

"Except we didn't reject it," I said, starting to understand at least some of what he was saying.

"Exactly. We bought in, hook, line, and sinker. God thought he was setting Wallace up as a patsy, but something went wrong. Darwin moved in."

"Who's Wallace? And who was he a patsy for?"

Bueber looked at me oddly, then sighed and explained, speaking slowly, as if to a not-very-bright child. "For God, of course. Alfred Russel Wallace came up with a less inclusive theory of evolution, and was nearly ready to publish when Darwin found out about it and rushed his version into print. If Wallace had been first, then evolution would have been presented in a less compelling manner and would have had far less impact. That was God's original scenario. The bogus fossil record would have been explained away, and faith would have been challenged, but not overturned. All the resultant social and technical innovations would never have happened, and God wouldn't be in trouble now."

"How is it He is in trouble?"

"I told you the fossil record wasn't perfect. It didn't need to be, because the scenario called for us to discover it, have it test our faith, and then have us dismiss it. We weren't supposed to examine it too closely. Darwin was a disciple of gradualism, don't forget, and that was the theory we were supposed to examine and reject. Species were supposed to change, but they were supposed to take endless amounts of time to do it, and move through endless intermediate forms as they did. *Except God never got around to forging the intermediate species*. There are all sorts of theories to explain why they aren't there, but their absence is a major stumbling block."

"How is it we weren't supposed to examine it too closely, but we did?"

"Because Darwin did a better job than Wallace was supposed to do. Someone or something set Darwin up as their useful idiot."

"I beg your pardon?"

"The whole damn thing was dropped in Darwin's lap, but he *still* had to be bashed over the head before he would produce. What are the odds on it all happening by chance? Darwin just happened to go aboard the *Beagle*. That ship just happened to put in on the coast of South America, where he could observe just the right geologic formations to start thinking about change over long time periods. Then, once he was in that state of mind, the *Beagle* just happened to deliver him to the Galapagos Islands, the *one* place in the world where it just happens to be easy to observe groups of closely related species that seem to have just recently emerged from root species."

"But he still went home and did nothing about what he found until Wallace wrote him. *Then* he rushed into print and turned the world upside-down. Caused much more tumult then Wallace's weaker theory would have. It set all sorts of things in motion that gave us much more wealth and advanced technology too soon. We had the money and the hardware to examine the fossil record too closely."

"What does advanced technology have to do with Darwin?"

"Isn't it obvious?" Bueber looked at me, and realized that it was not. He sighed and leaned back in his chair, and started again, more slowly. "Look, let me walk you through it backwards, and you'll answer your own question. What is the single mass human behavior that drives technological advance the hardest in the modern era?"

"War. War and military competition."

"Right. And the biggest war in history was?"

"World War II, of course."

"And what individual, the leader of what movement, was most responsible for starting that war?"

"Adolph Hitler, of course. The leader of the Nazi party."

"And Nazism was based in large part on paranoid theories concerning the struggle of superior races against supposed pollution of bloodlines. And what rather gloomy German philosopher was an inspiration to the Nazis?"

"I take it you are referring to Friedrich Nietzsche and his uebermensch—superman—ideas?" I asked.

"Very good. Last question: what then-recent theory inspired Nietzsche—and also inspired Hitler himself?"

"Social Darwinism," I answered reluctantly. "A spurious extension of the concept of natural selection into the realm of culture and human behavior." That was the trouble with Bueber. Every once in a while, he *could* tie it all together.

"There are plenty of other links I could demonstrate, but that one will do for now. I think you see my point."

"You keep hitting on technology," I objected. "But fossil hunting doesn't take much more than an eyeball and a shovel."

"That's what they'd have you think," Bueber said. "It's true as far as it goes. But it doesn't go very far at all. Yes, you can dig up all the fossils you want if you dig long enough—but you need computer technology to develop the data bases you need for comparative work, and for simulations and reconstruction, and all sorts of other things. You need CAT scanners and magnetic resonance imaging systems to examine the interior of a fossil and see what makes it tick. You need nuclear science to develop radioactive dating systems, and petroleum-industry-driven research to get a good base of geostratigraphic data. War and the threat of war drove all of the root technologies that made all those things possible."

"But sooner or later we'd have developed the technology and the research facilities that would demonstrate the flaws in the fossil record," I objected. "It was just a matter of time."

"Ahh, yes. Time. Don't forget there is not much of it left."

"Left until what?"

"Judgment Day, of course. June 6, 2036. The two thousandth anniversary of the day Christ was *really* crucified."

"June?" I asked. Bueber gathered breath, and I could see he was ready to explain *that* point in detail. "Never mind," I said hurriedly. "A side issue. But let me see if I understand your theory. God set up a fossil record good enough that it would not reveal itself as incomplete, and therefore spurious, before 2036, given the speed of technological development and degree of research effort he assumed would take place if Wallace put forward the theory of evolution. However,

Darwin did a better job in presenting the theory, with
the direct result of more intense research into the fossil record, and the indirect result of setting in motion
events that spurred technical development. As a result, we know more than we are supposed to about
the development of life on Earth—including the flaws
in the theory.''

"Excellent," Bueber said. "A superb summing up.''

"But hang on just a moment," I said. "You're im-
plying that someone deliberately manipulated events
to put Darwin in the right place at the right time to
come up with his theories. Who? And how?''

"Who is easy. The KGB and its predecessors, going
right back to the Czarist secret police.''

"You're saying that the theory of evolution was a
communist plot?''

"On the contrary. Communism was an *evolutionist*
plot. Yes, I know, Marx published before Darwin—
but both of them were being manipulated by the same
people. Doesn't it strike you as odd that the communists were so eager to seize on evolution as a model
for their ideals. Historical development of the urban
proletariat? Capitalism giving way to socialism, as feu-
dalism gave way to capitalism? The predestined
withering-away of the state? *Homo Sovieticus,* the new
Soviet man? Lysenkoism? All ideas clearly related
to—and perversion of—the theory of evolution.''

"But why?''

"I have no doubt that the Communist movement
was subverted for no other reason than to drive the
arms race—and thus technology—so that we'd find the
proof that the fossil record is false.''

"So you're saying the whole Cold War was just a
front operation to encourage fossil hunting?''

"Not exactly. To *manipulate* it. You'll recall that
the famous fossil hominid Lucy was found in the Afar
region of Ethiopia. Once the Marxists consolidated
their power in that country, they kept all foreign researchers out of the country for years on end. And
don't forget the Peking Man fossils vanished from
China. I assume those lost fossils would have sup-

ported some theory that certain parties did not wish to see advanced."

My head was starting to throb just a trifle. I decided to try and steer things back to where we came in. "Let's back up a bit," I said. "You said something about the dinosaurs dying out long before the asteroid that was supposed to kill them hit. But how could that be? I can see God not establishing every detail of the fossil record, but how could He miss something that big? Especially when the dinosaurs never existed in the first place."

Bueber nodded, something more than a bit manic about his gestures. "Ah, but they *did* exist."

"But you just said—"

"I know, I know. They did not exist in the historical past of the world as that past existed in 4004 B.C. They have existed in the past that has been in place since 4004."

"Gibberish," I said.

"Not if you accept the concept of a mutable past," Bueber said. "Think for a minute. I've walked you through enough scenarios. What's the best way to make it seem like someone slept in a bed, stayed the whole night there?"

This conversation was veering wildly from side to side, but I tried to hang on. "Well, you have some one do just that. Sleep in the bed, wear the pajamas, use the toothbrush."

"Exactly. If you just muss the bedclothes, pretend someone's been there, you're bound to miss a detail or two. The same thing if you want it to look like someone was shot—or that a planet evolved."

"Except your scenario calls for the planet to have been created in 4004 B.C."

"And so it was. But God is the master of space *and* time. If the Russians can invent time travel, so can He."

"Russians?"

"I'll come to that," Bueber said hurriedly. "In any event, in 4004 B.C., God created the Heavens and the Earth—and the past. A real, reachable past, full of animals that lived and died and ate each other and keeled over in streambeds. That's another thing. Haven't you ever wondered why so many creatures just *happened* to die in places like streambeds where their bones would be preserved? When was the last time you saw a deer or a squirrel drop dead by a streambed?

"In 4004 B.C., God created the appearance of a past by creating a past. But even if he slept in the bed and wore the pajamas, he didn't use the toothbrush. He cut corners, got sloppy here and there. And certain parties took advantage of that."

"As for example, with the dinosaurs," I suggested.

"With the dinosaurs," he agreed. "You see, the opposition knew that the past was a fake, no realer than Disneyland. Because it was created at the same time as the present-day world, the existence of the present-day world was not dependent on it. You could do what you liked to the prehistoric past with no fear of damaging the present. You'd move the rocks around under the ground, maybe, but you weren't going to erase history."

"You've lost me again," I said.

Bueber leaned closer and lowered his voice. "Do you recall the files I showed you a year ago? The ones on Soviet time travel experiments?"

"Oh, now we come to it," I protested. "You honestly believe in time travel?"

"Oh, absolutely. I have the proof of that, let me tell you." Bueber's eyes shifted nervously toward the floor, as if even the thought of that proof unnerved him. "However," he went on, recovering himself, "the tests I came across last year had nothing to do with the evolution conspiracy. Just low-level scientists performing lab trials. The experiments didn't come to anything—at least directly—but they *did* demonstrate that time travel was possible. Well, even if the Soviets never got it to work, somebody did. Someone with a score to settle, and a need for outside support. And they got it to work and put it to use in a big way."

"Who?" I asked, half-knowing the answer already.

After spending a bit of time with Bueber, I knew how his mind worked.

He leaned in closer and whispered so quietly I could barely hear him. "The Cubans," he said.

By this point my head was whirling. I had no idea what to say. The man was insane, no doubt about it. Neither of us spoke for at least half a minute.

"It all fits," Bueber said, after a sufficiently dramatic pause. He paused a moment longer, and then he spoke again, starting with one of his favorite rhetorical openers. "Haven't you ever *wondered* how the Cubans have hung on so long without outside support? The answer, of course, is they haven't. It's just that their support has come from a lot *farther* outside than we thought."

"Cuban communist time travelers," I said, making no further effort to mask my incredulity.

"Yes. Right. It all stands to reason. Their people did have access to the Soviet time travel labs. They had a chance to copy the technology. When the KGB staged the Soviet collapse, the Russians had the perfect excuse to grab back the blank checkbook they had given Castro, but it also gave Castro a great big motive for having his revenge on whoever was really behind the KGB.

"Once he established who *that* was, and found out that the one thing they cared about was promoting the theory of evolution as a means of eroding faith in God—well, all of a sudden he knew how to hit them where it hurt. He cut a deal. He would send his people back in time with the mission of disrupting the fossil record, in exchange for a series of miracles that would keep the Cuban economy running, at least for a while.

"He was constrained some by the historical fact of which fossils had already been discovered, but he still had a lot of room to work with inside that constraint. Remember, it was the asteroid that was supposed to have killed the dinosaurs. All Castro had to do was send some of his top people—team members from Angola, from his original revolution, from the Dallas operation—back into the period *before* the asteroid impact with orders to kill as many dinosaurs as possible, by the most mysterious means possible. Poison gas, germ warfare, radiation poisoning, anything that would leave no trace. I'll bet that a large number of them simply got the Argentinean treatment."

"The what?"

"The Argies used to disappear people, just like in *Catch-22*. The unmarked cars would roll up, the victim would be bundled in, and no one would ever see him again."

"My God," I said, not even sure what I was reacting to anymore.

"They're still at it, determined to wipe out every species they can before the asteroid impact, so that no one will ever find an example of that species surviving long enough to die when the big rock hits."

It was too much to keep straight. I seemed to have a slight buzzing in my skull, as if bees had gotten loose in my head. "Let me go back a bit. For the last hundred and seventy years or so, these certain parties of yours have been working to establish evolution, thus weakening the power of religion. Those certain powers would be—"

Bueber did not say a word. He just pointed his finger straight down, right toward the center of the Earth and all points below.

"I see," I went on. "And Castro is so determined to embarrass ah—*them*, that this good atheistic communist is willing to work hand in glove with God against the Devil?"

"Once again, my friend, you understand me completely. Quite a story, is it not?"

"It's quite mad," I said. "It's all insane. You have no proof, no evidence."

"Oh, but, yes, I do," he said, his voice cold and hard. "I have been working on this one for years. I've kept it quiet, but now I have the proof I need. And tomorrow, I will set it all out before the world. I'm going to blow the roof off everything from the Vatican to the American Museum of Natural History."

He stood and moved toward the window. He drew

the shade just far enough to get a look at the weather. "The rain is slowing down," he said. "I have to get going before it clears." He turned back to me and pulled his watch cap back on. "I came to you first, because you are a friend and because you would want to know. It *is* a fantastic story. I did not expect you to believe me without proof." He smiled without humor. "God demands faith. I do not. Tomorrow I hold a news conference, and the world will have all the proof it needs." He moved toward the door, turned, saluted me in the odd two-and-half-fingers-to-the-forehead manner of the unnamed military service in which he had allegedly served at some unspecified time in the past, and then was gone.

So ended the last of Bueber's visits. Most unsettling. I rose, opened the curtains, turned the overhead lights back on, and tried to get back to my book—not an easy task under the circumstances. There was something deeply depressing about a man that determined to live in a world no one else could see. I opened my book, but I did not see the type before my eyes. The imagery, the ideas, were too weird, too compelling. Vengeful Cuban communists, in league with God against Satan, stalking and disappearing the wild dinosaur to preserve the Lord's reputation. I stared at the door he had gone through, and the lateness of the hour, and the thunder of the rain, and the strangeness of the tale, filled my head with visions of tyrannosaurs being bundled into the back of unmarked Argentinean police cars driven by Joseph Heller. Mad nonsense— but no madder than what I had just been told.

I was in such a state of reverie, when the flash of light outside the window lit up the sky, and the deafening crack of thunder made me jump in my seat.

And, somehow, I knew what that lightning strike was for. In that moment, I suddenly did believe, believed everything, much as I did not want to.

They found him the next morning. A freak accident, the police told me. Struck by lightning, dead in an instant, the papers he was carrying incinerated. By a strange coincidence, his house was struck by lightning at almost exactly the same time, and burned to the ground, destroying Bueber's archives in the process.

And that should have been that. The end of the story.

Except for two tiny details. First, Bueber's whole thesis was based on the premise that God was not infallible. He was capable of missing a detail, making a mistake. If that were so, then logic indeed would dictate that Satan was likewise susceptible to error. If I could see that, then so could Bueber. And Bueber always allowed for contingencies, preferably with a deception plan to confuse and misdirect his enemies.

The second detail was that Bueber had "accidentally" left his Sam Browne belt full of hardware behind. It was not until a day or two after the funeral that I thought to examine it carefully. It was then that I found—*it*—carefully wrapped and padded, hidden in a flashlight with the batteries removed.

No, Bueber was not a man to take chances, and he was not above a spot of misdirection in order to fool his enemies. He was willing to risk—and lose—his life, if it meant that the Adversary could be fooled into thinking all the bases had been covered. Even with his house destroyed, and with the documents he was carrying ruined, he left something behind. Perhaps somewhere there is more, cached away somewhere. A file folder that explains what, exactly the object in question means. Or perhaps another bit of equally compelling physical evidence.

For the moment, the object I found is here. It exists. It is completely fossilized, and yet retains every detail of its original form, down to the veins on the wrapper leaf, and the form of the ash. I have arranged for every conceivable test to be run on it. I have dated it every way I know how. It is absolutely incontrovertible proof—but of what, precisely, I don't know.

But a sixty-five-million-year-old fossilized Havana cigar certainly must prove *something*.

FANTASY ANTHOLOGIES

Science Fiction Anthologies

☐ **FUTURE EARTHS: UNDER AFRICAN SKIES** UE2544—$4.99
  Mike Resnick & Gardner Dozois, editors
From a utopian space colony modeled on the society of ancient Kenya, to a shocking future discovery of a "long-lost" civilization, to an ingenious cure for one of humankind's oldest woes—a cure that might cost too much—here are 15 provocative tales about Africa in the future and African culture transplanted to different worlds.

☐ **FUTURE EARTHS: UNDER SOUTH AMERICAN SKIES**
  Mike Resnick & Gardner Dozois, editors   UE2581—$4.99
From a plane crash that lands its passengers in a survival situation completely alien to anything they've ever experienced, to a close encounter of the insect kind, to a woman who has journeyed unimaginably far from home—here are stories from the rich culture of South America, with its mysteriously vanished ancient civilizations and magnificent artifacts, its modern-day contrasts between sophisticated city dwellers and impoverished villagers.

☐ **MICROCOSMIC TALES**   UE2532—$4.99
  Isaac Asimov, Martin H. Greenberg, & Joseph D. Olander, eds.
Here are 100 wondrous science fiction short-short stories, including contributions by such acclaimed writers as Arthur C. Clarke, Robert Silverberg, Isaac Asimov, and Larry Niven. Discover a superman who lives in a *real* world of nuclear threat . . . an android who dreams of electric love . . . and a host of other tales that will take you instantly out of this world.

☐ **WHATDUNITS**   UE2533—$4.99
☐ **MORE WHATDUNITS**   UE2557—$5.50
  Mike Resnick, editor
In these unique volumes of all-original stories, Mike Resnick has created a series of science fiction mystery scenarios and set such inventive sleuths as Pat Cadigan, Judith Tarr, Katharine Kerr, Jack Haldeman, and Esther Friesner to solving them. Can you match wits with the masters to make the perpetrators fit the crimes?

Welcome to DAW's Gallery of Ghoulish Delights!

☐ **DRACULA: PRINCE OF DARKNESS**
Martin H. Greenberg, editor
A blood-draining collection of all-original Dracula stories. From Dracula's traditional
stalking grounds to the heart of modern-day cities, the Prince of Darkness casts
his spell over his prey in a private blood drive from which there is no escape!
UE2531—$4.99

☐ **FRANKENSTEIN: THE MONSTER WAKES**
Martin H. Greenberg, editor
Powerful visions of a man and monster cursed by destiny to be eternally at odds.
Here are all-original stories by such well-known writers as: Rex Miller, Max Allan
Collins, Brian Hodge, Rick Hautala, and Daniel Ransom.   UE2584—$4.99

☐ **JOURNEYS TO THE TWILIGHT ZONE**
Carol Serling, editor
From a dog given a transfusion of werewolf blood, to a cocktail party hypnosis
session that went a step too far, here are 16 journeys—to that most unique of
dimensions—*The Twilight Zone.*—by such masters of the fantastic as Alan Dean
Foster, William F. Nolan, Charles de Lint, and Kristine Katherine Rusch.
UE2525—$4.99

☐ **URBAN HORRORS**
William F. Nolan and Martin H. Greenberg, editors
Here are 18 powerful nightmare visions of the horrors that stalk the dark streets
of the cities and the lonely, echoing hallways of our urban dwellings in this
harrowing collection of modern-day terrors, stories by Ray Bradbury, Richard
Matheson, John Cheever, Shirley Jackson and their fellow fright-masters.
UE2548—$5.50

☐ **THE YEAR'S BEST HORROR STORIES**
Karl Edward Wagner, editor
More provocative tales of terror, including: a photographer whose obsession with
images may bring to life trouble beyond his wildest fantasies . . . a couple caught
up in an ancient ritual that offers the promise of health, but at a price that may
prove far too high . . . and a woman whose memory may be failing her with the
passing years—or for a far more unnatural reason.   UE2572—$5.50

DAW

Introducing 3 New DAW Superstars . . .

GAYLE GREENO

☐ **THE GHATTI'S TALE:**
 Book 1—Finders, Seekers   UE2550—$5.50

Someone is attacking the Seekers Veritas, an organization of Truth-finders composed of Bondmate pairs, one human, one a telepathic, catlike ghatti. And the key to defeating this deadly foe is locked in one human's mind behind barriers even her ghatta has never been able to break.

S. ANDREW SWANN

☐ **FORESTS OF THE NIGHT**   UE2565—$3.99

When Nohar Rajasthan, a private eye descended from genetically manipulated tiger stock, a moreau—a second-class humanoid citizen in a human world—is hired to look into a human's murder, he find himself caught up in a conspiracy that includes federal agents, drug runners, moreau gangs, and a deadly canine assassin. And he hasn't even met the real enemy yet!

DEBORAH WHEELER

☐ **JAYDIUM**   UE2556—$4.99

Unexpectedly cast adrift in time and space, four humans from different times and universes unite in a search to find their way back—even if it means confronting an alien race whose doom may prove their only means of salvation.

Attention:

DAW COLLECTORS

Many readers of DAW Books have written requesting information on early titles and book numbers to assist in the collection of DAW editions since the first of our titles appeared in April 1972.

We have prepared a several-pages-long list of all DAW titles, giving their sequence numbers, original and current order numbers, and ISBN numbers. Also included, of course, are the authors and book titles, as well as reissue information.

If you think that this list will be of help, you may have a copy by writing to the address below and enclosing two dollars in stamps or currency to cover the handling and postage costs.

DAW Books, Inc.
Dept. C
375 Hudson Street
New York, NY 10014-3658